MIDNIGHT
MELODIES

MEGAN CARTER

Bella
BOOKS
2008

Also by Megan Carter

Please Forgive Me
Passionate Kisses
When Love Finds a Home
On the Wings of Love

Writing as Frankie J. Jones

The Road Home
Voices of the Heart
For Every Season
Survival of Love
Midas Touch
Room for Love
Captive Heart
Whispers in the Wind
Rhythm Tide

Bella Books, Inc.
P.O. Box 10543
Tallahassee, FL 32302

Printed in the United States of America on acid-free paper
First Edition

Editor: Christi Cassidy
Cover designer: LA Callaghan

ISBN-10: 1-59493-137-2
ISBN-13: 978-1-59493-137-6

For Martha—Te amo con todo mi corazón.

Acknowledgments

I'd like to thank Peggy Herring and Carol Poynor for reading the manuscript. Carol, I apologize for giving you the manuscript just before you were scheduled to go on your cruise.

Thanks to Christi Cassidy for all her hard work and support. Your kind words came at exactly the right moment.

CHAPTER ONE
London, England
Wednesday, March 6, 1912

Her breath caught as the waves of pleasure engulfed her. She had delayed the climax as long as possible, intent on savoring every morsel of delight offered by the skillful hands of her lover. Every second of their time together was precious beyond words, because there was no way to know how long it would be before they would again share each other's company. Their relationship was based on stolen moments wherever and whenever they could arrange them. As her body quivered with the final ripple of joy she couldn't help but wonder how much longer they would be able to hide their relationship. Discovery of their unspeakable love would mean certain disaster. Strong, loving arms pulled her close and held her with a gentleness that caused tears to burn her eyes.

"I want to love you," she whispered. As always, she was very aware of how quickly the afternoon was passing. "Our time is slipping away."

1

"There's plenty of time. Let me hold you. Close your eyes. I'll be here when you wake."

The same hands that had only moments ago brought her such great pleasure began to stroke her hair. She tried to fight the drowsiness that was overcoming her, but the soft voice in her ear and soothing hands were too much. Content in the knowledge that for the moment they were safe, she leaned into her lover and gave in to the comforting cloak of sleep.

Bridget Sullivan woke to the sound of the teakettle and the rattle of china. She watched the woman she had fallen in love with two years ago—Ann Taylor. Simply thinking the name made a warm glow begin to burn inside her.

Ann glanced up and found her watching. "So my little sleepy-head has decided to rejoin me."

Suddenly jealous of the time she had wasted sleeping, Bridget sat up. "I'm sorry. I can't believe I fell asleep."

Ann handed her a cup of tea. "Nonsense. You were exhausted." She gave a small wicked grin.

Bridget blushed. "It's entirely your fault."

"I certainly hope so." She fluffed the pillow behind Bridget. "Get comfortable and enjoy your tea. I found a tin of biscuits. Would you like one?"

"Yes, please. I'm famished."

Ann's knowing smile brought another blush to her face. "You are priceless. After all this time you still blush so easily."

"It's only because you make me so happy." Bridget ducked her head and sipped her tea.

"I'll get those biscuits." Ann kissed the top of Bridget's head before walking away.

Aware of their precious time slipping away, Bridget asked, "What time is it?"

"It's only a little after three. We have plenty of time still."

Bridget glanced around her tiny apartment that smelled of freshly brewed tea mingled with the earthy aroma of raw clay.

Eight brilliantly shaded ceramic pots graced the crude shelf Ann had built and installed for her. The small bed and a chest of drawers filled one wall. Across the room sat a potter's wheel and a battered worktable. This was Bridget's home and studio. It was a rundown room located at the rear of an old theater, which was only open on Friday and Saturday nights. She had arranged with the owner to clean the theater after rehearsals and after each show for a small salary and the use of this room. For almost six years, the room had been her haven. She tried not to dwell on the fact that in gaining this place of safety she had lost her family. This refuge had grown even more important after she met Ann two years ago.

Ann placed the plate of biscuits in Bridget's lap and carefully balanced her own cup as she climbed back into bed. They sipped the tea and nibbled at the treats in comfortable silence for a long moment. Ann finally broke the stillness. "I've been thinking. Maybe we should leave London."

"Your father would never let you move away from home. Besides, how would we live?" She glanced at the ceramic pots on the shelf. Her work was just starting to sell.

"You know it's only a matter of time before he finds out. I've told you how deeply religious he is. He'd send me to Bedlam at St. George's Fields."

Bridget tried to conceal her shock. "Surely your father wouldn't send you to an asylum."

Ann shuddered slightly and rushed on without replying to Bridget's comment. "We could save our money. You could continue selling your pots, and I could ask for a bigger salary." She fidgeted with her cup.

Bridget knew that from early childhood Ann had worked at the general mercantile store owned by her extremely devout father. Over the years, her responsibilities had grown from dusting the shelves to keeping the accounts. Her father paid her a small salary that she used to purchase her first love, books.

"I know. I've been trying to convince him that at twenty-five, I'm certainly old enough to take care of myself." She shook her head. "And always, he comes back with that 'it's not proper for a young woman to be living alone.' If I'm not living in his home then I should be married so that some other man can take care of me." She took a deep breath and slowly exhaled. "I've told him a thousand times that attitudes are changing, but so far he hasn't budged an inch. He's absolutely convinced that my immortal soul will be condemned to hell forever if I'm not under his or some other male protection twenty-four hours a day."

"We're never going to be able to live together if you can't make him change his mind." She hated to sound like she was nagging. After all, Ann had used the excuse of visiting a sick friend to sneak over to see her on a rare weekday visit. Normally their time together was limited to a few hours on Sunday afternoon. On more occasions than she cared to remember, even those precious hours were taken from them because of some family matter Ann had to attend to. A secret part of her wished Ann could simply walk away from her family as she had done. She pushed the unkind thought away and reminded herself that she wouldn't have been able to walk away so easily had her mother still been living.

Bridget had never met Ann's father, but from what Ann had said, she didn't think he would ever change his mind. He appeared to be a very stern man, not cruel like her own father, but definitely a man who ruled his household with a firm hand. His strict control seemed to intimidate everyone except Ann's older brother, Hayden, who had developed a serious drinking problem.

Ann took her hand. "I can't stand being away from you. It's driving me crazy. I feel possessed—always plotting and scheming to find ways to get back over here." She stared into her tea. "Hayden has started asking questions about where I've been spending so much of my time."

"Your brother is a spoiled, massive pain in the hindquarters." Hayden was a spoiled man-child. He was given a much larger salary than Ann was, even though he seldom did any real work. Whatever money he had was wasted on alcohol. The constant lack of funds forced him to continue living with his parents.

Ann chuckled. "No one would argue that point with you. Still, if he gets too curious he could cause a lot of trouble."

A cold tingle ran along Bridget's spine. She'd had the misfortune of meeting Hayden briefly a few months earlier and had taken an instant disliking to him. He had been with one of his drinking cronies. They were both intoxicated. At first, Hayden tried to cozy up to her. When she made it obvious that she had no interest in him, he grew angry and insisted that Ann return home with him. Rather than cause a scene, Ann obeyed. That'd been the first time Bridget had seen any sign of weakness in Ann, and it had disturbed her for a long time.

After that encounter, Ann seemed nervous about venturing out of the apartment. It bothered Bridget that they were forced to hide away. It became a growing source of uneasiness between them. Luckily, the onset of cold weather took care of the problem, since it more or less forced them to spend their time together at the apartment.

Bridget turned her attention back to Ann. "He wouldn't try and follow you, would he?"

"I don't think he's that curious, yet. It's just that he has started to ask questions about how I spend my Sunday afternoons when I go out, and he takes special notice of whenever I take off early, as I did today. I think he's jealous that I might get something he doesn't. That's why he watches everything I do."

Bridget leaned her head against Ann's shoulder. "You must be careful."

"I try. There's so little time for us. I work late each weeknight, and Mother expects me to help at the house after the store closes on Saturday. Then there's Sunday morning Mass, and you know Father would die if I ever tried to skip Mass."

"We'll think of something."

"Let's sneak off to America and live in Texas."

Bridget blinked in surprise. "Texas. What on earth would we do in Texas?"

"We could be cowboys and carry six-shooters."

Bridget peered up at her. "Do they still carry six-shooters? Even if they do, I don't think we could be cowboys."

"I could be." Ann stretched her legs. "I think I could make quite a handsome man. Don't you?"

Bridget eyed Ann's small breasts and long lanky body. Years of standing and moving heavy merchandise at the store had given her muscles that Bridget had never possessed. "Perhaps, but I like you just as you are."

"It would be so much simpler if I were a man. I work as hard as my father does and harder than Hayden ever has. I'm as tall and nearly as strong as Hayden is, and I'm a much faster runner. Why shouldn't I be allowed the same freedoms? I've heard that there are women who pose as men and live their lives as they see fit."

Bridget didn't want to venture off into that area. Ann was so much more sophisticated about those matters. She would occasionally want to try some new sexual position she had read about in one of her naughty books. Bridget usually complied, but most of the time she was so embarrassed that she could barely keep her mind on what they were doing. She couldn't imagine how a woman could possibly go through life posing as a man. "I think it would be a hard life to always be hiding."

"Would you go to America if I did?"

Bridget tried not to show her distaste. She loved London and was quite happy in her small apartment. "I'd follow you to the ends of the earth." In truth, she had no desire to go to America or anywhere, and it wouldn't matter if she did. A trip to America would require much more money than either of them had. But, if it made Ann happy to think of living there, what harm was there in the little white lie?

Ann sighed. "I suspect that's where you think Texas is."

"Honestly, it wouldn't be my first choice of a place to live," Bridget admitted. It wouldn't even be in the top twenty-five, but she decided not to mention that fact. "You know I would love you no matter where we lived."

Ann set her teacup on the windowsill. "Don't fret. It's nothing more than a fantasy carried over from my childhood days. At the salary my father pays me, it would take me two lifetimes to save enough to immigrate to America." She turned back to Bridget with a look of longing in her dark brown eyes that clearly had nothing to do with Texas. "Now. If you're feeling properly nourished, I believe we have some unfinished business."

CHAPTER TWO

The rest of the week dragged along for Bridget. She tried to stay busy with her pottery, but even that failed to keep her mind off Ann. She rose early on Sunday morning to clean the theater. It wasn't as messy as usual and it only took her a couple of hours to put it back into shape. By Sunday morning, she was so desperate to see Ann that she considered taking a walk over to St. Bartholomew's Cathedral where she knew Ann and her family would be worshipping. Bridget had stopped attending church after her mother's death. She would gladly start going again if it provided her an opportunity to spend time with Ann. Aware that she couldn't simply show up at the cathedral and start talking to Ann, she paced. She rearranged items on the table so many times she soon had them completely out of place and had to move them back to their original location. Just before noon, she made tea for lunch and nibbled at a prune Danish. As she ate, she eyed the small potter's wheel tucked into the corner. She should pull it out and work or else she would have nothing to fire when the opportunity arose.

She had made an agreement with Akira Tanaka, a Japanese potter known for his magnificent glazing techniques. He allowed her the occasional use of his kiln in exchange for her assisting him three mornings a week. She didn't mind working for him because of the invaluable experience she gained. It had taken years before he even allowed her to watch as he dipped his pots in the secret glaze he produced. She didn't know the portions of ingredients used for the glaze, but she had kept a watchful eye on the numerous meticulously labeled bottles he kept in an unlocked cabinet in the back of his studio. Careful observation had shown her which of the bottle levels dropped after he prepared a batch of glaze. She didn't feel guilty about her spying because she knew she would never be a threat to his career. With her income, she struggled to save enough money to buy clay. It would be a long time, if ever, before she could afford to purchase the chemicals to make her own glaze.

Too restless to work, Bridget finished her tea and rinsed the few dishes she had used. Afterward, she grabbed her scarf and wrapped it snugly around her neck before pulling on her coat and hat. Maybe a walk would settle her down. Ann wouldn't be able to get away for hours yet. Her family always expected her to join them for a meal after church. She was in the process of pulling on her gloves when there was a noise at the door and Ann burst in laughing.

"You're early," Bridget said as she flew into her lover's arms before Ann could even make it into the room.

"Father wasn't feeling well and didn't want to eat. Hayden begged off as well. I was so restless after Mother and I shared a quick tea that she finally insisted I get out of the house for a while." She kissed Bridget again and hugged her. As she pulled away, she noticed Bridget's coat. "You were going out."

"No." Bridget started to unbutton her coat. "I was going crazy in the room missing you."

"Don't take your coat off. Let's go for a walk in the park. It's a beautiful day."

Today Bridget didn't want to share her time with Ann with any-

8

one else. Outside the room she wouldn't be free to touch her lover or kiss those beautiful full lips. Before she could resist, Ann was pulling her out the door.

Once they were outside Bridget's resistance disappeared as the weak sunlight began to warm her face. The air was a bit brisk, but there was little wind today and the sun gave promise of spring being just around the corner.

Ann slipped her arm beneath Bridget's as they strolled. "Don't worry," she whispered when Bridget tensed. "No one will think anything about us walking arm in arm."

Bridget made herself relax. Ann was right. None of the other strollers were paying them any mind, except for an occasional nod of greeting. They walked to the park in a comfortable silence.

"The trees will be budding out soon," Ann said as she leaned her head back and took a deep breath. "Did you know that in parts of Texas the winters are so mild the homes hardly need to be heated?"

Bridget shrugged. "No. I can't say that I know much about Texas."

"I've read that orange trees grow in people's yards. Imagine how it would feel to simply walk out your back door and pluck an orange off a tree."

Bridget smiled. It wasn't the image of herself plucking an orange that pleased her, but that of Ann doing so. "That would make you happy, wouldn't it?"

"Yes." She turned to Bridget and grabbed her shoulders. "Promise me that we'll do that someday—even if it's just for an extravagant holiday. Promise me we'll go to Texas together."

Ann's sudden seriousness made her uneasy. She pushed away the rational thought that they would probably never have enough money for such a trip and nodded. "Of course we can."

"Let's do it now." Ann's eyes blazed with such intensity that Bridget found herself shrinking away from them. "Let's leave here today while there's still time."

Bridget's concern was giving way to fear. "What do you mean while there's still time? We have plenty of time. We're both young and healthy." She stopped sharply. "Are you sick?" There was always some ghastly disease running through the city. Had Ann contracted one of them? Before her imagination could conjure even greater horrors, Ann stopped her.

"I'm not sick." She released her hold on Bridget and walked away quickly.

Left with no choice but to follow Bridget rushed after her. "Tell me what's wrong," she insisted when she finally caught up. She struggled to keep pace. "Ann, please talk to me. You're scaring me."

Ann simply walked faster.

Bridget was practically running. Finally, she stopped sharply. "Ann, slow down." To her surprise, Ann came to a halt and stared back at her. The look of pain in her eyes shocked Bridget, but when she saw the glint of tears, her heart faltered. She had never seen Ann cry. She rushed to her side. "Talk to me. What has happened to upset you so?"

Ann raised her arm as she started to speak but dropped it aimlessly.

Bridget ushered her to a nearby bench. "Sit down here and talk to me."

"I'm scared."

A cold wind seemed to blow through Bridget. She shivered and couldn't stop herself from glancing around them. She couldn't imagine Ann being afraid of anything—not her fearless, brave Ann. "Why?"

"Hayden has been dropping hints."

Bridget sat up sharply and looked around again. Everywhere she looked there were people—young couples strolling with their heads held close in loving conversation, old men and women sitting on benches feeding pigeons, children running and playing. She saw no one showing any special interest in them.

Ann seemed to sense her thoughts. "Don't worry. He's at home recovering from a hangover today. I checked to make sure he was sleeping before I left."

"What has he been saying?"

Ann shrugged. "It's not like it's anything directly, just little innuendos." She hesitated a moment. "Like the other morning at breakfast. Father was upset with Hayden, because he had been out so late the night before. Father had to make him get up. He wanted Hayden to help him uncrate a large shipment that had arrived the previous day. I was going to be working on the accounts and Mother was watching the counter. Anyway, Hayden was being more sullen than usual. Father became angry and started reprimanding him about staying out late and drinking. Suddenly Hayden jumped up and pointed at me and said that maybe Father should be more concerned about where I had been spending my time."

The cold in Bridget deepened. She couldn't stop the shudder that ran through her. If Mr. Taylor ever learned what was going on, he'd never let Ann leave the house again. She didn't even want to think about what would happen if her own father ever discovered her relationship with Ann. He would gleefully have her committed to an asylum, just to prove to her that he still held some power over her.

"We must be more careful," Ann said as she glanced around.

Bridget busied her hands by brushing at the imaginary lint on her coat. She couldn't help but feel that being careful simply meant she would be seeing less of Ann. The warm pleasantness of the day had disappeared for her. In its place was a looming sense of dread.

Maybe it was time they started thinking of a more extreme way to get away from Ann's family. It would have to be a drastic action, because Ann's father wouldn't simply let her leave on her own. He was too old-fashioned to accept the fact that his daughter could survive without him or some other man watching over her. London was an enormous city. It would be easy for them to disappear. She doubted Ann's father had the financial means for an exhaustive ongoing search for them. Her own father certainly had the means, but he didn't care what she did as long as she wasn't asking him for money and wasn't doing anything to embarrass him. She shivered again.

Ann stood suddenly. "Let's go back. I'm getting cold."

Once they were safely back inside Bridget's tiny apartment they tried to make love. They both flinched at every tiny noise from outside. Finally, they simply lay within the comfort of each other's arms. Bridget held on to Ann tighter than she normally did. She tried to loosen her grip, but the recurring thought that this could be the last time they would be together kept haunting her.

The sun was still high in the sky when Ann eased out of the embrace. "It's time for me to leave."

"Don't go," Bridget pleaded. "It's early still."

Ann kissed the top of her head. "I don't want to cause any undue suspicion." After pulling her thick auburn hair back up into the severe bun she normally wore it in, she began to dress.

Bridget swallowed her tears as she helped Ann with her corset. She would not let Ann see her cry. After tying off the corset, Bridget began to dress also.

Soon they were standing at the closed door kissing good-bye. "I may not be able to get away next weekend," Ann said quietly as she stroked Bridget's hair. "I love your hair when it's down."

The words began to eat through Bridget's determination not to cry. She turned away as she tried to speak, but tears choked off the words. All she could manage was a nod.

"Please don't be angry with me. I can stand anything but your anger."

Despite her resolve, Bridget turned and threw herself into Ann's arms. "I'll move to Texas with you. Or anywhere else you want to go." Tears flowed down her cheeks.

Ann lifted her head and wiped the tears away with her thumb. "Don't cry, my love. This is only for a while. If we don't give him anything to latch onto, Hayden will soon turn his attention somewhere else and forget all about me. Then we'll be able to see each other again."

For a few fleeting hours whenever you can sneak away. Bridget bit her tongue to keep from releasing her anger. She knew Ann was doing the best she could.

With one last kiss, Ann rushed out the door. As Bridget watched her leave, she realized that this was how their relationship would always be. At least until Ann's parents decided it was time she got married. Bridget closed the door. She didn't have the energy to face that demon.

CHAPTER THREE

Bridget tried not to think about Ann as she struggled through the next week. When Sunday came and went without so much as a word, she grew more despondent. After only a week without Ann, working with Mr. Tanaka no longer held any appeal, and cleaning the theater had become complete drudgery. Even her apartment had lost its sense of comfort. It seemed more like a prison now. As her anxiety grew, it became impossible for her to sleep for more than a couple of hours per night. The rest of the time she flopped around in bed trying to find a comfortable position or sat at the tiny table with a cup of tea and a pad, trying to determine how many pots she would have to sell so that she and Ann could immigrate to Texas. The faraway place that only a few days before had seemed so forbidding suddenly took on the aura of paradise. But, no matter how many ways she looked at the figures, they would be old women before they could afford to leave.

Somehow, she managed to get through the week and even managed to have two pots ready to fire when Mr. Tanaka told her she could use the kiln on Thursday. He was pleased with both her efforts, but to her they looked dull and lifeless. On Friday morning, she walked to the park where she and Ann had spent their last precious few hours together. She sat on the bench they had shared. As she stared out at children running in play and people milling around enjoying the warmth, a revelation hit her. She gave herself a swift mental kick before jumping from the bench and racing toward the tram stop. Why hadn't she thought about it before? Her father was one of the richest men in London. She would get the money from him. After all, he had come by the bulk of his wealth through her grandfather. She was entitled to something. In her desperation, she didn't allow herself to think about what she was going to say. There was nothing she wouldn't do to be with Ann.

When she reached the tall brownstone building that housed her father's vast network of offices, her bravado faltered. Not only was her father, Sean Sullivan, among the richest men in London, he was also a cruel man who had spent his life forcing everyone and everything around him into submission.

He was a man of moderate means when he married Jocelyn Miller, the only child of a kind-hearted and highly successful clothing manufacturer. Soon after the marriage, Mr. Miller began to suffer from stomach problems and within a year, he was dead. Sean Sullivan quickly took over the Miller clothing factories. He slashed wages and extended hours. If an employee protested the new working conditions, he was quickly replaced with a worker who didn't complain. Within two years, Sean Sullivan had tripled his net worth. He boasted that he had never failed in anything he set his mind to.

Bridget knew that was not true. Her father had failed to produce a male heir who lived long enough to take over his industrial empire. His first wife, Jocelyn, Bridget's mother, had given him a daughter and two sons. Both sons died before their first birthdays. When Jocelyn died, he quickly remarried a sour-looking woman named Agatha. Bridget had been seven then and held only the vaguest memories of the woman. After a three-year childless marriage, the doctors finally concluded that she was barren. Soon afterward Agatha was admitted to a sanitarium and within a year Sean Sullivan had been granted a divorce and had remarried. He was fifty-four when he married Louisa Wells. She soon convinced him to send Bridget to live with his sister, Colleen, in Yorkshire. Colleen was married to George O'Neal, a professor who had taught mathematics before health issues forced him to retire. He quickly took Bridget under his wing, and she became his personal solitary student.

In the meantime, Louisa bore a son, Sean Michael Sullivan, Junior, and a daughter, Lilly, who was only a few months old when she contracted measles. Sean Senior was in Liverpool on business and couldn't be bothered by mundane things that he felt should be taken care of by his wife—at least not until he received word that his son had also fallen ill. Then he immediately started for home, only to arrive too late and find that his wife and both children had died. Life had not beaten Sean Sullivan. Still determined to have a son to leave his legacy to, he went in search of another wife. At the age of sixty-one he married Eleanor Grimes, a young woman six months older than Bridget, who was by then eighteen.

Bridget returned to London to attend her father's wedding and decided to stay. Although she had grown to love her aunt and uncle, she was ready to face the world on her own. Times were changing and the views on what was and wasn't proper for women were slowly beginning to change. Thanks to George O'Neal's excellent tutoring, Bridget's education was superior to that of most men. And, although she would be forever grateful to him for all he had taught her about science, history and math, it was the love of the beauty of ceramics and glassware that her aunt had instilled in her that filled her every waking thought.

After her return from Yorkshire, she moved back into her room at her father's house. Things between her and Eleanor were tense but settled down some after Bridget met Mr. Tanaka and was away from the house three mornings a week. On one of those mornings, the rail system was undergoing repairs and she was forced to take an alternate route to Mr. Tanaka's studio. The new route took her past a theater. In the front window was a sign advertising a position for a charwoman. At the time, she did little more than glance at it. A few days later when the real problems at home began it would prove to be her salvation.

Her father had called her down to dinner, which was unusual. As they ate, he announced that he had decided it was time for Bridget to get married. She instantly told him she had no interest in marriage. Not one to be deterred, he ignored her objections and a few days later arrived home with a man nearly twenty years her senior. When her father pulled her aside and told her this was the man he wanted her to marry, Bridget's anger flared. She quickly showed Sean Sullivan that his eldest daughter had inherited much of his stubborn determination. After weeks of endless battles, he came home early one Friday evening and called Bridget downstairs. The argument began almost immediately, but this time he exploded in a fit of rage and slapped her across the room. He declared her too ugly for a suitable marriage and then ordered her out of his house.

Not willing to beg him for anything, she packed a small valise. As she packed there was a light knock on her door. Hoping her father had changed his mind, she opened it and was surprised to find Eleanor.

"Sean has left to go back to work. He wants you to leave before he returns." She looked away as if embarrassed.

"Fine." It was all Bridget could manage. She had almost no money and no idea where she would go. It was already late.

Eleanor reached into her apron pocket and removed something. She took Bridget's hand and quickly pushed the object into her hand. "It's not much, but it's all I have." Without waiting for Bridget to speak, she rushed off. The object was five pounds. Combined with the two pounds she had in her pocket, Bridget now had seven pounds to live on.

As she left the house, she decided to go to Mr. Tanaka's studio. There was a cot in the back. Maybe he would let her sleep there until she could contact her Aunt Colleen to see if she could go back and stay with them for a while. She was almost to the studio when she remembered the sign on the theater. She didn't want to leave London again. If she had a job, maybe she could find a small room to rent somewhere.

At the theater she knocked on the front door. When she didn't receive a response she made her way down the alley to the back door and knocked again. She was about to leave when the door was suddenly opened by a short, balding man with thick glasses perched on the end of his nose.

"I want to inquire about the cleaning position."

He looked her up and down before shaking his head. "It's not a job for the likes of you, lass." His voice carried a heavy Irish brogue.

"Mr. . . ."

"Cleary," he said.

"Mr. Cleary, I really need this job."

He shook his head. "The pay is only ten shillings a month."

"I'll take it."

He studied the valise she was clutching as he ran a hand over his head. "Are you runnin' away?"

She almost laughed. "No, sir. I'm much too old to be a runaway."

He chuckled. "'Tis ancient you are, then."

She glanced down, embarrassed. This man was clearly three times her tender eighteen years.

"I'll not have an angry husband come poundin' on me door."

"No one will be pounding on your door because of me. I promise."

After a long-suffering sigh, he relented. "We have a performance on Friday night, plus a matinee and evenin' performance on Saturday. You'll have to clean after each."

She smiled. "Thank you. I'll do a good job." She shifted the valise to her other hand. It was starting to feel heavy.

He cleared his throat. "'Tis no business of mine, but . . ." He hesitated. "'Tis a wee bit late for a lass of your character to be out and about." He pointed to the valise. "Would trouble be knockin' at your door?"

Bridget felt herself blush. "Nothing I can't manage."

"Me daughter Mary is about your age." He grabbed his head. "The good Lord was having a wee bit of fun when he gave me and the missus five girls."

Despite his words, Bridget saw his eyes light up when he mentioned his daughters. There was a stab of pain in her heart that she had never seen the same light in her father's eyes. "You love your daughters a great deal, don't you?"

He seemed taken aback by her question. "What father could say no to such a question?"

"Mine." Bridget hadn't intended to speak. The word just seemed to fly from her mouth.

As he rubbed his head again, she wondered if his hair had disappeared from normal loss or if the nervous habit had helped it along.

He pulled a small pipe from his jacket pocket and busied himself with filling it. After a long process of getting it lit and working properly, he cleared his throat again. "Meanin' no disrespect, miss, but do you have a place . . . what I'm meanin' is . . ." He took a long draw on his pipe.

Embarrassed, Bridget tried to shrug it off. "I'll find a room nearby. You needn't worry. I'll be fine."

"'Tis worried I'd be if you were me daughter Mary." He rubbed his head again. "If you were willin' to do a wee bit more work I might be able to help you out some." He motioned for her to follow him. "Theater people are an odd lot. Most of 'em believe they're more important than royalty, for sure. Before each new show we'll be havin' rehearsals two or three nights a week, and sometimes they make a bloody mess of the place. I usually have to clean up after 'em. I can't afford to pay you more, but if you could see yourself clear of takin' on that too, then, maybe we could do a little barterin'." He stopped and opened a door. "There's a cot in here from years back when I used to nip at the bottle a wee too much, but now"—he patted his stomach—"me constitution isn't so good." He flipped a switch and light filled the room. "'Tis not much, but 'tis yours if you like." He pointed to the light. "I had the whole place fixed up with electricity."

Bridget glanced around the room. It was empty except for a few boxes and a cot. On the cot was a pitifully thin mattress that looked old but clean. "It's a deal."

He rubbed his head again before bursting into a big smile. "Tonight you'll come home with me, and the missus will take care of everything. Tomorrow, I'll move this mess out, and we'll find you a wee bit of furniture."

Bridget held up her hand to stop him. "Mr. Cleary, you've done more than enough already. I'll be fine here tonight."

Appalled, he looked at her. "You can't be stayin' here and sleepin' on a bare mattress."

She patted the valise. "I have a cloak that will cover the mattress nicely."

It took her twenty minutes to convince him that she would be all right. Before he left her, he showed her where the water closet was.

Her life quickly settled into a comfortable groove and stayed that way for the next three and a half years. Money was always scarce, but under Mr. Tanaka's occasional tutoring and a lot of practice, her pottery continued to improve. She augmented her meager salary with the occasional sale of plain, practical ceramic mugs that she sold to local mercantiles. One shopkeeper had even allowed her to display a few of her decorative vases on a tiny shelf near the rear of the store. Surprisingly, a couple had actually sold. Throughout this time, her father never bothered to try to contact her. About a year after she left, she read in the paper that Eleanor had given birth to a daughter they named Clara. A couple of years later she saw another notice about the birth of their second daughter, Elizabeth. During those long and sometimes lonely years she began to wonder what was wrong with her. Not only had her father disowned her, but she still hadn't met a man who held her interest for more than a few minutes. Just when she was sure she was destined to spend her life alone she met Ann and gradually everything fell into place.

Bridget had gone to the Albert and Victoria Museum to see an exhibit of ancient Asian pottery. Near the end of the display, she became completely engrossed in a beautiful collection of painted Karatsu ware from the late sixteenth century. She hadn't noticed the woman beside her until she spoke.

"Did you know that offerings of tea were once made to the spirits of esteemed monks in Buddhist temples?" the woman asked.

Bridget turned and found herself staring into warm, dark brown eyes. To her mortification every logical thought she'd ever possessed disappeared. As she struggled to think of something at least halfway intelligent to say, the woman smiled suddenly.

"I must confess," the woman said. "That's all I know about tea other than I could really use a cup about now. Would you like to join me after we finish looking at the exhibit?"

Bridget nodded and managed to smile.

"I'm Ann Taylor." She offered a neatly gloved hand.

Even through the material of their gloves, Bridget could feel heat radiating from Ann's hand. "Bridget Sullivan."

In her nervousness Bridget missed the next several items, but as they made their way through the exhibit she began to relax, and by the time they were leaving Ann had her laughing and chatting as if they were long-lost friends.

She was snapped from her reverie by a dapper-looking young man who had stopped to hold the door open for her. She smiled her thanks and rushed inside before she could change her mind.

Since she didn't have an appointment, it took her almost two hours to get in to see her father. Sean Sullivan gave no special consideration to anyone. When she was finally ushered into his office she was surprised to see how much he had aged in the almost six years since she had last seen him.

He barely glanced up from the papers on his desk.

"I need some money," she said without preamble. She knew there was no need in beating around the bush with her father.

"I can't help you."

"You mean you won't," Bridget said. Her knees were practically knocking, but she was here for Ann, and nothing short of him tossing her out of the office was going to dissuade her. "All right then,

I'll settle for some of the money you stole from my grandfather."
She almost fainted beneath the steely glare he fastened on her. She couldn't stop herself from cringing back into the chair when he stood.

"I'm late for a meeting. I'm sure you can find your way out."
Before she could respond, he walked out of the room.

She cursed herself all the way back to her apartment. What had convinced her to approach him for money? He had tossed her out of his house without a backward glance, and he did so knowing she had nowhere to go. Why would he give her money now?

Her anger with her father was quickly replaced by her concern about Ann. When she entered her apartment, she immediately noticed a rather large bundle on the bed. Beside it, she found a scribbled note that she recognized as Ann's handwriting. Sick that she had missed her, she dropped to the bed and sighed in frustration. After a moment, she read the note. Not sure she had read it correctly she read it again.

Dearest Bridget,
Inside this bundle you will find some clothes and an envelope containing ten pounds. If you don't already have a traveling trunk use some of the money to purchase one. Pack these clothes and everything you value in the trunk as soon as possible and be prepared to leave. Please don't tell anyone about this. I will see you as soon as I safely can. Love, Ann

Bridget tore into the bundle and found several items of men's clothing and an envelope with ten pounds inside. She looked at the men's clothes, puzzled. What was Ann doing? What had she meant by she would see her as soon as she safely could? Was she in some type of trouble? Had Hayden guessed their secret and talked to Mr. Taylor? She read the note once more before slipping the money into her pocket. She trusted that Ann knew what she was doing. If she wanted her to buy a traveling trunk then that was exactly what she would do. Before leaving, she carefully wrapped all of the pots on the shelf and placed them inside a bag. Then, she walked to a nearby shop that sold used items. She had purchased all of her meager supply of furniture here.

The owner, Mr. Lewis, an older man with a thick bushy mustache and rotund middle and who was never lacking in a smile, met her as she came in.

"So you need some more furniture?"

She smiled and shook her head. "No, I'm looking for a steamer trunk today."

"Oh, you're taking a trip."

She started to nod but then thought better of it. "No. A friend of mine is going to Rome to visit relatives. She needs another trunk. I thought you might have a nice used one."

He nodded. "I have a beauty. It just came in last week. I don't know much about it. There's no label to indicate the manufacturer. But no matter, she's a beauty." He motioned for her to follow him.

"How much?" she asked as they walked.

He shrugged. "It's a beautiful mahogany trunk and seems very well made."

Bridget knew he was trying to soften her up for the price. "Mr. Lewis, I'm sorry, but I don't have a lot of money. In fact, I was sort of hoping I could barter these for at least a portion of the cost." She held up the bag of pots.

He stroked his moustache a moment before shrugging. "Let's see what you have."

A half an hour later she was back at her apartment. Mr. Lewis's nephew, who worked as his delivery boy, had hitched up the old mule to the delivery wagon that Mr. Lewis still used and given her a ride back to her room with the beautiful trunk. Mr. Lewis had taken the pots in an even trade for the trunk.

Once the trunk was inside, she began to pack. She wrapped the pearl necklace and emerald brooch that had belonged to her mother in a flannel square and slipped them inside a small pocket. She packed her meager wardrobe and scant personal effects, but they made very little impact in the enormous storage spaces of the trunk. Even with the clothes that Ann left, there was still plenty of space. After the trunk was packed and closed, Bridget made a cup of tea and sat down to wait.

CHAPTER FOUR

It was four days later when Ann finally barged into Bridget's apartment.

"Bridget, it's time. We have to leave. Hayden knows about us and he's going to tell Father."

Bridget could only stare. Even though she had suspected that this was coming, she still wasn't ready to accept it as fact. Hayden would talk. Now, others would know about them. How much would Hayden remember from that brief meeting? Would he remember her name? Would they be able to trace her back to her father? How diligent would they be in their search? She hadn't mentioned her father's name to the theater owner, Mr. Cleary, but Mr. Tanaka had once asked her father's name and what he did. At the time, there had been no reason to lie. Now she wished she had. She shook her head to clear away the thoughts. She was being silly. Hayden wouldn't know anything about Mr. Tanaka—unless he had been following her, too. The thought caused another shiver to run up her spine. If her father ever found out, he would make her life miserable.

"We can't stay here," Ann said. She looked around and saw the trunk. "Is everything packed?"

"How did Hayden find out?" Bridget asked. She needed time to think. How could they possibly run? They had no money. She didn't want to end up living in some rat-infested tenement.

"I don't know what got him started, but I was right. He has been following us." She glanced toward the window nervously. "He told me he had even been following you."

Bridget followed her gaze and frowned when she saw the window. She had cleaned it that morning and already the ever-present soot coated the pane. She tried to focus on the soot, because she didn't want to think about what Ann had just told her. Had Hayden been following her when she went to her father's office?

Bridget's frown deepened as thoughts of her father returned. What would he do if he discovered his oldest daughter was sinning against nature? Not that he cared about her so much, but the embarrassment it would cause him would be unforgiveable. He would still be angry about her visit. He was not a man to forgive and forget. He might decide to use the situation as an excuse to have her committed.

The smart thing for her and Ann to do was to leave London as quickly as possible, but to do so would mean giving up so much. She glanced at the potter's wheel where the piece she had been working on earlier still sat.

Ann seemed to read her thoughts. "You know I can't stay here," Ann said. A slight tremble in her voice betrayed her fear. "He'll have me locked away. I've told you how he feels."

"He wouldn't lock you away." Bridget tried to sound more certain than she felt. Ann's father did seem fanatical in his religious thinking.

"You don't know him and how fervent he is in his beliefs." Bridget saw the flicker of fear in Ann's eyes. She knew it took a lot to scare her. "We'll leave."

"We need to leave now."

Bridget glanced around the room that she had grown to love so. Her brain told her she had to leave, but her heart was still holding on to the happy memories she had here. Once they stepped out the door, everything would change. If they were going to have any chance of avoiding being found they would have to change their names. She would have to start over as a completely unknown artist. She closed her eyes. "We'll have to find a boardinghouse where we can stay until we decide where we want to go." She took a deep breath and let it out slowly as her thoughts scrambled in a dozen different directions. Everything was happening so fast. How could she just walk away? She needed to offer some sort of an excuse to Mr. Tanaka and Mr. Cleary. They had both been so sweet. She couldn't simply walk away with no explanation for her sudden disappearance. "Don't worry. We can find another place to live. Maybe even go to Paris or—"

"I want to go to America, now," Ann said.

Bridget blinked in surprise. "America? We can't just up and leave for America."

"Why not?"

"We can't afford it, for one thing." When Ann didn't respond she continued, "We'll have to wait. As soon as you don't come home, your father will start looking for you. If Hayden has been following you, eventually they'll come here. When they discover us gone, they'll start searching the train stations. Besides, we can't simply hop on a ship and go to America. I'm sure there's a proce- dure to be followed."

Ann began to pace. "I'm convinced it's the only place we'll be safe."

"Rubbish." Bridget started pacing in the other direction. "We could hide from them right here in London." She saw Ann's shoul- ders set into that determined stance she assumed whenever she made up her mind. Bridget knew that if she didn't do something quickly, they would be headed to America as soon as Ann was able to secure the necessary funds, which she would certainly do once she made up her mind. "All right," Bridget said. "We'll go some- place where we'll be safe for the next few days. Then we'll have time to decide what we want to do."

"I already know what I want to do."

"What about me? Does what I want matter?"

Ann stared at her for a long moment, but slowly the determination in her shoulders began to ease. "Of course it does."

After an uneasy moment, Bridget continued. "Then we need to find someplace safe to stay." She glanced around the room. "Where are your clothes? Did you leave them in the hallway?" She stepped toward the door. Ann started to speak, but Bridget cut her off. "Where are we going?"

"I don't know yet, but I'll think of something."

"How will we get there?" Bridget thought about her own meager savings of five pounds, tucked away in a sock beneath her mattress. Even combined with the ten Ann had given her earlier it wasn't going to get them far. They needed money, but where would they get it? She had the two pieces of jewelry that her grandfather had given to her mother, but she couldn't bear the thought of parting with them. Even if she did, the money wouldn't last long. How would they make a living? Ann had been working in her father's store for all those years. She might be able to find another sales position, but not if they were trying to hide. What would she do? Pottery was all she knew.

With only fifteen pounds between them, going to America was out of the question. With their low prospects of finding work, it was ridiculous for them to think about going anywhere. They had to have more money before they could leave.

Suddenly she thought about her father's wall safe hidden behind the painting in his bedroom. Her father had always been obsessed with keeping large sums of cash handy. The first thoughts about the cash were innocent, but gradually her thoughts became more menacing. She checked the small pendant watch she wore on a gold chain around her neck. The watch had also once belonged to her mother. Her father wouldn't be home for at least three more hours. She would have to work quickly. She dug beneath the mattress and retrieved the sock holding her money. Then she retrieved the ten pounds Ann had left for the trunk and gave it back to her. Ann started to ask questions, but Bridget quickly stopped her.

"I don't have time to explain now. I want you to wait for me here. If I'm not back in two hours, get a taxi and take the trunk to Waterloo station. I'll meet you there as soon as I can." She placed her carefully hoarded cash in her pocket. She would use some of it to take a taxi across town. If things didn't work out, she could take a tram back, but right now she needed speed.

"What are you going to do?"

Bridget held up a hand to stop her again. "I really need to leave now."

"Where are you going? Can't I come with you?"

"No. There's no time to explain."

"I want to tell you about a great idea I had."

Bridget pulled on her coat. "I'm sorry, but I don't have time right now. I have to take care of something. It shouldn't take long, but if I'm not back in two hours I want you to go the Waterloo station and wait for me like I asked."

"Why Waterloo? Won't they start looking for us at the stations?"

"Probably, but we don't have enough money for a hotel. It might cause too much suspicion if we arrived at a boardinghouse looking for a room late in the evening." She took Ann by the shoulders. "Remember to wait for me here for two hours and then go to the Waterloo station. If I don't show up by morning, then . . ." She trailed off. How could she explain what would happen if her father caught her stealing from him?

Ann wrapped her hand tightly around Bridget's wrist. "Are you planning on doing something dangerous?"

Bridget tried to smile and look relaxed. "Of course not. I'm just going to see a friend about collecting some money he owes me." She saw the flash of doubt in Ann's eyes.

"Who owes you money?"

Bridget pulled away. "I told you. I don't have time to explain. I have to hurry." She started to move away. "Remember what I told you."

Ann nodded, but the look of fear and doubt was still in her eyes.

Without giving herself time to change her mind or to examine too closely what she was about to do, Bridget rushed out of the door. As she went, she prayed her father still used the safe.

CHAPTER FIVE

Bridget approached the large Tudor-style house slowly. She had no idea how she would manage to get into her father and step-mother's bedroom without being observed. He wouldn't be there. He never came home before eight and often much later. Neither would there be a problem with the servants, because her father was too cheap and suspicious of having strangers in his house to hire any. Her stepmother, Eleanor, would probably be busy preparing dinner now. It might be difficult to get past her undetected.

Bridget realized the timing might work in her favor. The kitchen was in the back west side of the house. It might be possible to avoid Eleanor by slipping around to the east side of the house and entering from the garden. Her mere presence at the house would be enough to cause concern since after her argument with her father she was no longer welcomed here. She would have to be careful not to involve her stepmother in her deceit. She didn't necessarily have any feelings for the young woman, but Eleanor had been kind to her once and didn't deserve to be blamed for her deed. Her father wouldn't hesitate to take his anger out on whoever was closest.

The neighborhood remained blissfully quiet as Bridget carefully made her way around the side of the house into the large formal garden. The smell of newly turned soil greeted her. A quick peek through the French doors that led into the cozy sunroom told her she was alone. She eased inside and made her way toward the back stairs that led up to the second floor and her father's bedroom. The faint odor of kidney pie sent her stomach into an uneasy roll. It was her father's favorite meal, but she had never been able to tolerate it. How many whippings had she received from him over not eating the horrid stuff? She shook her head to clear away the memories. Now was not the time to start dragging up the past. With a final look down the hallway, she scurried up the stairs on her tiptoes. When she reached the landing, she stopped long enough to catch her breath and study the second-floor hallway. The nursery was next door to her father's bedroom. She peeked into the open doorway, but the crib was empty. As she eased toward her father's bedroom her heart began to pound so hard she could no longer hear anything except the roar of her pulsing blood.

She froze when she realized that nearly ten years had passed since she first found the safe. What if he no longer used it? Maybe he had moved it all to a bank. She dismissed the idea. He distrusted anything he couldn't control. He would use a bank to keep up an appearance, but he would have the bulk of his cash somewhere he could get to it quickly. Logic told her that it would still be in the safe. Ten years ago, it hadn't taken her long to find where he had written the combination on the wall behind another painting. Her father might be a genius in some areas, but he had always had to write things down in order to remember them.

A board squeaked beneath her foot and snapped her attention back to what she was doing. Thankfully, the bedroom was on the opposite side of the house from the kitchen, but she couldn't be sure where everyone was. She knocked softly on the bedroom door in case her stepmother was inside. She had no idea what she would say or do if Eleanor answered. Or God forbid her father flung open the door. Her knees began to shake at the mere thought of him being inside the house. When there was no response to her light tap she took a deep breath, eased the door open and peeked inside. She was surprised to find that it looked the same as it had when her mother had used the room. She tried not to think about the past as she slipped into the room and closed the door. Her mother had been a meek, shy woman who did her best to please. Unfortunately, her best had never been good enough for the tall overbearing man she had married.

A faded painting of sunflowers caught Bridget's attention. She ran across the room, removed the painting from the wall and almost laughed aloud when she found the safe there. She rushed across the room to the painting of children standing on a bridge. Behind it, she found the combination still visible on the wall. She read it twice before going back to the safe. Her hands shook so it took her two tries to get the safe open. Even after all these years, the staggering large amount of cash shocked her. How could someone with so much money live so frugally? She had never known hunger, but the family meals had always been simple. As a child, she had been expected to wear clothes until they were worn out or outgrown. There had always been coal for heat, but it had to be used sparingly and an extra layer of clothing was always needed to keep warm. She remembered times when her mother would put her in bed to keep warm during the coldest days. It was only after she had discovered the safe that she realized how wealthy they really were and what a miser her father was.

As she stood staring at the cash, she realized she hadn't brought anything in which to carry it. A quick peek into an armoire revealed a small blue-and-white-flowered needlepoint valise sitting at the back of the shelf. She grabbed it and stuffed two large stacks of bills inside. As she pulled the money from the safe, she knew she should feel guilty about stealing from her father. Instead, she focused on all the beatings she had taken over minor infractions and the beatings her mother had taken simply because he felt like lashing out. She had intended to take only a couple of stacks, but her anger fueled her into adding a few more. Most of his fortune had stemmed from her Grandfather Miller's factories. The money rightly belonged to her mother. She was doing no more than taking a small portion of the money that was rightly hers. If he kept this much in the house, how much was sitting in the bank?

When she was satisfied she had taken her fair share of the safe's contents, she closed it and hung the sunflower painting back in place. After a quick glance around to make sure everything looked as it had when she entered, she left the room, made her way back down the stairs to the sunroom and out of the house.

Bridget couldn't stop looking over her shoulder as she rushed back to her apartment. She knew what a mean and powerful man her father was. He wouldn't take the invasion of his home lightly. Guilt began to eat at her when she thought about what her father would do to her stepmother when he found the money missing. He would likely blame her, if not directly for taking the money, then for failing to protect it from being stolen. It wouldn't matter that she might not even know the safe existed. He would find out the truth. After he realized that Eleanor hadn't taken the money, how long would it take him to come looking for her? He would certainly put everything together if Ann's father should happen to make the connection between them. She prayed that her father wouldn't open the safe until she and Ann were safely out of his reach. She refused to think about what he would do to her if he ever caught her.

CHAPTER SIX

Rather than take the slower tram home, Bridget used her own money to pay for the taxi fare back to her apartment. She clutched the valise filled with cash to her breast as the taxi left the upper-class homes behind and headed toward the industrial section. She had stolen money from her own father. She waited for the guilt to hit her, but it wouldn't come. As she stared out the window she realized the only guilt she felt stemmed from her lack of remorse. Surely, she should be feeling some shame for having broken into her father's home. *Maybe I'm as cold as he is.* The thought shot a hot flame of fear through her. She shifted restlessly.

"Would you like the newspaper?" the taxi driver asked as he held the paper over the seat. "I've finished it already, and the old lady don't care to read them."

"Thank you." Bridget took the paper and idly flipped through it. She was too nervous to read. She was about to toss it aside when an advertisement caught her attention. After reading it over several times, she realized that Ann was right. What they needed was a completely new start. They couldn't spend the rest of their lives looking over their shoulders and worrying about when their fathers would catch up with them.

After paying the taxi driver and adding a nice tip, she tucked the paper beneath her arm. Throughout the transaction, she kept the valise tightly clutched to her breast. As the car pulled away, she anxiously scanned the street outside her apartment. She wasn't even sure what she was looking for, but when she saw nothing that triggered any concern she made her way inside. She was trying to think of a way to explain the cash to Ann as she pushed the door open. The sight of Ann's brother, Hayden, standing by the bed made her knees buckle. She grabbed the door for support and almost dropped the money.

As the two stared at each other, a smile gradually spread across Hayden's face. The familiarity of the smile made Bridget look closer. It wasn't Hayden after all.

"What in the name of God have you done to yourself?" She gasped as she peered closer into Ann's face.

"I fooled you for a moment, didn't I?" Ann asked. "I think this will be the perfect disguise. Everyone will be looking for two women, not a young married couple."

Bridget closed the door behind her. Ann's transformation was so complete she could only stare.

"Don't you like my new look?" Ann turned slowly. "I commandeered some of Hayden's old suits that he no longer wore. I told my mother I was taking them to give to the needy. That's how I got the ten pounds. Father heard me and gave it to me for the poor box. I know I should feel guilty, but I rationalize my dishonesty with the notion that I'm nearly insolvent. I realize it's an inadequate rationalization, but it soothes my conscience." She continued to turn. "The suit fits quite well, don't you think?"

Bridget took in Ann's new look. A silver cravat set off the waistcoat, a lovely silvery-gray pattern with elaborate lilac embroidered threads running through it. Gray pants worn over black boots made of soft leather flattered Ann's long legs. Bridget's breath caught as

Ann lifted the hat and her beautiful hair cascaded downward over her shoulders. She replaced the hat at a dapper angle.

"Well, what do you think?" Ann asked.

Bridget smiled. "I can't decide." She moved beside Ann, dropped the valise and newspaper on the bed and slowly made a circle around her. "It's a little strange to see you dressed as you are, but I must admit you're very handsome."

Ann removed the hat and tossed it onto the bed. "The idea came to me the other night. They'll be looking for two women traveling together. No one will give us a second look if we travel as man and wife." She leaned in and kissed Bridget's nose.

Bridget tugged on Ann's auburn hair. "I don't think you'll be fooling many people once they see these gorgeous locks."

"That's why you have to cut them off."

"What?" Bridget was certain she had misunderstood.

"If we're going to fool people, you have to give me a haircut."

"No. I won't do that." The mere thought of cutting Ann's beautiful hair hurt her.

"Where's your scissors?" Ann began opening drawers on the small chest of drawers until she found them.

"Ann, I won't cut your hair."

"You have to. Two women traveling will be much more conspicuous than a man and his wife." She stopped her search and took Bridget's hand. "Think about it. Everything will be so much simpler if we're a couple. No one will pay us any mind. We can walk into a restaurant and eat, check into a hotel, book a train to anywhere we want and no one will think anything about it. But if we do any of those things as two women, people will be more apt to notice and remember us."

She wanted to argue, but everything Ann said made sense. Bridget ran her hand through Ann's hair.

"It will grow back." She held the scissors out to Bridget. "Come on, we have to hurry. It's getting late. Father will be home in a couple of hours."

Thirty minutes later, they were standing in front of Bridget's small mirror studying her handiwork.

"It's sort of ragged in spots," Bridget said.

"On the contrary, I think you've done an excellent job."

Bridget smiled. "You're either being very kind or your eyesight is failing."

"My eyesight is perfect." Ann turned to kiss her.

As the kiss deepened, Bridget's hands made their way into Ann's closely cropped hair. Her pulse quickened when she heard Ann's sharp intake of breath. She felt her dress being eased upward but fought the urge to give in to the magic that she knew her lover's hands could create. Instead, she slowly opened the buttons on Ann's trousers and slipped her hand inside. Her first reaction was shock when she realized that Ann was wearing men's underwear. The shock rapidly gave way to pleasure when she discovered that her fingers weren't blocked by the normally burdensome layers of women's underwear. She quickly located the warm dampness of Ann's desire and soon had her lover's hips thrusting in unison with her stroking.

Bridget's desire grew as Ann came against her hand, but when Ann again reached for her, Bridget pulled back. "We don't have time now." For the briefest instant, she envied the freedom Ann's new wardrobe allowed her.

Ann's face grew serious. "You're right. We should leave before someone shows up looking for us."

They stood staring at each other.

"Where are we going to go?" Ann asked at last as she closed her trousers.

"America."

"We don't have enough money."

Bridget straightened Ann's tie. "We have plenty of money, but we need a plan if we're going to get away with this." She began gathering her scarf and gloves. "For now, we need to find some-place where we'll be safe for the night." She took Ann's arm.

"How much money do we have?"

Bridget paused. She couldn't lie to Ann, but she was ashamed to tell her about the money. "We have plenty of money," she said evasively.

"How much is plenty? Twenty pounds, thirty?"

"Quite a bit more than that."

Bridget felt Ann's body tense beneath her fingers.

"Bridget, where did you go?"

There was no point in trying to lie to Ann. She'd never be able to pull it off. "I went to my father's."

"Your father gave you money?" Ann was clearly flabbergasted.

"I got money from him," Bridget hedged. She could no longer meet Ann's gaze.

"You got money from him. You mean you borrowed it?"

"Sort of."

Ann grabbed Bridget's shoulders. "Stop playing games and tell me what you did."

"I went to my father's house and took an early withdrawal on my inheritance."

"Inheritance?" Ann's eyes widened and in a moment of uncharacteristic blasphemy she exclaimed, "My God in heaven, you've stolen money from your father."

"No. I took money that should have rightly belonged to my mother." Bridget pulled away. "Father made the bulk of his money from the mills he stole from my Grandfather Miller. I didn't do anything more than he did."

"How much did you take?"

Bridget bit her lip and glanced toward the valise. "I don't know. I just grabbed some." She picked up the bag and opened it.

Ann thumbed through one of the bound packets of bills. There was a quick intake of breath as her hand flew to her chest. "Bridget, these are thousand-pound bundles. There's a fortune in there." She raked her hand through the bundles in the valise. "Are they all thousand-pound bundles?"

"I didn't have time to stop and count it." She tried to keep the irritation out of her voice. She started to remind Ann that if it hadn't been for her brother, it wouldn't have been necessary to steal the money, but she bit back her remark. Accusations wouldn't help now.

Ann rubbed her forehead. "This is a horrible mess." She stared at the money. "Why did he have so much money at home?"

Bridget stared at the bag. "My guess is that he doesn't want anyone to know how wealthy he truly is. My father is not an honest man. I'm certain most of his fortune is from questionable means."

"That's all the more reason for us to worry. You told me how crazy mean he is. When he finds the money missing, he'll probably send an army of thugs after us."

"It won't matter because we'll be long gone by then." She pulled a bundle of bills from the bag and pushed them into Ann's hands. "I want you to keep this in case we get separated." She glanced at Ann's clothes. "You were right. Your disguise is exactly what we need."

Ann pushed the money away. "I don't want it. We can't keep this money. God punishes sin." She looked at Bridget. "We can't start our life together with stolen money."

Bridget took Ann's hand. "Listen to me. My mother's family was very wealthy. After Grandfather died, my father took over everything. From that moment on, my mother had to ask and sometimes beg for everything she ever had. Not once did he use any of that money to make her life easier." She struggled to keep her voice steady. "That greedy bastard killed my mother as surely as if he had put a gun to her head." She grabbed the valise and shook it. "Everything in here and more belonged to my mother. I did nothing more than take what already belonged to me."

"But he didn't give it to you. You stole it."

Bridget bit back her growing anger. "It wasn't his to give. I have as much right to it as he does. More," she added harshly.

Ann stood silent, but her face clearly revealed the demons she was wrestling.

"You have to take it." Bridget gave her a small grin. "You're the man. What will people think if your wife carries the money?"

After a moment Ann took the bundle and broke the band. After splitting the stack into two piles, she slipped them into both of the inner jacket pockets. "This business of being a man may be tougher than I thought. Maybe I should have taken some of my mother's old dresses and portrayed myself as your matronly aunt instead." She took a deep breath and slowly exhaled. "So, what do we do now?"

"We get out of here as quickly as possible." Bridget grabbed the newspaper from the bed and pointed to the ad she had spied in the taxi. "Look, it sails out of Southampton a week from tomorrow and we're going to be aboard."

Ann's eyes grew larger as she stared at the newspaper. "I've been reading about her. She's beautiful, but will we be able to get tickets on such short notice? And what about all that paperwork you were talking about?"

Bridget pointed to the bottom of the advertisement. "It says that accommodations are still available. We'll pretend to be a newly married couple setting off on our honeymoon. We'll holiday for a couple of months and see what we think of it. Hopefully, by the time we return they won't be searching for us so intently." Ann was nodding so Bridget rushed on. "If we like America, we can come back here and start making the necessary arrangements to immigrate there."

"That sounds good, but the trip will be expensive. Second-class tickets are twelve pounds each." She touched her jacket where the money rested. "But then, I guess we can afford it."

"We're not going second class," Bridget said. When she saw the small flicker of disappointment on Ann's face, she quickly added, "We're going over in a first-class suite."

Ann looked at the newspaper. Her eyes widened. "Are you out of your mind? First-class suites cost eight hundred and seventy pounds . . . each . . . one way."

"Think of it as a wedding present from my father."

Ann began to jump up and down, laughing hysterically. "We're going to sail to America on the RMS *Titanic!*"

CHAPTER SEVEN

An hour later, they were registering at a hotel near Waterloo station as Mr. and Mrs. Howard Franklin, newlyweds from Yorkshire who, in the excitement to begin their honeymoon trip to America, had arrived in London for a bit of sightseeing. The *Titanic* wasn't due to sail until Wednesday. Ann, now posing as Howard, looked properly embarrassed as she provided unplanned explanations as to why they had arrived at the hotel without reservations.

Bridget had little trouble blushing as she kept her gaze fixed on the floor, eternally grateful she wasn't required to deal with the issue. She marveled at Ann's poise in handling the arrangements for their extended stay. As Ann talked, Bridget glanced discreetly around the lavish room that she'd read so much about. The Goring had been built two years earlier and had the distinction of being the first hotel in the world that offered private bathrooms and central heating in each of the rooms. The hotel was located next to Buckingham Palace and was often visited by royalty and other notable guests.

Bridget had deliberately chosen the lavish hotel because it would be among the last places their parents would ever think to look for them. She doubted her father could even comprehend the concept of spending nearly eight shillings per night for a hotel room. Especially considering the average unskilled workers in London made less than twelve shillings per week. She was certain her miserly father paid his employees even less. With a touch of regret she thought about her tiny room. She would miss it and Mr. Cleary. She had left him a short note explaining that she was moving to Yorkshire to live with her aunt who had suddenly taken ill. She felt guilty about the lie and about leaving before he had a chance to hire someone in her place. To ease her conscience she told herself that he wouldn't have any trouble engaging a new charwoman. She had also posted a short note with the same message to Mr. Tanaka.

Ann had finished her somewhat lengthy explanation, and Bridget glanced up in time to see the clerk take in their appearance. Ann's suit was a little dated, but it was of a quality cut and her own dress, while simple, was still suitable for the occasion. She held her breath as his eyebrows seemed to merge when he studied Ann's recent haircut. He seemed to be on the verge of speaking when Ann leaned toward him and spoke to him in a tone so low Bridget could not hear.

The clerk looked at Bridget and smiled knowingly. "I believe we'll be able to find you a room," he said, suddenly all charm.

As soon as they were registered, a bellhop appeared to take their trunk. Bridget could barely contain her curiosity as they made their way to their room.

Her inquisitiveness was temporarily forgotten as she gaped at the elaborate furnishings. The crowning glory of the room was a magnificent brass bed displaying cameo medallions that had been hammered out in both the headboard and footboard. In one corner sat a pair of walnut armchairs also of rococo style. Exquisite deep carvings of roses and leaves graced the top crest of the chairs. The gold fabric was a perfect complement to the red and gold striped upholstery of the Venetian Rococo hand-carved settee, which sat across from the chairs. A carved gilt console table stood in the center of this sitting area. The table's beveled marble top rested on a base intricately carved with flowers that accentuated the central carved shell on the front of the skirt. Beneath the shell sat a cherub holding a bow and arrow. Across the room, a beautiful armoire with an elegantly carved cresting along the top, front and sides filled an area between two floor-to-ceiling windows. Bridget went to stand in front of the armoire. "Look at this." She traced a gloved hand over the arched, mirrored door.

"Quite the place," Ann said after she returned from seeing the bellhop out. "I was beginning to think they weren't going to allow us to stay."

"That reminds me. What did you say to him?" she asked.

Ann grinned. "I told him that you thought my hair needed trimming and that you had insisted on doing the chore yourself."

Bridget frowned. "I'm not sure I like you portraying me as the incompetent wife."

Ann's arms slid around her and pulled her close. "Can we save this until later? Right now I have something else on my mind."

Bridget ran her fingers through Ann's hair. "I think I like this," she whispered.

"Let's hope you like this better." Ann's thumb began to move across a swollen nipple.

Soon clothing was scattered in hastily discarded heaps around the bed. They didn't take time to turn down the bed but simply fell across it. Bridget closed her eyes and hugged her lover closer to her as Ann's fingers slipped into her. As her passion grew, everything else was forgotten. When she came, she buried her mouth against Ann's creamy shoulder and clutched her closer.

It was hours later before they found time to talk.

"We should go to the ticket office first thing tomorrow morning," Ann said as she idly traced her fingertips along Bridget's thigh.

"What if they ask us for something we don't have?"

"Such as?"

"I don't know. Health records or something."

"I really don't think the White Star Line is going to be asking its first-class passengers to produce papers declaring they are free of lice and other vermin." Ann chuckled.

Bridget ran her fingers through the back of Ann's cropped hair. "Do you suppose we'll be traveling with someone really famous?"

"I should think so. According to what I've been reading about the ship, she's supposed to be the most luxurious vessel ever launched."

"How long are you planning to keep up your masquerade as Mr. Howard Franklin?"

Ann's hand stopped. "Does it bother you?"

Bridget thought about it for a moment before answering. "No. It doesn't really. I actually think you make quite a handsome man, and I freely admit I love the freedom it is allowing us."

"How would you feel about me continuing to live as Mr. Howard Franklin for as long as I can get away with it?"

Bridget gave it a moment of thought. "It would make our lives much simpler, but what happens if you get sick and need a doctor?"

"I suppose that's something I would worry about when the need arises."

Bridget turned and kissed Ann's cheek. "In that case, my dear husband, you will need some more clothing. In fact, if we want to fit in with the rest of our fellow first-class passengers we both need more clothes," Bridget said as she sat up suddenly. "We have to go shopping tomorrow. At the very least you'll need a couple of new dinner jackets, shoes, a few more shirts . . ." She began ticking items off on her fingers.

"I have plenty of clothes."

"You've only been a man for a few hours and you're already getting difficult."

"That's not fair. I've never liked shopping for clothes."

"If we're going to travel first class without attracting undue attention, we'll have to dress the part." Her mind was clicking. "I'll need new hats, dresses, scarves, gloves and shoes. We'll need another trunk and a couple of valises. Then there's the matter of toiletries we'll need and—"

Ann pulled her down and kissed her. "Right now, all I need is this." Her hand slipped up the inside of Bridget's thigh.

"You're just trying to distract me."

"My dear Mrs. Franklin, are you already trying to avoid your recently acquired wifely duties?"

Bridget blinked at the use of their assumed name. "Good Lord, and above all, we have to remember our new names."

The next morning, under the guise of Mr. and Mrs. Howard Franklin, Bridget and Ann enjoyed a leisurely breakfast in the hotel's elegant dining room.

"Do you think it'll be safe for us to be out shopping?" Ann asked. "I don't think my parents would recognize me, but your father would certainly know you."

"My father rarely leaves his mills during the day. I seriously doubt he will be anywhere near Harrods, and unless he has changed considerably he certainly wouldn't have opened an account for my stepmother there. I don't think I'll have to worry about encountering anyone I know."

"Still, we should be careful."

Silence fell between them for a long moment.

Bridget broke it after gazing around at the luxuriously furnished dining room. "This place is beautiful. I feel like a queen," she whispered as she took Ann's hand.

"You shall always be my queen," Ann murmured, kissing the back of Bridget's hand.

Unused to the public displays of affection, Bridget blushed and started to withdraw her hand, but Ann held on to it.

"Now, now, Mrs. Franklin, you are going to have to become accustomed to my small public displays of affection." She kissed Bridget's hand again.

Bridget stared at Ann and shook her head. "It's amazing how much freedom a haircut and a pair of pants can make. Maybe I should try it."

Ann nearly choked on her tea. "What a tangled mess that would be—two women posing as two men." She shook her head.

"Come on. I've had enough of this chattering. We need to locate a ticketing agent and then go shopping."

Ann folded her napkin and placed it beside her cup before rising and offering Bridget her arm. "All right, but please don't expect me to stand idly around in Harrods while you spend hours in the hat department."

"I don't expect you to stand idly around," Bridget replied. "I expect you to go over to the men's department and procure all the items you'll need for the trip."

"Do you suppose they sell Stetsons?" Ann asked.

Bridget patted her arm. "No, dear. I suspect you'll have to wait until we arrive in Texas before you can purchase your Stetson and six-shooter."

Ann sighed. "Very well. As for the tickets, there is an agent a couple of blocks over. I suggest we go there."

"How do you know that?"

She leaned close to Bridget's ear. "It's a man thing, my dear." When Bridget didn't respond, she continued, "I went down and inquired at the desk while you were bathing."

When they stepped out of the hotel, the weather was pleasant so they walked to the ticketing agent's office. Bridget stood quietly as Ann asked about the availability of first-class suite tickets.

"Oh, yes, sir," the young man working at the window replied. "There are still accommodations available." He adjusted his eyeglasses.

"Excellent," Ann replied. "I would like to book passage for my wife and myself."

"Final destination?"

"America."

The clerk nodded. "Visiting family, are you?"

"No." Ann turned to Bridget and smiled. "We're on our honeymoon."

He smiled shyly and ran a bony hand over his pale, thinning

44

hair. "Oh, congratulations. You've chosen the absolute perfect ship. She's a real beauty. The finest ever built by anyone." He began to prepare their tickets. He handed over a pamphlet. "You're very fortunate to be sailing on her maiden voyage." He glanced at Bridget and smiled shyly. "It's a story you'll be able to tell your children and grandchildren."

Bridget felt her face begin to color and looked down.

The clerk didn't seem to notice as he continued with his praising of the ship's amenities. "Did you know that she is two hundred and sixty-eight meters in length and has nine decks total?"

"I read somewhere that it's a rather large ship," Ann replied.

The clerk looked up startled. "Large? Sir, she is tremendous. She has a *heated* swimming pool. The first *ever* built on a ship. There's a squash court, Turkish bath, electric lights and heat in every stateroom, four electric elevators, a veranda café"—he leaned forward in his excitement—"with real palm trees, and an authentic Parisian café complete with French waiters."

Bridget was afraid he would faint if he didn't take time to breathe soon.

"There's a smoking room for the gentlemen, a reading and writing room for the ladies. There is a first-rate gymnasium with all the latest equipment, which includes a mechanical horse and mechanical camel. They even have an infirmary that includes an operating room and—"

"Are there lifeboats?" Bridget asked, more to interrupt his tirade than out of actual interest.

He stopped sharply and looked at her as if she had grown an extra head. "Ma'am, I can assure you one won't be needed. This is the safest ship ever built. It has . . ." His face softened as he blushed deeply. "So sorry. I tend to get carried away. It's just that she's such an amazing vessel. I do wish I could sail with her." He settled down and quickly prepared their tickets. After he discovered they were staying at the Goring Hotel, he handed Ann a card. "Give us a call on Tuesday and we'll make arrangements to pick up any luggage you'll want stowed. It'll save you the bother of having to deal with it." He turned his attention to Bridget. "We encourage passengers to pack separately all items not needed during passage. Those pieces of luggage will be so marked and stowed below." He held up a hand as if expecting questions. "Of course, should the need arise any or all stowed items can be brought to you during the voyage." He turned back to Ann. "What about passage to Southampton? Will you be taking the boat train on the day she sails?" Apparently seeing the look of uncertainty on Ann's face, he continued, "I highly recommend you do. It's much more convenient that way. The train leaves from Waterloo Station at nine o'clock on Wednesday morning." He glanced up. "That would be Wednesday the tenth, of course, and it takes you directly to the ship in Southampton. The trip is about an hour and forty minutes. Some passengers choose to go the day before and spend the night at the South Western House. I've heard that it has excellent accommodations." He paused. "Of course, it's a much older establishment and not quite as elegant as the Goring." He leaned forward and lowered his voice. "I understand that both Mr. Ismay, the chairman of the White Star Line, and Mr. Thomas Andrews, the chief designer of the grand ship, will be staying at the South Western on the eve of departure."

Ann turned to Bridget. "Would you mind leaving London a day early?" Her eyes held the look of a child on Christmas morning.

Bridget knew Ann was anxious to see the ship that everyone had been talking about for so long. "I think that's a marvelous idea. We'll be right there and not have to worry about getting to Southampton on the day the ship sails." Bridget would have preferred to stay away from the train stations as long as possible. She was certain their families were looking for them by now. They still had six days before they would travel, so maybe it would be all right. As Ann and the clerk continued with the preparations, Bridget studied the woman she had fallen in love with. At first, it had been rather disconcerting to see her dressed as a man, but she had to admit she was quickly growing to like the new look. There was something very dashing about Ann's dark looks, and she loved the way the long line of the jacket accentuated Ann's height. Earlier, on the stroll over from the hotel, she hadn't failed to notice the less than covert glances that some women sent their way. She smiled to herself when she thought about what their reactions would have been had they known what those trousers truly hid.

Ten minutes later, they were back on the street waiting on a tram that would take them to Harrods. They stood off to the side by themselves.

"I was very impressed with the way you handled that," Bridget said as she slipped her hand beneath Ann's arm.

"I was afraid I'd make a horrible mess of it."

Bridget squeezed her arm. "Nonsense. You looked as though it was something you did on a daily basis." She leaned her head against Ann's arm. "You know, at first I wasn't too sure you could pull off this little charade, but you are really very good at it. You are handling everything magnificently."

"Well, let's hope I manage to handle purchasing a pair of trousers with the same finesse."

"I could purchase them for you. Mother occasionally did my father's shopping."

Ann smiled down at her. "Thank you, but no. It's something I have to do. If I'm going to live as Mr. Howard Franklin, I need to be prepared for whatever comes my way." She looked down at Bridget. "I also intend to take full advantage of every other benefit that's offered to my new gender."

"Such as?"

"Such as kissing you whenever I like." She softly kissed Bridget's lips.

CHAPTER EIGHT

Late that afternoon Bridget and Ann lay sprawled across the luxurious bed. Around the room sat literally dozens of packages from Harrods that had been delivered by a small army of delivery boys. Amazingly, most of the packages were purchases Bridget had made. Ann's clothes were being tailored and weren't due to be sent to the hotel until Friday morning. Ann had also taken the time to get an appropriate haircut and purchase an additional steamer trunk.

"Was there anything left in the store when you finished shopping?" Ann asked, her voice thick with exhaustion.

"If there was I can't imagine what it might have been. How was your shopping experience as Mr. Franklin? What did you buy?"

Ann yawned. "You'll have to wait for the fashion show, but the overall experience wasn't nearly as bad as I had imagined. There were a few anxious moments. It's truly amazing how much better service men receive. Although I nearly fainted when they measured my inseam. Then there was a moment when a salesclerk measured my foot. He actually almost said I had a foot like a woman."

"What did you do?"

"Oh, I acted properly tweaked and he was quick to soothe my masculine ego. I suspect his sudden need to placate me had more to do with the couple of hundred pounds' worth of merchandise I had already selected than it did with my actual manliness."

Bridget wanted to laugh but was too tired. "My feet are killing me," she said. "I don't even have the energy to take my shoes off."

Ann stood slowly. "I'm going to run us a hot bath. It'll make us feel better."

A few minutes later Bridget, dozing, felt her shoes being removed. She sighed in contentment as Ann began to massage her aching feet.

"Come on. Hop up. The bath is ready."

Ann helped Bridget up and gently undressed her.

Bridget was surprised to see that Ann had already stripped. As she eased into the hot water, she couldn't suppress the sigh of pleasure that escaped. "This feels so good," she breathed as she eased forward to let Ann slip in behind her.

"Lean back on me and rest," Ann said as she pulled Bridget against her.

"This was so sweet of you."

"It was the least I could do. I remember how painful women's shoes are."

"Are men's clothes as comfortable as they look?"

"Much more so. Losing that cursed corset is the real blessing."

"What I wouldn't give to burn mine."

"I never understood what purpose they served," Ann said.

"They keep women from thinking."

"How's that?"

"They're so bloody uncomfortable that we can't think when we're wearing them. That's why men insist we wear them. Although my mother always said they help keep your shape."

"I think you should throw yours away. Your shape is perfect.

You have no need for them."

Bridget chuckled. "Now wouldn't that cause a proper scandal?"

"Do you think women in Texas wear corsets?"

"I would imagine so. After all, they have to maintain a slim torso if they're going to wear those six-shooters."

"Ah, now you're teasing. I've already told you. Women don't wear six-shooters."

Bridget's eyelids were drooping. It took all her energy just to keep them open. When Ann began massaging her shoulders, she could no longer fight the exhaustion.

The water had cooled when Bridget opened her eyes. The room was nearly dark. Ann's head was lying upon her shoulder and she could tell by the steady breathing that she too had fallen asleep. She roused her gently.

"Oh." Ann groaned as she tried to push herself up into the tub more. "My neck is aching. How long did we sleep?"

"I'm not sure but it must be getting late." She eased herself from the tub and pulled the drain plug before helping Ann out.

"I hope we haven't missed dinner. I'm famished."

"So am I."

Upon discovering they still had time to go down to dinner they started getting dressed.

"Are you sure you want to wear this?' Ann asked as she helped Bridget lace her corset.

"No, I don't, but until the world comes to its senses, or I get brave enough to borrow your trousers, I'll keep wearing it."

Ann kissed her head. "I love you."

Bridget waited until the corset was secure before she turned and folded herself into Ann's arms. "I love you, too."

"Hurry and get dressed. I really am starving."

Bridget chose one of her new purchases, a beaded ivory satin and tulle evening gown with a flowing train. She had fallen in love with the gown's magnificent beadwork.

"That's a beautiful gown," Ann said as she pulled on a black dinner jacket and buttoned it over a bibbed white shirt. She touched the jacket's side pocket, then began digging into one of the packages of her purchases.

"You bought a pocket watch," Bridget said as Ann removed a beautiful gold watch.

"Yes. I've always wanted one, but I could never find a dress with an appropriate pocket."

Bridget laughed as she noticed Ann repeatedly touching her jacket pocket. "What's in your pocket?" she asked as she fussed with her hair.

Ann looked at her and smiled. "Aren't you a curious bunny?"

Bridget ignored her as she made one last check of herself in the armoire mirror. She knew she would discover what Ann had soon enough. Ann never had the patience to keep a secret.

"I bought you a present today." Ann removed a small box from her pocket.

From the size of the box, Bridget knew it was jewelry. "What is it?"

"Just a little something I thought you might like to wear."

Bridget tore it open and stood dumbfounded as she stared at the wedding ring. It was a wide gold band with a delicate wreath-like design engraved into it. Her jaw dropped even more when Ann bent down on one knee. "I know it's a bit late to be asking this, but, Bridget Sullivan, would you do me the honor of being my wife?"

Tears blurred Bridget's vision as she stared down at the woman she loved more than life. In answer, she knelt down with her and kissed her. "Yes," she whispered as she held the ring out to Ann. "Put it on me, please."

The ring slipped on her finger and fit perfectly. Ann pulled another package from her pocket and opened it to display a matching band. "I thought that since we're posing as man and wife, we should make it as realistic as possible." She handed Bridget the second ring and held out her hand as Bridget slipped it on her. A shadow of sadness crossed her face. "I won't ever be able to make it right by giving you a big wedding in a church and all, but you'll always have my heart."

Bridget couldn't stop the tears of happiness from flowing down her cheeks. "And you have mine," she whispered.

They remained on the floor for a long moment embracing. Ann finally pulled away. "I hate to be an ogre, but I swear if I don't eat soon, I'm going to collapse."

Bridget giggled and wiped her eyes. "Mercy, that honeymoon didn't last long."

CHAPTER NINE

The following morning they slept in and then went down for a late breakfast.

"What would you like to do today?" Ann asked as she spread a healthy dollop of first cream and then jam onto a scone.

"I suppose we should go through all of our purchases and start packing."

"It's only Thursday. They're not going to pick up the luggage until next Tuesday."

"I know, but the room is such a mess now and it'll only be worse when the rest of your clothes are delivered from the tailor. I want to get my stuff sorted and put away."

"You're right," Ann said. "I'm being lazy. I was hoping for a relaxing day today. I don't think I've recovered from yesterday yet."

"You seemed quite recovered last night." Bridget smiled when she saw the slight flush spread across Ann's cheeks. After dinner the previous evening, they had gone for a short stroll in the gardens before turning in for the night. They both had fallen asleep almost immediately. In the wee hours of the morning, she had turned over. As soon as her hand came into contact with Ann's bare back she had been struck with a wave of desire so strong she had to act on it. If Ann had been surprised by the interruption of her sleep, she hid it well. In no time at all, Bridget was on her back with Ann's mouth bringing her to levels so high, she'd had to cover her head with a pillow to smother her cries of pleasure.

"You can't hold me responsible for that," Ann replied. "I was resting peaceful when suddenly I was attacked by a highly impassioned woman. With all that noise you were making, I'm surprised the people next door didn't complain."

It was Bridget's turn to blush.

After breakfast, they returned to the room and spent the next several hours opening the bundles from Harrods and sorting them for packing. It quickly became apparent that they had both been rather extravagant in shopping.

"We have enough clothes here for the entire voyage and then some," Bridget said as she gazed around at the clothing that draped and covered every available spot of the room. "I never realized you were such a shoe fanatic." She nodded to the eight pairs of new shoes Ann had purchased.

Ann picked up a pair of calfskin boots. "Men's shoes are so much more comfortable than women's. They don't pinch the feet as badly."

"Is that the reason you felt you needed eight pairs?"

"No, I decided to buy several pair in order to delay the ordeal of having to buy more."

Bridget nodded. "In an odd way that makes sense." She picked up a bundle of gloves. "Let's get this stuff put away. The sun is shining brightly out there and I want to take a walk."

By early afternoon, they had managed to get the majority of the items packed away. They would still have to pack Ann's clothes once they arrived from the tailor's, but there was still plenty of room in the second trunk that would be used for the clothing they would need while onboard the ship. The used trunk Bridget had purchased would be stowed.

"That's enough for today," Bridget declared as she pushed away a stray lock that had worked its way loose from her upswept hair.

"Wonderful. Let's go for that walk now," Ann said as she reached for her jacket.

Bridget brushed a hand over her clothing. "Just let me change my blouse and do something with this hair."

"I'll be right back," Ann said. She was gone before Bridget could ask where she was headed.

After changing her blouse for a pale peach-colored one, over which she added a matching crocheted jacket, she began working with her hair. As she fussed with trying to tuck the stubborn lock back into place she felt a slight stab of jealousy at the simpler maintenance required with Ann's much shorter hair. Ann's decision to masquerade as a man had granted them amazing freedom. Bridget marveled at her lover's ability to continue with the guise. She would have been too petrified to attempt such. "Not that I could have gotten away with it," she muttered as she glanced at her ample bosom. Without a doubt, Ann's height and boyish build helped, but there was also that air of confidence Ann possessed. She wondered if Ann's responsibilities at the mercantile had helped to instill her sense of self-assurance or if it was something she had been born with.

Before she could ponder the subject further, Ann called to her from the main room. "Aren't you ready yet?"

Bridget rolled her eyes. "You know you're even starting to sound like a man."

Ann stepped into the bathroom and held up two bags. "I'll have you know that while you were fussing with your beautiful curls, I was downstairs sweet-talking Mrs. Stimpel into preparing us two picnic lunches."

"Who is Mrs. Stimpel?"

"She's in charge of the kitchen staff." Ann started out of the room.

"Wait a minute," Bridget said, rushing after her. "How is it you know this woman?"

Ann smiled. "A gentleman never kisses and tells."

Bridget placed her hands on her hips. "If I ever catch you spreading your kisses around elsewhere, you won't live to tell."

Ann leaned forward and kissed her softly. "Of that you have no worries. Let's go. My nose tells me there's a roast beef sandwich in one of these bags."

The park was crowded with playing children and watchful parents and nannies.

"Did you want children?" Ann asked suddenly as they strolled past the bulk of the crowd.

Bridget shrugged. "Sure, I've thought about it. I mean, I just assumed that I would have them someday."

"Will it bother you not to?"

"A little, but I'll be all right." She squeezed Ann's arm, wishing she could remove the trace of sadness she saw there. "I love you. If not having children is the price I have to pay, then so be it."

"You're a beautiful woman, Bridget. It's still not too late for you to be married."

Bridget stopped sharply. "I'm not with you because I couldn't find someone to marry." Her anger cooled. "Are you trying to divorce me already? I thought Catholics decried divorce."

"I'm trying to be serious," Ann replied rather sharply.

"Then be serious. I don't want a man. I want you. Besides, it's not completely out of the realm of possibility that I could have married a man unable to father children. Who knows? It's even possible I might be barren."

"I doubt that."

Bridget doubted it also but didn't want to argue the point. "Why are we discussing this?"

"I don't know. I guess I'm getting a little nervous."

"Are you having second thoughts about us?" A tiny finger of doubt began prodding Bridget.

"Not about the way I feel for you. I . . ." She faltered. "What if I can't make a decent living? What if I can't find a job? How will we live? How—"

"Stop it!" Bridget practically stomped her foot. "If you're trying to talk your way out of this relationship, say so. Otherwise, I don't want to hear another word."

"Well, you don't have to worry about those things."

Bridget stepped closer to her. "Ann Taylor, have you forgotten who you're talking to? I may give in to you a lot, but I'm not some timid little flower that will snap with the first gust of wind. If we're going to have a relationship it's going to be equal." She stabbed a finger into Ann's chest. "Do you hear me? Equal." She shook her head furiously. "Besides, I don't know what you're worried about. We have enough money to last us for years if we're careful."

"That's just it," Ann replied. "We aren't being careful. We're spending it like there's no tomorrow."

Bridget stopped and frowned. "You're right," she said eventually. "We have been going a little crazy, but I want this trip to be one you'll remember for the rest of your life." She grabbed Ann's hand. "We'll be more careful if it'll make you feel better."

Ann rubbed her forehead. "It's not just that. What are we going to do? Later I mean. Once we get back. I have to find a job."

As they started walking again, an idea suddenly came to Bridget. "You know lots about operating a mercantile. What if we opened our own store? It's something we could work together at. We have the money."

Ann nodded and took a moment to answer. "That's perfect, actually."

Bridget watched the frown leave her lover's face. A look of anticipation and excitement replaced it.

"Why didn't I think of that?" Ann asked. "It's absolutely perfect." She raised her hand to point out an empty bench and seemed surprised to see she was still holding the lunches. She leaned forward and kissed Bridget's forehead. "I'm sorry. I've spoiled our outing."

"You didn't spoil anything. From now on when you're worried, I want to know. We should be able to talk about anything." She glanced up at Ann. "I'm completely serious about this relationship being equal."

• • •

The afternoon slipped by quickly. By the time they had returned to their room it was almost dark, but Bridget felt their relationship had reached another level, one that brought them closer together and a little more secure in their love.

The conversation had also served to tear open a bubble of fear that Bridget had been struggling to keep under control. Long after they had gone to bed and Ann had fallen asleep, she lay staring at the ceiling. She knew that they were both worried about running off. The fact that they rarely mentioned it didn't lessen their fears. She could only guess at how Ann must feel about her parents. They were probably worried sick about her. At the same time it was terrifying to imagine what would happen if they were caught. She couldn't fathom living without Ann in her life.

In less than a week, they would be aboard the *Titanic*, sailing toward America and a long holiday. Maybe they would feel safer then. Even with that promising notion, she still shivered when she thought about her father and his anger. She knew he would never stop searching for the money she had taken from him. For a brief moment, she regretted taking the money, because a part of her would forever be looking over her shoulder, watching for him. Yet the money was allowing her and Ann to build a life. All she had to do was to stay one step ahead of him, she told herself. With that thought, she finally settled into a restless sleep.

CHAPTER TEN
Tuesday, April 9, 1912
Southampton

On Tuesday morning, the boat train ground to a stop behind the South Western House in Southampton. A swarm of porters hovered alongside the tracks, ready to usher the passengers into the hotel.

Ann handed one of the porters a stub. "Have our luggage taken to the room. We'll be back shortly."

"Can't wait to see her, huh?" the man asked as he winked. "She is a beauty, sir, if I do say so myself."

Ann slipped the porter some coins before taking Bridget by the arm and leading her through the crowd.

"I can't believe you," Bridget said. She clutched her hat as they practically ran around the building toward the dock. "You're worse than a child."

"You don't understand," Ann said. "This is the biggest ship ever built. In fact, it's the largest moveable object ever built by man."

"Slow down. I can't breathe." She was about to protest further when they came around to the side of the hotel. Ann stopped so sharply that Bridget almost knocked her down. With one hand clutching her hat and the other clutching Ann's arm, Bridget stared at the colossal ship before them. Her gaze traveled ever upward to the four buff-colored funnels that gleamed in the midday sunlight. She blinked, unable to believe her eyes. Never had she seen anything so massive. Even though she had read that the *Titanic* was as tall as an eleven-story building, the sheer size of the ship still astounded her. How would they ever get something that gigantic to move, much less float? She didn't know how long they stood there staring before a voice brought them back.

"Isn't this the most exciting adventure ever?"

Bridget turned to find a young couple standing beside them. The woman held a baby. The man had spoken.

"Quite amazing," Ann replied.

The man rushed on. "She's two hundred and sixty-eight meters long with a gross tonnage of forty-six thousand, three hundred and twenty-eight tons. Fully loaded, her total capacity is three thousand five hundred and forty-seven passengers and crew. There are nine decks. She uses eight hundred and twenty-five tons of coal per day and needs—"

"Trevor," the young woman beside him interrupted.

Bridget struggled not to roll her eyes. What was it about men that made them memorize all those numbers? Wasn't it sufficient to say the ship was gigantic?

He stopped and smiled sheepishly. "So sorry. I'm Trevor Sheffington." He extended his hand to Ann. "This is my wife, Emma, and our daughter, Amelia."

"I'm Howard Franklin," Ann replied with only the slightest pause. "This is my wife, Bridget."

Bridget nodded to the man and smiled at the pale, painfully thin woman. An awkward silence overtook the group. "How old is your daughter?" Bridget asked to ease the situation.

"She'll be six months next week," Emma replied as she lifted the corner of the blanket encasing the baby.

"She's beautiful." Bridget touched a finger to the baby's tightly closed fist.

"Isn't that just like women?" Trevor said. "Here we are standing before the engineering marvel of the decade, of all times even, and they start chattering about babies."

"Personally, I think my daughter is much more of a marvel than some silly boat," Emma replied as she gave her husband a look that made his cheeks turn scarlet.

He cleared his throat. "I'm sorry. I was a bit crass." He glanced at Bridget and shrugged.

"Go along and have a look-see," Emma said. "I know you're about to bust a seam." Ann and Trevor took off like schoolchildren at the end of the day.

"Your husband seems to know a lot about the ship. Was he involved in building it?"

"Mercy, no. Although, he would have loved nothing better than to be able to see it every day. He has been obsessed with the *Titanic* from the first moment he heard about it. I think he has read everything ever printed about her. He even wrote letters to the White Star Line asking questions." Emma lowered her voice. "Now that I see it, I must say it is rather amazing."

"I never dreamed it would be so . . . so . . . big!" Bridget said. "I mean, I've read about it in the newspapers, but words don't do it justice. And who would have thought there would be so many people here?"

"It seems as though everyone wants to see her before she sails."

"Are you and your husband immigrating to America?" Emma asked.

Bridget couldn't stop the flush that crept into her cheeks. She was going to have to get used to hearing Ann referred to as her husband. "No. We're taking a holiday." She stopped. "We're on our honeymoon."

"How fantastic. Do you have family there?"

Bridget glanced toward Ann and Trevor, who were several steps ahead of them. That was the problem with lying. Once you started, the lie took on a life of its own, until it finally took over everything. She and Ann obviously needed to work on their story better. They hadn't really discussed their subterfuge in much detail. They should have realized that they would be conversing with strangers on the cruise, strangers who in good manners would certainly be asking questions. She tried to hedge her answer in case she needed to retract it later. "Not really. What about you?"

"We're moving to California." The baby whimpered and Emma fussed with her for a moment. "I had a rather hard time with Amelia and the doctors suggested a warmer climate would be better for me." She glanced toward her husband. "Trevor worked with his father. They had a very successful fish market at Billingsgate, but Trevor was miserable there. All he has ever wanted to do is farm. It's all he ever talks about, but land here is so expensive. When his father died several months ago and left everything to Trevor, he decided America would be the answer to all our problems. So, we sold everything."

"Won't you miss your families?"

"There's really no one left. My parents died when I was a child," Emma said. "Trevor's mother died six years ago. He has an elderly uncle, but he's never really kept in touch." Emma was clearly tiring, so Bridget offered to carry Amelia for a while.

"Thanks," Emma said as she eased the sleeping child into Bridget's arms. "Trevor normally helps carry her, but he's so excited about traveling on this ship, he has forgotten everything else."

"Howard is the same." Bridget let the name dance around in her mind for a moment. It seemed odd to refer to Ann as Howard, but she guessed she would eventually get used to the idea. "He doesn't say much about it, but I can tell he's really excited."

"I must admit, I'm a little nervous," Emma said quietly.

"According to everything I've read, the ship is extremely safe."

Emma pushed a stray wisp of hair from her gaunt face. "Oh, I'm not concerned about the safety of the ship." She nodded toward the *Titanic*. "Look at it. What could possibly damage something as enormous as that? I'm worried about becoming seasick. I've heard dreadful stories." She tried to tuck the wayward hair back into place. "I've never been on a ship, so I don't know how I'll do."

Bridget shifted the baby in her arms. How could such a small thing get so heavy so quickly? "I'm sure you'll be fine. If not, there are doctors onboard who can help you."

"Trevor insisted we buy a first-class ticket. It was so expensive. I tried to convince him to purchase less-expensive tickets, but he was worried about me." She ducked her head. "He says I'm a bit too conservative with the money."

Bridget wasn't comfortable hearing about the Sheffington's financial situation. If they could afford first-class tickets then apparently Trevor wasn't worried about a lack of funds. "Which deck are you on?"

"B Deck. I believe Trevor called it the Bridge Deck."

"That's the same deck we're on."

"Wonderful," Emma exclaimed. "I'll feel so much better knowing someone else onboard." She reached for the baby. "Let me take her for a while. To be such a little thing she certainly can get heavy."

Bridget gratefully handed the baby over. Her arms were aching.

Trevor and Ann had finally reached the rail that prevented the curious sightseers from venturing any closer to the ship. When Bridget and Emma joined them, Ann slipped an arm around Bridget's shoulders.

"Have you ever seen anything so magnificent?" she asked.

"Just think," Trevor began as he took the baby from Emma, "in less than twenty-four hours we'll be aboard and headed to a new home."

The four stood staring at the ship until Emma leaned her head against Trevor's shoulder. "I think we'll be heading back to the hotel," he announced. "I'm afraid I've nearly worn my little Emma out."

They said their good-byes. Ann and Bridget watched them walk away.

"How about a bite to eat?" Ann asked. "I'm starving."

Bridget chuckled. "You're always starving."

CHAPTER ELEVEN

The following morning the sky had just begun to lighten when a low incessant humming woke Bridget. Ann stirred beside her.

"What's that noise?" Bridget asked sleepily.

Ann slipped out of bed and made her way to the window. "My gosh. Come and look at this."

Bridget scurried to the window. A large crowd of people had already started to form along the dock. "What's going on?"

"I guess they're here to see the ship set sail."

"Already! It's not scheduled to leave until noon." Bridget was tired. She hadn't slept well. In fact, for the past two nights her sleep had been restless and troubled. Last night, she had dreamed that seconds before the ship sailed, Ann's father had arrived with a large contingent of police officers. Mr. Taylor had tried to drag Ann off the ship. When she continued to resist him, the police officers had joined the melee. In the midst of the scuffle, Ann's shirt ripped open and exposed her breasts. When the other passengers saw Ann's true gender, they started hissing and throwing things at her. Bridget tried to fight her way to Ann, but her attempt was useless. The angry mob was impenetrable. The frightening sense of helplessness swept back over her as she stared out the window at the crowd. A shiver ran up her spine.

"Are you cold?"

Bridget turned away from the window. "We have lots of time yet. Let's go back to bed."

As soon as they were snugly beneath the covers, Ann pulled Bridget into her arms. "Come here. Let me get you warm." She rubbed Bridget's back. "Are you getting nervous about the trip?"

"Not about the trip." She stopped. "Well, maybe a little."

"Sea travel is much safer now than it has ever been."

"I'm not concerned about the ship. I suppose I'm a little nervous about going to America. It's so big and . . . and . . . wild."

Ann chuckled. "I doubt if it's any wilder than certain areas of London."

"In London, I know which areas are undesirable. How will we know which areas to stay out of in America? We won't know where to go."

"Darling, they speak English. We'll simply ask someone."

Bridget realized she was worrying about the petty things to avoid thinking about her real concerns.

"Talk to me. What's really bothering you?"

She told Ann about the dream.

"I'd be lying if I didn't admit that I've worried about that too," Ann said. "I guess it's because we're so close to leaving. In my heart, I know we'll be safe once the ship sails. No one will ever think to look for us in America."

"What about when we return?"

"We'll just have to be careful." Ann shifted slightly. "I have to confess something. I've been feeling guilty. I don't want my parents to worry about me. I know they are worried sick now, because they don't know what's happened to me. What if I sent my parents a letter when we reach New York? I could tell them I have moved to America. That I want to start a new life there."

"They'll come looking for you."

"No. It's too far away. I don't think they will. I know they'll be hurt. My father will be furious, but they'll both be so relieved that I'm safe, I think they'll leave me alone."

"What'll happen once we come back here?" Bridget was certain she already knew the answer.

Ann sighed. "I don't know." She eased her arm from beneath Bridget's head and sat up with her back propped against the headboard. "We didn't think this through very well, did we?"

Bridget wasn't sure if she was supposed to answer or not, so she waited. She didn't have the same responsibilities to a family that Ann did.

"I didn't want to alienate my family," Ann said. "Yet here I was ready to sail away without letting them know where I was or if I was even alive still. I feel so torn. My parents are suffering because of my sudden disappearance and yet, it's their refusal to let me live my life that has led me to this drastic decision. I don't know if Hayden followed through with his threat. If I go back and he has, my father will do something drastic. Especially now that he knows I might try to run away again. If he didn't say anything to them, then how do I explain my disappearance?"

Bridget sat up also. "You're right. You should send your parents a letter and let them know you're all right, but send it from here, not New York. That will alleviate some of your guilt. We'll go to Texas and see what we think of it," she said. "Once we've made our decision then you can decide the best way to deal with your parents."

"What if they trace us to the ship?"

"There's no record of Bridget Sullivan or Ann Taylor being on that ship. Mr. and Mrs. Howard Franklin will mean nothing to them."

Ann placed her fist against her forehead. "You are so right. I'm such a fool."

"You're just worried. Write the letter and we'll post it when we go down for breakfast."

• • •

At eleven thirty, Bridget and Ann, along with several other passengers who had stayed the night at the South Western House, made their way across to the ship. Their luggage had been taken to the ship over an hour ago. The sky was overcast, but the temperatures were mild enough to be comfortable.

As they made their way toward the ship, Bridget again felt overwhelmed by its colossal size. Almost as disconcerting was the seemingly endless wall of people who lined the dock. It appeared the entire town had turned out to witness the monumental event.

"Would you look at all those people?" she said to Ann, who looked extremely dapper in one of the new suits she had purchased from Harrods.

Bridget knew Ann was trying to act as nonchalant as most of the other men who were making their way to the ship, but Bridget could feel her muscles trembling. Perhaps Ann was overly excited that the eagerly anticipated day was finally here, or perhaps she was as scared as Bridget was.

As they made their way forward a man with a large seaman's bag bumped into Bridget. She lost her footing and for the briefest instant feared the crowd would trample her, but Ann's protective arm tightened around her waist and held her upright.

"I don't like this crowd," she said, her voice shaking.

"It'll be fine," Ann said. "I'll be right beside you the entire way."

Bridget started to respond until she realized they were on the gangplank. She clung to Ann's arm and tried to corral the nearly overwhelming nervous excitement building within her. After a short trek up the slight incline, they stepped through an opened door and found themselves in a rather disappointing entranceway. Her disappointment was soon forgotten as they moved on through another set of doors and suddenly before them gleamed the most impressive staircase she had ever seen. It was a large double stairway separated only by a banister. One set of steps curved upward and to the right while the other led to the left. Intricately crafted wrought-iron designs supported the gleaming oak banisters.

"It must be over fifteen feet wide," Ann said in awe.

A steward in a sparkling white suit appeared beside them. "Welcome aboard, sir, ma'am. My name is Gordon and I'll be happy to assist you." He turned his full attention to Ann, giving Bridget the freedom to continue admiring the staircase. She made her way up the first few steps and couldn't resist running her gloved hand over one of the bronze cherubs that served as lamp supports on the middle railing. When she moved farther up the staircase, she gasped in wonder at the colossal glass dome that flooded the area with natural light. A large chandelier hung from the center of the dome. At the landing, a clock was nestled into an intricate oak carving. Bridget moved closer to observe the remarkable workmanship.

"It's beautiful, isn't it?" Ann said beside her.

"What do you suppose it represents?" Bridget asked.

"I read in one of the brochures that it's Honor and Glory crowning Time."

Bridget stared at the two angels standing on either side of the clock face. One was waving a palm frond over the other's head, while the second angel concentrated hard at writing on a tablet. At the feet of the waving figure was a wreath. "Do you suppose the wreath is the laurel of victory?"

"Victory over what?"

Bridget shrugged. "I don't know, but look how it rests against the newel post that supports the clock. Maybe it's intended to represent White Star's belief in their supremacy over time."

Ann leaned closer and lowered her voice. "If that's the case, then I'm certain the one with the tablet is tallying the company's profits."

Bridget giggled. "It must be a very long tally, and that's why the other angel is fanning her."

"Do you think that the ball beneath the foot of our accounting friend is supposed to represent the world?" Ann asked.

Bridget studied the object for a moment before replying, "Maybe, or perhaps it's just a large pearl, although I'm not sure if there are any pearl-producing oysters in the North Atlantic."

"Obviously you've forgotten how much we paid for these tickets." Ann took her hand. "We can explore later. Let's go out and wave to all the poor souls who are missing this grand adventure."

"Shouldn't we go to the room to see if our luggage arrived safely?" Bridget asked as they made their way back out.

"No. I have our suite number, and I'm sure the luggage is fine. The trunk we sent from London should be already in the hold."

They made their way to the rail. Below, thousands of people waved up at them from the dock. As they waved back at the excited crowd Bridget experienced a sense of peace that had been absent for several days. "Thank you for taking care of everything," she said as she leaned her head against Ann's arm. "I don't know what I would have done without you." She looked up into Ann's sparkling eyes and smiled. "You really are excited about this, aren't you?"

Ann smiled and nodded. "Imagine. In seven days . . . seven days, we'll be in America." She shook her head. "It's almost beyond belief that a ship this large and elegant could be built. I've heard that even the third-class quarters are better than some ship's second-class accommodations. You and I are participating in a historic event." She put her arm around Bridget's shoulders and pulled her closer. "I can't believe we're really going." She glanced behind them. "I keep expecting someone to come along any moment now and tell us to leave."

Bridget recalled the nightmare she'd had and shivered again.

"Don't worry," Ann quickly assured her. "Everything is going to be fine. Remember, we're on the largest movable object ever built by man." She squeezed Bridget in her excitement. "I want us to enjoy every minute of this voyage. Someday we can look back and tell people that we were on the maiden voyage of the magnificent *Titanic*."

CHAPTER TWELVE

As Ann and Bridget stood waving to the crowd below, the Sheffingtons joined them. Trevor was so jovial that Bridget began to wonder if perhaps he wasn't slightly intoxicated. Emma on the other hand looked paler and more exhausted than she had the previous afternoon, but she was smiling and seemed genuinely pleased to be aboard ship.

Suddenly the all ashore whistle filled the air. The noise level from the dock rose to a deafening frenzy as final good-byes were shouted and nonpassengers raced off the ship. Millions of gaily colored paper streamers filled the air. The gangplanks were pulled away. A dozen tugboats began to slowly haul the majestic liner away from the White Star dock and out into the channel of the River Test.

"This is it," Trevor yelled above the bedlam. "America, here we come." He grabbed his wife and hugged her tightly.

Bridget looked up at Ann and was surprised to see tears glistening in her eyes. Ann glanced down at her and smiled softly. The din made it impossible to speak at anything lower than a scream, but neither of them needed to speak. They each knew what the other was thinking. They were safe.

Bridget was turning back to the rail when she noticed the two docked ships that were bobbing like toy boats in the water. The *Titanic* passed so close to them that she could easily read the names of the ships: *Oceanic* and SS *New York*. Suddenly, there was a loud explosive pop. The cheering from the dock changed to screams.

The three-inch steel hawsers securing the *New York* to her mooring had snapped and hurled through the air, landing a few feet from the horrified spectators. Ann pointed down at the smaller ship as it began floating toward the larger vessel.

Onboard the *Titanic* passengers watched as the *New York's* stern swung toward them. An eerie hush settled over the passengers as the two vessels drew ever closer.

Bridget heard bells from somewhere deep in the *Titanic* and then the noticeable change in the sound of the powerful ship's engines. A few minutes later several crewmen raced passed them and down the stairs.

Trevor leaned so far out over the rail that Ann grabbed onto the back of his coat to keep him from falling. "It looks as though they're rigging collision mats," he said as he drew back.

For the next several minutes, they watched in silence as the distance between the two ships slowly began to widen. A collective sigh of relief followed by a hearty cheer floated up from the *Titanic* as a tugboat finally gained control of the loose ship.

Trevor pulled a handkerchief from his pocket and dabbed his face. "That was a bit close."

"I thought we were going to hit her for sure," Ann said.

Trevor started chattering something about suction caused by the *Titanic's* enormous propellers, but Bridget tuned him out. Her attention centered on Emma, who looked like she was on the verge of collapse. It was obvious that Trevor did not intend to shut up, so Bridget simply interrupted him. "I could use a cup of tea. How about you, Emma?"

"They should be serving lunch in the dining room now," Trevor said as he checked a small gold pocket watch.

"I'm not hungry, but a cup of tea would be wonderful," Emma said.

"There should be a café on this deck." Trevor turned in a circle as if to get his bearing. "This way, I think."

"That's an excellent idea," Ann said as she took Bridget's arm. Together the four went in search of refreshments. They hadn't gone far when they spied the Café Parisien, a charming, brightly lit veranda. Trelliswork lined the ceiling and walls, giving the space the aura of a quaint sidewalk café in Paris. Large picture windows provided stunning views of the sea.

A few people were already seated, but the two couples were still able to get a table by one of the windows. A waiter appeared to take their orders.

"Is it possible to lower the window?" Trevor asked. He turned to Emma, who was fussing with the baby. "Will it be too cool on Amelia?"

"I have her bundled up quite well, but it might be too much."

Trevor was clearly disappointed but gave in. They ordered tea and a selection of biscuits.

"I should be starving," Bridget said. "We had an early breakfast. I guess it's all the excitement."

"I must admit," Emma said, "I was too energized to eat breakfast."

For the first time, Trevor seemed to notice how pale his wife looked. "Did you take your medication, Emma?"

She looked at him pleadingly. It was obvious that she was embarrassed to be the center of attention. "Please don't start. You know how sleepy it makes me. I couldn't possibly have taken it and still managed to stay awake this long."

"As soon as we've had our tea, I think you should go rest for a while."

She nodded. The waiter arrived with their order and saved her from having to say more.

They had a few minutes of blissful silence while they ate, but as soon as Trevor polished off the last of his biscuit, he began again. "I certainly hope that little incident isn't an omen," he said.

"Now, Trevor, please don't start that again. It might frighten them." The baby was getting restless and Emma was having difficulty trying to eat and handle the child.

"Would you like for me to hold her while you eat?" Bridget offered.

"Are you sure?" Emma asked.

"Positive. I love children."

Emma handed the child over, clearly relieved at getting a break.

Trevor waved his wife's earlier protest aside. "No one takes seriously the rumor of the ship being cursed." He looked to Ann for confirmation.

"I'm afraid I don't know anything about a curse," Ann said.

Bridget nearly kicked her under the table, because that was all it took to get Trevor started again.

"It's all nonsense," Trevor began. "I don't believe in curses. But it does give one a pause, especially considering the ship was never officially christened."

Trevor's attention was temporarily distracted as several noisy young men rushed passed. For the briefest moment, Bridget thought they had gotten a reprieve from his story, but no such luck.

As soon as the clamor died away, Trevor turned his full attention to them. "Have either of you ever read a book entitled *Futility*, by Morgan Robertson?"

Ann and Bridget shook their heads.

Trevor was practically rubbing his hands in glee. "Well, in eighteen ninety-eight, Robertson published a novel about the world's largest ship hitting an iceberg." He leaned closer. His actions reminded Bridget of a child telling a ghost story. "Here's the juicy part," he said. "The accident happened on a cold April night in the Atlantic Ocean."

"I dare say he chose that over a cold July night in the Pacific," Bridget said. She didn't want to hear any doomsday stories. Her sarcasm was lost on Trevor or else he simply ignored her.

"The name of the ship was the Titan." He waited for a response from his listeners. When he didn't receive the anticipated reaction, he continued, "All right, here's another. In the March eighteen eighty-six issue of the *Pall Mall Gazette* there was a fictional story by William T. Stead, who just happens to be a British spiritualist. The story was entitled 'How the Mail Steamer Went Down in the Mid-Atlantic, by a Survivor.' It's the tale of a large steamship that hits another ship and sinks. Several lives are lost due to a lack of lifeboats." He rushed on before anyone could speak. "Stead also wrote 'From the Old World to the New.' This story was also about a ship sinking after it struck an iceberg." He smiled slightly. "In his book, the ship that picked up the survivors was captained by none other than our own Captain Edward J. Smith."

Despite her intentions to ignore him, Trevor's stories were beginning to bother Bridget. She tried to focus on playing with the baby, who was now watching her and smiling.

"If Captain Smith did the rescuing then I'd say we're in good hands," Ann replied as she stood. "I hate to rush away, but we should probably see to our room, in case something is amiss."

Bridget handed Amelia back to Emma and stood.

They started to leave but Trevor wasn't finished. "If you have the time later, maybe we could talk to Mr. Stead."

"Are we holding a séance?" Bridget asked.

Trevor laughed. "Absolutely no need to, my dear woman. William T. Stead is very much alive, and it just so happens that he's a passenger on this very ship."

All three members of his audience blinked in surprise. Clearly pleased that he had finally gotten the response he had wanted, Trevor bid them farewell.

CHAPTER THIRTEEN

Bridget and Ann made their way back to the grand staircase and down a long corridor until they located their suite.

"Look at this," Ann said with a small whistle as she stepped through the door.

Bridget couldn't stop the small squeal of pleasure that escaped when she saw the lavish room that was decked out in exquisite Italian Renaissance décor. Two armchairs of carved and gilded walnut sat at a refectory table, a long narrow piece with a sturdy crosspiece close to the floor that served to strengthen and brace the table's two massive legs. The table held a vase of fresh flowers and an electric lamp. Across from the table was a horsehair sofa with similar carvings on the legs. Pale rose-colored carpeting covered the floor. The walls were lined with rich oak paneling. She switched the lamp on and danced around. "Can you believe this?" She dashed into the adjoining room and gave a squeal of delight when she saw a bed twice the size of the small one in her apartment. There was a smaller table with two straight-back chairs at the foot of the bed. Their onboard luggage had been placed across the room beside a hulking wardrobe that stood on four carved legs. A closer examination of the piece revealed detailed carvings of human figures. Before she could fully inspect them, she spied the bathroom through yet another door. "I'm getting used to the luxury of a private bath. As soon as we settle into a home of our own, that's the first thing I want to add."

Ann grinned. "I think that's an excellent idea."

"I feel like the Queen of England."

Ann's arms slipped around her waist. "I want you to always be as happy as you are at this moment."

Bridget turned to face her. "As long as you're by my side, I will be." She stood on tiptoe to kiss her lover.

Ann held her close for a moment before she pulled away and removed her coat. "What did you make of Trevor's story?"

"I think he has an overactive imagination. What's the purpose of christening a ship?"

"It's to ensure good luck to the ship and crew throughout the life of the vessel. I understand that every new ship is christened before it's launched."

"Then I'm sure White Star did everything they were supposed to do."

"Not according to Trevor."

Something in Ann's voice made Bridget turn to look at her. "You don't really believe what he said, do you?"

"I say, you never tempt fate."

Bridget shivered.

Ann came over and put an arm around her. "Don't worry. This is the most modern, best built ship ever to leave a port. Besides, we'll soon be out in the middle of an ocean. What could possibly go wrong?" She planted a kiss on top of Bridget's head. "Why don't we unpack and then take a stroll before we have to get ready for dinner."

• • •

That evening Bridget chose an ivory silk damask evening gown that was beautifully decorated with glittering paste stone. The graceful drape of the garment seemed to float around her as she walked. She chose a pair of matching beaded multistrap shoes with cutouts on the toes. The cutouts allowed a suggestive glimpse of stocking.

Ann came out of the bathroom wearing a bib-front white collarless dress shirt beneath an evening dress waistcoat of powder blue. She held up a collar. "Can you help me with this?" She stopped sharply. "Look at you. You're absolutely beautiful."

Bridget gave a small twirl. "I'm glad you like it."

Ann continued to stare at her. "Why don't we skip dinner?" she said as she stepped in and slipped an arm around Bridget's waist.

"I thought you were hungry."

"I am, but I seem to have everything I need right here." Ann kissed her as her fingers caressed her breast.

Bridget felt the heat began to build. "I think you'd better give me that collar before this gets out of control."

Ann reluctantly handed over the collar and stood patiently while Bridget got it fastened.

"All right, you're all set."

"Thank you." Ann stepped back to look at Bridget again. "You look exquisite, Mrs. Franklin," she said and kissed Bridget's fingertips.

"As do you, Mr. Franklin." She fussed with Ann's cuff links. "Which reminds me. There's something I've wanted to talk to you about."

"It sounds serious."

"No." She hesitated. "It's a bit silly really." She tipped her head to one side slightly. "I'm not sure what I should call you."

Ann blinked. "What on earth do you mean?"

"I'm having a problem calling you Howard, especially when we're alone. I'm deathly afraid I'm going to slip up and call you Ann in front of someone."

"I see. That might be a little awkward." She led Bridget to one of the chairs and then sat across from her. "I know we discussed it a little and we've pretty much decided that I would continue with my masquerade as Howard at least until we return from America."

"I remember."

"I've been thinking. Would it trouble you greatly if I continued with the pretense?"

"For how long?"

"Forever."

Bridget frowned. "You mean live the rest of our lives as Mr. and Mrs. Howard Franklin?"

Ann nodded.

"I don't know." She tapped a finger upon the tabletop. "I suppose it doesn't really bother me. After all, you're still the same person underneath it all. My biggest concern is that I'll use your true name before I think, or refer to you as *she*. What would happen if you got sick?"

"I've been giving it some thought. If I got ill, I could go to another town, change back to my female clothes and no one would be the wiser."

Bridget wasn't sure the solution was viable. "What if there was an accident and there wasn't time for you to go to another town?"

Ann took her hand. "There will always be problems and I know we're taking a big chance, but think about how easy the past few days have been. I truly believe that those problems will be far smaller than those we'd face as two women. It'll be much easier for me to get a job, and no one will question why we live together."

"But if people discover what we really are—"

"Would they be any harsher on us if they discover I'm not a man than they would be if they learn we are lovers?"

"No. I guess they wouldn't." After a moment, she added, "Can I think about this a few more days before I decide?"

Ann hopped out of her chair. "You can think on it for the next couple months if you like. After all, this is our honeymoon and we're supposed to be having fun." She held out her arm. "May I escort you to dinner?"

"Yes . . . Howard, that would be lovely." She giggled as she rolled the strange name around in her head. She must get used to saying it. She grabbed her hat and gloves from the table.

They strolled back to the stairwell and made their way to the D Deck where the first-class dining room was located. When they entered the lavish reception room where first-class passengers gathered before dining, Bridget tried not to gawk. The room ran the full width of the ship. White paneling delicately carved in low relief covered the walls. Luxurious carpet covered the floor. Plush, durable Chesterfield chairs were scattered about the room. Full-bodied tones resonated from a grand piano and provided an additional layer of poise and elegance to the room.

Ann plucked two glasses from a passing waiter. "There are a couple of empty seats over there," she said and nodded.

The empty chairs were in a cluster where a small group of people already sat. Bridget would have preferred to sit somewhere by themselves, but there didn't seem to be many empty chairs left. As they made their way across the room, she heard a voice call out Howard's name. She recognized the voice immediately and suddenly the empty chairs at the table with strangers looked very appealing.

"We could pretend we didn't hear," Ann mumbled as they continued across the room.

"That would be rude, and besides—"

Before she could continue, Trevor raised his voice to the point that no one in the room could ignore him.

Bridget tried to hide her embarrassment as she and Ann turned to the voice. There was Trevor motioning them over. He was sitting with two other men. The older one was broad through the shoulders, as if he was a man used to hard work. His most striking feature was a thick mane of snow-white hair. The other was tall and lanky with deep laugh lines on either side of his mouth. As soon as they approached, both of the strangers stood and offered Bridget his seat. She thanked them and quickly sat down in the nearest one.

"Where is Emma?" she asked.

"She wasn't feeling well, so she stayed in the room with Amelia."

Bridget wondered if she should join her.

"This is Mr. Miles Delaney and his brother Zack." Before any-one could speak, Trevor rushed on with the introductions. "The Delaneys own a ranch in Texas."

"I'm Howard Franklin and this is my wife, Bridget," Ann said. "Where in Texas is your ranch?"

"Down in South Texas," the older man, Miles, drawled. "The closest town is a little dot on the map called Whitehall."

His face reminded Bridget of tanned leather. It was obvious that he had spent many hours in the sun. There was a telltale white line at the top of his forehead where she was sure a hat would normally sit.

"Do you run cattle?" Ann asked.

Zack smiled. "Yes, sir. I'd say so. Right now we have about three thousand head." His cornflower blue eyes sparkled.

Ann's eyes widened. "That's amazing. I've always wanted to go to Texas. Is it really as the books describe it to be?"

Miles chuckled. "Well, I'm not sure how it's described, but I can tell you I've never seen a prettier place." He winked at Bridget. "'Course, I could be a mite biased."

The group chuckled.

"Are there still gunslingers there?" Bridget asked. "Howard is forever going on about those novels of the Wild West. He is abso-lutely enthralled with them."

"No, ma'am. Not really," Zack said with a wide smile. "We're pretty much civilized now. Oh, on occasion, a body can still run into one of those old codgers, but mainly they keep to themselves out in the wilds somewhere. Most of them never cared much for towns anyway."

"What brought you to England?" Ann asked.

"My wife," Miles said with a slight grimace before smiling to Bridget apologetically. "When I married my wife, Louise, I prom-ised her that as soon I was financially sound I'd take her to Europe. She wanted to see Paris and London and all those other places that women seem to like so much." He rubbed his neck. "I avoided it for a long time, but she finally caught on to me and"—he held out his hands and shrugged—"here I am."

"Since Miles and Louise were going, nothing would do for my wife, Betty, but we go too," Zack said.

"Are you still complaining?" A short, curvaceous woman with flaming red hair appeared at Zack's side.

"If Miles weren't complaining about something I'd think he was dead for sure." A second woman appeared. She would have been called petite by most, but as she shook everyone's hand, Bridget saw a sense of strength in her face that suggested she could hold her own in just about any situation. "I'm Louise and this is my sister-in-law, Betty." She glanced at Miles and winked. "What have these two galoots been saying?"

"We were just telling them about our wonderful trip," Zack said and held out his hand to offer the empty chair to his wife.

There was a moment of awkwardness as Louise was left standing. Finally, Ann nudged Trevor's shoulder and motioned for him to get up.

As they were shuffling the seating arrangement, the dining room doors opened.

"Looks like it's time to eat," Zack said as he held his arm out for Betty. "I sure wish I had a thick, juicy Texas steak." Betty elbowed him. "What?"

"Don't be rude."

Zack glanced at the rest of the group. "Well, I didn't mean nothing by it. I'll bet you if they were in Texas for a month they'd be missing their favorite foods, too."

"I agree," Bridget said. "I've heard that Americans aren't nearly as fond of tea as we Brits are."

"I think most of us are more partial to coffee," Louise said.

"Then I'm sure that a month from now, I'll be longing for a nice cup of tea with the same intensity as Mr. Delaney has for his steak," Bridget said, earning a hearty round of laughter.

A small ripple of appreciation ran through the group when they stepped into the immense dining room.

"It's as though every room I enter on this ship seems to get larger," Bridget said. There were a number of intimate recessed areas about the room where couples could dine. She hoped she would be able to share at least one private dinner with Ann. The soft white walls were topped by ornately molded ceilings. Even though the outside light was fading, the room gave the appearance of being bathed in sunlight. It took her a moment to realize that the sunlight was nothing more than an illusion produced by carefully placed lights.

"It looks as though they could feed an army in here," Ann said.

"They can seat five hundred and fifty diners at a time," Trevor began.

A slightly rotund man suddenly appeared at their side. "Will you ladies and gentlemen be dining with us tonight?"

"Yes," Trevor said. "I know we have assigned tables, but since it's not very crowded tonight, would it be possible that we have a table together?"

The man nodded. "Certainly. Right this way, please."

"Trevor, how is it that you know so much about the ship?" Zack asked after they had settled into their chairs.

"I've read everything ever published about this ship. Once she arrived in Southampton, I spent every free moment I had around the docks talking to anyone who knew something about her."

"Where is the captain's table?" Betty asked.

"It's at the forward end of the room." Trevor nodded toward the front of the dining room. "His table seats six. Did you know that Captain Smith is known as the millionaires' captain?"

Betty leaned forward. Trevor had finally found someone interested in his stories. "Why is he called that?"

"He is given the grandest ships, which of course are the ones that the millionaires sail on. This will be his final voyage. He's retiring."

Before Betty could respond, Miles lifted the tablecloth and peeked underneath. "These tables are made from good solid oak. They'll last a lifetime."

"It's certainly a beautiful ship," Louise said as she patted her husband's hand to make him release the tablecloth. "At first I was upset that our plans had been changed."

"You had to change your plans?" Ann asked.

"Oh, no, we didn't change them. White Star made the change."

"We were scheduled to sail back on the *Adriatic*," Miles said. "The company told us that due to the coal shortage caused by the strike all the coal stocks and passengers from the *Adriatic* and the *Oceanic* were moved over to this ship."

Trevor seemed upset that someone other than himself had slipped in a detail. "That's right. They didn't want to jeopardize the *Titanic's* maiden voyage."

Zack glanced around. "Personally, I would have preferred to sail on a ship that had already been tested a few times."

Betty patted his arm. "I'm sure they've already checked the boat for leaks, dear."

CHAPTER FOURTEEN

The group chatted about the Delaneys' travels as they dined. Ann and Bridget were fascinated about all the Americans had seen, but Trevor didn't seem to be enjoying the conversation. They were just finishing the main course when the ship arrived at Cherbourg, France. As soon as the table had been cleared in anticipation of dessert, Trevor looked at his watch and stood.

"If you'll excuse me, I believe I'll go out and have a look around. We should be docked by now. I believe I'll go watch the process. I'm sure there will be some passengers disembarking and others boarding the ship. Plus, I understand we're to pick up mail here." He leaned toward the Delaneys and practically whispered, "I have it on very good authority that Mr. John Jacob Astor himself will be boarding here. I'm sure he's not going to be very happy as we are already running behind schedule. That little incident with the *New York* back at Southampton was most unfortunate."

"Well, if you should see the gentleman," Zack began, "ask him if he'd like to invest a few of his millions in some beef. I know of this little place down around—" He grunted and turned to his wife. "What was that for?"

She blushed and he grunted again.

"On second thought, I guess I don't have a message for him," Zack mumbled. "My ankle couldn't handle it."

"Tell Emma if she needs help with the baby to let me know," Bridget said. "I hope she gets to feeling better soon."

Trevor nodded and made a hasty retreat.

"That man sure does like this ship," Miles said as they watched Trevor leave.

"I *like* the ship," Ann said. "I'm afraid Trevor is obsessed."

"You mentioned a sick baby," Louise said.

Bridget shook her head. "No. The baby, Amelia, is fine. It's his wife, Emma, who isn't feeling well."

"Being out on the water does cause some folks a lot of discomfort. If you talk to her, you might suggest she try sucking on a lemon. Chamomile tea will also help ease the queasiness."

"Louise is a pretty fair doctor," Miles said. "We don't have a doctor nearby. She takes care of all the hands." He winked. "Heck, she's even been known to cure a stray animal or two." This brought on a chuckle from all the Delaneys.

"Our oldest son, Kevin, was always dragging home stray animals," Louise explained.

"How many children do you have?" Ann asked.

Instantly, Miles and Zack whipped out their wallets. By the time the dessert arrived, photos of their children and grandchildren covered the table. Many were worn around the edges as though they had been handled a lot.

Ann picked up one of the photos. "I'd never stopped to think about how amazing photos can be. I saw a man and a young boy earlier today. They were taking photos aboard ship."

"My sister's oldest son has a camera and he is crazy about it," Betty said. "That's how we ended up with these." She waved at the photos.

Bridget looked at the images that had been captured on the

small pieces of paper. "That must be an amazing feeling to create something like this." She examined each photo in detail. When she looked up, she found Ann watching her and smiling.

"What takes you folks to America?" Zack asked.

"We're on holiday . . . our honeymoon, actually," Ann replied. Bridget couldn't stop the blush that was rushing up her neck.

"Newlyweds," Betty exclaimed. "How wonderful."

"Where are you planning on visiting?" Louise asked.

"We're not absolutely certain where all we'll be going." Ann glanced at Bridget.

"Howard is dying to see Texas," Bridget replied. "Sh . . . He's been talking about it for ages." She bit her tongue over her near slip. She studied the Delaneys carefully, but no one seemed to have noticed.

"If you get near our neck of the woods, make sure you drop by for a few days," Miles said. "We've got plenty of room." He nodded toward Ann. "We'll even make a cowboy out of old Howard here."

"He would love that," Bridget said.

"What I absolutely must have is a Stetson," Ann said, getting into the playfulness of the conversation. "Like those worn by the heroes in your Mr. Zane Grey's novels."

"That can be arranged," Miles assured them. They spent the next several minutes talking about Texas. Bridget watched the sparkle in Ann's eyes and knew she'd do whatever it took to keep it there.

After dinner, the group split up and went their separate ways.

"If it's not too cold would you like to take a stroll around the ship?" Ann asked as she slipped an arm around Bridget.

"That would be wonderful." She lowered her voice. "I know I'm being horribly rude, but if you should happen to see Trevor . . . well, I'd rather not run into him again tonight."

"He is sort of singleminded, isn't he?"

"I wonder if he rants on endlessly about this ship to Emma."

"Perhaps that was part of her malady tonight."

Bridget recalled Emma's paleness and the dark circles around her sunken eyes. She had a sad feeling that Emma's health issues were much more serious than her merely being tired of listening to Trevor. She made a note to drop by to visit her if she wasn't up and around by tomorrow morning.

When they stepped outside the air was brisk but bearable. In the distance, they could see the light from Cherbourg. As they drew closer to the rail, Bridget noted that the two tenders that had ferried the passengers out to the ship were still alongside.

"What did you think of the Delaneys?" Ann asked.

"They seem like very nice people." Bridget had a hunch she knew where the conversation was headed.

"I have so many questions to ask about Texas. I could have talked all night, but it seemed rude to keep peppering them with my queries."

Bridget patted Ann's hand. "It's a long trip to America. I'm sure you'll have plenty of opportunities to talk to them."

Ann gave a long contented sigh. "I can hardly believe we are here. It simply amazes me. To think that a little over a week ago, I was behind a counter feeling about as blue as I've ever been in my life. I was certain that I would never be able to control my own life. Now, I can't remember ever being happier. I can't envision how I could ever be any happier than I am at this very instant. I wish I could burn this moment into a tangible thing that I could physically hang on to forever. Something I could take out and relive whenever I'm sad."

Mental images of the photographs of the Delaneys' children came back to Bridget as she leaned into her lover. "You sound as if you're approaching a hundred years old. There are thousands of these moments still ahead of us, and each of them will live in our memories. Wait until we get to Texas." She felt a ripple of excitement run through Ann's body. "See what I mean? Merely thinking about it excites you."

Ann leaned down to whisper in her ear, "I wasn't thinking about Texas. I was thinking about that nice big bed we have waiting for us and what I'm planning on using it for very soon."

This time it was Bridget who shivered in pleasure. "How long did you want to stand here looking at those ships?"

They practically ran back to their room, which was delightfully warm thanks to the electric heater. The door latch was barely in place before they started stripping. With all the buttons, corset laces and undergarments, Bridget was at a distinct disadvantage. She was busy trying to free her stockings from the garters when Ann came to help.

"Let me help you," Ann said as she unlaced the corset. As soon as she removed it, she slipped her hands around Bridget's waist.

A jolt of desire swept over Bridget as Ann's naked body pressed against her back. She bent her head to receive the lips that traced warm patterns along her neck. She started to finish undressing, but Ann stopped her.

"Let me."

As the clothing dropped to the floor, Ann's lips and hands roamed freely over her body. She was slowly lowered to the bed and then Ann's long supple body was over hers. Time seemed to stand still as they kissed—long lingering kisses that gradually intensified as their desire built. Warm hands caressed her skin and made it tingle with desire. She lost track of the number of times she teetered on the brink of pleasure, only to be denied relief at the last moment. Finally unable to bear the exquisite agony any longer, she begged for release. "Please, my love, now."

Ann's knee parted Bridget's thighs and long, slender fingers slipped inside her. Ann's body began a rhythmic rocking against her and soon they were both caught up in a surge of sensations that left them drained and clinging to each other.

CHAPTER FIFTEEN

Bridget swam in the warm haze of half sleep.

"Wake up, sleepyhead. It's after eleven, and I have it on good authority that we'll soon be arriving at the Queenstown harbor where, of course, we'll be picking up and dropping off passengers—to say nothing of taking on more mail."

At the clinking of china, she opened one eye slightly to find Ann fully dressed and busy setting out food on the small table she'd moved to the side of the bed.

"I suppose that means you've already had the pleasure of bumping into Trevor," she mumbled as she pushed herself upright on the bed.

"That would be a correct assumption," Ann said as she handed her a plate filled with cheese, thin slices of meat and breads.

On the table, Bridget could see a bowl filled with fresh fruit and a pot of tea. She dug into the food. They had made love long into the night and she was famished.

"While you were whiling away your time here in dreamland, I went out, had breakfast with him and Emma, took care of a little business and found a kind soul who prepared this wonderful feast for you." Ann poured tea into a delicate china cup and held it out to her. Then she plucked a slice of apple from the fruit bowl and sat on the side of the bed. "You should have seen their faces when I explained that my wife wasn't able to join me at breakfast, because you were too exhausted after a long and, I must say, marvelous night of lovemaking."

Bridget nearly choked on a bite of cheese. "You are horrible."

"Now, now, that's not what you were screaming only a few hours ago." Ann held up a hand. "That reminds me. Our neighbors to the side have asked if you could possibly try and hold the noise down for the remainder of the trip."

Bridget stuck out her tongue. "You weren't exactly silent." She sipped her tea. "What business were you attending to?"

"I almost forgot." Ann reached into her jacket pocket and removed a slip of paper. "I noticed your reaction to the photographs last night and thought you might enjoy this."

"What is it?" Bridget set her plate in her lap and took the paper.

"Our pal Trevor gave me the idea. It seems there is a fully equipped darkroom for amateur photographers to test their skills."

Bridget started to speak, but Ann stopped her.

"I realize you don't have a camera or film to be developed, but with Trevor's help I managed to locate a Miss Rachel McCormick. It seems as though she came aboard with several rolls of exposed film that she took while on holiday in France. Now, unfortunately, Miss McCormick's camera became inoperative just prior to her boarding the ship so you won't be able to see how the actual taking of the photographs is handled, but she is an apparent genius in the developing process." Ann pointed to the paper. "She will meet you at the grand staircase at two o'clock this afternoon."

"How exciting. I must admit that I've never given photography a second thought, but last night there was something about looking at those images that made me want to try it." She picked up a bit of ham. "Thank you. This was very thoughtful of you."

"I hope you enjoy the lesson. According to our friend Trevor, Miss McCormick has made something of a name for herself as a photographer. He says her photos fetch a handsome price."

They sat in comfortable silence as Bridget finished eating breakfast. As she placed her dishes back onto the tray, Ann pulled her watch from her pocket.

"It's a rather nice day. After you're dressed, would you like to take a stroll? I've heard that the view of Queenstown harbor is quite lovely, but you'll have to hurry. We should be arriving in about forty-five minutes."

Bridget hopped out of bed. "Take out my lilac tea gown, please. I'll have a quick bath and be ready in a few minutes." After kissing Ann's cheek, she raced off to the bathroom.

They were standing at the rail when the ship dropped anchor approximately three kilometers from Queenstown, Ireland. They watched in silence as passengers and cargo were transported between the vessels.

"It's rather amazing that this ship is too large to anchor in the actual harbor," Bridget said.

"I suppose they will eventually have to dredge the harbor to make it deeper. Especially if ships this size are to continue. Our parents grew up traveling in horse and buggies. For them a trip across the ocean meant extreme hazards and several weeks of travel. We'll make the crossing in seven days."

Bridget glanced at Ann. "That really impresses you, doesn't it?"

Ann nodded. "I can't stop thinking about what might be possible ten, twenty, thirty years from now. Who knows what we'll be capable of accomplishing."

Before Bridget could respond, the Sheffington family joined them at the ship rail.

Trevor immediately engaged Ann in a conversation about the

need for deeper harbors where the new super ships could drop anchor. Bridget and Emma made their way to a couple of deck chairs where they could relax and enjoy the warmth of the sun.

Bridget took Amelia to give Emma break. "How are you feeling today?"

Emma lay back on the deck chair and closed her eyes. "Better. The doctor gave me some medicine before we left Southampton. I hate taking it, because it makes me ill, but Trevor insists I follow doctor's orders." She hesitated a moment. "He won't accept the fact that I won't be getting better."

Bridget stared at her. "What's wrong?"

"I have a heart condition. The doctors suspect I was born with it. The strain of the pregnancy made it worse." She opened her eyes and gazed at the baby. "Don't misunderstand me. I'd do it all over again for her. She's my life."

Bridget wondered where that left Trevor in the hierarchy of Emma's world.

"I love Trevor," Emma said, almost as if she had read Bridget's thoughts. "He can be trying at times, but he's a good husband and father. I don't know what's going to happen to him when I'm gone." The casual tone in her voice shocked Bridget more than the words.

"Aren't you afraid?"

Emma closed her eyes and smiled faintly. "I'm terrified, but not for myself. I worry about Amelia and Trevor. He doesn't know how to raise a baby. Besides, a child needs a mother. I've always felt that a child needs a mother more than a father."

"What about your mother? Couldn't she help?"

Emma shook her head. "I have no family. There's only the three of us now. That's why we're moving to America. Trevor thinks everything will be better there." She seemed to want to talk, so Bridget sat quietly and listened as she stared down at the sleeping baby. "I know it's awful of me," Emma said. "When I'm gone, I don't want Trevor to wait a year or more before he remarries. I want my daughter to grow up with a mother. If Trevor remarries right away, Amelia will never know what it's like to be without me."

Emma's cold, calculated thoughts made Bridget shiver. The movement woke the baby and for a moment she seemed to gaze directly into Bridget's eyes before she smiled and fell back asleep. Bridget slipped her finger into the fold of the blanket and gently lifted one of the tiny hands. Her mother had died when she was six. Her father remarrying hadn't helped ease her pain. If anything, it had made it worse, but she couldn't very well tell Emma that. All she could offer was a lame, "Maybe the doctors in America can help you."

Rachel McCormick was nothing like Bridget had imagined her. Despite the fact that her clothing looked more suited to a long day of housecleaning, the woman was astonishingly beautiful. The biggest surprise came when she spoke. Rather than the Irish brogue Bridget had anticipated, there was a soft American Southern drawl. Her surprise must have shown on her face, because Rachel laughed.

"I can see that Mr. Franklin didn't tell you everything about me. My family immigrated to America in the early eighteen hundreds. They settled in Chatham County, which is located along the Georgia coast. They made a God-awful fortune in cotton." She gave a small throaty laugh. "But as my dear granny used to say, 'Don't get too fond of what the good Lord gives you, 'cause he's liable to take it back just any minute.' In our case, it wasn't the Lord who arrived to take it away, but a devil of a man named Sherman. He destroyed everything, including my papa—the last surviving male of a long and proud line." She looked at Bridget and shrugged. "'Course, I don't remember any of that. Mr. Sherman had been gone over a decade by the time I appeared."

Bridget's brain automatically did the calculations. She couldn't hide the surprise that hit her when she realized Rachel McCormick must be almost forty years old.

"Surprised you again, didn't I?" She suddenly took Bridget by the arm. "Come on and don't mind me. Most folks think I've spent too many years sniffing developing fluids." Without giving Bridget time to respond, she rushed on, "Now, tell me. What made you decide that you want to take photographs?"

"I really don't know." Bridget related the experience she'd had with the Delaneys' photographs.

"So you're only interested in family photos." Rachel sounded slightly disappointed.

"I really don't know what I'm interested in. Until the other night I'd never given photography much thought, but since then . . ." She trailed off.

"Can't get it out of your mind, huh? I know the feeling. I went to the Eiffel Tower and while everyone else was standing around oohing and aahing about the architecture and the grand view it made, I was walking around looking at angles and shadows, or how light hit the girders." They stopped outside a door that Rachel unlocked. "I want to show you something before we begin."

Once Bridget stepped into the room, she knew she would never look at another photo in the same way again. Photographs covered every single area of the small single room.

"Did you take these?" she asked and cringed at the inference that Rachel would show her someone else's work. She recognized scenes of the Taj Mahal, the Great Pyramids, the Parthenon and dozens of other famous sites. Most of the shots were of buildings or landscapes, but scattered in among them was the occasional photo of a person. The portraits were the ones that truly grabbed Bridget's attention. Never had she seen photographs that showed so much emotion and yet held an alluring hint of mystery to them. She lost track of time as she studied photo after photo.

When she finally looked up, Rachel was sitting on a chair with a book in her hands, but she was watching Bridget.

"I want to be able to do this," Bridget said. Never had anything material struck her with such intensity. Not even Mr. Tanaka's beautiful pottery had moved her the way these images had. "Where do I start?"

Rachel stood. "When we land in New York, buy yourself a Brownie camera and as much film as you can afford. Then everywhere you go use that camera. Keep notes on the lighting conditions and refer back to them when you get your photos back from the lab. Learn how the light affects your shots."

"Are Brownies expensive?"

"Not really. They cost about a dollar apiece and the film runs about fifteen cents a roll."

Bridget did the currency conversion in her head and frowned. "I want a real camera."

Rachel gave the rich throaty laugh that Bridget would always remember her by. "It is a *real* camera. Besides, it's not the camera that makes the photograph. That's made here and here." She tapped the spot over her heart and then her eye. "I'm not going to show you how to process film."

Bridget bit her lip to keep from crying out in disappointment.

"I'm not trying to be mean or anything, but before you start worrying about processing, I want you to start looking at things as a photographer would. From now on, I want you to look at everything you see. I mean really look at it. Get down on your knees and watch bugs crawl. Watch mothers tending their babies, whether they be human, animals or whatever. Study the way light hits objects. Don't look at it from just one angle. Move around it and look at it from every possible direction. If you can move it, study the way it looks when placed on different surfaces." She took a deep breath and slowly released it. "Sorry, I can get a little carried away."

Bridget smiled, but it was hard. She was bitterly disappointed that Rachel wasn't going to show her how to develop film.

Rachel handed her a book. "This is the only training I've ever had. It taught me the fundamentals of photography and film development. Read the first part over and over until you have it down. Don't read the last section until you've reached the point that it's time to start developing your own photos."

Bridget took the book. "How will I know when to start?"

Rachel smiled. "The same way you know how to breathe."

Confused, she frowned.

"Photography has a way of getting into your blood. When you're ready you won't need anyone to tell you."

CHAPTER SIXTEEN

Time flew by. Bridget spent Friday and Saturday with Ann enjoying all the amenities the ship had to offer. They spent a lot of time with the Delaneys and the Sheffingtons talking or playing cards. Betty Delaney and Trevor would point out celebrities and fill the group in on the latest gossip about each person. Occasionally Rachel McCormick would join them and regale them with stories of her faraway travels and adventures.

The *Titanic's* maiden journey was proving to be perfect. The water was calm, providing an unbelievably smooth journey. The weather was chilly but nice. From the jovial mood aboard ship, passengers and crew alike seemed to be enjoying the trip.

On Sunday morning, Ann and Bridget went to the morning divine service. Bridget considered begging off, but it seemed important to Ann so she went. Rachel was the only member of their little group who did not attend. After the service they all made plans to meet that night for dinner. Louise Delaney offered to stop by Rachel's cabin to invite her. Ann and Bridget decided to take a stroll. As they stepped out, the brisk temperatures caused Bridget to pull her coat tighter around her body.

She shivered. "It feels as though it's getting colder."

"I think this would be a good day to stay inside." Ann gave her a knowing look.

"I swear you only have one thing on your mind."

"I didn't hear you complaining last night." Ann leaned closer. "Unless I misunderstood your pleas of 'Oh, no. Don't stop.'"

Bridget swatted her arm. "You're being shameful. You shouldn't talk like that on Sunday."

Ann laughed aloud. "Let's go over to the library so I can pick out a book. Then we can spend a quiet, leisurely Sunday in our room . . . reading."

Bridget hid her face in the collar of her coat to keep from laughing at the woeful look on Ann's face.

To Ann's evident delight, she found a copy of Zane Grey's *The Young Lion Hunter* that had been released the previous year. "I've been searching for this," she said as they made their way back to the room.

"Will you have time to finish it before we reach New York?"

"I'm sure I will, if you don't object to my keeping the light on until the wee hours of the morning."

"Look how quickly you've changed your mind."

"What?" Ann looked at her innocently.

"A few minutes ago you were all sad that you couldn't rush right back to the room to ravish my body and now you can't wait to get back there to read your book."

Ann glanced at the book in her hand before giving a mischievous grin. "I'm practically ambidextrous."

Bridget stopped short. "What good would that do you?"

Ann leaned closer and spoke in a near whisper. "I can hold the book in my left hand, and with my right hand, I can—" She wiggled her fingers suggestively.

Bridget felt her neck grow warm as she scurried toward their cabin.

They spent the rest of the day reading. Occasionally one of them would stop to discuss something she had read. Bridget could hardly wait until they reached New York where she'd be able to buy herself a camera. She intended to document every stage of their journey. She deeply regretted not having a camera with her now. It would have been wonderful to be able to practice with it onboard the ship.

At six that evening they began to dress for dinner. As they dressed, Bridget remembered the first time she had seen the dining room and how she had hoped to share a nice romantic dinner with Ann there. "Can we have dinner alone tomorrow?"

"Sure. Any particular reason?"

"I just think it would be romantic to have a quiet evening alone."

Ann kissed her cheek. "Tomorrow night, I'm all yours." She slipped on her shoes. "In fact, why don't we skip the dining room tomorrow night and go to the restaurant. It's supposed to have excellent food, and it won't look as though we're being standoffish."

"I'd also like to go by the barbershop tomorrow," Bridget said. "Louise had mentioned that they were selling postcards there." She was already thinking about the photo collection she would put together for Ann. Maybe she would give it to her for Christmas. The postcards could serve in place of the photos she was missing.

The Delaneys and Rachel were already in the reception area when Bridget and Ann came in. Ann got a glass of sherry for herself and a glass of Champagne for Bridget.

"We were just sitting here talking about home," Louise said. "We've been gone for so long and now that the trip is almost over, I can't wait to get home."

"We still have a long train ride ahead of us," Miles reminded her.

"To say nothing of the trip from San Antonio to home," Zack added.

"It has been worth it, though," Betty said. "I've had a wonderful time."

"Rachel, where are you off to next?" Ann asked.

"I'm exhausted. As Louise mentioned, the trip was great and I have some wonderful photos, but now I'm ready to go home to rest for a while."

"We'll cherish these memories forever." Louise squeezed Miles's hand before looking up. "And you two lovebirds are just beginning. Think of all the fantastic adventures you still have before you."

Bridget smiled as Ann raised her glass. "Here's to many, many more happy memories for us all."

A chorus of "Here, here" echoed around the group.

"What's all the noise about?"

They turned to find Emma and Trevor.

"We were making a toast to happy memories," Betty said.

Emma raised her glass of wine. "I'll drink to that." Once more, the glasses were lifted.

"Where's Amelia?" Bridget asked as Emma slipped into the seat next to her.

"A woman from steerage is watching her."

"You look like you're feeling good," Bridget said.

"I'm having a good day," Emma replied. "I think—" Before she could continue, dinner was announced and they rose to join the other hungry travelers.

The group was seated and menus passed out. When Bridget read the list of options, she blinked in surprise. All of the prior meals had been topnotch, but this one was nothing short of marvelous.

Zack gave a low whistle. "They're putting on a spread tonight."

"This is a ten-course meal," Rachel said.

Bridget read the menu, noting the lavish dishes—consommé Olga, poached salmon with mousseline sauce, filet mignon Lili, roast duckling with apple sauce, roast squab and cress, cold asparagus vinaigrette and pâté de foie gras. All to be topped off with a dessert of either Waldorf pudding, peaches in chartreuse jelly, chocolate and vanilla éclairs or French ice cream.

"Mercy," Betty said. "I think I'll just start with dessert and work my way backward."

"We'll all have to be careful and not walk on the same side of the ship at once," Trevor said. "After a meal like this we could cause her to list."

For the next three hours, conversation ebbed and flowed as the group relished the fancy meal. A different wine was served with each course and before long they were all feeling a little tipsy. Fresh fruit and cheeses followed the tenth course. Coffee, along with cigars and port for the men, had in turn topped off the fruit and cheese.

"I certainly hope they don't have any more meals like this one," Ann said as they all sat in a stuffed stupor. Bridget wished she could loosen her corset.

"Don't tell me you didn't like it," Trevor said.

"No, it was wonderful," Ann said, "but if I have many more meals like that I'll have to leave the ship wearing a bed sheet."

"All of us parading down the gangplank wearing sheets," Louise said and chuckled. "Wouldn't that be a sight to see?"

"The Romans got away with it," Zack replied. "You can wear anything you want as long as you give it a fancy name."

"I hate to break up the party," Emma said, "but we need to go pick up Amelia."

Slowly the group drifted away.

"I have to walk for a while," Ann said as they left the dining room. "Do you think it will be too cold on deck?"

"If we bundle up I think it'll be all right."

They went back to their room and put on their heaviest coats.

Bridget noticed Ann pulling at something at her waist. "What's wrong?"

"The money belt is digging into me." Ann had purchased the belt at Harrods during her shopping spree.

"Why don't you take it off for a while?"

Ann looked around as if uncertain. "Do you think it'll be safe?"

"It's too late for any of the staff to be coming through, and if we lock the door no one will bother it."

She started to take it off but stopped. "Maybe I shouldn't."

"Nonsense. It's making you miserable."

Ann unbuttoned her shirt and removed the belt. She slipped it into the wardrobe behind their clothes. After she buttoned her shirt, she checked the time. "It's almost ten thirty."

"We can sleep late tomorrow morning if you like."

Ann patted her stomach. "That would be nice. I can't imagine either of us will be hungry for breakfast."

When they stepped out onto the deck, the skies were perfectly clear. "Look at the stars," Bridget said in awe. "Have you ever seen them look so brilliant?"

"There's no moon to dim them," Ann replied as she took Bridget's arm. They walked alongside the rail. "Look at the water. It's perfectly calm."

"It has gotten a lot colder, but it feels good."

"Let me know if it starts getting too cold for you," Ann said.

They strolled for several minutes, each lost in her own thoughts.

Ann finally broke the comfortable silence. "I'm getting chilled. Are you ready to go inside?"

"I'm cold, but I hate to go in and miss all this beauty."

"We still have two more nights. Maybe the clear skies will hold."

"I hope so." As they started back to their room, Bridget squeezed Ann's arm. "I'm going to miss this. It has been so wonderful to spend all my time with you."

Ann kissed the top of her head. "We have the rest of our lives together. Nothing but the cold grip of death could take me away from you."

A hard chill ran through Bridget. "Don't say things like that." Suddenly tears blurred her eyes.

"I'm sorry. I didn't mean to upset you." Ann hugged her and ran a comforting hand over her back. "Don't be scared. I plan on living for a very long time yet."

Another chill ran through her.

"You're freezing. Let's get inside."

CHAPTER SEVENTEEN

Bridget had begun to doze when the bed suddenly jarred violently. At first, she thought Ann had jumped onto the bed. When she reached over and found Ann lying peacefully beside her she sat up.

"What was that?" Ann asked.

"I thought it was you jumping on the bed."

Ann turned the bedside lamp on. "Why would I be jumping on the bed?"

"I don't know. I was asleep and that was my first thought."

Voices from the hall filtered into the room.

"Something must be wrong." Ann stood and pulled on her robe. "Wait here. I'm going to see what's going on." She started toward the door but stopped. She stood still for a moment, slowly tilting her head from side to side.

"What's wrong?"

She turned back around. "I don't know, but I think we should get dressed."

Something in her manner frightened Bridget. "Why? What did you hear?"

"It's not what I heard," Ann said as she began stripping off her pajamas. "Bridget, I think you should get dressed quickly."

Bridget scrambled out of bed. Fear gripped her throat. "I wish you'd tell me what was happening."

"I'm sure it's nothing to be overly alarmed about, but listen closely. The engines have stopped. We aren't moving."

With Ann's help, Bridget was dressed in record time.

"Put on your warmest coat and that beaver pelt hat you bought," Ann said. "Make sure you bundle yourself up good and tight." She found the money belt and tied it back on under her shirt before she pulled on her heavy black wool coat. She was still buttoning it when a knock sounded at the door.

For a long moment, they stood staring at each other until Ann finally went to answer the door. Bridget tried to hear the conversation, but she was too far away. When Ann returned her face was pale. "That was a steward. They want everyone to put on a life jacket and go out on deck."

Bridget's heart began to pound and suddenly the multiple layers of clothes seemed much too warm.

Ann retrieved the life jackets from their storage area. "Here, let me help you." Her hands trembled as she buttoned Bridget's jacket.

"Ann, are we going to be all right?"

Ann ducked her head as if to concentrate on fastening her own jacket, but she wasn't quick enough to hide the fear in her eyes.

The mere fact that something could scare Ann terrified Bridget. She grabbed onto Ann's hand. "I don't want to go out there." Suddenly everything seemed sinister. "Please, let's just stay in here until they fix whatever's broken. We can sleep late and in the morning we'll have a wonderful stroll on the deck before we go for a cup of tea." Tears were streaming down her face.

Ann held her tightly and shushed her softly. "Look at you. You've worked yourself up into a complete frenzy." She ran a hand

103

over Bridget's back. "We don't know what's wrong yet. It could be many things. They need us to go out on deck, so let's go see what's going on."

Bridget wiped her eyes and nodded. "I'm sorry. I didn't mean to fall apart."

Ann kissed her forehead. "Everything will be fine." She picked up her white wool scarf and wrapped it around her neck. "Are you sure you're warm enough?"

Bridget nodded and they headed out.

When they reached the deck, Bridget was surprised and pleased to find there was an almost party-like atmosphere. Everywhere she looked she saw sharply dressed men and women wearing the ridiculous-looking life jackets. Her fears began to melt away. Ann had been right. There was nothing to worry about after all. Whatever was wrong couldn't be too serious.

They milled around until they bumped into Trevor and Emma. Amelia was wrapped in a tight little bundle.

"What's going on?" Ann asked Trevor.

"No one seems to know. Every time I ask someone on the crew, they tell me to stand by."

"I wonder why the engines have been cut," Ann said.

Trevor shrugged. "There could be a lot of reasons. Maybe we threw a propeller."

Rachel McCormick joined them. She held up her life jacket. "Can someone please help me with this thing? I can't seem to get it to work correctly."

Ann helped her get the jacket on.

The Delaneys arrived before she was finished. "We came over to this side to see if you all knew who called this party," Zack said.

Bridget noticed that beneath his coat he was still wearing his pajamas. He life jacket was thrown over his shoulder.

"You should put that on," Trevor said, pointing to the jacket. "The captain ordered you to do so."

"Why? We don't need it unless the boat sinks, and from what I've been hearing this thing is unsinkable."

Miles scratched his head. "Has anyone said what's going on?"

Bridget glanced at each member of the group. They were all shaking their heads.

Miles rubbed his jaw. "I know this sounds crazy, but it felt like we hit something."

"We're in the middle of the North Atlantic," Trevor snapped. "What is there to hit?"

"I don't know," Miles said, "but something almost tossed me out of bed and for once it wasn't Louise."

There was a nervous rustle of laughter.

Bridget noticed Zack putting on his life vest. All of the women seemed to move closer to their husbands.

"We felt something," Ann said. "Your room is on the starboard side, isn't it?"

Miles nodded. "If you felt it all the way over to the other side of the ship . . ." He let the sentence trail away as a sudden flurry of activity began behind them.

They all turned to look. Bridget felt her knees weaken as members of the crew began to remove the tarps from the lifeboats.

Trevor rushed over to where they were working. "What's going on?" His voice was pitched higher than normal.

The group slowly moved closer.

"We're preparing the lifeboats, sir. Please, step back."

"I can see you're preparing the bloody lifeboats," Trevor yelled. "Why?"

The young man turned to him and even from where she was standing Bridget could see he was frightened. "Sir, we've hit an iceberg and Captain Smith has ordered that all lifeboats be made ready in case they're needed."

"That's ridiculous," Trevor scoffed. "This ship won't sink. It has sixteen watertight compartments." He stormed back to the group. "Come on, Emma. Let's go back inside where it's warm. You and Amelia don't need to be out here in this freezing weather."

Emma glanced at the people around them. "Trevor, I'm frightened. I think we should stay here."

"There's nothing to be frightened of," he assured her. "I'm telling you it would take something a lot more destructive than an iceberg to sink this ship."

"Amelia and I are warm enough. Can't we stay here, please? At least until we know for sure what's going on."

He finally relented. "All right, if you want to stand out here and freeze for absolutely no reason." He put his hands into his coat pockets. "I have every intention of writing the White Star office and letting them know how inconvenient this has been."

From one of the other decks a ragtime band began to play.

"See," Trevor said. "If anything was wrong the band wouldn't be playing."

They waited for a few more minutes.

"Nothing seems to be happening," Zack said. "Maybe Trevor's right."

"Of course, I'm right," Trevor snapped. "I know as much if not more about this ship than most of the crew and I'm telling you, there's nothing to worry about."

Bridget looked around. Other than the uncovered lifeboats and the passengers standing about in their life jackets, nothing seemed amiss. As the minutes ticked by more and more passengers began to go back inside to escape the cold. She looked at Ann, who simply shrugged.

"If I could have all the women and children over here, please."

They turned to the voice. Bridget recognized the officer, but she couldn't recall his name.

"What's going on here?" a man called out.

"The captain has ordered all women and children into the lifeboat, so please everyone move this way and we'll get you loaded."

Frightened, Bridget grabbed Ann's arm. "I don't want to get into that little boat," she whispered. Her sentiment seemed to match that of everyone around her, because no one moved toward the boat.

After a lot of coaxing, a handful of women and children climbed into the lifeboat, which was lowered over the side. Suddenly the night sky filled with light.

"They're shooting off fireworks," someone shouted nearby. Several people began to clap.

"Oh, dear God."

Bridget turned to find Trevor staring at Emma in horror.

"It can't be," he mumbled.

"What's wrong?" Ann demanded.

"It's not possible—the airtight compartments—three million rivets." He turned to Ann and shook his head. "It's simply not possible."

Miles grabbed Trevor by the arm. "What are you babbling about?"

Tears began to stream down Trevor's face. "Those aren't fireworks. They're distress flares. It's sinking," he said. "The ship is sinking."

They all stared at him as they processed his statement.

Then his eyes grew larger. "Dear God," he whispered. "There aren't enough lifeboats for everyone."

For the briefest instant Bridget froze. Miles and Zack broke the spell at almost the same instant as they grabbed their wives and began rushing them toward the lifeboat that was being loaded. Rachel followed them. Emma took Trevor by the arm and pulled him aside.

Bridget took Ann by the arm. "Come on. We have to leave."

"Yes." Ann nodded. "Yes, we do." Suddenly she grabbed Bridget and kissed her harshly. "Come on."

Betty and Louise Delaney were arguing with their husbands when Ann and Bridget arrived. "I'm not leaving without you," Louise insisted as Miles tried to help her into the boat.

"It'll only be for a little while," Miles said. "They'll either get the problem fixed and bring you all back onboard or another ship will be sent to pick us up."

"What about what Trevor said?" Louise asked. "There aren't enough lifeboats."

Miles waved her protest away. "This big old tub could float for days. There's nothing to worry about. Now, please get in the boat."

At that moment, Zack took a more direct route and simply picked Betty up and set her in the boat. "You two are holding up the line," he said as he leaned forward and kissed his wife. "You be careful out there and don't start fishing without me."

With Betty in the boat, Louise reluctantly gave in and followed.

Trevor and Emma had been talking quietly off to one side.

"Ma'am," the officer called to her. "Will you please get into the boat?" Emma nodded and handed Amelia to Trevor while she climbed in. Trevor kissed the child's bundled head before handing her back.

They all turned to Bridget. She reached back and took Ann's hand. "Come on."

Ann stood fast.

"What's wrong?" Bridget turned back to her.

Ann pulled her close. "It's women and children only," she said softly as her finger traced Bridget's cheek. "You'll have to go without me."

Bridget panicked. "I'm not leaving without you."

"You have too. It'll be all right."

Bridget shook her head. "Fine. If that's the case, I'll stay here with you."

Ann shook her head. "You can't do that."

Tears were blurring Bridget's vision. "Please don't ask me to leave you."

Ann smiled. "Who said anything about you leaving? I'm sure it's nothing more than a safety measure. They'll launch the lifeboats and let them float around until they get things straightened out. Then they'll bring them all back in."

"Don't lie to me." She stomped her foot. "This is crazy. Tell them. Tell them that you're a—"

Before she could complete the sentence Ann clamped a hand over her mouth and whispered into her ear, "I chose to live as a man. Please don't take that away from me. No matter what happens I want you to remember that I love you, and know that these past few days have been the happiest days of my life. Regardless of how this ends I want you to know I wouldn't change one minute of this trip. You've allowed me to live a freedom I have never known possible. I wouldn't have had the courage to do it without you beside me. Please don't take that away from me."

Slowly the fight in Bridget died. She clung to Ann for another moment. "You'd better take care of yourself, Howard Franklin. You've talked about Texas so much that I'm actually starting to look forward to going."

Ann smiled again and nodded. They held hands as they made their way to where the group waited. Ann squeezed her hand slightly before helping Bridget into the boat. Their gazes locked as the lifeboat slowly began its descent to the dark water below.

CHAPTER EIGHTEEN

Bridget held Ann's gaze as long as possible. Just before she lost sight of her, Ann nodded slightly and mouthed a silent *I love you.* Bridget held up her gloved hand in response. As they descended, Amelia began to whimper.

"Ladies, please sit down. We can't have one of you falling overboard into the icy drink." The young crewmember tried to sound cheerful, but the quiver in his voice was plain to all who cared to listen.

Clearly dazed, everyone complied. Bridget sat beside Emma. Louise and Betty were behind them. Rachel sat next to a young woman holding a small boy. There was a bit of a jolt when the boat hit the water. Bridget looked up to try to catch another glimpse of Ann.

The crewmembers began to row away from the hulking ship. Bridget sat facing the ship. As the lifeboat pulled farther away from the ship, Bridget finally spied Ann, Miles, Zack and Trevor staring down at them. Their brave smiles warmed her. She waved and smiled back as brightly as she could manage. She was determined to be brave. She wouldn't have Ann worrying about her. Louise and Betty twisted around on their seat so they could see. Only Emma kept her head down.

As long as Bridget could still see the vaguest image of a face, she refused to take her eyes off the ship. It was the only link she had left to Ann. Twice she thought she saw Ann standing at the railing waving to her, but she knew the lifeboat was too far away for her to recognize anyone.

They had rowed out approximately a half-mile from the liner. Suddenly the ship no longer looked majestic. It had taken on a darker, more sinister persona. Bridget closed her eyes and tried to picture herself on a lake and the body hunched beside her was Ann. The bitter cold of the night air refused to let the image blossom. Beside her, Emma began to gently rock and sing. It took Bridget a moment to realize Emma was talking, not singing. She leaned closer to hear.

"They aren't filling the lifeboats to capacity," Emma muttered. "They can't afford to have empty seats."

"Emma, don't be scared. I'm sure the crew knows what they're doing."

"They're all lost. Trevor's gone."

"What do you mean?"

Emma pulled Amelia closer to her chest. "The men, there's not enough lifeboats for them. The ship is sinking and they're only letting women and children in the lifeboats."

A chill shook Bridget. She tried to keep control over her fear. "You heard Zack. The ship will float for hours."

Emma was shaking her head. "Look. It's already sitting lower in the water."

Louise and Betty must have heard her because they both turned completely around.

"My God," Betty screamed. "It is sinking." She turned to the nearest crewmember. "We have to go back. The ship is sinking. Our husbands are still onboard."

"I'm sorry, ma'am," a leaden voice replied. "We can't go back."

Bridget fought the pounding voices in her head that were screaming at her to tell them Ann was a woman and shouldn't have been left on the ship.

Suddenly the lifeboat gave a violent lurch. Bridget grabbed the side of the boat with one hand and placed an arm across Amelia with the other.

"Betty, sit down," Louise shouted.

There was a brief flurry of scuffling behind her, but Bridget didn't turn around. She stared at a strange glow in the water alongside the ship for several minutes before she realized that what she was seeing was the lights from the lower decks. They were beneath the water. The *Titanic* was indeed sinking and doing so very quickly.

Time disappeared. Bridget saw a few lifeboats ease over the side, but she couldn't see who was on them. She prayed that Ann was among them. Soft strains of music drifted across the water and an occasional rocket would flare high into the sky, providing the night with a macabre sense of splendor. Bridget was aching from the cold, but thanks to Ann insisting she dress in her warmest clothes, she was in much better shape than most of the others in the boat.

Emma sat hunched forward as if trying to protect Amelia from all the dreadfulness. No one on the lifeboat spoke. All they could do was watch as the mighty ship steadily settled deeper into the water. The lower the ship sank, the louder the screams and cries for help grew. Beneath all the screams came the incessant bittersweet sound of music.

Bridget tried not to think about what was happening onboard the ship or what the remaining passengers must be going through. To do so was to go mad. She glanced up at the overwhelmingly beautiful sky—the same sky that she and Ann had been admiring only a few hours ago. Questions hammered within her head so fiercely she ached to scream them aloud. How could something so lovely remain unmarred by the terror that was unfolding beneath it? How could a sea smooth as glass cause such devastation? How could such a mighty vessel be destroyed by ice? Above all, how could she face life without Ann by her side?

Despite the heavy coat and fur hat, the cold seeped through and numbed her body. Her feet, hands and face had become home for a thousand needles. She welcomed the pain. It kept her sane. At some point, she realized the rockets had stopped firing. The ship sat low in the water. It was sinking at an alarmingly fast pace.

The passengers in the lifeboat sat in their own private hell until the ship's lights blinked off. For the briefest moment the night was silent, and not even the music could be heard. Then the lights flickered on and with them came the noise of the doomed. Everyone in the lifeboat seemed to lean slightly forward when the ship's lights came back on. Even Emma emerged from her stupor. It was as though the ship had deliberately pulled their attention back to witness its final moments. Weary, Bridget watched in morbid fascination as the forward funnel slowly collapsed and crashed into the water, crushing everything and everyone in its path. The air filled with screams. Without warning, the bow plunged beneath the dark water, causing the stern to rise high above the ocean's surface. Tiny, almost inhuman figures were tossed around like toys. Hundreds jumped or fell into the water. A low rumble escalated into a frightful noise. The lights blinked off again. This time the broken giant remained dark. No one moved as the ship broke into two sections. The bow sank. The stern seemed to hang suspended in space for a moment before settling back into the water and righting itself. For a few seconds it seemed as if the beautiful lady wasn't ready to surrender to Neptune's beckoning arms. The stern again tilted high into the night air, as if reaching for the diamond-bright stars. This time the water's pull was too great. The glittering gem of the White Star Line seemed to take one last shuddering breath before she finally admitted defeat and slipped from sight.

A deafening silence followed. The music was gone. A strange sense of peace hovered over the area for a brief moment. Then, as if the gates of hell had torn open, the night was filled with agonizing cries of pain, terror and helplessness as hundreds of people thrashed about in the frigid water. Bridget tried to cover her ears, but she couldn't move. Surely, no sound so ghastly had ever been heard by human ears. It tore through her, ripping at her soul with razor-sharp talons. Somewhere in the madness was her beloved Ann. Her dear gentle Ann was alone out there somewhere. It didn't require Trevor's great knowledge of the ship to know that anyone who had remained on the ship had next to no chance of survival. She knew Ann well enough to know that she wouldn't have climbed into a lifeboat until the last woman and child on the ship had been taken off. Guilt clawed at her. She should have stayed with her. Ann would never have left her there alone. Her ears ached from the din of people crying out for their loved ones, frantic pleas for help and prayers to God for mercy, but there was no release for her. She had been struck mute. Her throat ached from the fruitless effort of trying to release the excruciating torment trapped inside. Without Ann that pain would be lodged in her heart forever.

She was only vaguely aware of Louise and Betty turning away from the carnage, and of Emma fumbling at something beside her. She didn't even respond when Emma thrust Amelia into her arms.

"Take care of her. I'm not strong enough to do this on my own." In one fast lunge, Emma threw off her coat and flung herself overboard. Maybe the cold had slowed everyone's reflexes or perhaps it was the fact that the move was so sudden and rash. For whatever reason, Emma managed to swim several feet before everyone could react.

"For the love of God," a crewman cried as Bridget gasped. "Ma'am, you can't be swimming out there. You'll freeze to death, for sure." The crew struggled to turn the boat to follow her, but it was too late. Emma had already slipped beneath the water and disappeared.

"Why did she do that?" Betty cried as she partially stood. She seemed to be having trouble breathing.

"Sit down," Louise said. "Lean against me and relax. It'll be okay."

"No," Betty said as she obeyed. "It'll never be all right again. I need Zack."

"The men will be along when they can," Louise said. "You have to calm down or you'll make yourself sick. You have to be brave."

Bridget stared at the tiny bundle in her arms. What would become of the poor child now? She had no one. Emma had taken off her lifebelt and tied it as best as possible around the baby. Emma's coat lay at Bridget's feet. As she stared at the coat, she thought about her mother's jewelry that had been left on the ship. She wished she had thought to take it with her. It had been the only tangible thing of hers left, and now it was at the bottom of the ocean. Suddenly, it became very important that she keep the coat for Amelia. It was all the baby could ever hope to have of her parents. Bridget removed the lifebelt from the baby before wrapping the child in Emma's coat.

She clutched the baby to her chest. They were both alone now. Neither of them had a home to go to or a family to love them. She began to rock as Emma had done earlier in the evening. Slowly the horrible cries of the dying gave way to an even more frightening sound—silence.

CHAPTER NINETEEN

The night grew colder. Occasionally shouts from other lifeboats would ring out across the water. Women would start shouting inquiries as to whether their husbands were aboard or not. Always the answer came back—no. Finally, they stopped asking.

Bridget remained sane by watching over Amelia. At some point, Louise eased over beside her. "Let me hold her. You should try to sleep."

Bridget tried to speak but no sound would come. She shook her head. Finally, Louise gave up and moved back to sit beside Betty.

"What was that?" a weary voice asked from somewhere in the front of the boat.

Bridget looked up in time to see the dying tail of what appeared to be fireworks. Everyone stared into the darkness until a few minutes later another rocket went off. A flurry of excitement ran around the boat.

"It's a rescue ship," one of the crewmen yelled. "Heave to."

They started rowing toward the fading light.

After several minutes, a tiny flick of light appeared on the horizon. They continued toward it. The light gradually took on a green glow. Another fifteen minutes passed before the outline of a ship materialized. Passengers in the lifeboat started screaming and waving, trying to catch the ship's attention. Bridget wanted to join them, but she didn't have the strength to do so. Behind her, a seaman's torch flared for a few precious seconds. A few seconds later, a light on the ship began to flash.

"They saw us," a crewmen said.

There was laughter and rejoicing, but Bridget didn't feel like joining in the merriment. What was there to be happy about?

They approached the anchored ship with what seemed like an agonizing slowness. As soon as they were alongside a rope ladder was tossed over for them to climb. Ropes were tied around women's waist to keep them from falling. Rachel and Betty were among the first ones out.

Louise tried to help Bridget up, but she had no desire to move. Louise sat beside her while the others eased their way around in the lifeboat to the rope. "I never took you for one who would give up so quickly."

Bridget raised her head slowly.

"I heard what Emma said about the lifeboats, but there's still a chance that the men managed to get a seat on one of them. Heck, knowing Miles the way I do, he probably built his own boat." Despite her brave words, a touch of fear in her voice rang through. "We have to have faith in them," she said. Then she looked Bridget in the eye. "I know they fought hard to survive. We have to do the same."

Bridget wanted to ask if Louise really thought there was a chance that anyone left on the ship had survived, but she didn't have the courage.

"And God forbid, if the worse has happened, then you have her to think about." Louise patted the bulky bundle that hid Amelia in its depths.

Bridget tried to speak, but all she could manage was a nearly soundless whisper. She shook her head. "Can't," she whispered. She watched as a rope swing was lowered to hoist an older woman who couldn't navigate the ladder.

"I know she has no family. Without you, she'll end up in an orphanage."

Bridget's arms instinctively tightened around the baby.

Louise gave a small smile. "That's what I thought. Come on now." She helped Bridget up. "We need to get some hot food into you and your baby."

The words bounced around in Bridget's head as she made her way up the ladder while Louise held the baby. She held her breath as Amelia was placed inside a sack and hoisted up. By the time they were both safely on board, Bridget had made up her mind. She would keep Amelia as long as she could.

The rescue ship was ablaze with lights. Despite the fact that the deck was crowded with people, there was an eerie silence. Somewhere off to the side, a baby was crying. She tried not to see the haunted, stricken eyes that stared back at her as she searched in vain for Ann. The crowd looked like a crazed sideshow, with people in their nightclothes standing next to someone in formal garb. Some had blankets wrapped around them while others were wearing coats that clearly didn't belong to them. One woman wore a monstrously elaborate hat that was studded with peacock feathers that surrounded a large white dove. Another wore a seaman's jacket that was at least two sizes too small. Beneath the jacket, she wore a gold and white silk brocade evening gown along with several strands of pearls.

Gentle hands eased her forward and a steward pushed a cup into her hand. "It's strong, hot coffee with a wee bit of brandy. It'll help chase the chill away." He glanced at the bundle in Bridget's arm. "Is there a child in there?"

Bridget gulped the hot coffee and nodded. "Where are the others?" she croaked.

Clearly uncomfortable, the man glanced away. "This would be all we've found so far, ma'am."

Louise, Betty and Rachel appeared beside her. For a moment,

they seemed unsure what to do. Louise broke the spell by taking a large swallow of coffee. "They'll be along soon," she said, taking another sip.

"Sure they will. There're still several boats out there," Betty said. "The men will be along shortly." She grabbed onto Louise's arm. "You know Zack has never been one to miss a meal." Suddenly, she began to cry.

The steward turned quickly. "Mrs. O'Leary, I need your help, please."

A short, heavyset woman with salt-and-pepper hair made her way over. She took one look at the group and quickly ushered them into a salon where breakfast was being served.

"Sit here, dearies. I'll see to it that you're brought food." She gasped as Bridget began to unbundle Amelia. "Mercy me, that's a child. I thought it was a blanket." She turned. "I'll be back."

They sat in exhausted silence until Mrs. O'Leary returned a few minutes later with a baby bottle filled with warm milk.

Bridget stared at the bottle. She should have been the one to think of it. What kind of mother would she make?

"We're searching for some nappies for the wee one." Mrs. O'Leary patted Bridget's shoulder. "Not to worry, we'll find something for you."

Bridget cradled the baby in her arms and began feeding it. What had she been thinking of? She didn't know anything about raising a child. Emma hadn't literally meant for her to take the child. She had just handed her over. Amelia would be much better off with someone who knew how to care for her. She was a sweet, healthy baby and would probably be adopted right away. The thought of handing the infant over to someone else made her sad. She looked down and found herself being observed by piercing blue eyes that seemed to bore into her thoughts. A short stab of guilt hit. Did babies have some sort of extra-keen sensory perception? Did Amelia know she was thinking of sending her to an orphanage? The baby's tiny feet began to kick.

Bridget glanced away quickly and told herself to stop being silly. Amelia was only six months old. She had no comprehension of what was going on. She couldn't possibly understand all the events of the past few hours. *Neither do I*, Bridget realized. Perhaps she was merely seeing her own fears reflected in the baby's eyes. She looked down and smiled. The bottle was empty and the baby was sleeping soundly. As Bridget set the bottle aside, she became aware of the rest of the group watching her.

"Why did she do it?" Rachel asked in a hollow voice.

"She was sick and knew she didn't have long to live," Bridget said. Her voice seemed to be somewhat stronger. Perhaps the coffee and brandy had helped. "She was certain Trevor wouldn't make it and she was scared."

Louise and Betty ducked their heads.

Bridget realized that her last statement had described not only her own, but their worst fears also.

The awkwardness of the moment was broken when a woman dressed in evening clothes complete with an expensive-looking diamond necklace brought a pot of tea to the table and poured them each a cup. "I thought you might like this more than the coffee," she replied.

They thanked her as she rushed off to another table.

Two men toting a large pot of soup and a stack of bowls arrived soon afterward.

Bridget drank the tea but only picked at her soup. She began to observe the other people in the room. Most were women. Only a few men sat hunched over cups or bowls. Their one commonality was that they all looked lost and exhausted. A few were crying, but several were simply staring into space.

"They're in shock," Louise said. "I guess we all are."

Mrs. O'Leary returned with a bundle. "Here are some flannel squares. One of the passengers had some flannel yardage she had stowed away below." She was out of breath. "I had to find a couple of boys to bring the trunk up. That's why it took us so long." She ran her hand over the material. "Quite soft they are. I wouldn't mind having a nice pair of drawers from this meself." Her hand flew to her forehead. "Jesus, Mary and Joseph. I'm so tired me mouth is taking over."

"Don't worry, Mrs. O'Leary," Louise said as she took the bundle. "Right now, I think we would all enjoy a new pair of drawers."

They were interrupted as a man wearing a red-checkered bathrobe over his clothes burst into the room. "They've spotted another boat." There was a mad dash from the room. Bridget grabbed Emma's coat to toss over Amelia before she ran out.

The four women clung to each other as the survivors were brought aboard. Again, most were women. There were a few familiar-looking faces but not the ones they were looking for. They returned to the salon where the torturous routine would be reenacted nine more times.

As the night wore on, Louise helped Bridget bathe Amelia and change her diaper. Mrs. O'Leary had reappeared with a couple of nightshirts for the baby. They were a little snug, but Amelia didn't seem to mind. In talking to Mrs. O'Leary, they learned that five boats had arrived before theirs. That only left five boats still to be found.

They were sitting in the salon drinking yet another cup of tea when Louise's head suddenly snapped up. "Miles," she whispered, then leapt out of her chair.

Bridget looked up, expecting to see him standing in the doorway, but there was no one. She frowned at Rachel and Betty, thinking perhaps she had failed to hear the announcement, but they seemed as puzzled as she was. They exchanged glances before they stood as one and raced after her.

The sun was midway up the horizon when they stepped out onto the deck.

"Boat approaching on starboard side," a lookout yelled from high above.

They tried to reach the rails to look over, but the deck was packed with people. With a little effort, they finally made their way to stand beside Louise, but they still couldn't see the boat. After what felt like an eternity, a rope ladder was tossed over the side. The crowd surged forward slightly in anticipation. Bridget held her breath as the crown of a hat appeared over the rail. She had to fight the urge to cry out in frustration when she saw it was a much older man. He was drenched and could barely walk. A steward ran out with a blanket to throw over him before he was led away. The next head appeared. It was also a man. From behind them, a shout of elation rang out and a young woman shoved her way to the front. Bridget was ashamed of the almost overwhelming feeling of jealousy that washed over her. When a snow-white head appeared over the rail, Louise took off. Miles had barely stepped onto the deck when she threw herself into his arms.

Betty clutched Bridget's arm. "Zack will be next," she whispered, "and then Howard."

Neither Zack nor Howard was among the next three men to climb aboard. Bridget turned to see Miles talking to Louise. She saw the way Louise's body slumped against him for the briefest instant. Then he told her something else and she turned toward them. Bridget's knees weakened when Louise looked directly into her eyes. Slowly Louise squared her shoulders before she started toward them with tears streaming down her face.

Betty took a step back. "No," she cried, and Rachel took her arm.

Miles and Louise drew closer. Bridget saw the glint of tears in Miles's eyes also. Betty began to scream. Bridget wanted to run. She didn't want to hear the news she knew was coming. She bit her lip and stared straight ahead as Miles and Louise went to Betty. She ached as they told Betty that Zack had been killed when the funnel collapsed. She heard the words, but all she could see was a limp figure wearing a black wool coat with a white scarf being lifted up over the railing from the lifeboat below. It was Ann.

CHAPTER TWENTY

The ship's deck gave a sickening spin. Bridget could feel herself swaying. Afraid that she would drop the baby, she tried to steady herself. Louise grabbed Amelia and handed her off to Rachel.

Louise was talking to her, but she couldn't make sense of the words. She pushed Louise aside and started toward Ann. The trip across the deck seemed to take forever. She cried out when two men began to wrap Ann's body in a blanket. Even from a distance, she could see Ann's face was blue from the cold and her clothes were wet, as if she had only recently been pulled from the water. Bridget fell to her knees beside her and pulled her glove off so she could feel Ann's skin once more. She flinched when she touched Ann's face. It was no longer warm with life. Tears flowed down her face as she leaned down and kissed her lover's lips one last time. She raised up to discover Ann staring at her. A short scream escaped her before she realized that Ann was still alive. Before she could say anything, Ann was out again.

Bridget threw her arms around her. "Don't you dare die on me now."

Someone was pulling at her. "Be careful of his leg, ma'am."

"What's wrong with his leg?" Because of the blanket wrapped around Ann, she couldn't see the leg.

Louise helped Bridget up. "Howard needs medical attention." When Bridget started to ask questions, Louise cut her off.

The small group trailed behind as Miles and a steward lifted Ann and carried her into a room with a sign declaring it to be the second cabin dining room. They placed her on one of the cots that lined one wall of the room. On the far side, sheets draped over tall objects had created smaller private areas. A man in a white coat rushed over to them. "I'm Dr. Andrews. What's wrong?"

"He may have a broken leg," Louise said. Without waiting for a doctor, she lifted the blanket from the lower portion of Ann's legs.

Amelia began to fuss so Bridget took her from Rachel.

The doctor checked Ann's pulse before he pulled her eyes open and peered into them. He turned back to Louise. "Do you know what you're doing?"

"I've set more than a few bones," Louise said.

"Thank goodness, because I have more than I can handle," the doctor said. "There's a stack of blankets over there on that table. Get him out of those wet clothes as soon as possible and keep him warm."

"I'll get some blankets," Miles said as he rushed off.

The doctor turned back to Louise. "If his condition changes or you find more than you're comfortable dealing with, send someone to find me. I'll be around all night." He looked at Bridget. "Are you and the baby all right?"

"We're fine."

He turned his attention to Betty. "Ma'am, I think you need to lie down." He motioned to the row of cots along the wall. "Remember, I'll be around if you need me." He left just as Miles returned with a couple of blankets.

"Miles," Louise began, "would you pull another cot over here for the baby, please? I'm going to need Bridget to help me."

Miles did as she asked.

"I'm going to need a pair of scissors, something to use as a splint and binding strips," Louise said.

"I'll find them," Miles said as he rushed away.

Betty was still standing by the bed.

Louise looked at Rachel and nodded toward Betty. "Can you help her?"

Rachel nodded and led Betty across the room.

"Will she be all right?" Bridget asked. She placed Amelia on the cot and covered her with Emma's coat.

"Given some time, she will be." Louise turned her attention back to Ann. "Grab one of those blankets. We need to get these wet clothes off him."

Bridget held her breath. This scenario was the one that had worried her most about Ann's masquerade.

"You don't have to worry. I already know," Louise said softly.

Bridget stared at her, not sure she had heard correctly.

"Help me get this coat off."

The wet coat was hard to remove, but together they finally managed to get it off without having to jostle Ann too much. The task of removing her shirt while trying to keep her covered with the blanket proved much more difficult.

"I wish Miles would hurry up with those blamed scissors," Louise grunted as she struggled to wiggle Ann's arm out of a sleeve.

They were both perspiring by the time the stubborn garment came off. Once the shirt was removed, the money belt and the binding Ann had put around her breasts were revealed.

"I'll let you handle the rest while I take a look at his leg," Louise replied as she tucked the blanket more firmly under Ann's chin.

A moment later, Miles came by and handed her a pair of scissors. "I'm still looking for the rest," he said before hurrying off again.

Louise took the other blanket, spread it over Ann's body and glanced around once more. "I'm going to have to cut the pants off."

Bridget nodded as she fumbled with the strings on the money belt. They were wet and impossible to untie. She finally took the scissors Miles had found and cut both the strings and the wrap around Ann's breasts. She rolled the money belt as inconspicuously as possible and slipped it beneath the coat covering Amelia.

"When he's better we'll make a breechcloth out of a sheet for him to wear," Louis teased.

Bridget smiled. "He's so enthralled with the West, he probably wouldn't mind. In fact, since he has become so fond of comfort he may not want to go back to wearing pants." They both gave a weary chuckle.

Louise took the scissors and knelt by the cot. "If we cut the pants loose on the injured leg, we can probably slip them off the other side without hurting him." She went to work cutting the pants along the outer seam. When she had finally cut all the way to the waistline, she cut the underwear loose as well. Then she motioned to Bridget. "See if you can pull them off now. If not, we'll have to cut the other trouser leg also." She held the blanket in place while Bridget slipped first the pants and then the underwear off.

Louise folded and tucked the blanket until only the lower half of Ann's right leg was exposed. The knee was badly bruised and swollen.

"How did you know?" Bridget asked.

"I grew up with six brothers, and I've worked around ranch hands most of my life. I think it was the hands I noticed first. After that it was just little things that most people wouldn't notice. The way he would sit with his knees together. He tends to cross his legs at the ankle rather than the knee." She shrugged. "Like I said, it was just little things." She gently probed the area around Ann's knee before she slipped a hand beneath Ann's thigh and slowly eased it up until the knee flexed.

"Is he going to be all right?" Bridget wouldn't refer to Ann as a female, even though Louise knew the truth. Ann had stood noble and faced the same dangers as every other male on that ship. She had earned the right to be treated the same as any of them would be.

"I think so. Nothing is broken. I think it's just a badly twisted knee."

"What are you going to do now?"

"I'll bind the knee. Then we'll take turns watching him as the doctor asked."

"Why are you being so understanding?" Bridget asked, unable to believe Louise or anyone else would ever accept them.

"There are several reasons. First, we liked you both from the beginning. You seemed like nice, decent kids." She brushed a strand of hair from her face. "My youngest brother is . . . was different also." She shook her head. "My father was a strict man and he had no tolerance for anything he didn't understand. Lord knows he never understood Danny. They were such different spirits. I really can't ever remember hearing my father laugh, but Danny was always laughing. He was such a gentle soul, much too gentle for Papa's world." She eased the blanket down to cover Ann's leg. "There was an incident. Papa caught Danny with a man." She took a deep breath and slowly exhaled. "Papa shot the man and beat Danny half to death. That night he made Danny stand in front of us while he told us what had happened. Then he informed us that we weren't allowed to speak to Danny again until he begged God for forgiveness. Later that night Danny tried to talk to me, but I was scared of what Papa would do to me, and I walked away from him. The next morning I went to the barn to milk the cow, as I did every morning, and there was Danny hanging from a rafter. I've always wondered if I had just defied Papa that one time, could I have saved Danny?"

"Maybe you couldn't have saved him, but you didn't kill him either."

Louise gazed at her a moment and nodded. "But the main reason I'll always be there if either of you need me is because Miles told me Howard saved his life. I don't know the entire story, but for that, he will always have my undying gratitude." She glanced around the room. "Now, where is that man?"

"Does Miles know? About—" She nodded toward Ann.

"Yes. We talked about it. I'll admit he was a little confused by

127

the whole idea at first, but Miles is an even-tempered man. That's one of the things that made me fall in love with him."

They stood in silence for a moment.

"Would you mind if I asked you a question?" Louise asked.

Bridget hesitated a moment before responding. "No. I guess not."

"Why does he do it? It has to be hard, hiding your entire life. I mean, is it that hard for two women being together? People don't seem to notice it as much as they do when two men live together."

"I don't know that it's easier for women. Maybe it is once they're older. All I know is that once Ann became Howard things became easier. We could travel without being harassed. We could sit in a romantic restaurant without people staring and pointing at us. We could hold hands in public." A spark of anger took hold and Bridget had to stop to keep it from flaring. Louise wasn't the problem. She forced herself to remain calm. "Besides, as Howard it'll be easier for him to find work." She brushed Ann's hair back from her forehead. "And he really likes men's shoes." She smiled as she wrapped a tendril of hair around her finger. "He says that if women ever discover how comfortable men's clothes are, they'll never wear another corset or dress again."

"Now there's an idea." Louise patted her waist. "I wouldn't mind losing the corset."

Miles returned with the items she had asked for. "How is he?" he asked.

Louise took the strips and began to wrap Ann's knee. "I don't think anything is broken after all. It's just a nasty twist."

"What happened?" Bridget asked.

Miles shook his head and sat on the end of the cot where Amelia was sleeping. He rubbed a hand over his face. "After you all left in the lifeboat, Trevor became really agitated. He was obsessed with that ship. You would have thought he'd designed it himself. We were all talking about how the accident could have happened. Then, all at once, he took off running and went back inside the ship. We tried to catch him, but he was like a crazy man. He kept going deeper and deeper. We followed him until the water got so deep that it wasn't safe anymore." He sighed. "We went back up to the port side to see if there were spaces in any of those boats, but by then the boats had all been launched. Zack wanted to try to swim out to one of the boats that had left with empty seats, but Howard told us we'd freeze to death before we could get to one."

"He was right," Louise said.

Miles went on. "We started looking for something we could use as a makeshift raft. All we needed was something big enough to hold the three of us. We were up near the—" His voice broke, and he struggled to regain control. "When the funnel collapsed, Zack was underneath it. We tried to get to him, but it was too late. After that everything sort of went crazy. People were screaming and praying. We decided we would stay on the ship as long as we could, then once we hit the water we would strike out for one of the boats. We were standing at the rail when the ship broke up. We were holding on for dear life, but something crashed down on me. I remember hitting the water and being pushed down. Whatever it was on me was heavy. I couldn't fight my way from beneath it. The next thing I knew, Howard was hauling me across the hull of an overturned boat. Then he helped a couple of other men up before he crawled onto it. We hung on until another boat finally came along and picked us up."

Louise had moved over beside him and put her arms around him.

Bridget stared at Ann. "I'm sorry about Zack," she said.

Miles nodded slowly. "He was a good brother. I'm going to miss him a lot." He glanced at the baby and frowned. "Where's Emma?"

Bridget sat on the side of Ann's bed and stroked her hair while Louise told Miles their story.

Around noon, two crewmembers came into the room and began making their way from bed to bed. Bridget pretended to be concentrating on feeding the baby, but she heard them asking passengers their names. She considered waking Ann up. She needed her help. This wasn't a decision she should make on her own. As one of the men drew nearer, she placed Amelia on the bed and stood.

The man nodded as he approached. "The captain has asked that we compile a manifest of all survivors." He looked at Ann. "Is this your husband?"

"Yes."

"Could I have his name please?"

Bridget glanced at Ann once more, willing her to wake up. Then she turned and replied, "Sheffington. Trevor and Emma Sheffington. This is our daughter, Amelia."

The man neatly printed the names onto a sheet of paper that had been divided into two columns. "Just one more question, if you please, ma'am." He cleared his throat softly as he flipped to a different sheet of paper where a long list of names, four columns wide, had been written. "Was there anyone else in your party? What I mean is, anyone who didn't . . ." He trailed off.

"No. It was just the three of us."

He seemed relieved not to have to enter another name to the gruesome list. "Thank you. I hope your husband is up and around soon." He nodded and left.

Bridget sat back down on the cot. The baby's bottle was empty so she set it aside, picked up the infant and slowly rocked her. "Amelia," she whispered. "If the stress of this trip doesn't kill me, your new father may." Her concerns were met with a gurgle of laughter and a resounding burp.

CHAPTER TWENTY-ONE

The next morning, Bridget sat in the dim light of the makeshift hospital. She was on the cot beside Ann's bed, watching Amelia sleep. The baby was lying on her back with her hands tucked beneath her chin and seemed completely at peace. Bridget wished she could find the same peaceful sleep. She had dozed a few times, but each time she did she started to dream. There wasn't even peace when she was awake. It had gotten so bad at one point that she had actually resorted to trying to wake Ann. She needed to talk to her. The decision to use the Sheffingtons' name yesterday was weighing heavily on her. What if someone was waiting in New York to meet Trevor and Emma? Once she gave the matter some thought, she realized that she and Emma hadn't really talked that much. Maybe there were things that she hadn't told her. Bridget shook her head. She distinctly remembered Emma saying that she was worried about what would become of Trevor if she died, because there was no one else for him to turn to. Then a more frightening thought hit her. According to Miles's story, no one had actually seen Trevor die. What if he was onboard ship right now, and they had somehow missed each other? What if she was stealing his daughter and he was still alive? At a little after five when Louise tiptoed in with a cup of hot tea and a bundle of clothes, Bridget was on the verge of screaming.

"I managed to find a set for you and Howard," Louise whispered so as not to disturb the other patients who were still sleeping. "How's he doing?" She placed a hand on Ann's forehead before checking her pulse.

"He slept straight through the night." She tried to push her demons away.

"There's no fever and the pulse in normal. He's just exhausted."

Think about someone who has worse problems than you do, she told herself. "How is Betty doing?" She took a sip of the tea. The warm liquid provided a soothing sense of familiarity.

"She rarely says anything," Louise said. "She just stares into space most of the time. Rachel seems to be the only person who can get through to her." She rubbed her arm. "I guess she doesn't really associate Rachel with Zack. It's as though she's caught in some sort of limbo. I don't think she has accepted the fact that he's gone, and so she can't grieve for him." She sighed. "I pray that she'll get better. Maybe she just needs to get home to grieve in private."

"What about you and Miles? Were you able to get any rest?" Bridget asked.

"We're okay. We slept for a few hours."

Bridget wrapped her hands around the steaming cup. It gave her a sense of comfort. She didn't think she'd ever complain about being hot again. "Where are they putting everyone?"

"There were a few spare rooms, but not many. They've put all the women into the first-, second- and third-class dining rooms— by class, of course." She shook her head in disgust. "The men were put in the smoking rooms, which aren't large enough to hold everyone, so people are pretty much scattered all over the place.

Miles and I snuck off and found ourselves a cozy spot in a little storage area behind the first-class galley. After almost losing him, I wasn't about to let them separate us."

"I don't blame you." She leaned forward. "I know you're going to think we are completely insane, but I suppose I should warn you that I've changed our names again."

Louise looked at her and blinked.

"It's because of Amelia, really. I want to keep her and live in America. When they came around yesterday taking names of passengers I didn't know what to do and panicked. I told them we were the Sheffingtons."

"What about your families in England? I mean, I'm assuming you both have families."

Bridget looked down at her sleeping lover and made a quick decision. Louise had been so good to them and right now Bridget needed someone she could talk to about all the madness that was rattling around in her head—someone who would listen and not condemn her. She told Louise everything that had transpired in the past few crazy weeks.

When the story had been poured out, Louise patted her hand. "No one could accuse you two of living a boring life."

"But that's what I want."

"What does he want?" She nodded at Ann. "How will he feel about Amelia?"

"I think it'll be all right. We never really discussed *having* children. Our concern was would we be all right in *not* having children." She leaned toward Louise. "What if we're not the right parents for Amelia? Even I admit that we've not been very responsible recently. I'm certain most people would find us completely unstable and therefore unfit to be parents."

"Bridget, I have a secret to share with you. Only an unstable person would intentionally become a parent."

Bridget's chin dropped.

"Don't look so shocked. I love all my children, and I thank God for them every day. At least, I do now that they're grown and out of the house. There were days when they were younger that I would

133

find myself wondering what I had done to deserve such punishment." She patted Bridget's hand again. "I'm not trying to frighten you. I think you and Howard will make wonderful parents. You just need to realize that parents aren't perfect. Thirty years ago Miles and I were standing in the same shoes you two are today." She stopped suddenly. "Well, not exactly."

They both burst into giggles that they had to smother behind their hands.

"We're shameless," Louise whispered as she wiped tears from her eyes. "These poor people are trying to sleep." She grew serious. "All I'm trying to say is that children don't come with instructions. You'll feel like you're just muddling your way through most of the time. The secret is to keep love and respect always at the forefront of it all. That's how you'll all continue to grow as you move through life together. That's the incredible beauty of it all."

Bridget gave her a quick, awkward hug. "Thank you."

Louise waved her off. "Why don't you go change? I'll stay here with these two if you want to take a break and stretch your legs a bit. There's a bathroom at the far end of this hall. As of about an hour ago, not many people had found it yet."

Bridget thanked her, then grabbed the clothes and Amelia's empty bottle. She had a bit of trouble finding the bathroom, which was probably why it was still empty. She took a quick bath before putting on the clean clothes. On her way back, she made a slight detour to the kitchen, where she found a steward who was more than happy to prepare a fresh bottle of milk for Amelia. When he returned with the bottle, it was on a tray containing a steaming pot of tea, with a cup and a plate of biscuits and jam, along with a few cold slices of ham.

"It's all we have ready right now," he said. "Breakfast won't be served until eight."

"Thank you. This is most kind." She begged the use of one more cup and hurried back. She and Louise shared the tea and food.

After drinking the last of her tea, Louise stood. "I guess I'd better go. I'm supposed to meet the others for breakfast. Do you want me to bring you anything?"

"No. They brought trays in for the patients last night. So, I'm sure they will again this morning."

The sun hadn't broken the horizon yet. The room was dim with only a few shaded lamps scattered about. Most of the occupants were still sleeping, although here and there she could barely detect the soft whisper of voices. When Amelia was finally asleep, Bridget poured herself another cup of tea and quickly devoured the last biscuit.

Despite everything that had happened in the past few hours, she felt a strange sense of contentment. Ann and Amelia were safe and it felt wonderful to just sit and sip her tea. She couldn't remember a time when it had felt so good to have a bath and clean clothes, even if the clothes belonged to someone else. The passengers and crew of the *Carpathia*, the ship that had rescued them, had opened their hearts, suitcases and wallets. Their kindness and generosity had been overwhelming.

Suddenly Ann said, "Where am I?"

Bridget eased off the cot so as not to disturb the baby and set her tea down. "We're on the *Carpathia*. Everything is fine now."

"Are you all right?"

"Yes, I'm fine. We're both fine."

Ann blinked a couple of times. Her face drew tighter and she began to shake.

Bridget tucked the blankets more securely around her. "It's all right. We're safe now."

"Zack and Trevor—"

"I know. Miles told us what happened."

Ann squeezed her eyes shut. "We couldn't get to him."

Bridget made a soft shushing noise. "Please, don't think about it now. There'll be time later, when you're stronger." She brushed Ann's hair back from her face. "Do you feel like sipping some tea?"

"Please." Ann sat up slowly and grabbed the blanket as it started to fall. "What happened to my clothes? Who took them off me?" She clutched the blanket to her.

"It's all right. I was here. Louise helped me." Bridget placed an extra pillow between Ann's back and the wall. "Lean back and relax."

"Louise? She knows?"

Bridget smiled and nodded. "She doesn't care. She figured it out while we were still onboard the *Titanic*."

"How?"

Bridget looked at her. "Are you sure you're up to all this now?"

"I feel fine, except for my knee. It hurts."

"Louise thinks you twisted it." She retrieved the shirt Louise had brought over for Ann. "If you're going to sit up, you'd best put this on."

The two of them managed to get the shirt on Ann without exposing her secret. As she was buttoning the shirt, Ann asked about the money belt.

"Don't worry. It's safe." Bridget poured tea from the pot into the cup. "I'm afraid it's not quite as hot as you like it." She handed the cup to Ann.

"It's perfect."

They sat gazing at each other. The dim light helped hide their disheveled appearance. It was almost possible to believe that it all had been a horrible nightmare. Bridget didn't know how to bring up all the things she needed to tell Ann.

"I wouldn't have made it without you," Ann said softly. "Every time I felt like giving up, I'd remember your face, and just the promise of seeing you again made me hang on. I swear I thought I heard you calling my name a few times."

"I was so scared," Bridget said, "I couldn't even speak."

"I'm sorry you had to go through all that. It was all my fault."

"Nonsense."

"I pushed you to take this trip. You were perfectly contented living in your apartment and—"

"Stop it. I'm where I want to be."

Ann finished the cup of tea. "Will you lie here beside me for a while?"

Bridget cast a quick glance at the still sleeping Amelia before lying down beside Ann, being careful not to bump her knee.

Ann laughed softly. "This cot reminds me of that tiny little bed in your apartment." She kissed the top of Bridget's head. "Once we're settled I'm going to buy the biggest bed I can find."

"You don't need one too big, because I don't plan on letting you ever get too far from my side."

Amelia began to fret. Bridget sat up quickly to pick her up before she started crying.

"Is that Amelia?" Ann asked when Bridget returned.

"Yes." The baby quieted down as soon as Bridget picked her up.

"Where is Emma?"

Bridget took a deep breath. She knew she should probably wait until Ann was stronger before she told her everything, but there simply wasn't time. She started with Emma, and how she jumped from the boat and swam away.

"Where was she trying to go?"

"Who knows? I think it was all just too much for her."

"What's going to happen to Amelia? Trevor told me that neither of them had a family."

Bridget looked down into the face of the sleeping baby. "How would you feel about us keeping her?" Even in the dimly lit room, she could see Ann's eyes widen.

"No one would ever let us adopt a baby," she finally sputtered. "We don't even know which country will decide to keep her since Trevor and Emma were immigrating to America. It would be extremely complicated."

"I didn't say anything about adopting."

"You just said—"

"Please hear me out." She leaned closer to Ann. "I've been thinking about this, a lot. Since the *Titanic* was headed to America and we're much nearer there than we are to England, I'm sure this ship will take us on to Ellis Island where they will process everyone through."

Ann nodded.

"When we dock, there's going to be complete chaos. There will be hundreds of people there to meet the families from both ships. I'm sure reporters will be there. Everything will be in disarray. Suppose we just walked off the ship and got ourselves lost in the crowd. I don't know how the system works there, but there's a chance we could simply walk away." She took a deep breath and told her about how she had given their names as Sheffington. She had intended to confess telling everything to Louise, but when she heard a small groan slip from Ann, she decided it might be best to wait a while before making a full confession. After a long stretch of silence, she placed a hand on Ann's arm. "It's for the best. Whether we simply walk away from Ellis Island or whether we leave as the Sheffingtons, we could keep Amelia. We wouldn't have to go back to England. If by some weird twist of fate our parents ever managed to connect us to the Mr. and Mrs. Howard Franklin who boarded the ship in Southampton, there would be no record of us leaving this ship in America. They would stop looking for us."

Ann rubbed her cheek. "I don't know that I like the idea of letting my parents think I perished on the ship." They sat in silence for a few moments. "On the other hand, if my father ever found me . . ." She didn't finish. For a moment, she gazed at Amelia. "What would we do in America?"

Bridget shrugged. "Move to Texas, open our own mercantile and raise our daughter."

CHAPTER TWENTY-TWO

Ann spent the rest of Tuesday in bed resting. As the morning wore on, Bridget finally got around to mentioning her talk with Louise. Ann took it much better than she had anticipated. They played with Amelia and talked for hours. Late that afternoon, most of the *Titanic* survivors gathered on deck to pay their last respects to three of their fellow passengers who had not survived their injuries. Bridget made sure Ann didn't hear of the service for fear she would try to attend. She wanted her to stay in bed and rest as long as possible, but on Wednesday morning, Ann insisted on getting up.

"I think you should rest another day," Bridget said as she watched Ann struggling to pull her pants on beneath the blankets.

"No. We should be docking in New York tomorrow night. I can't very well disappear into the crowd if they have to carry me off the ship. If I stay in bed, my knee will only get stiffer. I need to get up and move around. Besides, I couldn't stand another day of having to be shuttled around every time I need to take care of my business."

Bridget tried not to smile, but getting Ann to the toilet the day before had required a joint effort of all their friends.

Miles had scrounged a single crutch late yesterday afternoon. Bridget could only hope that there wasn't some poor sod onboard who only had one crutch this morning.

Ann finally managed to get the pants on and eased out of bed. The pants were a little too large, but they would do until she could do better. She leaned against the wall as she tucked her shirt in and buttoned up. She had been able to repair the strings on the money belt by tying strips of rags onto the severed ends of the strings. "Would you hand me the jacket please?"

Bridget handed it to her.

It was too large also, but it hid the slight bulge of her breasts and the belt. "How do I look?" she asked as she tucked the crutch under her arm.

"You're as handsome as always."

"Let's see if I can make it to breakfast. I'm starving."

They found their four friends already seated when they entered the dining room. There were no clues to indicate that only a few hours ago the female survivors from the *Titanic* had used this room as a sleeping area.

They exchanged pleasantries and placed their meal orders. Betty sat staring straight ahead like a zombie. Bridget wondered how long it would take her to rebuild her life.

"I heard we should reach New York around nine thirty tomorrow night," Rachel said.

Ann sipped her tea. "Is it true that the line at Ellis Island can be quite long?"

Miles shook his head. "We're not going through Ellis Island. I was talking to one of the pursers. The shipping company wants to get the sick and wounded to the hospital as quickly as possible, so the American authorities gave them permission to dock in the North River."

Bridget glanced at Ann. Perhaps this would make it much easier for them to slip away undetected. "What about the passengers who were immigrating? How will they be processed?"

"I don't know. Everything is a mess. The *Titanic's* original manifest was lost and it seems that the roll that was taken on Monday doesn't match the copy that was kept by the White Star Line main office."

"Why wouldn't they match?" Louise asked.

"Who knows," Miles said. "It's a terrible mess that will never get straightened out."

"I suspect part of the problem is due to language difficulties," Rachel said. "We were transporting quite a diverse group of passengers."

"Do you suppose it was because so many people had their travel plans changed due to the coal strike?" Bridget asked. The question seemed to dangle in the air for a moment as she gave herself a mental kick for asking such an insensitive question. The Delaneys had been on the *Titanic* due to the coal strike. She glanced at Betty, who continued to stare into space. "I'm sorry. I didn't think."

"It's okay," Louise said.

Rachel placed Betty's teacup into her hands. Betty automatically moved the cup to her lips and drank. Thankfully, their food arrived and the group fell silent as they ate.

Bridget discreetly watched as Rachel continued to place things in front of Betty to encourage her to eat.

The dining room's occupants began to thin out as the *Carpathia's* original passengers returned to their rooms. With nowhere to go, the survivors were in no hurry to leave. The ship was so crowded there wasn't enough room to do much except sit, and at least here they each had a chair.

After they had eaten and the plates were removed, the waiter brought out fresh pots of tea and coffee.

"May I hold Amelia?" Louise asked after the waiter left.

Bridget carried the baby around to her.

"Mercy." Louise grunted as she took Amelia. "How many bottles a day are you feeding her?"

Bridget chuckled. "That little girl has an appetite. We're going to have to buy a cow to keep her in milk." Everyone at the table except for Betty stared at her.

"So," Louise began, "it sounds as though you've made a decision."

Ann took Bridget's hand. "I know this may sound a bit odd, but after the past few days, I've come to think of each of you as a second family."

All heads nodded in agreement except for Betty's.

"Bridget and I have done a lot of talking, and we feel that we can give Amelia a good home. But we may need a bit of help from you."

"You know you can count on me," Miles said immediately. "Tell me what you need."

Ann told them about Bridget using the Sheffingtons' name. "I think it would be better if we could simply step off the ship and disappear. This will be much easier to do, I think, if we don't go to Ellis Island."

Rachel nodded. "I'm sure the dock will be crowded. Everything will be a mess."

"Exactly," Bridget added.

"We'll get you out of there somehow," Miles assured them. He leaned back in his chair. "So, where in Texas are you planning on living?"

Ann frowned. "I don't rightly know. I've never really given an actual town much thought." She shrugged. "I suppose I never really believed I'd ever go."

"Have you given any thought to how you'll earn a living?" Miles asked.

Louise slapped his arm.

He looked at her, surprised. "What? It's an important question. You sure as heck wouldn't want to move to Dallas if you were a shrimper or El Paso if you want to grow corn or—"

"We get the picture," Louise said. "I'm sorry I interrupted."

"We want to open a mercantile, nothing fancy, just basic dry goods and such for now," Ann said.

Miles glanced at Louise and she gave a slight nod. He cleared his throat. "Well, if you don't have your heart set on any particular place, I think you'd find Whitehall a nice place to live. It's a small town, but the people are friendly. They're good neighbors. They know when to mind their own business. It's not a rich community, but we do okay. We help each other out when help is needed. There's a decent school and a couple of churches." He looked directly at Ann. "It's a place where you can raise your family and be safe."

Ann looked at Bridget. "It sounds nice, but I'm sure the town already has a mercantile and I wouldn't want to move in on someone, especially in a small town where the potential for sales is so limited."

Miles nodded. "That's really decent of you. I think the current owner might be willing to sell. You see, he's an older gentleman." He turned to Louise for confirmation. "How old do you think Mr. Wheedle is?"

"I'm not sure, but he had half-grown kids when I was a little girl. I'd think he's at least sixty-five, sixty-six."

"Why don't you go on down with us?" Miles said. "You can have a look around to see how you like the place. Have a talk with Mr. Wheedle. I'll teach you how to ride a horse and maybe we can even take a trip up to San Antonio and find you a Stetson."

Whitehall. Bridget let the word roll over her tongue. She thought about the people sitting at the table with her. Until a few days ago, they had been complete strangers, but now, she had grown to think of them as family. She thought about Emma and Trevor and for the briefest instant, she thought she heard Zack's hearty laugh. She glanced up to find Betty looking at her and suddenly she knew that they all would be lifelong friends. They would all share in both the good times and the hard, but somehow their lives would be forever bound.

CHAPTER TWENTY-THREE
Whitehall, Texas
Present Day

As soon as the dog began to bark, Erica removed a hefty ball of raw hamburger from a plastic bag and tossed it to him. As always General Lee, the seventeen-year-old, nearly blind, totally bald English bulldog dropped to the ground like a lead weight. "Good boy," she whispered as she tiptoed past him and over to the back gate. The fence separated the yards of the Misses Wilkerson and Hudson. The two had never married, and both still lived in their respective family homes. They had been carrying on their feud ever since the then ten-year-old Janie Wilkerson brought home the first General Lee back in 1934 and he proceeded to chew the hair off Ida Sue Hudson's favorite doll. The current General Lee, who was busy gumming the hamburger to death, was actually the fourth.

From the pocket of her hooded jacket, she pulled out a small can of spray lubricant and squirted each of the hinges. They squealed slightly as she opened the old chain-link fence gate. She froze and held her breath. The last thing she needed now was for the eighty-four-year-old Miss Wilkerson to come tearing out with her grandfather's Civil War relic shotgun. The slightest ruckus would cause an immediate defensive reaction from her geriatric peer, Ida Sue, who was a bit more modern in her choice of weaponry and was widely known for her skill with the rifle her father had brought home from World War I. In case there was anyone who doubted her marksmanship, Ida Sue kept a framed newspaper clipping hanging in her living room that described how she had shot the earlobe off a misguided, would-be burglar back in 'seventy-two. Of course, that occurred before her eyesight began to fail. Now the poor thing was lucky to see the broadside of a barn much less hit it.

After a few seconds, Erica eased the gate shut, thankful that it no longer shrieked as it had the previous night. It was September and the recent lack of rain over the summer months had caused the ground to shift and throw everything off kilter. She checked the latch on the gate to be sure it was secure. If General Lee got loose, the entire town would be called out to search for him, and as a member of the volunteer fire department, she would be expected to be there. She sprinted to the end of the hedgerow behind Raul Sosa's house.

The next stretch of her almost nightly obstacle course would be more difficult. She had to cut through Jason Moore's backyard. Just yesterday, the idiot had brought home a Doberman. Everyone in town knew he'd bought the dog to protect the single, straggly marijuana plant he had growing in the middle of his mother's totally organic vegetable and flower garden. The law didn't bother him because he didn't raise the plant to sell, or use. He grew it because he thought it made him a bad boy. He liked to walk around town wearing a cheap imitation leather jacket and sporting a ragged bandanna tied around his head. By June, the south Texas heat made the jacket so rank that no one would get near him. His mother would eventually sneak the jacket out of his room and burn it. Then he would dig out his two favorite black Def Leppard T-shirts with their ripped-out sleeves and torn necklines. According to his mother, he had gotten the shirts out of a box of rags she had bought at a church bazaar over in Poteet. Jason would wear the T-shirts until December when the Wal-Mart over in Floresville ran their winter special on imitation leather jackets.

Erica swallowed the goose egg of fear in her throat and slowly approached the fence. The blasted dog had almost taken a chunk out of her rear end the night before. Just thinking about the dog scared the bejesus out of her. She looked back toward her own home with longing. How much longer was she going to allow herself to carry on with this charade? She was thirty-one and this little adventure had long since lost any excitement factor it might have once possessed. She carefully scanned the yard, but there was no sign of the dog. Maybe Jason's mother had made him get rid of it. There was no back gate to the Moores' fence. She always had to jump over it. She placed both palms on the crossbar and slowly eased her body over the fence. Her feet had almost touched the ground when she heard a low snuffling sound nearby. She froze and went instantly deaf as her heart jackhammered every ounce of blood directly to her eardrums. As she hung on the fence, she had a vision of the lead story in tomorrow morning's *Whitehall Gazette*. *A local business owner and school board member, Erica Winfrey, was hospitalized last night after a Doberman chewed off her ass. The dog is the property of Whitehall's drug kingpin, Jason Moore. Both Ms. Winfrey and the dog were doing fine as of this morning.*

She continued to hang from the fence until her arms began to burn so she could no longer hold on. Since she was still alive and her butt still seemed to be attached, she slowly relaxed. She had obviously let her imagination get the better of her. She eased her way off the fence until her feet rested firmly on the lawn. After a deliberate count to three, she turned slowly and scanned the yard. There was no sign of the dog—at least not until she took a step and her feet flew from beneath her. The nonorganic aroma that met her nose told her immediately that she hadn't slipped on some wayward banana peel.

She started to stand up and in doing so placed her hand firmly in another pile of Doberman crap. It took a moment of struggling and some fancy maneuvering for her to stand without placing either of her hands back on the ground. When she finally managed to get up she smelled like an outhouse. "Son-of-a—" Before she could finish she saw two cold glassy eyes staring at her and they were less than ten feet away. She cleared the fence with one leap, and unfortunately so did the Doberman. As she raced past Raul Sosa's hedgerow, she could hear the dog's feet pounding behind her. She didn't bother to unlatch the gate to Miss Wilkerson's fence but vaulted over it. Poor General Lee must have thought the Yankees were invading again. He began barking with the strength of a dog half his age. By the time she had cleared the Wilkerson side fence the peaceful night air was shattered by the booming percussion of a Civil War-era double-barrel shotgun. Within seconds, the tree limbs behind Miss Hudson's house began to explode as the Springfield M1903 returned fire.

God, she prayed, *please don't let them accidentally kill each other.* And with that, she barged through her back door and into the kitchen.

Her grandmother was sitting at the kitchen table looking at the latest edition of *Playgirl* and sipping a glass of bourbon. "How was your date?" she asked without looking up.

"I don't want to talk about it."

"Oh, she wasn't in the mood, huh?"

"Grams, I mean it."

"It sounds as though the widows Wilkerson and Hudson are at it again." She flipped the page and smiled. "You'd better hurry and get yourself cleaned up. I'm sure you'll be receiving a call soon."

"Grams, I can't do this anymore."

"I'm not the one you should be talking to." She sniffed and wrinkled her nose. "I think you may have stepped in some canine byproduct."

Erica struggled not to lose her temper. It wasn't her grandmother's fault that she had just made a complete fool of herself. The unpleasant odor finally penetrated her anger. She leaned down and removed her sneakers. She wasn't about to go outside to remove them, for fear the Doberman was standing out there waiting for her. She made her way into the garage and then on back to the laundry room. She set her shoes in the garbage can while she stripped naked and threw her disgusting clothes into the washer. She scrubbed her hands until they were red. Then she scraped as much of the mess off her shoes as possible before tossing them into the ancient porcelain laundry tub and turning the hot water on. She found a small plastic stiff-bristled brush on the shelf and used it to scrub the shoes clean. After she was satisfied the shoes were clean she set them on the floor and tossed the brush into the trashcan.

She made her way back to the garage. "Grams," she called out, "are you alone?"

"Ain't I always?" her grandmother called back.

"I'm naked so don't look."

"Your secrets are safe with me."

Erica zipped across the living room and was just slipping into her bedroom when she heard her mother.

"Great gods in the morning, what is going on out here? I was right in the middle of my oatmeal bath when I heard the misses cut loose. They're going to kill somebody one of these days. Erica, why are you running through the house naked?"

Before Erica could respond, she heard her grandmother call out, "She's practicing for the Indy Five Hundred, Judith. Now, go on back and sit in your oatmeal. Everything is under control."

"Mother, are you reading that filthy magazine again?"

"It ain't filthy yet. I just got it today. Give me a few days. My hands aren't as nimble as they used to be."

"Oh, Lord, help me. Mother, you should be committed. I swear I don't know how I have managed to survive in this family. You all are going to drive me to an early grave." She stomped back to her room and slammed the door.

Erica stifled a laugh and went to shower.

CHAPTER TWENTY-FOUR

When Erica stepped out of the shower, she heard her cell phone ringing. She considered not answering it. She already knew who it would be. If she didn't answer, Alice would just keep calling until she did.

"Where are you?" Alice asked as soon as Erica picked up the phone.

"I'm standing naked in the lobby of the Peabody Hotel in Memphis," Erica replied drily.

"There's no need to be catty."

"Oh, please do not make any animal remarks to me."

"I've been waiting on you."

"Well, I won't be there tonight."

There was a brief pause before Alice said. "I really wanted to see you."

Erica could hear the hurt in her voice but refused to give in to it. "Alice, I'm tired of sneaking around like a teenager. If you want to be with me, you know my address. Or I'll drive over and park my car in your driveway and we can spend a wonderful night together in each other's arms. We are adults. Adults have sex. And sometimes adult women have lesbian sex."

"Stop it. There's no need to be crude. We've gone through this a thousand times and you know I can't—"

"Yes, Mayor Goodman, I know you think you can't."

"It's easy for you. You don't have to depend on the public for your livelihood. What's the worst that would happen? You'd have to resign from the school board. Your store might lose a few customers for a while. Even that wouldn't last. They would return as soon as they grew tired of driving twenty miles to another hardware store. I, on the other hand, would be crucified if anyone ever found out that I'm . . ."

Erica rubbed her forehead. It was useless to point out that the same people who Alice was worried about crucifying her were also customers of Franklin's. "You can't even say it. Alice, you're a lesbian, and you will be tomorrow and the day after that and the"— the phone went dead—"day after that." Erica hung up.

She slipped on a baggy jogging suit and went back to the kitchen to find the one person she could always depend on to understand— her grandmother, Emily Gertrude Ashcroft Boyd, better known around Whitehall simply as Gerti or Miss Gerti. At seventy-two, she was still one of the strongest women Erica had ever known. With her five-foot-two-inch frame and gray Prince Valiant haircut, she might appear frail to anyone who had never tangled with her, but there was power, both emotionally and physically, in that tiny body. She had married James Boyd, her high school sweetheart, and had five children with him. He was thirty-four when a drunk driver crossed the centerline, killing him and two of their boys. She raised the three surviving children alone and still managed to take over Franklin's Mercantile, the family business, and turned it back into the thriving business it had once been. Over the years, she changed the name from Franklin's Mercantile to Franklin's Hardware and Supply, but you could still find everything from anvils to zippers on their shelves. As soon as Gerti's children were old enough, all three had fled Whitehall for the more glamorous life of the bigger cities. Sharon moved to Dallas and married an investment banker. William married a woman he met while in college and moved to Wisconsin to work in her father's law firm. Judith, Gerti's oldest child, married a man in Whitehall and soon left for Houston. After a messy divorce, she returned to Whitehall in 1979 with two small children. She changed her name back to Boyd and picked up her life as if she had never left the town of her birth.

Erica went back to the laundry room to throw her clothes in the dryer. It took several tries to get the dryer to kick on. "That dryer is on its last leg," she said as she returned to the kitchen, where she found a peanut butter and jelly sandwich and a glass of milk waiting for her. She sat down. "How many times do you think you and I have sat here like this?"

Her grandmother tossed the magazine onto the table and took a sip of her bourbon. "A few thousand, I suspect."

Erica picked at the sandwich. "Grams, it's not working."

"Alice is in a difficult position."

"Do you think anyone around here would really care if they found out she was gay?"

"It's hard to say. I know it wouldn't matter to most. There are some who would be upset that she didn't come out before the election, but they would probably get over it. Then there are a few narrow-minded jackasses out there who wouldn't want a lesbian mayor."

"What am I going to do?"

"Sorry. I can't help you there. I still haven't figured out what to do with your mother."

Erica laughed. "What a trio we make."

"How were sales today?" Gerti asked. Gerti usually spent two or three mornings a week at the store and the rest of her time was spent on a multitude of civic issues. She always had a project of some sort.

"Good, but I wanted to talk to you about the Mercks' account." Franklin's was the only store in Whitehall where individual credit accounts were still available. Erica sometimes wondered if any other small business in the world still offered store credit to its customers. Soon after she was given more or less full rein to run the store, she had announced to her grandmother that she intended to stop the practice. That had been the only time she could remember her grandmother speaking harshly to her. Gerti had pointed out that many of the clients were farmers and ranchers who didn't have a steady income coming in weekly. These people depended on Franklin's and had for decades.

"What's wrong with the Mercks' account?"

Erica shrugged. "It's getting pretty high. They owe the store over two thousand dollars."

"Is the store still making enough money for us to live on?"

"Don't be sarcastic, Grams. You know it is."

"Then leave the Mercks alone. They've always been good customers. They'll pay when they can." She tapped her fingers on the table as she always did when she was thinking. "Things have been rough for them since Richard hurt his back. The insurance company is giving them a hard time, and Becka is having to do everything on her own. Dick Junior is supposed to leave for college in May, but if the insurance company doesn't step up and meet their obligations, his college fund will have to be used to pay the hospital."

"How do you know these things?"

Her grandmother put a finger to her forehead and in a wavering voice said, "I am the great and powerful Gerti. I know and see all."

"You're a great bullshitter," Judith said as she stepped into the kitchen. She patted Gerti's shoulder as she walked by. "She knows these things because she sits over at Lili's Tearoom sipping *cordials* and gossiping all afternoon."

"Well, I might learn a few things that way," Gerti admitted and winked at Erica.

"What happened next door?" Judith asked as she poured herself a glass of apple juice.

"The South tried to rise again," Gerti said. "Fortunately, the misses are too blind to hit anything."

"Those two are a menace," Judith said. "They ought to be committed."

"You think everyone over the age of sixty should be committed." Gerti looked at Erica and winked again. "I wonder how she'll feel in six years when she turns—"

"Why is that filthy porno magazine on the kitchen table?" Judith interrupted.

"I thought you might like to take it back to your room and glance through it," Gerti said. "A few hours with it would probably be a lot more relaxing than sitting in oatmeal."

"Mother, will you please stop being vulgar."

The doorbell rang. "That'll be Sheriff Fart Face." Gerti sighed.

"Mother, for goodness' sakes, I've told you a thousand times the man's name is Bart Case."

"Why don't I get the door?" Erica said. She left the two alone so they could continue their bickering. They were complete opposites. Gerti was petite but strong as an ox. She never worried about getting her hands dirty, and her idea of a beauty regimen was getting her hair trimmed every few weeks. She would, as she put it, gussie up when the occasion called for it, but her clothing of choice consisted of simple blouses and baggy slacks with elastic in the band. She enjoyed her nude male magazines and bourbon and possessed a sharp-edged tongue that could slice steel when she wanted to.

Judith, on the other hand, was big-boned like her father. The vanity in her oversized bathroom could have served as a display case for a major cosmetic center. Her walk-in closet was bulging with clothes that rarely saw the light of day after being worn a couple of times. She had a standing weekly appointment with her hairdresser, and once a month she drove to Corpus Christi for her spa treatment. She strived to portray herself as a Southern woman of impeccable taste and breeding. Unfortunately for her, a tiny streak of Gerti's DNA had carried forward into her genes and every once in a while someone would push her too far and trigger the Gerti strain. When this happened, her impeccable taste and breeding were blown out the window.

Erica had always thought she had gotten the best of both women. She had gotten her mother's height and less volatile temper, along with Gerti's strength and confidence that allowed her to be herself.

Erica tuned the bickering out as she opened the door. The caller was indeed Sheriff Case, a painfully thin man who didn't seem to know the purpose of an iron. His uniform—white shirt and black slacks—always looked as though he had taken it directly out of the dryer and put it on. "I came by to see if you ladies had seen or heard any prowlers around tonight."

"No. We haven't noticed anything unusual."

He nodded and hooked his thumbs over his belt. "Miss Wilkerson said someone tried to steal General Lee."

Erica couldn't keep from smiling at the thought of anyone wanting to steal the poor old dog.

"Yes, ma'am, I know it sounds a little strange, but I think someone might have actually been out there tonight."

Erica tensed slightly. "How do you know?"

"We found this in her backyard. She says it doesn't belong to her." He held up a plastic bag containing the can of lubricating spray that she had used on the hinges.

"Oh, that wasn't left by a prowler," Gerti said as she walked up and took the bag. "I threw this can at that old gray tomcat that was a-howling this morning." Before he could protest, she opened the bag and handed the can to Erica. "Put this back in the garage for me, please."

The sheriff looked a little put out. "If you ladies see or hear anything let me know." He tipped his hat and left.

As soon as the door closed, Gerti took the can from Erica and looked at it. "So, this is what lesbians use." She handed the can back to Erica. "You girls ought to try Vaseline. It's cheaper."

CHAPTER TWENTY-FIVE

The following morning, Erica was on a ladder stacking cans of paint when Alice came in. She watched as sunlight from the front window turned Alice's chestnut hair into gleaming strands of gold. She loved running her hands through Alice's hair. A small yelp of pain escaped her as she pinched her hand beneath the can she was holding. She focused her attention back on what she was doing.

There were already several customers in the store. She considered pretending she hadn't seen Alice in hopes that someone else would wait on her, but Gerti was talking to a group of women by the checkout counter, and Fred Zuniga, one of the two full-time clerks, was helping a customer with a plumbing problem. Erica looked around for Angela Green, the other clerk, but didn't see her either. There was no way for her to avoid helping Alice. She came down the ladder and moved behind the counter. "What can I do for you today, Mayor?" Dark circles smudged beneath Alice's slate blue eyes.

Erica brushed her hands off on the seat of her jeans. One of the great things about owning a hardware store was that no one expected you to dress as though you were ready to spend a long day sitting at a desk. Erica's usual wardrobe of jeans, boots and a long-sleeved shirt worked perfectly.

"I need some C-cell batteries," Alice replied as her gaze traveled the length of Erica's body.

Erica nearly missed being checked out, as she was busy throwing Gerti a warning glare to stop the comment she knew was coming about the batteries.

Gerti gave her a nasty look and turned away.

Erica went with Alice to the large spinner that held the batteries.

"Will I see you tonight?" Alice whispered.

"You do realize that I have to cut through Jason Moore's backyard to get to your back door, don't you?"

"So?"

"He acquired a Doberman day before yesterday and I almost got my ass bit off last night. While I was trying to outrun him, I scared poor General Lee half to death and was almost target practice for the misses."

Alice actually blanched. "I'm sorry," she whispered.

To Erica's surprise, tears began to stream down Alice's face. "Oh, God. Please don't cry." She glanced about. There were too many people around. Alice would go into a convulsion if she were to touch her in public. Finally, Erica gave in as she always did. "Don't cry. I'll think of something." She found the card of batteries that Alice had asked for and took them back to the counter where Alice paid for them and made a hasty exit.

Erica was headed back to finish stacking the paint cans when Gerti called her over to where she was chatting with the women. Erica nodded to each of them again, even though she had greeted them when they came into the store.

"Someone stole the Moores' Doberman last night," Gerti announced.

"They tried to steal General Lee too, but Janie and Ida Sue cut loose on them and scared him off," Leola Gaines said. Her cheeks glowed with excitement.

"Don't you suppose the dog just jumped the fence?" Erica asked, earning a disappointed look from the group. Whitehall was a sleepy little town and juicy tidbits like dognapping didn't come along too often. Gerti's narrowed eyes told her she'd better get with the program. "Of course," she said, "Dobermans are expensive dogs. I can see why someone might be tempted to steal one."

Now that she had seen the light, the ladies huddled around her.

"I heard that it was the mob," one of them whispered.

"Mob?" Erica asked, dumbfounded.

"Yes," Leola said. "They were after the"—she leaned in and whispered—"marijuana. He grows it in his backyard, you know. His poor mother doesn't know what it is."

Erica struggled to keep her face neutral.

"That's right," another said. "It was all drug-related."

"I sure hope he doesn't wake up some morning and find that poor dog's head on his pillow like that guy in that *Godfather* movie did," Leola added.

All of the women gasped in horror, making the red patches on Leola's cheeks shine brighter.

"Ladies, I'm sorry," Erica said. "This is just too ghastly for me to even think about. If I listen to any more of this I'll be too scared to even walk home alone." She hurried off before they could stop her.

As she rushed off, she heard Leola say, "Oh, dear, I hope we didn't frighten her. I never knew she was the nervous sort."

"She has to sleep with a light on," Gerti replied loud enough to ensure that Erica heard.

As Erica climbed back up on the ladder, she wondered what the penalty would be for dropping a can of paint on her grandmother's head.

Erica continued to work around the store. It was almost ten when her mother phoned to tell her that a special meeting of the city council was being called and the mayor's office had asked them to attend. "All of us?" Erica asked.

"Yes, that's what Joanie said."

Joan Ayers was Alice's secretary. She was almost the same age as Judith, but because her mother had also been named Joan, she would forever be called Joanie.

"What time?"

"Six o'clock."

"Okay, I'll see if Fred or Angela can close the store for me. If not, I guess I'll have to close early."

Erica didn't have time to go home and change before the city council meeting. An order of electrical fixtures had arrived and she had lost track of time while she was entering the stock into the computer.

They were waiting for her when she hurried in. She saw the look of disapproval on Judith's face. Gerti was standing off at the side talking to one of the councilmen. "Sorry I'm late." She waved to Joanie, who was sitting at a table in the corner.

"That's all right," Alice said, beaming. "I think we can get started now." She waited until everyone found a seat before she glanced at Joanie and smiled. "Since this is not an actual meeting of the council I'd like to make a motion that we dispense with the regular rules of order and proceed with an informal meeting."

The motion was quickly seconded and approved.

Alice folded her hands on the table. "First off, I just want to say how honored I am to be the one to make this announcement."

Gerti looked at Erica with questioning eyes. Erica had no idea what was going on and shrugged.

"As you all know," Alice said, "our community will be celebrating its sesquicentennial next year, and in honor of the event the decision has been made to rebuild the town square." She looked at each of the five council members and smiled. "There will be a groundbreaking ceremony for the new square on Saturday morning. At that time we will announce that the city is going to erect a statue in the town square to honor your family. We're doing so to show our appreciation to your ancestors Howard and Bridget Franklin for all they did for Whitehall during the Depression and those awful years following it."

Judith literally squealed with happiness.

Gerti, on the other hand, looked unusually pale. "What did you have in mind?" she asked.

Alice and the council members seemed to rise as one. Even Joanie stood. "If you will join us over here," Alice said, motioning them toward Joanie. "We think you'll be very happy with what was chosen."

For the first time, Erica noticed that something large was on the table beside Joanie. A dark cloth draped over it had prevented her from being able to see what it was.

After everyone had gathered around the table, Alice nodded and Joanie removed the cloth to reveal a statue approximately twelve inches tall of a man and a woman.

"Now, this is just a model, of course," Alice explained. "We wanted to get your approval before we show it to the general populace. The artist has assured us that the statue will be ready in plenty of time for the unveiling at next year's sesquicentennial celebration. We're all so excited."

"I think it's absolutely wonderful," Judith gushed. "I feel so honored that you all would do such."

"No," Gerti said sharply.

Everyone turned to her in stunned silence.

"You mean you don't like it?" Aaron Reed, one of the council-men, asked.

"I mean that Howard and Bridget would not have wanted this."

"Well, how can you be so sure?" Reed persisted.

"Because they were simple people who helped their neighbors because it was the right thing to do," Gerti said. "Not because they wanted some statue in the town square."

"All the more reason they should be honored," Alice said.

"I agree completely," Judith said.

Gerti looked to Erica, but she had no idea what she was expected to say. Erica realized that they were all looking at her. She swallowed and tried to read the signal Gerti was sending her. "Um," she began slowly, not taking her eyes from her grandmother's face. "I'm sure the actual statue would be very expensive."

Gerti nodded slightly.

Encouraged that she was on the right track, Erica continued, "So maybe the money would be better spent on something for the entire community."

Gerti smiled.

Erica relaxed until she saw the looks that her mother and Alice were shooting her. "On the other hand, maybe the citizens would enjoy a statue in the new town square."

Gerti glowered.

"Maybe a horse with a dead general on it would be better suited," Erica added lamely as everyone in the room turned to glare at her.

CHAPTER TWENTY-SIX

"What on earth put a burr up Gerti's butt?" Alice demanded as soon as Erica slipped in the back door.

"Well, hi, darling. I'm glad to see you, too," Erica snapped. Part of her anger was guilt. She had broken one of Alice's cardinal rules by approaching the house directly from the street. Always before she had been careful to cut through the backyard to make sure no one would see her, because that was the way Alice wanted it. Tonight she had simply walked the few blocks that separated them and then snuck through Alice's side gate when she was sure no one was looking. She was sick and tired of slinking through the neighbors' yards.

"I don't get it," Alice said, ignoring her. "Judith was happy. Why wasn't Gerti?"

Erica took a beer from the refrigerator and twisted the top off. She rarely drank, but if Alice was going to rant and rave, she had to find something to do. She went into the living room and sat on the sofa.

"And what was that crap about a dead general on a horse?"

"Alice, where are we going with this relationship? Or more to the point, are we going anywhere with it?"

"What do you mean?"

"I mean where do you see us five years from now?"

Alice sat in a chair across from her. "Here, I guess."

"By that do you mean both of us physically living here in this house together?"

"I suppose so."

Erica leaned her head against the back of the sofa.

"Is there someone else?" Alice asked in a low voice.

"No. There's no one else. I've already told you a dozen times that I'm tired of sneaking around."

"You knew how it would be from the very start. You knew I had to be careful. I never pretended otherwise."

"Alice, there's careful and then there's paranoid."

"I'm tired. I don't know what I have to do to please you. You're here almost every night. How would I explain that if someone ever saw you?"

"I'm allowed to sneak through my neighbors' backyards to spend a few hours with you, and then, I'm allowed to sneak back home before daylight."

"Let's go away this weekend."

Erica sat up. "You mean it?"

Alice nodded. "We can go down to Corpus to my Uncle Nolan's beach house and spend the weekend together."

"Just the two of us? No one else will be around?"

Alice laughed. "Yes, silly, just the two of us."

Erica knew she was being placated, but the truth was that she loved Alice Goodman in a way she never dreamed possible. "Will you leave your laptop and cell phone here?"

Alice tilted her head. "I'll compromise. I'll leave the laptop, but I have to take my cell phone in case there's an emergency and Joanie needs to reach me."

"Short of a national emergency, you promise no conference

calls the entire weekend?" Erica countered.

"That's agreeable."

Erica smiled. "Will you make the sautéed shrimp with butter sauce?"

"Will you give me one of those wonderful backrubs afterward?" Alice moved to sit beside her.

Erica leaned over to kiss her. "That's very agreeable."

As the kiss deepened, Erica let her hand slide down Alice's back and then slowly around to caress her breast. As her fingers touched her breast, Alice immediately pulled away and stood. "Let's go upstairs." She held out her hand.

The interruption of the moment peeved Erica, but she should have known better. Alice wouldn't dream of having sex anywhere other than her bed, and even then, the lights all had to be off. Rather than upset the uneasy peace they had established, Erica took her hand and led her upstairs.

Sex with Alice was different. Erica didn't consider herself worldly, but she'd had a couple of short relationships. The first had been in college and the other with a woman who lived on a small farm outside of Whitehall. In both of the previous relationships, she had enjoyed making love, but she had never experienced the toe-curling, eyes-rolling, world-imploding experience that everyone always talked about. Then she met Alice. Despite all her modesties, Alice could cause all those things and then some. In her weaker moments, Erica oftentimes wondered if she was in love with Alice, or what the woman did to her. It wasn't as if the mechanical aspect of the act was so different. It was something else. Something she couldn't explain. Whatever it was she always came back for more.

Once they were upstairs, Alice headed off to the bathroom where she would change into a gown that she would refuse to remove no matter how much Erica pleaded. Erica stripped off her clothes and crawled into bed. She would have to make some sort of excuse to her mother to explain her absence this weekend. Not that Judith particularly cared, but she never left town without a reason, which usually involved the store, so Judith was certain to ask. She could always tell her that it was personal, but that might pique her mother's curiosity a bit too much. Of course, she would tell Gerti why. She had always told Gerti everything. Her grandmother was one of the few people who knew about her lifestyle. Somehow, she had never been able to tell her mother. Maybe it was because public image meant so much to Judith.

Erica sighed and turned over. It hurt to admit, but in some ways, she wasn't any different from Alice. She was just as closeted, although maybe not to such an extreme. *Who's sneaking through backyards?* a little voice asked. She flopped back over and ignored it. She did that because Alice was so insistent. After all, hadn't she boldly walked right down the street to come here tonight? *You waited around until no one was looking and then you slunk in the back door.* She pushed the thoughts away and concentrated on the trip that weekend. In two days, they would escape to the coast for a few hours of time. She wondered what it would be like to spend the entire night with Alice. Suddenly it struck her that they had never spent an entire night together. She sat up and leaned back against the headboard.

"Alice," she called.

Alice opened the door and came out. As soon as she sat down on the side of the bed, she turned out the bedside light.

"How long have we been seeing each other?"

"Let's see. I met you when you were helping on my campaign. As I recall, Judith was hosting a fundraiser and you came by the campaign headquarters to drop off something. So I've known you about three years." She slipped into bed. "What I do remember is that I noticed you right away. You had on a pair of jeans and a long-sleeved shirt with the sleeves rolled up." She made a small sound of pleasure as she reached for Erica. "Why are you sitting up?"

"I was just thinking." Erica slid back down into bed. "Do you realize we've never spent an entire night together?"

"Nonsense. We've spent lots of nights together."

"Name one."

Alice sighed and turned over. "All right. Let's see. There was . . . no . . . um . . . no."

"There hasn't been a single night," Erica said.

"If you'll just give me time to think, I'm sure I'll remember."

Erica locked her hands beneath her head and waited.

Finally, Alice dismissed the problem. "The issue will be solved this weekend."

"The issue. Is that how you see us?"

Alice sat up. "All right. You're determined to pick a fight so have it your own way. I thought that getting away this weekend would make you happy, but apparently it's not enough." She began to cry. "No matter what I do, it's never enough."

Erica squeezed her eyes shut. Alice was right. She was in a crappy mood. She reached for Alice and pulled her to her side. "You're right. I'm sorry. I'm just . . . frustrated."

"It won't always be like this."

Erica wanted to ask when it was going to change but knew it was useless. As long as Alice was in the public eye, it would never change. She told herself to get up and end the fiasco, but then Alice was kissing her. In seconds, the wonderful warm tension began to build and then without warning she was pushing her face into a pillow screaming for God.

CHAPTER TWENTY-SEVEN

By eleven on Friday morning, Erica was driving toward Corpus Christi. On the seat beside her was a map to the beach house, a bottle of Cabernet, a long, white box containing a dozen long-stemmed red roses and a tastefully wrapped package containing a black negligee that was anything but discreet.

Alice had left the previous day, insisting she wanted to get the house aired and cleaned before Erica arrived. Erica knew the real reason. Alice was afraid people might talk if they both left the same day. She had made a solemn oath to herself that she wouldn't do anything to spoil their weekend. She had left Whitehall sooner than they had discussed so that she could buy the items in Corpus.

The beach house was located on a three-thousand-acre parcel of land that belonged to Alice's uncle, Nolan Goodman. The Goodman family was among Whitehall's original settlers. Alice's father, Arden, had been a career army officer and settled his family in Dallas after he retired. Alice had gone to law school and been lured back to Whitehall by Nolan's offer of an immediate partnership in his law firm after she passed the bar exam. Two years after she arrived in Whitehall Alice took on the State of Texas when a group of legislators tried to use eminent domain to obtain a large section of land at the edge of Whitehall in order to build a new highway from San Antonio to Brownsville. Alice's research quickly revealed that by locating the new road closer to Highway 35, which was the current roadway into the valley, the route would be both cheaper and more direct. The lawmakers argued that their proposed route was needed in order to bring more business to the small towns along the way. After long exhaustive research, Alice discovered that under the guise of dummy corporations these same legislators had acquired several other parcels of land. The corporations had in turn sold the land to the government for the more expensive route.

Nolan Goodman was now in a nursing home in San Antonio. He had been placed there after he was found standing guard duty in front of the courthouse early one morning wearing nothing but a Civil War-era saber and his boots. Erica often wondered how the modern-day South could survive without its hallowed relics from the Great War of Yankee Aggression.

Erica turned off from the main highway and followed the directions on the map Alice had drawn for her. She had driven several miles before she came to the large gated entry. She keyed in the security code she had been given and watched as the gate slowly slid open.

"Fancy schmancy," she muttered as she entered. She had to drive almost three miles before she finally reached the house. She whistled when it came into sight. She had been expecting some little fisherman's cottage, but this place looked like it would be more at home on some beach in New England. The two-story structure boasted a recently acquired coat of sky-blue paint, with almost blinding white wooden shutters and trim. A balcony encircled the second floor and a wide screened-in porch wrapped around the lower level. The front yard was beautifully landscaped with flowering crepe myrtles, oaks and lacy-looking saltwater cedars. The back opened directly onto the beach of the Gulf Coast.

Alice ran out of the house to meet her.

Erica got out of the car and walked around to the other side to get the things from the front seat. She couldn't hide her shock when Alice grabbed her and kissed her soundly on the mouth. "Whoa." She laughed when Alice finally released her. "I wasn't expecting that. Who are you and what have you done with my girlfriend?"

"Don't be mean," Alice said. "This is my haven. There's no one but us for miles and miles."

"Good, then maybe I'll get to see lots of this." Erica pulled the gift box out of the car.

"A present?" Alice practically squealed with excitement as she tore at the wrapping. She blushed a deep crimson when she pulled the sexy garment from the box. "I can see what you have on your mind," she said as she leaned into Erica and kissed her again.

"I even brought these along to help break down your defenses." Erica held up the wine and the box of roses.

Alice gave her a coy look. "You might find that alcohol won't be required to break down my defenses."

They went inside. "The roses are beautiful," Alice said as she placed them in a tall, crystal vase.

Erica was staring out the patio window at the beach. "The water looks wonderful. Let's go for a walk along the beach." She quickly changed her jeans and boots for shorts and sandals. On the way out, she grabbed her sunglasses from the car.

As they walked along the water's edge gulls and sandpipers scurried a few steps ahead of them. "What did you tell Judith and Gerti about this weekend?"

"I told Mother I was going to visit an old college friend and I told Grams the truth."

"I still can't believe she is so open about our relationship."

"Grams is okay. She says she has too many other things to worry about to be concerned with who's sleeping with whom."

"I wish everyone was that open."

Erica chose to let the subject drop. They would never agree on it anyway. They walked for over an hour before finally returning to the house.

"I didn't know how hungry you would be so I made a seafood salad," Alice called as she busied herself with rinsing the sand off their shoes.

"I'm fine for now," Erica said as she stretched out on a large hammock hanging on the back sunporch. She took a deep cleansing breath and let it carry away all her concerns. The warm breeze off the water caressed her face. She closed her eyes and listened to the distant sound of the birds.

When she opened her eyes again, it was almost dark. She swung her feet over the edge and sat up, upset that she had slept away most of their first afternoon together. It took her a moment to locate Alice. She was sitting down on the beach next to a small fire.

Erica slipped on her shoes and ran down to join her. "I'm so sorry I fell asleep." She kicked off her shoes before stepping onto the brightly hued Mexican blanket that had been spread out to protect them from the sand. The thick weave of the blanket felt rough beneath her feet. She sat across from Alice, who was leaning against an ice chest. Next to Alice was a wicker basket with a glass of red wine sitting on top. Nearby lay several chunks of wood waiting to be added to the fire.

"Don't apologize. I took a nap myself." She patted the blanket beside her. "Are you hungry?"

Erica smiled. "I'm starved, actually. This is very nice. I don't think I've ever had a picnic on the beach before."

Alice dug into the ice chest and removed two small bowls of seafood salad and an open bottle of Merlot. "I thought we'd save the wine you brought and have it with dinner tomorrow." After setting the items on the blanket, she removed a glass and some silverware from the wicker basket and handed them to Erica.

"Wine, food, a campfire . . . It looks as though you thought of everything." Erica opened one of the bowls. She noticed a spare blanket next to the ice chest and thought about how wonderful it would be to make love to Alice here on the beach. She dismissed the idea. If Alice wouldn't make love with the light on, an open beach was definitely out of the question.

Alice poured wine into Erica's glass. "I try."

They ate and watched the sun slip behind the water. As the sky exploded in a glorious riot of hues, Alice rested her head on Erica's shoulder.

"I wish we could stay here forever."

Erica squeezed her hand.

"When I was a kid, we used to come here almost every summer," Alice said. "We would go through Whitehall and visit with Uncle Nolan for a few days and then come here for two weeks. My brother, Devon, and I would spend every possible minute on the beach. We couldn't get into the water unless Mom or Dad was around, but we didn't care. There were so many other things to do, but most of all there was space and freedom from all those judging eyes." She sat forward and hugged her knees. "Since Dad was a senior officer we always lived on base. It was all right, but we could never really just cut loose and be kids. We always had to be aware of how loud we were and what we were doing. Dad insisted we be better than the other kids—better behaved, better grades, better athletes, better everything. Here there was no one to impress. Even Dad relaxed when we came here." She stared out across the water. "God, I love this place."

Alice rarely mentioned her family, and to Erica's knowledge, they had never visited her in Whitehall. She was hesitant about prying, but she was curious. "You don't seem very close to your family."

Alice's back tensed.

Erica mentally cursed herself for destroying the light mood they had been enjoying. She started to apologize.

"They no longer wish to have anything to do with me."

"Oh." Erica didn't know what else to say.

Alice lay back and rested on one elbow. "There was a small incident. Two weeks before I was scheduled to graduate from law school I was caught with a woman professor and asked to leave. When my parents found out, they pretty much erased me from their lives. Even Devon stopped talking to me. Uncle Nolan was the only one who stuck by me. In fact, he's the reason I was allowed to graduate. He called the president of the college and told him he intended to go public with the fact that the school hadn't adequately protected their students from—as he stated it—'lecherous professors.' I was allowed to graduate and the incident was removed from my records. When Uncle Nolan asked me to move to Whitehall and work with him, I didn't see how I could refuse him." She traced the pattern on the blanket with her finger. "At first, I didn't intend to stay very long, maybe a year or two to get some experience. Then, I fell in love with the place and with you."

"You're afraid to come out because of how your family responded, aren't you?"

Alice shrugged. "I guess that's probably part of the reason. Basically, I don't believe people are as dependable as you think they are."

Erica tried to imagine how she would have handled the situation if Gerti had turned on her all those years ago when she finally came out. Suddenly it struck her that maybe that was why she resisted coming out to her mother. "I haven't been very fair to you. I'm sorry."

"Let's not talk about it anymore." Alice got up and put another log on the fire before lying down beside Erica. "Tell me what's going on with Judith and Gerti."

"What do you mean?"

"Why is Gerti so adamantly opposed to the statue?"

Erica rolled her eyes. "Your guess is as good as mine. You would think she'd be as ecstatic as Mom was. Well, not quite as much, but you know what I mean. It surprised me that she got so upset."

"Did she say anything about it later?"

"No. In fact, I've hardly seen either of them since. They're both busy with different projects for the sesquicentennial celebration."

"Sissy Jamison wants to compile a biography on Howard and Bridget and have brochures to pass out at the grand opening ceremony."

Sissy Jamison had appointed herself as the unofficial historian for Whitehall. She spent most of her time digging through county archives for some tidbit of information. She and Judith frequently butted heads over who was in charge of the small city museum that was located in a back room at the courthouse. "Mom won't be too thrilled about that. She won't think Sissy's up to the task."

"Why don't you write it?"

Erica looked at her and frowned. "I wouldn't even know where to begin."

"Start at the beginning. Where did they come from? Where did their families come from? All that good stuff that people always want to know."

Erica lay down beside Alice and stared at the stars that were beginning to shine through. "I don't really know anything about them."

"What were they to you?"

"Well, let's see. My Grandfather Boyd's mother was Howard and Bridget's only daughter." She hesitated a minute. "That's about all I know. We don't really talk about it much."

"Why not?"

"I don't know. I never really gave it much thought."

"So you don't remember any of them?" Alice asked.

"No. My Grandfather Boyd and two of their sons were killed in a car accident almost ten years before I was born. Mom was the oldest child and she was only around fifteen then. I may remember Grandfather Boyd's mother. I have a dim memory of Gerti getting my sister, Camille, and me all dressed up and we'd go over to this big house. It must have been over by the high school, because I vaguely remember a band playing." She shrugged. "I could be completely wrong. It was so long ago."

Alice sat up and pulled her shirt off over her head, then stood and unfastened her shorts. As the shorts slid to the ground, she looked down at Erica. "Let's forget about families and history for a while."

CHAPTER TWENTY-EIGHT

The boldness of Alice disrobing on the beach shocked Erica so, she could only stare as Alice kicked her shorts from around her ankles. When Alice began removing her panties, Erica's libido kicked into high gear. She didn't know what had come over Alice, but she sure as heck intended to take full advantage of whatever was going to be offered. She scooted out of her shorts so quickly the rough fibers of the blanket burned her butt.

She reached for the spare blanket that was lying beside the ice chest.

"Unless you're cold, you won't need that," Alice said as her fingertips traveled slowly up Erica's legs.

"I'm . . . I'm not cold," Erica stammered as Alice began to place small kisses across her stomach. The trembling in her body had nothing to do with being cold. In fact, she couldn't remember ever feeling so hot. She lost track of time as Alice explored her body, seemingly intent on exploring every inch of it, first with her fingers, then her lips and finally her tongue. Each time Erica reached for her, Alice pulled back and told her to be patient. They had all night. She lost track of the number of times she came. Her cries of pleasure blended with the sound of the waves lapping against the shore. Just when Erica was certain she couldn't continue, Alice finally lowered herself onto Erica's waiting hand and a new surge of energy overtook her. At some point, they rolled off the blanket in their acrobatic dance to obtain the best position. Erica was vaguely aware of the sand against her back, elbows or knees, but she no longer cared. Never in her life had she wanted to possess and be possessed by a lover as she did with Alice there on the sandy beach. They came together in one shattering, quivering climax.

After several minutes, Erica tried to move. It felt as though her muscles had been replaced by the sand that was now starting to make its presence known in every crevice of her body. Had there been such a thing as a bankcard for orgasms, Erica's would have been severely overdrawn. She didn't know how long they lay there before Alice slowly rose and helped her up.

"Come on," she said. "I'm not finished with you yet."

Erica thought they were heading to the house, but Alice obviously had other plans as she headed for the water.

"It'll be too cold," Erica protested weakly.

"Only for a moment. I promise you won't be cold for long." She turned and kissed Erica hungrily.

Erica allowed Alice to lead her out into the waist-deep water. With cupped hands, they playfully splashed water over each other until most of the sand was washed from their bodies.

Alice stepped forward and molded her body to Erica's as she kissed her again. A surge of desire shot through Erica so intense her legs began to tremble. Alice's hand slipped beneath the water and eased between their bodies. Her other hand held the back of Erica's head as she kissed her with a renewed vigor. The hand beneath the water slipped between Erica's legs. She struggled to remain upright as Alice's kisses and fingers worked their magic once again.

Much later, they made their way back to the blanket. They used the spare blanket to wrap around them as they lay staring into the fire that Alice had added more wood to.

"What happened to the ultra-modest woman who won't even leave the light on at night?" Erica asked. She was exhausted, yet strangely energized.

"I'm sorry. You must think I'm psychotic." Alice snuggled closer against her. "I know this may sound weird, but this is the only place where I feel safe enough to really be myself. When we're at home, I feel as though the entire town is watching me. Not literally, of course." She chuckled. "That would be psychotic. In Whitehall, everything I do is subject to scrutiny."

"You're the mayor. Everything you do at work affects someone."

"I'm not just talking about work. For instance, last week I was in the grocery store. They had a new shipment of some Texas wines that I had never tried before. I couldn't make my mind up as to whether to try the white Zinfandel or the Merlot. So I got both. I also bought a six-pack of beer. I keep it in that small refrigerator I have out in the garage for Mr. Walthrop. He likes to have a cold beer when he's finished working."

"Walthrop? He's the guy who mows your yard?"

"Yes. While I was in the store, I ran into Clara Higgins. She spent twenty minutes complaining about the light from the new pole that was installed at the corner of her street. Anyway, I noticed she kept glancing at my basket, but I didn't give it much thought until the following day when Reverend Pawlik called me. He chatted for a while before casually mentioning that the church was considering starting an Alcoholics Anonymous program."

Erica started laughing.

"You see. You already know where this story is going. I'm telling you it's not funny. Sometimes I get this crazy urge just to do things that will get the entire town in an uproar."

"Such as?"

Alice waved an arm in the air. "Something like going to the grocery store and buying a big jar of pickles, a quart of ice cream and a pregnancy test kit. Or going over to the drugstore and buying one of those sleazy magazines that Gerti likes, along with one of those silly vibrating bug-looking things that they advertise as a back massager." She was clearly on a roll. "I want to put seventeen concrete lawn ornaments on my front yard and paint them all lavender." Her frenzy disappeared and she seemed to deflate. "I don't know. I feel like I'm living under a microscope."

"You only have a little over a year left as mayor. You don't have to run again."

Alice gave a long low sigh. "I know."

Erica rose up onto one elbow and gazed down at her. "You also love it, don't you?"

Alice tried to hide her face. "I do. Not the part where I have to deal with the crazies, but I love being in a position where I can do things that benefit Whitehall and the people living there."

"Oh, shit." Erica dropped back down. "I'll still be jumping backyard fences when I'm eighty. I can see it now. I won't have a walker. I'll have a small stepladder that I'll drag from fence to fence. When my eyesight starts to go, we'll have to string a clothesline from my back door to yours so I don't lose my way. Maybe I should start digging a tunnel from my bedroom to your kitchen. I could carry out the extra dirt in my pockets, and let it trickle out and down the inside of my pant leg as I walk to work like those guys did in that old war movie."

"I've already promised you that I wouldn't run again."

"But you want to, don't you?"

"I'm starting to get cold." Alice sat up. "Let's go back up to the house." She kicked sand into the fire to douse it. "Everything else can stay here until morning."

Erica jumped up. "Can we just back up a few minutes and start over? I don't want the rest of our weekend to be ruined."

Alice squeezed her hand. "It's not ruined. If you like you can use the shower in the guestroom to wash off." She walked away quickly.

Erica stared after her. She started to call out to suggest that they could shower together but hesitated. She finally picked up their discarded clothes and headed toward the house.

●　●　●

By the time Erica had showered and made her way to their bedroom the light was out and Alice was breathing evenly. If she wasn't asleep, she was at least doing a great job of pretending. Erica lay staring at the ceiling for a long while. There didn't seem to be a solution for their problem. Alice felt she couldn't come out as long as she was mayor, and it was obvious that she wouldn't be happy giving up the office. Of course, there was always the possibility of her being defeated, but unless something dreadful happened between now and the next election she couldn't see that happening. In truth Alice was a good mayor and had done a lot for the town. Her constituents loved her. Everything narrowed down to the fact that Alice couldn't come out and Erica couldn't keep sneaking around. She fell asleep trying to find a solution. The obvious one stared her in the face when she woke the next morning alone in the big bed.

They spent Saturday lying on the beach relaxing. They were both very attentive to the other, but there was no reference to, or repeat of, the marathon lovemaking they had shared the previous night. On Sunday, Erica left shortly after breakfast, using the excuse of having to help Gerti with a new ad she wanted to place in the newspaper.

Alice walked her to the car and kissed her softly. "I won't be back until Tuesday morning. There's a seminar in Corpus tomorrow that I want to attend."

Erica nodded and tried to think of something to say, but there didn't seem to be anything left. As she drove away, she watched Alice's image grow steadily smaller in the rearview mirror. When she could no longer see her, she began to cry.

CHAPTER TWENTY-NINE

Erica heard the uproar coming from inside the house long before she opened the door. Gerti and Judith's rows weren't news, but what she found when she opened the door surprised her.

Gerti was standing in front of the sofa with a large umbrella that she was swinging like a saber at Judith, who was standing on the sofa with the broom and one of the pillows from the sofa. She tried to use the pillow to deflect Gerti's attack, but Gerti hit it with the umbrella so hard that Judith lost her grip on it and the pillow fell to the floor.

"What in the name of Saint Michael is going on in here?" Erica asked as she dropped her suitcase.

The battle temporarily ceased as they both turned to stare at her.

"Don't look at me like I've sprouted two heads," Erica said. "What are you two trying to do? Kill yourselves?"

"Your mother has lost what little sense God gave her," Gerti sputtered before turning and giving an unsuspecting Judith a quick rap on the rear end with the umbrella.

Judith swatted back with the business end of the broom, but Gerti skillfully warded off the attack.

Erica slammed the door. "Stop it. Both of you."

They ignored her as Judith practically fell off the sofa trying to avoid Gerti's unerringly accurate umbrella assault.

"I said stop it." Erica stepped forward to grab the umbrella from Gerti and was just in time to catch Judith's broom squarely in the head. As she reeled from that blow, the umbrella came swinging back in preparation for another frontal attack and caught her on the other side. She stepped back, tripped over the pillow Judith had dropped and down she went.

"You goofy old fool, you've killed her." Judith bounded off the sofa.

Gerti dropped her weapon and rushed to Erica's side.

Anger blew respect and good upbringing completely out the window as Erica raised both hands. "Stop! Don't either of you crazy people touch me."

They were both talking at once, asking if she was okay.

"No. I'm not okay," she yelled. She struggled to get up, and they rushed to help. In their haste, they somehow managed to knock her down again. The smoldering ember of anger that had slowly been building over the past few days suddenly burst into a raging inferno. She grabbed the pillow and swung it wildly back and forth in front of her. They both quickly moved away and stood huddled together as Erica jumped up and shook the pillow at them. "It's not enough that I live in a town filled with gun-toting, pot-growing maniacs, or that I fall in love with a crazy, closeted woman who has to have the friggin' light out before we can have sex. Oh, no. I have to come home and find you two reenacting *War and Peace* and seemingly hell-bent—"

She stopped. Had she actually said what her ears just heard? She glanced at the other two. From the slack-jawed expression on Judith's face, and the "oh-crap" look on Gerti's, she was pretty sure she had just come out to her mother.

After what felt like an eternity, Judith raised one perfectly man-icured finger to her chin. "Did I understand what you just said?"

"If you understood her to say she's a lesbian, you got it right for a change."

Erica glared at Gerti. "Grams, I don't think I need any more of your help right now."

"Oh, what's the big deal?" Gerti asked. She straightened her blouse and tucked it back into her slacks. "So she bangs women."

"Mother!" Judith exploded.

"I do not *bang* anyone," Erica countered.

Gerti shrugged, "That's probably why you're so grumpy."

"Can we just get back on topic here?" Judith asked.

"We certainly can," Gerti replied as she turned on Judith. "I want you to call that woman right now and tell her not to come down here."

"I will not. I've already made the arrangements and we have plenty of room. In fact, I already have the guest room ready for her." She pointed at Erica. "I want you to explain yourself, young lady."

Gerti shook her finger at Judith. "She's a lesbian. I explained to you what that meant years ago, and I'm sure nothing has changed since then. Now, I'm your mother and I'm telling you to call that woman and put a stop to this entire mess."

Erica's head began to hurt as she looked from one to the other of them. She wondered if they had finally slipped over the edge.

Judith placed her palm against her forehead. "I don't have time to deal with you, Mother. I have just discovered my daughter is a lesbian."

Erica waved her arms in the air. "Stop it. Everybody just stop." She was so surprised they listened that she almost forgot what she wanted to say. "Why don't we all sit down at the kitchen table and discuss this like rational adults?"

Gerti started toward the kitchen immediately. "I'd better go hide the knives, before you two have that rational adult talk."

Judith started to speak, but Erica held up a hand. "Mom, please. I've wanted to tell you for a long time, but I knew it would upset you."

"I suppose she already knew." Judith motioned toward the kitchen.

Erica could see the glimmer of tears starting to build. "Yes. I told her a long time ago. You were so busy and—"

Judith turned away and started toward her room.

"Mom, please. Can't we talk about this?"

Her only answer was the soft click of Judith's door.

"Uh-oh. That's not good," Gerti said from the kitchen doorway. "It's a lot less scary when she slams the door."

Erica stomped her foot. "Damn, damn, diddly damn."

"Come on into the kitchen," Gerti said.

Erica stared toward the hallway for a long moment, wondering if it would do any good to go and try to talk to her mom, but she knew Judith wouldn't be talking to her again until *she* was ready to do so. She turned and slowly made her way to the kitchen. "Man, I've really messed up things now."

Gerti placed two glasses on the table, poured them each a shot of bourbon and handed one to Erica before she sat down. "Give her some time. She loves you and will eventually come around."

"I don't know. She looked awfully hurt."

Gerti tapped her fingers on the table. "Yeah, she did."

They each took a healthy slug of their drink.

"I should have told her a long time ago."

"You can't start second-guessing yourself. If you do, you'll never stop. You made your decision, now live with it."

Erica rubbed her hands over her face. "Why does everything have to be so blasted complicated?"

"It's called life. It's a little joke God plays on all of us. He gives us free will. Then, he sits back and laughs as we walk around slamming into the decisions we made like a bunch of Keystone Kops." She took another sip of her drink. "I gather from that minor meltdown you had in the living room that things didn't go well this weekend."

Erica shook her head. "Grams, I don't know what to do. One minute everything was wonderful, and the next thing I know, it was

181

like we were passing this bomb around, each knowing the slightest jar would cause it to explode in our faces."

Gerti patted her hand. "Alice is in a tough spot."

"I know, and I want to be supportive, but all this sneaking around is driving me insane."

"No, you get the insanity from your mother."

"She thinks I get it from you," Erica said as she leaned back in the chair.

"No. It's definitely from the Boyd side of the family."

Erica recalled the conversation she'd had with Alice on the beach. "Did Grandfather Boyd's mother live near the high school?"

The sudden change in conversation seemed to throw Gerti for a moment. "No, she lived here."

"Here?" Erica shook her head. "I'm confused. You used to take Camille and me to visit an older woman. I seem to remember she lived in that big house down by the school, because I remember hearing a band playing."

"No. We came here to visit James's mother, Amelia. The band you remember hearing was probably the brass band that used to play in the town square every Sunday afternoon." She tapped her fingers. "You're probably confused because back then there were two big oak trees out front. A tornado came through here in nineteen eighty-three, which was the year after Amelia died, and blew them both over. One of the trees hit the front corner of the house. Your mother and I decided we'd have more room if we moved in here. That's when we built the porch across the front and added on the two rooms that your mother uses. After the renovations were finished we moved here."

"Why didn't we live here while Great-Grandmother Amelia was living?"

Gerti shrugged. "I had a house, the one where James and I lived. I didn't want to leave it."

"Why did you change your mind after she died?"

"It just made more sense. This house was bigger and it was the family home. We thought you girls should grow up here. At the time, I thought your Uncle William would be coming back to live

182

in Whitehall after he graduated from college. I thought he would want to live in my old house."

"Alice was asking me about Howard and Bridget and I'm embarrassed to say I didn't know anything about them. I don't remember hearing you talk about them very much."

Gerti suddenly seemed to grow tired. "They were James's grandparents. They were good people and neither of them would hesitate to give you their last penny if you needed it."

Erica waited but Gerti sipped her drink and stared at the table in front of her.

"Tell me about them."

Gerti looked at her for a moment. "I remember Howard walked with a slight limp. He was a quiet man. If anyone ever needed help, you could bet he'd be the first one in line to offer a hand though. I can remember my own parents talking about how they wouldn't have survived the Depression without the credit line that Bridget and Howard let them carry." She became more animated as she continued. "My father and a lot of other people back then would have walked through fire for either of them. Bridget and Howard were both hard workers. Even in their mid-seventies, they still went to work at the store every single day. Right up until the day he died." She wiped her eyes suddenly.

"How did he die?"

"He had a heart attack. It was early spring. He was helping a customer load bags of seed corn and he just fell over. James and I got to him as quickly as we could, but it was too late. Bridget had us bring him back here to the house. She wouldn't let anyone else touch him. Old Mr. Prichard, the funeral director then, begged her to let him prepare the body, but she refused. She prepared his body for burial herself. He was laid out in the parlor." She motioned toward the front of the house. "Bridget sat right there beside him. She never left his side until after he as buried." She wiped her face. "After that she just seemed to give up. It was as though she was lost without him. She died a few months later."

"What about Grandfather Boyd's father? What do you know about him?"

"His name was Roger Boyd. He was sort of an odd bird. Never did talk much either. He just sat around and smoked his pipe. He was about twenty years older than Amelia. He owned a sawmill that was located outside the north end of town. They had four kids. Your grandfather James was the oldest, then Edwin who died from influenza when he was two. Rachel married a carpenter and moved to California. The last I heard she was still living." She paused for a moment. "I guess she would be about sixty-eight or sixty-nine now. Then the youngest, Howard, was killed in Vietnam."

"Grams, I don't understand something. You seem to have so much respect for Howard and Bridget, why are you so opposed to the statue?"

Gerti drained the last of her bourbon and put the glass in the dishwasher before replying, "Erica, sometimes it's better to let sleeping dogs lie." She walked out the room.

Erica sat staring into the amber liquor for several minutes before going to her own room. They each spent the rest of the day in their rooms. Erica spent most of her time sleeping. It wasn't until much later that night that she remembered she had never found out what Gerti and Judith had been fighting about when she arrived home.

CHAPTER THIRTY

The following morning Erica showered quickly and slipped out of the house early. She didn't want to take any chances of setting off another round of arguments. Her mom would settle down eventually. The problem was, would it be a week or a decade? Until then, it was useless to try to talk to her.

Erica didn't take time to enjoy the beauty of the little town. Today she simply wanted to get away from the house before the other two started moving around. The smell of bacon tickled her nose. Her stomach quickly responded and reminded her that she hadn't eaten anything since the burger she had grabbed on her way home from the coast the previous day. She made a slight detour to Jimmy Kwan's Taco Emporium and Pancake House. Local rumor purported that Jimmy had paid more for the elaborately painted sign than for the original building that housed the now-expanded eatery.

Jimmy Kwan was another chapter in Whitehall's colorful history. She had arrived in Whitehall on a Greyhound bus, according to Gerti, sometime during the early years of the Nixon administration. Within days, she purchased a small rundown building that had once been a cobbler's shop. The records over at the courthouse indicated she paid four hundred dollars for the building and lot. The fact that she was mute quickly spread throughout the town and added another layer of intrigue to the young stranger. Depending on who was gossiping, her age ranged somewhere between fifteen and twenty. Her history encompassed everything from her being a wealthy Asian princess in-hiding to her being in the witness protection program.

For the next two weeks, curious townspeople strolled by the building assessing the outside progress as the strangely silent young woman worked long into each night. Their curiosity reached an almost fevered pitch when her renovations turned to the inside of the building, because before she began she covered each of the windows with ripped-open brown paper bags. From inside the building, the sounds of hammering and the occasional steady scrape of a handsaw could be heard. The intrigue grew when she was seen purchasing several small cans of paint from the mercantile. After she was spotted buying yet more paint, speculation reached such a high point that the sheriff started making an extra round each evening to gently move along the crowd that seemed to gravitate toward the mysterious building.

Then the day arrived when two burly men in a truck bearing the name of a sign company all the way from San Antonio arrived. Everyone gathered to see the new sign, but strangely enough, there didn't seem to be one on the truck. They watched in confusion as the men went inside and stayed for several minutes. There was audible gasp as the men stumbled out carrying an enormous brightly painted sign reading "Jimmy Kwan's Taco Emporium and Pancake House."

Right away, there was a problem. The sign was so large that if it was placed on the front of the small building it would hang too low over the sidewalk. Any pedestrian over five-nine would bang their head. The problem was solved when Amelia Franklin Boyd arrived with a twelve-foot utility pole dragging along behind the store's old delivery truck. The pole was installed in front of the building and the sign was hung. Years later after the building was enlarged and the ceiling raised enough to accommodate the sign, it remained on the pole. Every other year, Jimmy would climb a ladder to touch up the paint on the sign, and every five years the Taco Emporium and Pancake House received a fresh coat of paint inside and out.

Curiosity drove the first few customers in to try the new eatery, but the excellent food brought them back. Word spread and soon people were traveling in from out of town to catch a peek at Whitehall's newest resident and experience the unusual restaurant, which had one more quirky characteristic—no menus. You told Jimmy Kwan what you wanted to eat and if she knew how to make it, fine, and if not, you asked for something else.

Her muteness caused few problems. She carried a notepad in her pocket and if forced to she would scribble a few words. Soon customers no longer gave much thought to her not responding vocally. Her smile, frowns and hand gestures conveyed everything she needed to say.

A local reporter back in the 'Eighties had gone into the restaurant every morning for two months and each day he would ask her why she had chosen the name. Each time she would shrug. Finally, she'd apparently grown tired of him asking and shocked everyone by whipping out the pad and writing, "Because I like sound of it."

When Erica entered the restaurant, Jimmy was where she always sat behind the register. As her business grew, so did her staff. She now employed over a dozen full-time employees. Despite the early hour there were already several customers having breakfast.

Erica waved. "Good morning, Jimmy. How are you this morning?"

Jimmy smiled and waved back, then pointed toward the corner.

Erica turned to see Gerti sitting in a booth eating a bowl of fresh fruit. "Thanks, Jimmy." She went back to the booth. "Mind if I join you?"

"Not as long as you're buying," Gerti replied. "Otherwise, move along so I can pick up some cute sailor."

"There's probably not a sailor within a hundred miles of here," Erica said as she slid in across from Gerti.

"Well, no wonder I'm not having any success. I was beginning to worry it was because I was getting old and losing my girlish figure."

"You'll never get old."

"It's the bourbon," Gerti said. "They probably won't even have to embalm me when I croak. So you make sure the mortuary doesn't overcharge you."

"Quit talking about death." Erica grimaced. "You know I hate it when you talk like that."

"It's a fact of life, kiddo."

A waiter arrived with a steaming cup of coffee for Erica. "Thanks, Walt. I'll have two eggs over easy with three strips of extra-crispy bacon, hash browns and toast."

"Why don't you just order a heart attack on a plate?" Gerti asked.

The waiter chuckled. "If she keeps eating like this, she's never going to make it as long as you have, Ms. Gerti."

"Neither will you, Walt, if you keep reminding me how old I am." Gerti speared a grape and popped it in her mouth.

He laughed. "I'll be back in a few."

Gerti shook her head as he left. "Kids now don't even have time to finish a sentence."

Erica sipped her coffee while Gerti finished eating the fruit. "So, what was going on between you and Mom yesterday?"

Gerti frowned and her lips tightened. "I don't know how I ever gave birth to such a bullheaded, self-centered she-devil." She put her fork down and pushed the empty bowl away. "There must have been some mix-up at the hospital." She nodded. "As I recall, Lydia Perkins was giving birth to her little Dottie at the same time I was there. I'll bet they got those babies mixed up. That sweet little Dottie is probably really my child."

Erica smiled. "Grams, Lydia Perkins is African American. I

don't think the staff would have confused the babies."

Gerti waved her off. "Then the only other explanation is that your mother is some sort of genetic throwback."

"Grams, that's not a very nice thing to say about your own daughter."

"I know, but she never ceases to amaze me."

Walt brought Erica's food. After he had left, Erica turned back to her grandmother. "Why don't you just tell me what happened?"

Gerti took a slice of toast off Erica's plate and smeared butter on it. "She got a knot in her tail when she found out that Sissy Jamison was going to write up that biography on Howard and Bridget. So, Miss Prissy Priss called her friend Tiffany something or other, who works for the state historical commission. Tiffany tells her about this hotshot woman genealogist slash historian slash writer from Dallas. Of course, Tiffany doesn't know her personally, so they *network* until they find someone who does and somewhere along the way Judith invites this woman to come down here and live with us while she writes a family history brochure. Now mind you, all this has to occur by this coming Thursday. Judith has already bullied Mr. Acosta over at the print shop into agreeing to work overtime if necessary to have this thing printed by Friday night, so she can pass it out at Saturday's ceremony."

Erica nearly choked on her food. She had ignored the entire tirade except for one small line. "You mean she's going to *live* with us?"

Gerti snared a strip of bacon and crunched it. "I don't like bacon this crispy."

"I'll try to remember that the next time I order *my* breakfast."

If Gerti noticed the dig, she ignored it. "That's right. Since Whitehall doesn't have a hotel, Judith told her she could stay in our *guest suite*."

Erica tried not to smile, but Gerti had mimicked Judith's tone perfectly. "Did the woman accept?"

"Of course she did. Judith is going to San Antonio later today to pick her up at the airport."

Erica made a slight face. "I wonder what she's like. Did Mom say anything else about her?"

"Nope. She never even talked to her."

"What do you mean?"

"I told you. One person called another person and yadda yadda."

"So Mom knows nothing about this woman?"

"Just that she's supposed to be a hotshot historian."

"I guess it's safe to assume she not an ax-murderer," Erica said as she watched Gerti take her last slice of bacon.

"A pen can kill you just as quickly as an ax," Gerti grumbled as she gobbled down the bacon.

Walt came by with a pot of coffee. "Wow," he said as he freshened Erica's cup. "You really were hungry."

Gerti slipped out of the booth. "Erica, you really should eat a better-balanced meal." She took off before Erica could respond.

CHAPTER THIRTY-ONE

It was well after nine before Gerti arrived at the store. She went directly to the office and closed the door. Erica was so busy on the floor that she didn't have time to go back to talk to her. At shortly before eleven, Judith tore through the front door as if the hounds of hell were on her heels. Erica was on a ladder trying to fix a flickering fluorescent light.

"Erica," Judith shouted, causing several customers to turn toward her. "Get down here right now. I need you to go to San Antonio."

"Right now?" She turned and her irritation faded when she noticed that Judith's normally perfectly styled hair was mussed and her jacket appeared to be buttoned crooked. Something was obviously wrong. Erica nearly fell from the ladder in her haste to get down.

"What's all the racket?" Gerti asked as she came out of the office. When she saw Judith, her demeanor changed to one of concern. "Judith, are you all right?" She rushed to her side just as

Erica skidded to a halt beside her.

Judith grabbed Erica's hand and shoved a piece of paper into it. "Here's all the information. Now hurry." She started pushing Erica toward the door.

"Where am I going? Erica protested.

"Read the paper as you run home for the car," Judith insisted. "No. Wait. Better yet, take my car." Her handing over the keys to her precious Mercedes scared Erica so much, she grabbed onto the counter to keep from being shoved any farther.

"Judith." Gerti grabbed her daughter by the arm. "What in God's name is going on?"

Judith grabbed her head. "Oh, it's . . . I'm so overwhelmed. I don't know where to begin."

"Try the beginning," Gerti said.

"I went to my meeting of the Women's League. You know we meet the first Monday of—"

"Judith!" Gerti snapped. "I didn't ask for a reading of the minutes. What the hell is wrong with you?"

"Naomi Jensen's mother is ill, so she has to fly to Detroit." Judith fanned her face with her hand. "Naomi was in charge of the luncheon that will be held for the attendees of the groundbreaking ceremony for the new town square. Since she had to leave, I've been nominated to host the luncheon."

They both stared at her.

She quivered in frustration. "This is an enormous honor for me. Not only will every prominent family from the county be invited, but the governor may attend, also. Perhaps even someone from the state legislature. This is my moment to shine and finally show that boorish Sara Bell Hogg what true elegance is. That woman has been trying to upstage me ever since we were in grade school. It's sickening the way she's always trying to pretend that she's descended from the line of our dearly beloved Governor James Stephen Hogg. This is my chance to show her a thing or two. Who knows where the original Franklin line began? And, it will all be revealed at my glorious luncheon." She seemed almost to float for a moment. "I think perhaps a nice light meal. Yes. Nice but unassuming. Something that says South Texas. I could have fresh seafood flown in from the coast and—"

"What are you carrying on about? The coast is less than two hours away, I don't think a Cessna will be needed," Gerti snapped. "I can't believe you scared the dickens out of me just to tell me about some dinner you have to cook."

"It's not a dinner. It's a luncheon," Judith snapped back.

"Mom, the luncheon is Saturday. Why hasn't Naomi already planned it?"

Judith waved her off. "Oh, she had, but I'm going to cancel all that and make my own arrangements. Mercy, it's hot in here. Why don't you turn up the air conditioner?"

"The air conditioner isn't going to cure your hot flashes," Gerti said.

Judith ignored her. "I didn't come here to tell you that. I came— oh, dear Lord." She grabbed her forehead and spun toward her daughter so quickly that Erica jumped back in surprise. "You need to get to the San Antonio airport before noon to meet Ms. Richardson."

"Oh, no." Erica said, backing up. "I'm not driving all the way to San Antonio. You know how I hate to drive there. You invited her down here. You go get her."

"I don't have time. I just told you I have to plan a luncheon and there are a million things I need to do today." She seemed to be surprised to see her car keys in Erica's hands. She took them back. "Now get going or you'll be late. Make sure you get her back here as quickly as possible. There's not a minute to waste." She turned and blew out the door as quickly as she had blown in.

Erica stared after her mother for a long moment before she turned to complain to Gerti, but she had disappeared also. She glared at the paper her mom had given her before she threw it on the floor and stomped it. After a moment, she picked it up and headed for home to get her car. It would take her almost an hour to get to San Antonio.

• • •

193

Erica felt like a complete idiot as she stood with her small, hastily made cardboard sign bearing the word *Richardson*. She was hemmed into the middle of a large crowd of people awaiting the arrival of the passengers from the American Airlines flight. The plane had landed ten minutes ago, but no one had yet entered the waiting area. There was a collective sigh of relief when the first passenger came around the corner. Erica held the sign high over her head as people jostled against her while trying to reach their parties. She was beginning to think that her mom had somehow gotten the flight wrong when a short, skinny woman approached her boasting a crewcut and more earrings that Erica could possibly count in a polite glance. She had a backpack that looked large enough to hike across Europe with strapped to her back, and what appeared to be a briefcase dangled from one shoulder. There was a large rainbow flag sticker on the bag.

"I'm Rae Richardson. You must be Judith Boyd."

Erica had to fight to keep from laughing. "No. I'm Erica Winfrey. Judith is my mother. Something unexpected came up and she sent me to meet you." She motioned to the backpack. "Can I help you with that?"

"No, thanks. I have it. How far away is Whitehall?"

"It's only about an hour's drive."

"Cool. I'm looking forward to getting started. I love history—any history, small town, city, people, places, whatever. I love history."

They left the terminal. "You don't sound as though you're from Dallas. Your accent, I mean."

Rae threw her a puzzled look and then smiled. "Oh, I'm not from Dallas. I've been there the past few months working on a couple of projects. I actually live in New York."

Erica nodded. This was getting better and better. She could hardly wait until Judith discovered that she had hired not only a dyke, but a Yankee to boot, to write the family history. Despite her eagerness to get back to Whitehall, she didn't forget her responsibilities to her guest. "Have you eaten?"

"No. Actually I'm starved, but I should warn you I'm a vegetarian."

It just doesn't get any better than this, she thought as she helped Rae put her backpack into the trunk.

"What's the gay scene around here like?" Rae asked as they crawled into the car.

The question caught Erica off guard for a moment.

"Sorry if I offended you. I just thought you were . . ." Rae shrugged.

"You didn't offend me, just surprised me. I guess we move a bit slower around here."

"But you are a lesbian, right?"

Erica glanced at her. "Yes, I am, but, um . . . you might not want to ask anyone else that question." She pulled out of the parking lot. "And for the record, I'm not out at home to anyone other than my grandmother and sort of to my mom."

"Cool. I can keep quiet. Don't you find it rather confining to live that way? How can we expect the world to accept us if they don't know we exist?"

The question hit a raw nerve and Erica had to struggle to remember her manners. "There's a place up ahead that has a nice salad bar. We'll stop there for lunch."

Apparently, Rae got the message because she let the subject drop.

The restaurant was crowded and it took them a while to be seated. Erica knew Judith would be anxious for their arrival, but she hated driving in San Antonio and had no intention of going in search of another restaurant.

As they ate, Erica answered as many of Rae's questions about Whitehall as she knew answers to. She found herself talking about the Misses Wilkerson and Hudson and a host of other colorful characters. Time slipped by unnoticed. It was almost two when Erica realized that they were among the last customers.

After they left the restaurant, guilt began to prod Erica. Rae seemed like a nice person. She felt as though she should at least warn her about what she was about to get into.

"I guess I should warn you that Whitehall isn't exactly a gay Mecca."

"You mean as far as you know it's not. Of course, everyone could simply be in the closet."

Erica tried to imagine her mother's friends as closeted homosexuals, but the image made her laugh. "There are a few of us, but we are definitely the minority."

"Will I be in physical danger?" Rae asked in a light tone that indicated she wasn't seriously concerned.

"Of course not. You're a guest."

Rae nodded. "I do love the South. You may hate everything that I stand for, but I'll be treated with nothing but the utmost respect while I'm here." She made a dismissive noise.

"That's right." Erica glanced at her. "We do respect a guest, but we also expect the same respect in return."

"Touché." She grinned at Erica and winked. "I'll put my best foot forward." She turned slightly. "It's your family I'll be researching, correct?"

Erica nodded. "I don't mean to be rude, but why was it important for you to actually come to Whitehall? I mean, aren't copies of county records kept in Austin?"

"I came for a couple of reasons. First, I never turn down an opportunity to go to new places. I love meeting people and seeing where they live. Second, since this project has such an incredibly short deadline, I thought it would be quicker if I came here so I could interview family members and people around town that have known your family. I hope you understand that I can't guarantee how much data I could collect on such a short notice."

Erica realized Rae was in for a struggle. "My grandmother is the oldest living relative. Grams, Mom and I are the only descendents left in Whitehall. We're a very small family."

Rae pulled a small pad from her pocket. "Tell me what you know about your family."

Erica chuckled. "You'll only need about a page of that little book. I'm afraid I don't know much." She quickly repeated what

Gerti had told her the night before.

"So Howard and Bridget grew up around Whitehall?"

Erica frowned. "I don't know." She glanced over, embarrassed. "I guess that sounds pretty weird to you."

"No. Most people don't know their family history for more than one or two generations. I've met people who didn't even know where their parents were born." She put the pad back in her pocket.

"How did you get interested in doing this?"

"I love history, but I didn't want to teach and I didn't want to end up in some stuffy little government office processing applications for historical markers. One of my exes was really into researching her family tree and she turned me on to it. That's when I found a way to combine the two and still make a decent living. I compile family histories and flesh them out by incorporating the history of the community. After I've finished with each job, I use the data I collect on the community as research for articles that I write for various historical journals, travel magazines, et cetera." She stared out the window. "Then about eight years ago, I got another break when another one of my exes who happened to be a member of a rather prominent family in New York asked me to help her family. They had tried to have their family history documented but all the researchers hit a dead end after a couple of generations. I started researching them as a favor to her really, but I took the time to interview a distant cousin that no one else had bothered to follow up on. I discovered that the eldest known patriarch had changed his name. From there I managed to trace the family back to Europe, where thankfully they were poor but honest farmers. I compiled a booklet, handed it over to the family and earned their seal of approval." She shrugged.

"So how did that lead you to my mother?"

"I had just finished a project for a client in Dallas when an ex from the historical commission called and told about the job."

"I don't mean to be rude, but how many exes do you have?" Erica asked bluntly.

Rae laughed before shaking her head. "I'm not into counting. I believe in having fun whenever the opportunity presents itself."

Erica could feel Rae's eyes assessing her. "You and I could have a lot of fun, I'll bet."

Erica nearly ran off the road. "I don't think I would be comfortable being added to your list of exes." She tried to hide how much Rae was flustering her.

"Would you be opposed to me trying to change your mind?"

Erica's heart pounded. Never before had she been so openly propositioned. She thought about Alice. "I'm sort of involved."

"Sort of . . . that's sounds interesting. Why don't you tell me how you're sort of involved? The only thing I find more intriguing than history is dyke drama."

Erica tried to ignore Rae. In spite of her best efforts, she couldn't help but be curious about this woman who so openly displayed a sense of pride in her lesbianism. She gave in and told her a little about her relationship with Alice, all the while being careful not to say anything that would give Alice's identity away.

CHAPTER THIRTY-TWO

When they reached Whitehall, Erica said, "I'd drive you around to show you the town, but you'll be able to see most of it from your bedroom window."

"Maybe we can take a walk later on and you can show me the sites." She stopped. "Listen, if it's going to cause you trouble or embarrass you to be seen with me, I'll understand."

"Thanks. I appreciate the offer." She looked at Rae and smiled. "I'll have to remember to extend the same courtesy to you if I should ever come to New York."

Rae's eyebrows lifted. "Oh. Does that mean you might come to visit?"

Erica's face burned. That hadn't been what she'd meant. "We're home." She quickly parked the car and jumped out to get the bag from the trunk.

They made it into the living room before Judith breezed out to meet them. Anyone who didn't know her well wouldn't have noticed the slight falter in her step. Or the way she paled a shade or two when she saw her guest for the first time. But Judith never missed a beat as she shook hands.

"Ms. Richardson, I'm so glad to finally meet you. I've heard nothing but rave reviews about your wonderful work."

"Please call me Rae."

"Is that a Northern accent I detect?" Judith asked, her voice only a slight bit higher than normal.

"I'm from New York."

"Oh, how interesting. I've never been to New York, of course, but I've heard so many things about it." Judith motioned to Erica. "Take Ms. Richardson's . . . ah . . . Rae's luggage to the guestroom, please." She quickly turned back to her guest. "I thought you might be hungry after your flight, so I took the liberty of preparing a light dinner." She waved a hand. "It's nothing fancy, just some stuffed bell peppers."

"Mom, we ate in San Antonio. That's why we were a little late." Erica debated adding the rest, but what the heck. Moments like these didn't come along very often. "Rae is a vegetarian."

Judith actually swayed a little at that final blow. She quickly regained her composure. "Oh, dear." She was saved from any further comment when Gerti walked into the room. "Mother," Judith began, only the slightest tremor in her voice. "This is Ms. Rae Richardson. She's from New York." Judith's composure slipped another notch. "She's a vegetarian."

Erica held her breath as Gerti looked Rae up and down before offering her hand. "Well, it's a pleasure to meet you." She glanced at Judith with a glee-filled grin. "I can't tell you how much my daughter has been looking forward to your arrival. I do believe she has promised to introduce you to nearly everyone in town."

Rae shook Gerti's hand. "Thank you. I'm looking forward to meeting everyone."

As much as Erica would have loved to stay and watch the exchange between Judith and Gerti, she picked up Rae's backpack. "Come on. I'll show you where you'll be staying." She led the way to the back of the house. She placed Rae's backpack on the foot of the bed. "The bathroom is through there. I'm sure Mom has stocked it with everything you can imagine, but if you need anything just let us know." She knew Judith was probably having seizures by now, but Erica couldn't simply walk away without extending an offer for Rae to join them. "There's not much to do here at night. We normally just sit around and talk, or read. You're welcomed to come out and join us anytime you like."

"I do most of my writing at night." Rae grinned slightly as she moved to within inches of where Erica stood. "Unless, of course, something else should happen to distract me."

"I doubt anything will be distracting you," Erica said, unable to keep from smiling. Before she realized what was happening, Rae leaned forward and kissed her. To her further embarrassment, there was the briefest moment when her lips responded. She started to leave.

"Come back anytime you want to finish that."

"It's already finished," Erica replied as she closed the door. She went back and found Judith and Gerti sitting at the kitchen table. As soon as they saw she was alone, Judith dropped her head onto her folded arm. "Dear God in heaven, I'm ruined. I'll be the laughingstock of the entire county. How could Tiffany not tell me that this woman was a . . . a . . . oh, I can't even say it."

"Vegetarian," Gerti said in an exaggerated whisper.

Judith raised her head and glared at her. "This is all your fault."

Gerti blinked in surprise. "My fault? How could it possibly be my fault?"

Erica slid into an empty chair.

Judith shook her head and started wringing her hands. "I haven't figured it out yet, but I know you're responsible for this."

"Mom," Erica said. "It's not that bad. She'll only be around until she gathers enough information for the biography and then she'll be gone." She rubbed a hand over her lips to try to erase the slight tingling warmth she still felt from Rae's kiss. "The quicker she gets the information, the quicker she leaves."

Judith stopped wringing her hands. "You're right." She looked at Gerti. "Mother, you have to tell her everything you know immediately."

Gerti peered at her hands. "For me to tell her everything I know could take weeks. I've lived a full and active—"

"The family history, Mother. Tell her what you know about Howard and Bridget Franklin."

"Oh, that. Well, that won't take much time at all, because I don't know very much about them. In fact, it probably wouldn't take me five minutes to tell her." She started to stand. "Should I go tell her now?"

"Mother," Judith said with narrowed eyes. "I'm warning you. This is important. That woman is going to prepare a wonderful family history that will be read at the sesquicentennial opening-day luncheon. It will be read again a year or so from now when the new statue is dedicated." She stopped sharply and stared into space.

Erica was starting to get concerned by the time Judith finally snapped her fingers.

"I knew something had been bothering me." She turned back to Gerti. "I need that diary."

Gerti flinched. "What diary?" If there was one thing that Gerti was not accomplished at, it was lying.

"The one you and Dad had that awful fight over."

"I don't know what you're talking about."

"Mother, please stop being difficult. I distinctly remember hearing you two fighting over a diary. Dad kept saying something about giving it to Grandmother Amelia, but you didn't want him to."

"You were probably dreaming," Gerti said as she stood. "I don't remember anything about a diary." She walked out of the room.

"I swear I'm going to stick that old woman in a nursing home someday."

"Mom, please. You know you would never do that."

"No. But I can dream, can't I?" She turned to Erica. "Why is she being so difficult about this?"

"How should I know? She told me to let sleeping dogs lie."

Judith frowned. "What did she mean by that?"

"She wouldn't say anything else."

Judith tapped her fingers in a gesture so similar to Gerti that it made Erica smile. "Maybe she knows something." She peered at the empty doorway where Gerti had disappeared. "No. She's just being difficult to get to me. She knows how much this means to me."

"Mom, why would she do that?"

"Who knows why she does most of the things she does?"

"Listen, I want to apologize for last night. I never meant for you to find out that way."

Judith jumped up. "I have work to do. I can't talk now." She raced off.

Erica stared at the empty doorway and found herself wishing that Alice was home so that she could go over and talk to her. She finally got up and started out of the kitchen. When she reached the living room, she stopped and for a long moment stared toward the back hallway that would lead her to Rae's room. She tried to tell herself that she would just go back to check on her, but deep down she knew if she went back there, things would probably go too far. Not trusting herself to stay in her room, she grabbed her keys and walked to the store. There was always enough work there to keep her mind occupied. It was well after midnight before she returned.

CHAPTER THIRTY-THREE

The following morning Erica woke up much later than usual. She knew she should get to the store, but the day clerks had keys and they were both dependable, so she took her time. When she went into the kitchen, she found Rae dressed in a pair of men's pajamas sitting at the table reading the paper.

"Good morning," Rae called over the paper. "There's a fresh pot of coffee, if you're a coffee drinker."

"How did you sleep?" Erica poured herself a cup of coffee.

"Great, after I got used to the lack of noise."

"Can I fix you something for breakfast?"

"No, thanks. Your mom made me an omelet before she went out to clean the garage."

Erica's cup stopped midway to her lips. "Clean the garage? That's odd. I thought she was busy planning her luncheon." She excused herself and went to the garage.

Judith was digging through a large plastic box that was clearly marked on the side as items that once belonged to Amelia.

"Mom?"

Her mother gave a small squeal of fright as she spun toward her. "You nearly scared the pee water out of me."

"What are you doing?"

"I'm looking for the diary that your grandmother insists never existed."

"Whose diary was it?"

Judith looked flustered. "Well, I don't rightly know, but I do remember hearing my parents arguing about it, and it must have been important if Mother doesn't want me to have it."

"That's not much to go on. It could have been anything."

"I might have believed that if Mother hadn't lied about it last night."

Erica nodded. It was obvious that Gerti hadn't been telling the truth about the diary. So maybe there was something to it. "Okay, well, you have fun. I'm heading out to the store."

Judith stopped. "No. You can't. I promised Rae that you would show her around today. She wants to see the town. When you've finished with that, take her over to the county clerk's office and introduce her around. She mentioned wanting to go through some sort of old records."

"All right." She went back inside. "Whenever you're ready to leave let me know. It looks as though I will be your official tour guide for the day."

"Am I taking you from your work? I can find my way around on my own."

"No. Actually, I don't much feel like working today anyway."

"Great. Let me get dressed and I'll be ready."

Erica toasted a slice of bread and ate it as she waited. She had finished her coffee and was rinsing her cup when Rae reappeared wearing a pair of slacks and a cotton shirt that she had tucked in.

"Do you think I'll blend in with the locals?"

Erica glanced at the short spiky hair and the multitude of earrings and chuckled. "Outsiders probably wouldn't be able to tell the difference."

They had no sooner stepped out the door than Miss Wilkerson and General Lee came hobbling toward them. Miss Wilkerson wore a billowing pink housedress several sizes too large for her withered frame. As she grew closer, Erica could see where someone had used a large safety pin to gather the neck opening. A pair of lime green, fuzzy house slippers peeked from beneath the dress.

Erica smiled to herself. The poor thing had probably been standing by her window all morning waiting for them to leave. As soon as they drew closer, she made the introduction.

Before the older woman could say a word, Rae held out her hand. "Would you by chance be related to the great Civil War hero Colonel Archibald Wilkerson?"

Miss Wilkerson's eyes widened. "Why, yes. That would be my grandfather. How is it you know his name?"

"Ma'am, I would be a poor historian indeed if I wasn't familiar with such a distinguished fighting man."

"I have his shotgun, you know, as well as many other of his personal belongings." She practically wiggled with joy.

Erica looked at General Lee, who had flopped down on the sidewalk and dozed off. She considered doing the same as the two rattled on for ten minutes about Civil War battles.

When Erica finally managed to separate them, she looked at Rae. "How did you know all that stuff?"

Rae slipped her hands in her pockets as she walked. "Yesterday when we were driving in you mentioned several different townspeople. Last night, I went online and did some research." She tilted her head toward Erica. "That's what I do, after all."

"You've certainly won her over."

As they walked around town meeting others, it quickly became apparent that Rae had looked up more folks than she had mentioned.

"This is getting creepy," Erica said after Rae had spent five minutes discussing the tornado that caused so much damage to the town—the same tornado that Gerti had been talking about only a few days before.

"There's nothing creepy about it. Your local paper has done an excellent job of putting their back issues online. I scanned various headlines and picked out the major events. When something happens in a small town, there's a ripple effect that touches everyone there in some small way." She stopped to gaze up into a mesquite tree. "Oral histories are getting harder to do. People have become paranoid. They don't like to talk about themselves to strangers." She shrugged. "I can't blame them. I've found that if I can share even one item of interest with another person, then they are much more willing to share more of themselves with me."

Erica nodded. "So you look up a story about Miss Wilkerson and discover her grandfather. Now she feels safe enough to take you into her home and share all her family secrets."

Rae made a face. "You make it sound sinister and sleazy. I'm not a tabloid writer. I honestly care about preserving stories. Nothing would please me more than to sit down and hear the stories of every person in this town." She kicked a pebble along the sidewalk. "I could care less about who slept with who back in the day, or any of that stuff. I want to know where all of these people came from. How did they happen to land here in this particular place? What made them leave their countries, their families and whatever securities they might have enjoyed to come here? Who did they find when they got here? What happened to them?" She turned and looked Erica in the eye. "I'm not here to take advantage of anyone. Why don't you trust me?"

"I guess it's hard for me to imagine that anyone outside of Whitehall cares about any of those things."

"You're wrong. I care."

They walked in silence for a few minutes.

As they approached the courthouse, Rae pointed to the gleaming brass cannon that sat on the lawn. "What's the story behind that?"

"It's another one of our treasures from *The War*."

"I've never seen a cannon look that shiny before."

"Billy Dawson keeps it like that." She thought about the man who arrived each morning like clockwork to polish the old relic. "Billy's father owned a large ranch outside of town. Billy was supposed to take it over until he a lost a leg in Korea. After he came home, he sort of wandered around aimlessly for a while. Then one day he moved into a small house at the end of town and each morning he came over in his wheelchair and polished the cannon. He's in his eighties now, but he still shows up every morning at exactly six thirty. I've seen him out here when it has been pouring rain. He sits there with an umbrella in one hand and a rag in the other."

Rae stared at the cannon. "What a wonderful story that would make."

They continued toward the front of the square.

"That's a beautiful courthouse," Rae said as they drew closer.

"Come on. I'll you show around inside."

As they were going up the steps, Rae leaned toward Erica and lowered her voice. "I have a confession to make. My great-grandfather was a cavalry soldier. He fought for the Union Army."

"I do hope he wasn't among those terrible Yankee transgressors who tried to burn our courthouse in 'sixty-three," Erica said, mimicking Miss Wilkerson's voice as closely as she could.

"No, he served in the eastern campaign."

"That's good, because the store is running short on tar and feathers this month."

They were laughing when they opened the door to the courthouse and Erica nearly bumped into Alice.

"When did you get back?" Erica asked.

Alice's gaze locked on Rae. "I got back about an hour ago."

"Oh, sorry." Erica quickly made introductions. "Mom hired Rae to compile and write the biography for the ceremony." She turned back to Rae. "Alice is the mayor of Whitehall." A thin sweat broke out along Erica's hairline as Alice and Rae continued to stare at each other. "Rae will be staying with us while she's here." Erica cringed and cursed her motormouth when Alice glared at her for a moment before turning back to Rae.

"It was nice to meet you, Ms. Richardson. I hope you enjoy your stay in Whitehall." She shoved the door open and stormed out.

Erica watched her head down the steps.

"Um . . . I think you should probably go after her," Rae said.

Erica hesitated.

"Look, I've been in hundreds of courthouses. I can find my way around. Why don't you go on? I'll find my way back to the house when I've finished here."

Erica nodded. "Thanks. I'll see you later." She started out the door but stopped long enough to remove her house key and give it to Rae. "Take this in case there's no one home when you get there." She raced down the steps and managed to catch Alice before she crossed the street. "Hey," she called out. "Wait up."

Alice slowed only slightly.

"Why are you so mad?"

Alice stopped and turned to her. "Is that what you want from me?"

Erica frowned. "I don't know what you're talking about."

"That woman. Is that what you want?"

"Alice, I was taking her to the courthouse to introduce her to—"

"I heard you laughing a block away."

"When did it become illegal to laugh?"

"If that is what you want, then fine."

"Stop it," Erica hissed. "You're being completely unreasonable."

Alice stopped and took a deep breath. "Look. I planned on calling you later, but I may as well tell you now." She looked down at the sidewalk for a moment before staring Erica in the eye. "I've decided to run for reelection. I think it would be best if you didn't come over anymore."

"You're dumping me?" Erica asked, dumbfounded. "Just like that?"

"Stop acting as though this is a brand new concept. We've been moving toward this for months. You said so yourself the other night at the house."

"Can't we find some way to compromise on this? I mean, everything was so good the other night at the coast."

Alice held up her hand. "Let's not make this any harder than it has to be. I have my career to consider."

"In other words, your career is more important to you than I am."

Alice looked away. "The two aren't compatible. Please don't try to contact me again unless it's in an official capacity." She turned and walked away.

CHAPTER THIRTY-FOUR

Erica went to the store and started shelving a new shipment of hand tools. Afterward she went into the office and tried to work on the accounts, but the numbers refused to make sense. She finally gave up and sat staring at the computer screen. She told herself that Alice had made the smart decision. Their relationship had stalled almost as soon as it started. How could she have ever dreamed of having any sort of normal life with Alice? Even if they never actually came out, they could never live in the same house, go on vacation together or anything else that other couples did, at least not as long as Alice was in politics. She knew of a few lesbian couples who lived in the surrounding area who led relatively normal lives. There was no reason why she shouldn't be capable of doing the same thing. All she had to do was meet someone who wasn't in the public spotlight the way Alice was.

She thought about Rae, who so proudly displayed her lifestyle. The townspeople they'd met that morning all seemed to be completely taken with her, but she was a stranger who would be leaving in a few days. Of course they would be polite to her. Consumed with her musing, she completely lost track of time. When Fred came in to say good night, she was surprised to find that the computer had sat idle so long it had shut itself off. She stood and stretched her stiff body. As she cleared her desk in anticipation of leaving she realized that the thought of going home and listening to her mom and grandmother bicker was almost more than she could stand. She tried to think of somewhere else she could go. None of the logical options appealed to her. It was over an hour's drive to San Antonio and nearly two hours to Corpus Christi, not that she felt like going to those places either.

She turned the lights out and locked the store. As she crossed the street, she saw Rae waving at her. Erica went to meet her. "How was your day?"

Rae tilted her head. "Judging from the way you look, my day was much better than yours."

"I'd rather not talk about it."

"Sure, I can understand. Hey, I saw a great-looking place that I'm dying to go to. Will you go with me?"

Erica frowned. She didn't feel like going back into San Antonio. "Where is it?"

Rae glanced around as if to get her bearing. "Down that street, I believe."

"You mean Jimmy Kwan's?"

"Yeah, that's the place. Is the food any good?" She stopped. "Will your mom be expecting us home for dinner?"

"No. We're usually so busy with our own schedules that we rarely eat together." As they walked to Jimmy Kwan's, Erica filled her in on the few details she knew about the owner.

Jimmy did a double take when they entered the crowded restaurant. Then she pointed to an empty table near the front.

"Where did all these people come from?" Rae asked as she took a seat.

"Most are farmers and ranchers from the surrounding area."

A young woman with long red hair worn in a single braid down her back came to the table with two glasses of water. She spoke to Erica before turning to Rae. "I guess you'd be the historian everyone's talking about."

Rae smiled. "I hope they're being nice in what they have to say."

"Rae Richardson, meet Tina Delaney. Tina's family was one of the original settlers of Whitehall."

"What can I get for you all tonight?" Tina asked.

"I think I'll just have a couple of fried pork chops with some green beans and mashed potatoes," Erica said.

"Can I really order anything I want?" Rae asked.

"As long as the cook knows how to fix it you can."

"Then I'd like some spaghetti with tomato sauce, no meat, some garlic bread and a small side salad, but no meat, please."

Tina smiled. "Yeah, I heard you were a vegetarian."

When she went to wait on the next table, Rae turned to Erica. "What's the deal with my being a vegetarian?"

"It's just one more way you're different. This is farming and ranching country. You won't find many vegetarians around here. I suppose it's because being able to serve meat, other than wild game, with a meal was once a sign of your wealth. Poor families couldn't afford it. Or maybe it's the inherent distrust we Southerners have of any food that's not fried."

As soon as Tina was out of earshot, Rae leaned forward. "I thought you were the only member of our alternative lifestyle here." She nodded toward where Tina had disappeared into the kitchen.

Erica shrugged. She had often wondered about Tina but felt the need to protect her. "I don't think she swings our direction," she lied.

Rae let the subject drop as she looked around her. "I can't believe that there are no menus. It must be a logistical nightmare for the cook."

"No. If you look around it's not much different from any other restaurant. People are pretty much creatures of habit. I'll bet if you got up and looked around, you'd find that half the people in

here are eating green beans and mashed potatoes as side dishes."
She shook her head. "In all the years I've been coming here I don't
remember once ordering anything that I couldn't find on a menu
at any restaurant that serves home cooking."

"Why not? Don't you ever want to try something different?"

Erica looked at her closely to see if they were still talking about
food. She didn't see anything in her face or eyes to indicate that
there had been another meaning behind the question. Finally,
she shook her head. "No. I've been ordering the same things for
so long I wouldn't even know what else to ask for." She quickly
changed the subject when she realized she wasn't certain she was
still talking about food. "You should talk to Tina and her family.
Some of her family members were on the *Titanic*."

Rae's head shot up. "How did I miss that in my research last
night?" She looked toward the kitchen where Tina had gone. "Do
you think she would talk to me?"

"I don't see why not."

"How much do you know about them?"

"I know that Tina's"—Erica thought for a moment—"I guess
it's her third or fourth great-grandfather or something like that,
died during the disaster. I think his name was Zack. Afterward, his
widow, Betty, became active in trying to help improve the working
conditions for migrant workers." She sipped her water. "Grams
used to have an old scrapbook that had a lot of photos of Betty
Delaney in it."

"Do you think it would be all right for me to see it?"

"Sure, I don't see why not. It used to be in the den. I'll find it
when we get back to the house."

A few minutes after Tina arrived with their food, a thin, elegantly clad woman approached the table. Erica struggled not to
groan in frustration.

"Hello, Sara Bell." Erica introduced the two women.

Sara Bell eyed Rae as if she expected her to develop horns at
any moment. "I understand you're here to do a history for Judith
Boyd."

"Yes, that's right," Rae said.

"Well, you might be interested in knowing that my own illustrious family descends directly from one of this great state's most beloved forefathers. He's none other than the famous Governor James Stephen Hogg."

Rae nodded. "You're Arthur Hogg's wife, if I remember correctly."

"Why, yes, I am," she gushed.

"Then technically your husband would be the descendent of Governor Hogg."

Sara Bell bristled but quickly remembered her manners. "Well, *technically*, I suppose that's true." No one had ever accused Sara Bell of knowing when to retreat. She pulled out a chair and sat down. "I could tell you so many stories about the governor." She giggled into her hand. "He was such a jokester. He named one of his daughters Ima. Can you imagine anything more appalling than going through life with a name like Ima Hogg?" She waved her hand. "Of course, what can one expect? After all, his sister was named Ura."

Rae leaned forward. "Governor Hogg named his daughter Ima after the heroine of a Civil War poem entitled *The Fate of Marvin*. The governor's older brother, Thomas, wrote the poem. The story of him having a sister named Ura is nothing more than a legend. And, I'm sorry to inform you that there's no Arthur Hogg in the governor's direct line."

Erica froze as Sara Bell's face cycled from several shades of pale back to a hue of red so fiery Erica half expected her to spontaneously combust. She knew she should do something to stop this, but it was too late.

Sara Bell exploded from the chair. "You, madam, have the manners of a Yankee pig."

"I'm sorry if I've offended you, but I'm a genealogist and historian. I'm confident you can appreciate how frustrating fictitious ancestral pedigrees are to me."

Erica didn't take her eyes off Sara Bell. From the deafening silence in the room, she knew that everyone else was watching as well.

The skin on Sara Bell's face twitched as she struggled to regain control. Then, without warning, she spun on her heel and stomped between the tables of gawking diners with all the finesse of General Sherman marching through Georgia.

Once the sweet tea from overturned glasses and a bowl of spilled soup were mopped up, the diners went back to their meals, but there was a low hum around the room that hadn't existed before.

Erica slowly released her breath. She had witnessed the birth of another vignette in Whitehall's history. She didn't need psychic powers to know that what had just occurred here would become the story of how the odd Yankee girl had upset Sara Bell Hogg's applecart. It would be a story that would be repeated for decades. A slight chill ran down Erica's back as she watched Rae calmly eating her spaghetti. She had never seen Sara Bell so angry, and she wasn't the sort of person who would take the slaughter of her public image lightly. She might have lost the battle, but there had been no signs of surrender in her exit. Erica speared a green bean with her fork and prayed that Sara Bell didn't come charging back in with the cannon from the courthouse lawn.

CHAPTER THIRTY-FIVE

The house was quiet when they returned from the restaurant.

"I'll see if I can find that scrapbook and then meet you in the kitchen," Erica said as she headed down the hall toward the den. She finally found it in one of the bottom cabinets. There were a couple of other old albums, so she took them also, thinking they might be useful to Rae's research for Judith.

When she got to the kitchen, Rae wasn't there yet, so she put on a pot of coffee and sat down at the table. She idly flipped through one of the books while she waited.

"I can't believe you started without me," Rae scolded as she came in again dressed in men's pajamas.

"I should have changed while I was waiting on you."

"Go change. We're not on a timetable."

Erica hopped up. "I won't be a minute." She stopped and pointed. "The one with the red binder has some old newspaper clippings about the Delaneys and the *Titanic*."

She headed to her room where she changed into a pair of sweats and an old T-shirt bearing the Whitehall Dragons' school logo. Rae was completely engrossed in the articles when Erica returned to the kitchen.

"Would you like some coffee?" Erica asked.

Rae declined and continued reading the article. As she read, her finger stayed at the edge of the article and trailed down quickly as if she were skimming the material. Within a matter of minutes, she had gone through every article in the book. She closed the book and leaned back with her eyes closed. After a moment, she opened her eyes and placed her hand flat on the cover. "Who put this together?"

"I think Bridget did. Why?"

"These articles are from several different newspapers." She flipped the book open again. "The first one is from New York, then Columbus, Ohio, Chicago, St. Louis, Little Rock, San Antonio and then here. On each article, the date gets progressively newer. It's as if the papers were being purchased while they were traveling."

"Maybe the Delaneys bought them when they came home," Erica said.

"Could be. But why would they buy them and then give them to Bridget?"

"Perhaps newspapers were scarce, and they let her have them after they had finished with them."

Rae shook her head. "I don't think so. I went through the county records from eighteen fifty-eight, when Whitehall was established, through nineteen sixty-five when Bridget died."

"All of them?" Erica asked doubious.

"Yes, every single word, in fact."

"That's impossible."

"Maybe for the average reader, but I can read faster than most people think, and I'm blessed or cursed, whichever way you wish to view it, with an approximate ninety-seven percent recall." She glanced up at Erica. "I don't mean that to sound as though I'm bragging. It's simply a fact."

"That's amazing."

"It certainly helps me whip through decades of data. Now, where was I? Oh, yeah, the first mention of either Howard or Bridget was in early May of nineteen twelve when they purchased a building and two lots from Ezra Wheedle. From that point on their names appear in the tax rolls all the way through to 'sixty-five, and their names appeared in the *Gazette* numerous times as well. Before nineteen twelve there was no mention of them in the newspaper."

"So?"

"Why would the Delaneys give newspapers to complete strangers?"

"What difference does it make where the papers came from?"

"It's a loose end, and those often lead me to the previous chapter of someone's life." Rae patted the book. "Howard and Bridget Franklin, two people with an unknown prior history, arrive in Whitehall and buy a store less than a month after the Delaneys' experience with the *Titanic*." She looked at Erica and wiggled her eyebrows. "Now, wouldn't your mother love to discover that a couple of her ancestors had survived the sinking of the *Titanic*?"

"I think you might be reading too much into a handful of newspaper articles."

Rae pulled another album to her and opened it. She closed it and reached for the other one. "This is the older of the two," she said almost to herself.

"How do you know that?" Erica asked as she refilled her coffee.

"Elementary, my dear." She held up the book. "These photos are monochromic, while the others are Kodachrome."

"Nobody likes a know-it-all."

"Sure they do. Just look at me. Everybody loves me."

"Maybe you should ask Sara Bell about that one."

"Was I too harsh on her?"

"Yes and no. She is a pompous ass, but a lot of her identity is wrapped up in her perceived connections to Governor Hogg."

Rae made a dismissive gesture. "She has her own family roots.

She should be proud of them."

"Isn't it more desirable to be the descendent of royalty as opposed to a common farmer?"

"That may be true for some, but tell me. If you were stranded on a deserted island with only one other person, which would you prefer, a king or a farmer?"

"Given the choice, I'd prefer the person be a shipbuilder."

Rae had already moved on to another item. "Do you know who took these photos?"

Erica peeked at the album that was filled with faces of people she didn't know. "I think Grams once told me Bridget took them. She was something of a photographer, I guess."

"Look at these," Rae said. "They're wonderful. These photos should be in a museum or gallery where they can be shared."

Erica leaned closer. As a child, she had never been very interested in this particular album because it had very few photos of people she knew. A shot of several people standing by a cotton field with long sacks filled with cotton resting at their feet caught Erica's attention. The workers' exhaustion seemed to radiate from the page. "Look at this one," she said, pointing to the photo.

Rae studied it. "At the restaurant you mentioned that Betty Delaney did a lot of work to help improve the lives of migrant workers." She tapped the photo. "I'll bet that's Betty right there."

They went through photo after photo. By the time Rae flipped over the final page, Erica felt as though she had been granted a special passage back through time. She had never noticed how extraordinary the photos were.

Rae closed the album and ran a hand almost reverently across the cover. "Promise me that you'll get these wonderful photos out of this binder. If you don't want to loan or donate them to a facility that can properly care for them, at the very least store them in an acid-free environment."

"It has been ages since I've looked at them. I honestly never realized how good they are."

Rae reached for another book and flipped it open. "Tell me who these people are."

As a child Erica had gone through this collection of photos countless times, bugging her grandmother to tell her all about the people in the old and sometimes faded pictures. She now realized that Gerti had appeased her by merely giving her the person's name and what their relationship was to Erica. She pointed to one. "That's Bridget and Howard. The little girl Bridget's holding is my mom. This is Amelia and her husband, Roger. That's Grams—she's holding William—and that's Grandfather Boyd, holding Sharon. The two boys sitting in front of them are Charles and Richard. They died in the accident with my grandfather."

"Do you have any idea when this was taken?" Rae was leaning close to the photo, peering at it.

"William is a tiny baby, so it's sometime during the early Sixties, I guess. Mom or Grams would know more. I think Grams once told me that this was the last photo taken of them all together."

"Look at Gerti. She looks like your mom does now."

Erica studied the photo. "You're right. I'd never noticed that before."

"Your grandfather has his mother's eyes." She kept staring at the photo. "It's funny. None of them resemble Bridget or Howard." She frowned. "Not even Amelia." She glanced up at Erica. "She was their natural daughter, wasn't she?"

"Yes. She was an only child."

Rae made a slight sound of acknowledgment. "All of these are Amelia?" She pointed to several other photos of Amelia, then leaned back and closed her eyes again.

Erica heard the sound of the garage door opening. "Mom's home."

Rae opened her eyes and rubbed her forehead. "Good. Maybe she can go through these photos with us."

There was a heavy thud of a door slamming just before she heard, "Erica Amelia Winfrey!"

Rae's eyebrows shot up. "You're in trouble," she whispered just as the door between the kitchen and garage flew open.

Judith shook her finger at Erica. "What is wrong with you?"

Erica turned her free hand upward. "I'm sorry. I don't

know—"

"I just saw Sara Bell and she's livid."

Rae started to slip out of her seat.

"Oh, no, you don't." She pushed Rae back into her seat before she turned to Erica with her fists on her hips. "What possessed you to embarrass her like that in front of everyone?"

"I didn't do anything," Erica protested.

"How does that make you any less guilty?" Judith shook her finger again. "In fact, that makes it even worse. You knew better." She hooked a thumb back over her shoulder toward Rae. "Being from the North and all, she at least has the excuse of not knowing any better."

"Excuse me, I'm sitting right here."

Judith turned to glare at her. "You might not want to keep reminding me of that fact, young lady." She took a deep breath. "Now, in the morning I want both of you to go back over to Jimmy's for breakfast and make a public apology to Sara Bell." She turned to Rae. "And you tell her you were wrong about your facts."

Rae stood up. "I will not. I'm not wrong. I've read extensive histories on Governor Hogg, and Sara Bell's husband, Arthur, was not among his direct descendents."

"Well, everybody knows that," Judith said, clearly exasperated. "What do you take us for anyway? We Southerners are the original genealogists. When I was nothing more than a cricket sitting at my daddy's knee I listened to the old folks rattling off their family histories all the way back to their European ancestors."

"If you knew she was lying, why are you so mad?" Rae asked, clearly confused.

"I'm not *mad*. Dogs go mad. I'm angry." Judith quivered with indignation. "You need to understand that here, what we know, and what we announce to the world, are very different things."

"So you walk around lying?"

Erica grimaced and stepped slightly to the side so that she would be in a better position to grab Judith's purse in case her mom decided to take a roundhouse swing at Rae. To her surprise, Judith dropped into a chair and set her purse on the table.

"We don't consider it lying," Judith replied, suddenly sounding more tired than angry. "We simply overlook certain things."

Rae looked at Judith. "I'm sorry if I embarrassed Sara Bell, but I have no intention of apologizing to her." After a long moment of silence, during which she sat staring down at the photo album, she added, "Maybe my being here wasn't such a great idea. Why don't I just write up the information I've found so far. From what I've read or heard about Howard and Bridget, about all of your family for that matter, the people of this community have had nothing but the utmost respect for all of you. What else do you really need to know?"

"Finally, someone has said something that makes sense."

Erica looked over to see Gerti standing in the doorway. She had come in unnoticed.

"I just came from a meeting with Alice Goodman and told her I wanted this whole statue business dropped."

Judith jumped up. "Mother, you had no right to do that."

"I had every right."

"No, you didn't. I want you to call Alice this very minute and tell her you've changed your mind."

Gerti stared at her as if she had lost her mind. "Do you know who you're talking to? You may be out of diapers, but I can still wallop your fanny." She stepped into the kitchen.

Erica shook her head when Rae gave her a look that said, "What should we do?" She knew better than to get between them.

"I'm still the head of this family," Gerti continued. "I'll decide what is and isn't good for it."

"Grandma and Granddaddy Franklin were Daddy's ancestors. It's not your decision to make."

For a moment, Erica feared Gerti would blow, but what happened was much worse than any explosion. The wind seemed to leave her grandmother's body, and it was as though she began to shrink before their eyes. Gerti suddenly looked every one of her seventy-two years.

Judith and Erica stepped toward her at the same time, but Gerti turned away. "Then do as you will and you can suffer the consequences." She went to her room and closed the door quietly behind her.

Judith continued to stare at the empty doorway for a long moment. "Erica, maybe you should go check on her."

Erica walked down the hall and tapped on her grandmother's door. "Grams, it's me. Are you all right?"

"Let me be, Erica. I'm tired."

"You know she didn't mean to hurt you."

"I told you to let me be."

CHAPTER THIRTY-SIX

Judith pleaded a headache and went off to her room.

"Is it always this intense here?" Rae asked.

"No. It's usually rather boring."

"I thought your mom and Sara Bell were archrivals or some such."

"They both want to be the town's queen bee." Erica rubbed her forehead. "I'm sorry to run off and leave you, but I'm tired. I think I'm going to turn in."

"Is it all right if I take these to my room and look at them?" Rae motioned to the photo albums.

"Sure. Just put them back in here on the table when you've finished." As soon as Erica got to her room, she picked up the phone and dialed a familiar number.

Alice answered on the second ring.

"I was afraid you wouldn't answer."

"I shouldn't have. I asked you not to call."

"Then why did you answer?"

"I heard what happened with Sara Bell and figured you would need someone to talk to."

"Alice, I miss you."

After a slight pause Alice said, "I miss you too, but that's not going to solve our problem."

"Can I come over?"

"No. I told you. That has to stop. Sooner or later, someone will catch on."

"So, that's it? Just like that we're over?" Erica sat on the bed.

"We can still be friends. I wouldn't want to lose your friendship."

Erica didn't want to think about not being able to touch Alice ever again. How could she possibly see her day after day and live with the fact that Alice no longer loved her? For the first time in many years, she considered leaving Whitehall. She pushed the thought away. She couldn't live anywhere else. This was her home. "I'm sorry I bothered you. It won't happen again." She hung up before Alice could respond.

She stretched out on the bed and stared at the ceiling. Maybe she could be friends with Alice someday, but not for a while.

Her phone rang. She grabbed the receiver, hoping it was Alice. It was Ed Raines, one of the other volunteer firefighters. A grass fire had been called in from the edge of town. He would pick her up in two minutes. Since Ed lived just a few of houses down, they normally rode to fires together. She grabbed the bag containing her turnout gear from her closet and then her cell phone. As she ran out to the sidewalk to wait for Ed, she dialed the next number on the phone tree, Arthur Hogg. When Arthur answered, she gave him the address to the fire. He was now responsible for calling the next person on the list. Erica could already see the emergency lights on Ed's truck flashing in the semidarkness. It would be completely dark in a matter of minutes. She hated fighting fires at night. They always seemed more ominous then.

He slowed enough for her to jump in. "Hey," he said by way of a greeting. As he drove, she slipped into her turnout gear. The fire-resistant clothing protected her from exposure to heat and flames, as well as chemicals. The suits were only a few months old. When Erica joined the volunteer force eight years ago, the equipment had been mediocre at best and had finally reached the point that the firefighters were in danger. She had convinced some of the members to go before the city council with her to request that something be done about replacing the decrepit equipment. The council had agreed and filed the necessary requests for state support. The new suits had cost a little over thirty thousand dollars. Slightly more than half of the money had come from a state grant. The people of the community had raised the rest by every means ranging from bake sales to donations.

"How big is the fire?" she asked.

"Don't know for sure. Joe Hadley called it in. He said he and his boys tried to put it out, but it was too big. The wind is going to be a problem."

"Yeah, but at least it's blowing away from town." She could feel the adrenaline start to build.

They saw the glow long before they arrived at the site. The fire engine and a few other volunteers were already fighting the flames. The fire looked as if it had started along the roadside and now involved about three acres. Someone had probably been careless about tossing a cigarette out the window. The lack of rain had turned the grass along the roadside into a tinderbox waiting to ignite. Erica grabbed a hose and started helping feed it out to the blaze. At one point, the chief came by and instructed her to go help a couple of volunteers who were clearing a firebreak between the fire and the Anderson home, which was less than a mile down the road.

"We don't want it to get any closer and frighten Ms. Sadie," he said.

Erica grabbed a chainsaw from the truck and jogged over to help. She was too busy to notice when the other members arrived, but within the hour, the flames were under control and before another hour had passed, it was out.

The volunteers straggled back to the engine and stored their tools. There would be a small crew of volunteers at the station to clean and prepare the equipment for the next fire.

Someone handed her a bottle of cold water. She turned to say thanks and found herself face to face with Arthur Hogg. "Hey, Arthur, I'm sorry about that mess earlier this evening."

He took a long drink from his water bottle before replying. "She's pretty upset." He glanced around as if to make sure no one was listening. "I've been telling her for years she ought to stop telling people that, but you know how Sara Bell gets. For some reason it was important to her." He rubbed at a spot of soot on his hand. "I don't know why my name ain't enough for her."

Erica didn't know what to say. "Would my going over to Jimmy's in the morning and apologizing to her help?"

"Probably not." He shuffled from foot to foot for a moment. "Listen, I just want you to know that no matter what happens, I think you're okay."

Just then Ed called out to Erica.

"I'll catch you later," Arthur said as he took off, leaving Erica to wonder what he meant by "okay."

Two fire-watchers stayed behind. They would continue to monitor the burned area for a while to make certain no stray embers flared back up.

When Ed dropped her off, she entered though the garage and went directly to the utility room rather than go through the house in her smoke-infused clothes. As she stripped off her gear to clean it, Gerti came out from the kitchen.

"Are you decent?" she called.

"In every way but smell," Erica replied.

Gerti and Rae came in together.

"Is everyone all right?" Gerti asked immediately. It was always the first question she asked when Erica came home from a fire.

"Yes. It was just a grass fire out near the Anderson place."

"Wow," Rae said. "You never told me you were a firefighter."

"Volunteer," Erica clarified as she finished cleaning her boots. The adrenaline rush was gone and she was exhausted.

"What happened?" Judith asked. She came in with the ritualistic cup of hot tea and handed it to Erica. The practice had begun after Erica's first run as a volunteer firefighter. Afterward she had been so hyper that Judith had made her a cup of tea to calm her and the tradition stuck.

Erica noticed that Judith and Gerti were careful not to look at each other. After all, they were still mad. They were just there to check on her.

"There was a grass fire out by Sadie Anderson's place," Gerti said as Erica drank the tea.

"Was anyone hurt?" Judith asked.

Erica shook her head.

"I can only imagine how frightened Miss Sadie must have been," Judith said.

Gerti nodded. "I'll take a cake out to her in the morning and sit with her for a while."

Judith waved a hand in front of her nose. "We need to install a shower out here for you to use." She patted Erica's arm and left.

"Glad no one was hurt," Gerti said. She also gave Erica's arm a pat before she left.

Rae gave a small chuckle after they were gone. "Your family is amazing. After what happened in the kitchen earlier, I didn't expect them to speak for days, but the minute they heard that fire engine you should have seen them come tearing out of their rooms. And your mom was on the phone in no time finding out what was going on."

"Just because they argue doesn't mean they don't still love each other."

"Is that what happened at the courthouse this morning?"

It took Erica a moment to remember that Rae was referring to her encounter with Alice.

"I'd rather not talk about that."

"She's the one you're 'sort of seeing,' isn't she?" When Erica didn't respond, she continued. "Come on. I'm not going to tell anyone. It's none of my business. I thought maybe you needed someone to talk to about it."

"There's nothing to talk about anymore. She wants out and

that's that." She turned away. "I'm sorry to be rude, but I need a shower."

"If you're sure it's over, do you need any help scrubbing your back?"

Erica stopped and for a moment gave the offer serious consideration. She didn't feel like being alone tonight, but images of Alice were still too vivid in her memory. "No, but thanks for the offer." She walked away quickly before she could change her mind.

CHAPTER THIRTY-SEVEN

Rae was at the kitchen table early the following morning waiting for Erica. "Would you mind if I walk to work with you? I need to talk to you about something."

"Sure, but can we talk while I have breakfast?"

Rae lowered her voice. "Your mom and grandmother are still home. I'd rather wait."

Normally, Erica would have suggested breakfast at Jimmy's, but with all that had gone on last night, combined with the fact that Rae had no intention of apologizing to Sara Bell, it might be best if they stayed away for a day or so. Sara Bell would certainly be there, if for no other reason than to pretend Rae's comments hadn't humiliated her.

"Come on," Erica said. "We can pick up doughnuts at the bakery, and I'll make coffee at the store."

As soon as they were out of the house, Rae began. "As you've seen, I only know one way to present something and that's head-on. So I apologize in advance for anything that you may find offensive."

Erica glanced at her. "That's a lot of drama to hand out before I've had my first cup of coffee."

"I think you'll handle what I have to say all right, but I'm not so sure about your mother and grandmother. That's why I decided to talk to you first."

"What's going on?"

"Something isn't right about your family."

"Excuse me?"

"Sorry. I meant your family history. Why is your grandmother so adamant about the city not commissioning this statue? I'd think it would be a huge honor. Especially considering she knows how much it would mean to Judith."

"I've been wondering about that, too."

"It was the scrapbook that really got me thinking. Too many things didn't add up. So, I decided to research the *Titanic's* passenger lists."

Something in Rae's voice made Erica stop.

"There was a Howard and Bridget Franklin onboard, but according to records they died when the ship sank."

Erica frowned. "What makes you think it has anything to do with our Howard and Bridget?"

"That's not all I found," Rae said, ignoring her question. "There was another couple named Trevor and Emma Sheffington. They boarded the ship with their six-month-old baby girl. Her name was Amelia."

Erica didn't like the direction in which this seemed to be headed.

"I searched immigration records, the passenger logs of ships returning to England for up to three months after the accident, the nineteen-twenty census records, veterans' records . . ." Rae shrugged. "I've checked every major database I can think of and I can't find a single record for the Sheffingtons. Now, obviously I haven't checked every county in the United States. There's a slim chance that they moved to some remote area and simply fell off the grid. I might still eventually locate them."

"I take it that you don't think you will."

"I'll concede that it's possible that Trevor and Emma's records are still sitting out there somewhere waiting to be found. There are millions of documents rotting away in courthouse basements all over this country. To say nothing of the ones that have been destroyed by fire, mindless nitwits and a dozen other problems." She shook her head. "I have a gut feeling that's not the case."

"We should probably move," Erica said as she started walking. "Nothing attracts attention like two people standing around talking."

Rae fell into step with her. "I found an article in the online archives of the *Whitehall Gazette* welcoming the surviving Delaney members home after the shipwreck. In the same issue there was a small 'Around Town' announcement welcoming Mr. and Mrs. Howard Franklin and their six-month-old daughter, Amelia. On a hunch, I ran a search for birth records as well as marriage records in the United Kingdom. I found a marriage record for Trevor Sheffington and Emma Dreyfus, but not for Howard and Bridget. I found birth certificates for Trevor and Emma. I even found the birth certificate for Amelia Sheffington, but again, nothing under Amelia Franklin."

Erica stopped again. "So you think Howard and Bridget's real name was Sheffington?"

Rae shrugged. "The *Titanic's* passenger list makes it clear that the Franklins and the Sheffingtons boarded the ship at Southampton, but after the accident, either Trevor and Emma changed their name or the Franklins left the ship with the Sheffingtons' daughter."

Erica suddenly remembered Gerti's comment about letting sleeping dogs lie. She pinched the bridge of her nose and wished she had waited until after she'd had her first cup of coffee before starting this conversation. "Please don't mention this to anyone else, including Mother and Grams."

"I have to give Judith something tomorrow."

"By tomorrow it may not be a problem, because right now

I'm seriously considering turning them both into mulch. If Jason Moore can get away with planting marijuana in his mother's garden, I'm sure no one would think twice of me planting those two." Her head throbbed. "I could have them freeze-dried and propped up in the new town square. The town would still have a statue, and it wouldn't cost a penny." She turned around.

"Where are you going?" Rae asked.

"I'm going to go drag my grandmother out of bed and make her watch as I start burning her twenty-year collection of *Playgirl*. I'm going to keep burning them until she tells me everything I want to know."

Rae followed her. When they reached the house, Rae insisted she had a lot of work to do and scurried off to her room.

Erica knocked on Gerti's door. When there was still no answer after the second knock, she eased the door opened. The bed had been neatly made. Gerti had already left. She went to the kitchen to check and found it empty also. She was about to leave when she noticed the note on the refrigerator door. She read it and discovered that Gerti had gone to Corpus Christi with a group of her friends to shop. They wouldn't be back until the following afternoon. Erica shook her head. These so-called shopping trips translated into a day at the track betting on the greyhounds, followed by margaritas at a bar that hosted male dancers several nights each week. She put the note back on the refrigerator where her mom would be able to see it.

"Maybe there will be a few hours of peace," she muttered as she left the house. It was time to get the issue with the statue settled once and for all so things would get back to normal. Erica made up her mind. As soon as Gerti returned, she would insist that her mom and grandmother sit down and work this mess out. If a valid reason for not wanting the statue existed, then it was time to make that reason known to the rest of the family. If Gerti was objecting just to be stubborn, then she needed to get over it and stop blocking the council's efforts.

CHAPTER THIRTY-EIGHT

When Erica stepped into the bakery, she noticed that everyone nodded politely but only two people out of the six or eight actually spoke to her. Then they looked away and didn't meet her gaze again. She assumed people were letting her know how they felt about Rae's confrontation with Sara Bell the previous night. Guilt by association, she guessed.

When the clerks, Fred and Angela, came in and seemed their usual cheerful selves toward her, she wondered if she had been overly sensitive about the incident at the bakery, and finally she concluded that she had been.

Since she had been away from the store so much in the past few days, she was behind in updating the accounts. She decided she would spend the day working on them. As she focused on entering the data into the computer, she was vaguely aware that the store was much busier than normal. The lack of noise from the cash register suggested that the customers were doing more browsing than buying. She was too busy to give it much thought. After finishing the updates to the accounts, she started preparing an order that would need to be submitted in a few days. As the morning progressed, Erica realized that no one had stopped by to see her. She normally had to close the office door if she wanted to work uninterrupted. Her suspicions were confirmed when she went to Jimmy's for lunch. Jimmy smiled and waved her toward a seat as always, but as Erica made her way across the restaurant several people pretended not to see her. Walt smiled when he came to take her order.

"Well, it's good to see one person is still speaking to me," she said, feeling somewhat better.

"Hey, it's no big deal to me. I think it was awfully brave of you."

Erica frowned. "Brave? I just sat there like a lump. I should have put a stop to the whole thing before it got so out of control." She took a sip of the water.

He shook his head. "I'm not talking about the mess with Sara Bell. I think it's great that you were brave enough to finally come out."

Erica choked on the water. After a vicious coughing attack, she stared at Walt in disbelief. "Where did you hear that?"

He shrugged. "I don't know. That's all anyone has been talking about all day. Heck, the mess with Sara Bell is already old news." He flipped open his order book. "So, what'll it be today?"

Erica felt eyes staring at her and wanted to slink out the door, but she couldn't. That would simply give the gossip mill additional fodder. Instead, she ordered a burger with fries. As soon as Walt left, she forced herself to hold her head up and meet any gaze sent her way. If the gawker was rude enough to stare, she gave them a polite questioning look that was, she felt, more than enough to remind them of their manners.

She didn't taste the hamburger or the cherry cobbler she ordered afterward. It was hard to sit there while people mumbled all around her. She knew what they were saying. Her fortitude was at least slightly rewarded when a few people looked her way and nodded politely as she left the restaurant. She forced herself to go back to the store and spend the afternoon working in the front rather than remaining in the office to finish placing the order she had started. Each time the phone rang, she expected it to be someone from the school board demanding her resignation. Each time the door opened, she expected it to be Judith storming in to murder her. Several times that afternoon she thought about calling Alice or Rae but held off. She'd have to fight this battle on her own.

Erica closed the store at its regular time and as casually as possible walked home. As she strolled down the street, she imagined she could feel eyes peering at her from behind window curtains. When she finally reached her house and closed the entrance door, she had to lean against it until her knees stopped shaking. The worse still lay before her. She braced herself for Judith and Gerti's anger. She was trying to put together her defense plan when she found Rae sitting at the kitchen table working on her laptop. Her backpack lay on the floor.

"Are you leaving?"

Rae nodded. "Your mom came in to say she'd changed her mind about presenting the history brochure. She paid me and said you would drive me back to the airport."

A glimmer of hope took life. A trip to San Antonio would postpone her meeting with Judith for at least two hours. "When does your flight leave?"

"Not until eight thirty tonight."

Erica tried to hide her glee. If she wasted enough time in returning she could time it in such a way that Judith would already be in bed. "Will you be going back to Dallas?"

"No. I'm going home to New York."

Erica sat down. She wondered if Rae had heard any of the rumors floating around. "Have you been out today?"

"No. I was busy working on the stuff for your mom until about an hour ago when she came to see me."

"She didn't say why she had changed her mind?"

"No. She said she didn't need the information anymore. Then she gave me a check. I feel bad because she insisted on paying me the full amount. So, I've compiled all my notes." She picked up a CD case from the table. "I've copied everything I could validate onto this."

"What sort of mood was Mom in?"

Rae glanced at her and shrugged slightly. "She seemed happy, bubbly even."

Erica started to tell Rae about what Walt had said, but then decided not to. The petty dramas of Whitehall were no longer Rae's problem. Suddenly, she wanted to get out of the house before Judith returned. She jumped up. "Why don't we leave now? We can get dinner there."

As they drove to San Antonio Erica wondered what it would be like to get on the plane with Rae and go to New York. She glanced at Rae and couldn't help but speculate what she would have been like in bed.

"It's not too late to find out."

Erica's face burned. "Dang, was I that obvious?"

"No. I was just hoping that was what you were thinking."

Erica chuckled. "I'm going to miss you. It has been nice to have someone to talk to."

"I can't believe I'm going to say this, but I was actually starting to get attached to the people of Whitehall and all their little idiosyncrasies."

"You're welcome to come back to visit anytime you want."

"Why don't you come to New York with me? You could stay with me as long as you like. We could have a good time."

Erica shook her head. "What happens in a few weeks when the good times aren't so good anymore?"

"You don't seem to have much confidence in my ability to maintain a relationship."

"Should I?"

Rae squirmed a little. "No. I suppose not." She looked at Erica apologetically. "I guess I'm not the happily-ever-after type."

"Maybe you just haven't met the right person." She added quickly, "Not that I'm suggesting I'm the right one, because . . . well, we both know I'm not."

"That's okay. Friends are harder to come by than lovers, so if it's all right with you I'd rather keep you as a friend."

Erica held out her hand. "That's a deal."

They stopped at the same restaurant they had gone to on the day Rae had arrived. They talked about everything except Whitehall. Afterward, when they arrived at the airport, Rae insisted that Erica drop her off rather than go inside to wait with her. As they stood at the curb, Rae gave her a hug. "You and the mayor should try to work things out. You both love the town and each other. You could make a difference there."

Erica knew that any chance she'd ever had of trying to live a hidden life with Alice was now impossible, but she smiled and nodded. "Maybe I'll look into that." She gave a wave and quickly left.

The thought of going home overcame her dislike of San Antonio traffic. She took her time and went to a mall where she tried on a half a dozen pairs of boots before deciding that she really didn't need to buy another pair and left. She turned off her cell phone and walked around the mall window-shopping until it closed.

As she drove home, she grew more nervous. She wished her grandmother hadn't gone to Corpus. Gerti would handle the situation without much fuss, but Judith was another matter. She would not be happy with the entire town knowing and whispering about her lesbian daughter. The closer she came to Whitehall, the more she wished she had gotten on the plane with Rae.

CHAPTER THIRTY-NINE

When Erica arrived home, she was relieved to find the house dark except for a lamp on in the living room. She tiptoed toward her room but stopped when she saw Gerti's bag sitting by the sofa. She wasn't supposed to be back until tomorrow afternoon. And it wasn't like Gerti to leave things lying around. She eased down the hallway toward Gerti's room and saw that the door was open. A closer peek revealed an empty room. Puzzled, she headed toward her mom's room.

Her concern grew when she discovered that her mom wasn't home either. Erica slipped the cell phone from her pocket and turned it on. There were no messages. She considered calling Gerti but quickly changed her mind. If anything serious had happened to either one of them or even both of them, someone would have called her. Grateful that she was going to get a few more hours' reprieve, she rushed to her room.

After a quick shower, Erica stretched across the bed with the lights off. She needed to think about how she would handle Gerti and Judith, but her thoughts kept drifting to Alice. Finally, she dialed the familiar number and let the phone ring until the answering machine finally kicked on. She considered leaving a message but decided not to and hung up. She lay staring at the faint shadows on the ceiling. Where was Alice? A small bothersome idea intruded. Had Alice already met someone else? A cold wave of discomfort twisted through her stomach. Was that what had really triggered Alice's decision to quit seeing her? She glanced at the glowing numbers on her bedside clock. It was after midnight. Where could she be? For that matter, where were Gerti and Judith? Again she thought about calling her mom's cell phone but chickened out. Instead, she crawled between cool sheets and finally fell asleep.

The house was quiet when she awoke the next morning. Concerned, she went to living room and saw that Gerti's bag had been removed. She walked into the kitchen, peered out the door leading into the garage and saw her mom's car. Even though she was relieved that they were both home, she still didn't want to run into either of them before she absolutely had to. Rather than taking a chance on waking them, she skipped making coffee and tiptoed back to her room, where she dressed as quietly as possible. Within minutes, she was at the mercantile.

By the time she got to work and started to prepare the coffee, she began wondering where Gerti and Judith had been so late the previous night. She tried not to think about what Alice might have been doing. Late hours and Whitehall really weren't synonymous. The phone rang as she spooned coffee into the filter-lined basket.

The caller was Larry Collins, president of the school board. "We're having a special meeting. We'd like everyone to be in attendance." There was a sense of formality in his voice that she'd never heard before.

Erica's heart skipped a beat. She forced herself to remain calm. "Sure. What time?"

"Right now. The rest of the board is already here in my office." Larry's real estate office was only a couple of blocks away.

It occurred to her that she could simply give her resignation to him over the phone and follow it up with a letter, but somehow that seemed cowardly. As she secured the filter container on the coffeepot and headed out the door, she told herself that this was what she deserved for being so insistent that Alice come out and face everyone. Now that it looked as though she was about to get the opportunity to practice what she preached, it no longer seemed like such a good idea.

The two-block walk to Larry's office was the longest she could remember ever having to take. Larry was waiting for her at the front door. He unlocked it to let her in and then relocked the door. "They're in the conference room," he said without looking at her.

She grabbed him by the arm. "Larry, I've known you my entire life. What am I walking into?"

He looked away clearly embarrassed. "I swear I did everything I could."

"It's that bad then?"

He finally met her gaze and nodded.

She took a deep breath and slowly exhaled. "All right." She straightened her back and held her head high. "Let's get this over with."

The other four members of the board were sitting around the table in the small conference room. She met the eyes of every member. Two of them, Allen Shears and Grady Blaylock, had gone to school with her mom, and they seemed uncomfortable meeting her gaze. Henrietta Garza nodded at her, but it was impossible to read her face. The final member, Ramona Cox, returned her gaze with an air of smugness that made the devil in Erica rise. Ramona and her husband, Bill, had moved to Whitehall about nine years ago. They bought the old Klaft place, which consisted of fifteen acres at the eastern edge of town. They proceeded to build an enormous two-story home, several barns and a swimming pool large enough to attract migrating geese. According to the rumor mill, Bill Cox had made a fortune during the dot-com era. The purchase of the land had been completed through an agent. An out-of-state contractor had shown up soon after the land was purchased and hired crews from San Antonio to build the home and pool. Once the house was completed, two women and a man arrived. They turned out to be the maids and a yardman. It was a couple of weeks after the construction was completed that Bill and Ramona finally arrived in Whitehall. The day after their arrival a small caravan of four horse trailers showed up with some of the most beautiful Appaloosa horses Erica had ever seen. It was then that the community learned that its newest members had come here intending to raise Appaloosas. Unfortunately, they hadn't bothered to check with the city zoning board before they purchased the land. They had been understandably angry when they discovered that since their land was within the city limits of Whitehall they wouldn't be allowed to keep horses on the property. A local rancher offered them the use of one of his barns until arrangements could be made for the animals and the three men Cox had hired to take care of the animals. Rather than admit their own lack of accountability in researching the limitations placed on the land, they threatened to sue because no one had warned them of the restriction. The San Antonio lawyer they hired had the undesirable duty of informing them that the city couldn't be held liable since it had no way of knowing what the land was to be used for, and that the final responsibility rested with them. The horse trailers and three men had eventually left and presumably returned to wherever they had originally come from.

Since then Bill had started a computer-consulting company that he operated from home and Ramona had tried to move into local politics. Over the years she had run for county clerk and city council and even took a stab at the mayoral race. She had lost in every race. Then, two years ago, she ran for school board and surprised everyone by winning a position. Almost immediately, she had started trying to take over the board and bend everyone's will to match her own views. She and Erica had clashed on more than one occasion.

Over the years, the people of Whitehall had simply incorporated the episode with the Coxes in with the rest of its colorful history, but Erica was certain that Ramona had never forgotten or forgiven them for not allowing them to keep the horses.

After seeing the smugness in Ramona's eyes, Erica decided then and there that when she left here it wouldn't be with her tail between her legs. She took the offensive. Her gaze never left Ramona's face.

"I guess you guys heard I'm a lesbian," she said.

Ramona's eyes nearly popped out of her head, and it took her a good ten seconds to recover enough to respond. "So you're admitting it, are you?" she asked, practically hopping up and down in her seat.

"I don't remember ever denying it."

Ramona glanced around at the others at the table. "Did everyone but me know?"

Erica knew she should resign and leave, but something pushed her on. She quickly answered before anyone else could. "Gosh, Ramona, I thought you knew. With you being such a sophisticated woman and all." In truth, no one seemed to know exactly where the couple had come from originally. The few tidbits the locals had been able to gather suggested that the couple had traveled a great deal. Gerti had wanted to suggest to Sheriff Case that he should run their backgrounds, but Erica had finally convinced her not to.

Ramona glared at her. "I don't see how you can joke about being a pervert."

"Ramona," Larry cut in. "We agreed that this was not going to turn into a name-calling session." He turned to Erica. "I'm sorry," he said. "We've received several calls." His jaw clenched. "Actually, I suppose it would be more accurate to say that some of us have apparently received calls from parents." He glared at Ramona.

Erica suddenly understood what was happening. She stopped him. "Larry, it's all right. I resign. I'll send you an official letter this afternoon."

"Wait a minute," Larry said. "You should know that not all of us wanted your resignation." He hesitated. "You could probably choose to take legal action."

Erica shook her head. She did not intend to fight the request. "No. That would be expensive for the board and there's really no need."

Ramona sniffed. "I told you she wouldn't have the nerve to go into court and admit what she is."

Erica's body began to shake with anger and hurt. Over the years, she had worked hard for this board. She forced her voice to remain much calmer than she felt. "What I am is a citizen of this town, one who cares a great deal about what happens to the kids here. I'll admit that I originally ran for this position because I was asked to. In the seven years that I've been on the board, we've expanded the computer lab at the high school and created a computer lab for the grade school. We've raised the funds needed to install a new floor in the gym. We've started a tutoring program that has been so effective other schools come here to study it. And we started a scholarship program that has allowed three young people from this community to attend college. Three kids who might not have been able to do so without the scholarship." She struggled to keep from glaring at Allen Shears. One of those three kids had been his nephew. She stood. "What I don't recall from those seven years is my *private* life ever interfering with me accomplishing the job I was elected to do." She held her head high and walked out of the room. As she went back to the store, she focused on recalling the items she needed to add to the store's next order. Her heart felt as though it would shatter, but she'd be damned if she'd let anyone see her cry.

CHAPTER FORTY

When Erica reached the store, she found Miss Wilkerson pounding on the door.

"Miss Wilkerson," she said, surprised. "What's wrong?" She held out a hand to steady the older woman as she turned. Erica experienced a moment of dread when she noticed that the ancient English bulldog wasn't with her. "Is something wrong with General Lee?"

"No. No. It's not that. I heard something and I thought I'd warn you."

Erica tried not to grit her teeth in frustration. "Miss Wilkerson, I just resigned from the school board, but thank you for being concerned."

The older woman grabbed Erica's hand. "Hush up and listen to me. I just got a call from . . ." She hesitated. "We'll just say a friend," she said primly. "Sara Bell Hogg has called a special emergency meeting of the Women's League. She is going to petition the league to have Judith's membership revoked."

Erica stared at the woman and wondered if perhaps the poor thing's memory was starting to slip. No one in her right mind would ever try to remove Judith Boyd's name from any membership. Judith was the sort of woman who always put in twice as many volunteer hours as anyone else. If there was a fundraiser to be held, Judith was the one to call. When she couldn't do the work herself, she knew the names of people to contact to get things done. "Miss Wilkerson, I'm sorry to have to ask, but are you certain you're not confusing the incident with the school board, rather than—" Before she could finish, the older woman grabbed her by the ear.

"Listen to me, you little sprout. Sara Bell is girding her loins for battle against your mother."

Erica wanted to laugh at the expression, but since Miss Wilkerson was still hanging on to her ear, she thought it was probably best not to antagonize her any further. She realized she was expected to say something. "What do you think I should do?" She wondered how many people were watching them from a distance.

"Rally the troops. Prepare your battle plan." She suddenly let go of Erica's ear. "I'd best get on back home. I need to get General Lee inside and batten down the hatches."

"I think you're mixing your metaphors," Erica said without thinking.

"Don't get sassy with me, young lady." She shook a bony finger at Erica. "I've known you ever since you were in diapers. I've paddled that bottom of yours more than once, and don't think I can't do it again."

"Yes, ma'am. I'm sorry." Erica kept her ears and bottom well out of Miss Wilkerson's reach. "I guess I'd best get on home and see if I can find out what's going on."

When Erica reached the house, nothing had changed. Both Gerti and Judith were still in their rooms. She decided she would wait and face them rather than continuing to avoid the confrontation that was inevitable. Within a matter of minutes, nearly everyone in town would know about her resignation from the school board. She went to the kitchen to make coffee. It had just begun to perk when the phone in her mother's room rang. A couple of minutes later, Gerti's phone rang. Then the cell phone clipped to her jeans began to ring. She glanced at the screen and saw Alice's name. For a moment she debated whether or not to answer, but she really wanted to talk to her. Her hand shook as she answered.

"It's me," Alice said in a near whisper. "You're going to get a call in a couple of minutes. Don't answer it. In fact, get in your car right now and go somewhere for the rest of the day."

"What? Alice, I've already been asked to leave the school board. So—"

"For once, will you please listen to me?" The call-waiting click sounded. "Damn, Erica, why didn't you tell me about this before?" It was obvious that Alice was pissed.

"I just found out this morning. I didn't know they were going to ask me to resign."

"I'm not talking about the school board." She made a sound of frustration. "I don't have time to explain. Just leave now." She hung up.

Erica's phone began to ring. She tried to ignore it, but curiosity got the better of her and she answered. The caller was Dorothy Lentz, the secretary of the Women's League. She seemed nervous as she rushed through her message.

"Erica, we'll be holding a special meeting this morning at nine and we would like for all members to be present. I have several calls to make so . . . um . . . good-bye." She hung up.

Erica went to her room and sat on the side of her bed. She and Gerti, like most women in town, were dues-paying members of the league, but it had been years since either of them had actually attended a meeting. Only the officers regularly attended. The other members were little more than worker bees who showed up to help at raffles and other fundraising events. Would they be petty enough to ask Judith to resign because of her? She shook her head. That didn't make any sense.

She heard someone moving around and went back to the kitchen to find Gerti pouring herself a cup of coffee.

"What's got Dorothy in such a tizzy?" Gerti asked.

Erica poured her coffee and took several sips. She started to tell Gerti about what had happened with the school board and about Miss Wilkerson's visit, but Judith walked in humming.

"You're certainly in a good mood this morning," Gerti said.

"It's going to be a glorious day," Judith said and continued to hum.

Erica realized that neither Gerti nor Judith had an inkling as to what had been going on. She wondered if perhaps Miss Wilkerson was wrong. "Did Dorothy say what the meeting was about?"

"She went stupid fast when I asked her what it was about," Gerti replied.

The smile on Judith's face seemed to brighten. She poured her coffee.

"Mom, do you know?" Erica knew she should mention what had been happening, but she wanted to put it off as long as possible, and besides, Judith was in such a good mood, she must know something Erica didn't.

"I suspect I do," she called merrily over her shoulder before leaving the room.

"Now, what is she up to?" Gerti asked.

Erica sat down at the table and quickly told her about Miss Wilkerson's visit.

Afterward, Gerti shook her head. "She must be confused. Even Sara Bell wouldn't be that goofy. Besides, the banquet is tomorrow and Judith is in charge. It would be crazy for them to upset everything at the last minute."

"Then it may have something to do with me." She told her about the experience with Walt.

Gerti frowned. "Who could have started that rumor?"

"Well, it's not exactly a rumor," Erica reminded her. "I have no idea who else could have known." She took a deep breath to tell Gerti about her resigning, but Gerti started talking before she could.

"What about Rae?" Gerti asked. "Maybe she told."

"No. She wouldn't have done that. She didn't agree with me staying the closet, but she understood the need for me to be careful."

Gerti tapped her fingers. "Maybe you and I should go on over to the center a little early and see if we can get to the bottom of this before Judith gets over there."

"What are we going to do if Miss Wilkerson is right?"

Gerti glanced toward Judith's room. "Well, let's pray that the old girl is wrong this time. I don't want to think about what it will do to Judith if she's not."

As Gerti went to get her purse, Erica promised herself that she would wait to tell Gerti about the school board until after this meeting was over. One problem at a time was enough.

It was around eight forty when Gerti and Erica strolled over to the community center and already there were forty or fifty women milling around outside.

"I wonder why everyone is standing out here," Gerti asked.

They soon discovered that the doors were still locked. Tina Delaney joined them.

"What's going on?" Erica asked. "Isn't anyone with a key here?" The coffee she had drunk was now trying to burn a hole in her stomach. She wished she had taken the time to eat a slice of toast or something.

"The entire board except your mom is already inside," Tina said. "They said they aren't letting anyone else in until nine."

"Do you know what's going on?" The heat rising off the sidewalk was making Erica feel dizzy.

Tina shook her head. "There are a lot of rumors, but I don't know if any of them are true." She gave Erica a look that suggested she might have heard rumors other than the one dealing with the Women's League.

"What are they saying?" Gerti asked.

Tina seemed to withdraw slightly. "Miss Gerti, you know how people like to talk. I'm sure it's nothing."

Erica tried to convince herself that it was nothing, but her brain wouldn't quite believe the bluff.

Gerti looked as though she was about to say more but let it go. They stood in silence for a few minutes before Judith arrived.

"Why on earth is everyone standing out here in this heat?" Judith asked. "It's going to fry your brains for sure."

"They aren't letting anyone else in until nine," Gerti replied.

Judith looked at her watch. "How asinine can they get? Come on, I have a key." She started making her way to the door. As soon as she unlocked it, she motioned for the group to follow her inside.

As Erica slowly shuffled her way toward the door, she couldn't help but think that her life was about to change. From high overhead, the roar of an airplane's engine made her think of Rae, who would be safely tucked away in her New York apartment by now.

CHAPTER FORTY-ONE

The board members of the Women's League were seated at a table positioned on an undersized stage at the front of the room. By the time everyone had made their way into the building there was already an uproar at the front of the small room. Judith and Sara Bell were going head to head. Dorothy Lentz sat at the table with the other four board members. All looked as if they'd had sour apples for breakfast. Alice Goodman, who wasn't on the board, sat off to one side. When she saw Erica, her lips tightened.

Erica waved, but Alice turned away and stared straight ahead.

"Looks as though the free-for-all started early," Tina said.

Gerti grabbed Erica and Tina by the arm. "Hold on to your hats, girls, we're headed for the front line." She pushed and squeezed them through until they were standing at the stage. "Settle down," Gerti yelled. A hush fell over the room. "Now, let's get this show on the road. I've got work to do."

A small chorus of agreement ran through the crowd.

Erica had never seen Sara Bell Hogg look so flustered. Not even after her encounter with Rae. Sara Bell, the league president, stared out at the large gathering before sending a withering glower toward Dorothy.

When she didn't move, Gerti again took matters into her own hands. "Sara Bell, call this meeting to order."

After one last almost desperate glance to the other board members, she picked up the gavel and gave a couple of half-hearted raps on the table.

Judith moved around her and took her seat at the opposite end of the table. The smile was no longer on her face.

Tina had found an empty chair and brought it to the front for Gerti. As the crowd settled, Tina and Erica moved to the side to stand along the wall.

Rather than call the meeting to order, Sara Bell cleared her throat a couple of times before she spoke in a voice so low that the women in the back began to shout out that they couldn't hear. She reluctantly picked up the table mike. "I was saying that there has been a mistake. This meeting wasn't intended to be a complete membership meeting but rather an emergency meeting of the board."

A rumble of complaints poured from the crowd.

Sara Bell looked fiercely at Dorothy again as she gaveled for silence. "I apologize. I know what an inconvenience this has been for everyone."

A few women started to stand when Alice stood and called out in a clear, loud voice, "Madam President, I would like to say a few words."

Sara Bell paled as she turned to Alice. It was obvious that she didn't want to yield the floor. "Um . . . well, Mayor Goodman . . . um . . . since this isn't an official meeting of the entire membership . . ."

Dorothy Lentz jumped up.

Sensing something juicy was about to start, everyone quieted down.

"I make a motion," Dorothy began, "that since the majority of the members-at-large are present that we declare this an official meeting of the entire membership and move on with the matter at hand."

"I second the motion," Judith declared before Sara Bell could say anything.

Even over the noise in the room, Erica clearly heard Gerti say, "If Sara Bell doesn't grow some big ones soon, she's going to lose control of this crowd."

Sara Bell obviously heard her also because she glared at Gerti and pounded the gavel sharply. "Fine," she said. "But I'm telling everyone right now that I'm not going to sit up here and put up with all these disruptions. If the members-at-large can't control themselves I'll have the sergeant-at-arms clear the room." She shook the gavel. "That's the only warning I intend on giving you all."

The crowd roared with laughter. Everyone knew that Luella Brock, the sergeant-at-arms, was at least seventy, and it was up for speculation as to whether her weight was higher than her age. Upon hearing Sara Bell's ultimatum, Luella gave the crowd a fierce look before cackling with laughter. Then she began to pose as though she were competing for the Miss Olympia contest. With each new wave of laughter, she became more outrageous. Finally, Sara Bell had put up with all she intended to. She pounded the gavel so hard that poor Luella jumped and almost fell.

"Can we dispense with all the mumbo-jumbo and get on with this?" Gerti yelled. "Alice, what have you got to say?"

Sara Bell threw the gavel down and slumped back into her seat.

Alice turned to the crowd. "Actually, Dorothy has already said all I had to say. I simply wanted to request that the membership be allowed to stay for the meeting." She returned to her seat.

Erica wished she'd had an opportunity to talk to Alice before the meeting. Alice had said that the events with the school board had nothing to do with this meeting, but what else could it be?

The board members all sat staring at the table.

After a long moment, Gerti chimed in again. "Hell's bells. Will somebody please tell us what's going on here?"

When Sara Bell continued to stare at the table, Inez Gutierrez, the vice president, leaned forward. "This meeting was called with the intention of asking Judith Boyd to resign from the board."

A collective gasp ran through the room. Erica watched her mother's expression change from irritation to confusion, to dismay and finally to annoyance. "On what grounds?" Judith demanded.

When Sara Bell continued to show no indication that she intended to take charge of the meeting, Inez reached for the gavel and called for order.

"On what grounds?" Judith asked again as the buzz in the room died down.

Inez glanced at the rest of the board, but they continued to stare at the table. Finally, she put down the gavel. "Since it was Sara Bell who came forward with the charge, I think she should be the one to explain." She sat back and folded her arms.

Cornered, Sara Bell's gaze jumped around the room. Cornered, she was careful to avoid eye contact with Judith, Gerti or Erica.

"Well?" Judith stood to confront Sara Bell.

"I never meant for this to be a public meeting," Sara Bell muttered, causing protests from the back again. "I said, I never meant for everyone and their brother to be here," she shouted. "I just wanted you to resign from the luncheon committee."

"Why?" Judith asked.

Sara Bell finally turned to her. "Because," she answered hotly, "you lied and tried to deceive not only this board but the entire town."

Erica tensed as Judith stood up. She wasn't looking forward to being caught in the middle of a catfight between those two.

"Sara Bell Hogg, how dare you call me a liar."

"Well, if the shoe fits."

"The only shoe that's about to be fit is the one I'm going to put up your rear end if you don't start explaining yourself," Judith said.

Sara Bell reached beneath the table and pulled out a large beige purse. After a moment of digging, she produced a book with a red binder.

Gerti was suddenly on her feet. "What are you doing with my diary?" she roared as she charged toward the stage.

Erica was so shocked it took her a moment to react. By the time she reached the stage, Gerti was already trying to crawl up onto it.

The members were certainly getting their dues' worth this go-around, Erica decided as she tried to convince Gerti to sit down, but the older woman wasn't listening. She was still trying to climb onto the stage. Finally, in desperation, Erica wrapped her arms around her grandmother's waist, picked her up and held her until Gerti stopped struggling.

Inez had practically pounded a hole through the table trying to get the room under control.

"Grams," Erica shouted over the uproar. "Will you please stop it before you hurt me?"

Gerti instantly relaxed. As soon as Erica released her grip, Gerti stomped down on her instep and took off again.

Erica hobbled after her and caught a smack upside the head from Gerti's purse. If something wasn't done to defuse Gerti's anger, she was either going to kill herself, Erica or Sara Bell, or possibly all three. Since the book seemed to the problem, Erica took a running start, jumped on the stage and grabbed the book before anyone could stop her. Then she grabbed Inez's gavel and slapped the table so hard the handle on the gavel broke. The head came back and popped her sharply on the arm.

"Sit down and shut up," she screamed as her arm throbbed with pain. The room fell silent. "I've had enough of this bull." Gerti was still standing. "Grams, please sit down. In fact, everybody sit down, please."

Surprisingly everyone obeyed.

Erica turned to the board members at the table. "Now, I want an explanation of what the heck is going on." When no one spoke, she continued, "All right if this has anything to do with the school board asking me to resign because I'm a lesbian, then this is bull. It has nothing to do with my mother."

From the sudden buzz that echoed around the room, she deduced that this meeting didn't, in fact, having anything to do with the school board. She glanced at Alice, who looked as though the grim reaper had just tapped her on the shoulder. Gerti and Judith were both staring at her as if she had lost her mind.

She shook her head. She'd worry about all that later. Right now she needed to get this mess straightened out. She held up the book. "Who does this belong to?"

"It's mine," Judith and Gerti answered at the same time.

Erica looked between the two. "In that case, I suppose it's mine too." She opened the front cover and read aloud, "'This is the diary of Howard Franklin'."

"It's mine," Gerti persisted as she stood and reached for it.

"Not until I find out what's going on," Erica replied as she turned to Judith. "If this belongs to Grams, how did you get it?"

Judith looked guilty. "I found it in her room."

A new round of accusations sprang to life between Judith and Gerti.

"If you two don't sit down and be quiet, I'll tote you from this room," Erica shouted. They both hushed, but they continued to stare daggers at each other.

Erica then asked Sara Bell how she managed to get the diary.

Sara Bell studied her perfectly manicured nails. "Judith gave it to me last night. She said she was going to have it published to pass out at the dedication of the statue that the city council wanted to have placed in the town square."

A small ripple of excitement ran through the audience. It took Erica a moment to remember that only a few people had known about the project, so this was news to most everyone here. Erica held up her hand. "I'm sorry. I'm confused. Was there something in here that caused you to suggest that Mom be removed from the board?"

Gerti started to rise until Erica gave her a warning look.

Sara Bell paled slightly and licked her lips. "I never intended to make the information public."

Erica tried to control her temper. "Then what did you intend?"

"I just wanted Judith to retire from the luncheon banquet and . . . and . . . I didn't want that statue to be put in the town square."

"Why not?" Erica asked.

Alice suddenly stood. "I think perhaps it would be best for us to stop right here."

Erica frowned as she looked around. Both Gerti and Sara Bell seemed as though they were on the verge of tears. She glanced out over the crowd. If she told them to leave now, she doubted they would. Even if they did, there would be all sorts of gossip and rumors, and nothing in the diary could be as bad as what would be floating around town within two hours. She rubbed her forehead and remembered the conversation she'd had with Rae about the confusing events that had occurred on the *Titanic*. If there was something in the diary that was embarrassing to the family neither her mom nor grandmother would ever forgive her. She looked down at Gerti, who was now staring straight ahead. After a moment, she turned to Alice. "Do you know what's in here?"

Alice slowly nodded.

"What should I do?" Erica asked.

Gerti suddenly stood up. "That's my property and I want it back." Then she grabbed her chest and slowly crumbled to the floor.

CHAPTER FORTY-TWO

Erica didn't remember jumping off the stage, but she found herself fighting her way to her grandmother.

"Grams," she cried as she knelt beside her. Suddenly she was grateful for all the life-saving courses she had been required to take as a member of the volunteer fire department. The slight movement of Gerti's chest told her Gerti was still breathing. Erica pressed her fingers against the side of Gerti's neck and felt a rapid pulse. As an added precaution she gently pinched one of Gerti's fingers and watched closely it quickly regained its color. That was a good indicator that blood was still being circulated through Gerti's body. She carefully brushed the stray lock of hair from her face. "You're going to okay, Grams. Can you hear me? Please, Grams, talk to me." She began to cry. "Oh, God, this is all my fault."

Judith knelt on the other side. "Mama, please speak to me. You're going to be all right. You hang in there. An ambulance is on its way." She lifted one of Gerti's hands and pressed it to her face.

The five minutes it took the ambulance to arrive seemed like an eternity. The ride to the hospital was one of the longest Erica could ever remember. Tina's car had been parked nearby, so Erica, Judith, Alice and Sara Bell all piled into the small lime-green Beetle and headed to the hospital. Erica sat in the front passenger seat. She could hear Sara Bell consoling Judith. Whatever animosity had existed between them only minutes ago was temporarily forgotten. It would undoubtedly reappear in a few days or weeks, but for now Judith was a friend and neighbor in need.

Gerti was taken directly to the emergency room. Her family and friends were sent around to the front to the waiting room. Erica tried to handle the admitting procedure but quickly discovered she didn't know enough about Gerti's insurance to answer the necessary questions. She had to go get her mother.

By the time they finished with the paperwork and went back to the waiting room, it was packed with people from all over town who had heard the news and rushed over to be with them. The atmosphere was no longer that of titillating suspense. These folks were here out of respect and genuine concern. Even Jimmy had left her restaurant to come and wait on news about Gerti.

Alice sat by Erica and held her hand. For once, she didn't seem to be worried about what someone else might think.

When the doctor finally came out, he stopped and looked around in surprise.

"How is she?" Judith and Erica asked as one. Several people moved toward him.

He held up a hand. "Miss Gerti is doing fine. We've already taken her to a room where she's resting."

"What happened?" Judith asked. "Was it her heart? I thought she was as strong as an ox."

"It wasn't her heart," he assured her. "She mentioned that she hadn't eaten breakfast. I think she merely fainted. I've scheduled a battery of tests, but I can tell you now that her heart is fine. There are no obvious signs of a stroke." He stopped. "I can't be absolutely certain until I get the test results, but as of right now, I don't see anything that would suggest a problem."

"When can we see her?" Erica asked.

"You and Judith can go back now, but I don't want a lot of other people going in." He turned to the group. "I know you all want to see her, but I have to ask that you give her time to rest. I'm keeping her overnight, and I'm asking that only family members go in."

There were understanding nods as Erica and Judith followed him back to the room where Gerti rested. Erica was the first one through the door. She was dumbfounded to see Gerti sitting up in bed. Her dismay quickly turned to irritation as Gerti fell back onto the bed and assumed her *I'm dying* act. Erica fought the urge to reveal her grandmother's charade, but she intended to speak to her later and she'd better have a danged good explanation for scaring them half to death. She stood to the side as Judith rushed in and planted kisses on Gerti's forehead.

"Oh, Mother. How are you feeling?" She continued to fuss over her until Gerti almost blew her act by pushing her away.

Erica stepped to the far side of the bed and carefully avoided the wires trailing off monitors as she leaned down to kiss her grandmother. She was so angry her voice shook. "You old faker," she whispered. "I'm on to you."

"Judith," Gerti said weakly. "Would you go get me some ice chips, please?"

Judith grabbed the small water pitcher from the bedside stand and rushed out.

As soon as the door closed behind her Gerti sat up. "You're not going to rat me out, are you?"

Erica glared at her. "What were you thinking? You nearly scared us to death. How could you do that?"

"I couldn't let Sara Bell tell everyone what was in the diary."

Erica rubbed her forehead. "Grams, don't you think it's time we got all this stuff out into the open? What could possibly be in that diary that was so bad that you faked a heart attack?"

"It wasn't a heart attack," Gerti corrected. "I collapsed."

"You nearly scared me and Mom to death." Her voice was growing louder. Gerti shushed her.

"Did you hear all those nice things your mother said?" Gerti asked. "I never knew she cared so much."

"Grams, she loves you. We both love you." She flung her arm out. "Hell, half the town is sitting out there in the waiting room worried sick about you."

Gerti at least had the decency to look embarrassed. "Well, I knew that you both loved me. But now I think Judith would actually miss me if I keeled over for good."

"You're impossible."

Gerti reached beneath the sheet and pulled out the diary.

"How in God's name did you manage to get that?" Erica demanded.

"You had it in your hand when you knelt down beside me. You left it on the floor and in all the excitement I just sort of slipped it under my shirt." She handed the diary to Erica. "I want you to take this and put it in a safe deposit box that your mother can't get access to." She continued to hang onto the book. "But first I want you to swear on my life that you won't read it."

"Grams! Enough already."

"I mean it."

There was a noise at the door and the diary quickly disappeared beneath the sheet.

For the next several minutes, Erica stood quietly by as her mother slowly fed chipped ice to Gerti. When the nurse came to chase them out of the room, Gerti called Erica back. As soon as they were alone she pulled out the diary. "Remember, you swore on my life," Gerti hissed.

"I did *not* swear," Erica said. Seeing the desperate look in her grandmother's eyes, she gave in. "All right, if it means that much to you, I won't read it." She carefully tucked the binder into the top of her jeans and arranged her shirt to hide it as best as possible.

Back out in the waiting room she sat quietly for a few minutes before she turned to Alice. "I need a cup of coffee. Would you mind going to the cafeteria with me?"

For the briefest instant, it seemed as though Alice might not, but she finally nodded.

As soon as they were out of sight of the others in the waiting room, Erica pulled the diary from beneath her shirt. "Will you please put this in your bag?" she whispered.

Alice frowned when she saw what it was. "Where did you get that? You didn't have it earlier."

"It's a long story. I'll tell you later. Just promise me you won't look at it or read any of it."

"I don't have to read it. I already know what's in it."

Erica blinked. In all the excitement, she'd forgotten that Alice had said she knew what was in the diary. She stared at the mysterious book. She had promised Gerti she wouldn't read it, but she hadn't agreed not to ask anyone else about what was so important in it.

Alice seemed to be reading her mind as she took the diary and slipped it into her bag. "You have my word I won't tell anyone. Not even you." She smiled slightly. "Do you still want that coffee?"

"Actually, I do."

They went to the cafeteria and each got a coffee. Alice surprised her by motioning to a table. "Let's sit in here for a while. They'll call us if there's any change in Gerti's condition."

"I'm fairly sure Gerti is going to be fine." Erica tried to keep the sarcasm from her voice.

Alice laughed softly. "I won't say I agree with her tactics, but the old girl sure knows how to stop a runaway train."

"No one would dare challenge Mom's right to host the luncheon now."

"Heck, right now they're all feeling so guilty, they'll probably let her host next month's luncheon as well," Alice said as she lifted the lid off the Styrofoam cup.

"She's lucky she didn't break her neck falling down like that."

"I never told you, but right after I came to Whitehall to live, Gerti took me to lunch at Jimmy's." Alice stared into her coffee. "Just out of the blue she came over and asked me. I have to admit, she intimidated me. She was practically Whitehall royalty."

"Lord, don't ever tell her that," Erica said. "There would really be no living with her then."

"She didn't ask a lot of questions. She talked about the town and people who lived here. Not gossip, just general information."

She looked at Erica. "It took me a while to realize that what she had basically done that day was make me a member of the community. If Gerti Boyd approved of me, then I was obviously okay." Alice gave Erica's hand a quick squeeze. "What I'm trying to say is that she'll always be very special to me."

Erica blinked back the rush of emotion that swept through her. "The school board asked me to resign this morning."

Alice gave a surprised intake of breath. "I'd completely forgotten to ask you about that. What on earth for?"

"Rumors about my lifestyle started circulating, and apparently parents started calling in and complaining."

"Oh, I don't believe that for one moment. I'll bet you ten bucks Ramona Cox is behind this."

"I won't take that bet, because I think you're right."

"That woman has been on a crusade of some sort ever since she arrived. Personally, I think she's trying to work herself into a position where she can influence the zoning board to change the restrictions on that land she owns."

"I don't know," Erica said. "Nothing seems to make sense anymore."

Alice leaned forward. "I've been doing a lot of thinking these past few days. I know Whitehall is a rural community, but with increasing coverage of television, movies and the Internet, that doesn't mean the same as it did twenty or thirty years ago. I can understand how maybe twenty years ago no one would have noticed you're gay, but today I don't get it. Why didn't people already know about you?"

Erica grinned. "Are you saying I'm that obvious?"

"Oh, please. You're about as obvious as the back end of a jackass. Just look at you. Your standard wardrobe is a man's white shirt, jeans and boots. I've never heard a single story of you dating anyone. How many other women in Whitehall do you know with that combination?"

Erica shrugged.

"All I'm saying is that no one said anything, because no one cared."

"Whoa!" Erica held both hands up. "Are you, Miss I-Can't-Come-Out-Because-it-Will-Destroy-My-Career, now saying no one would care? Because if that's where you're headed, let me remind you that I was asked to resign this morning."

Alice twirled the lid that was lying on the table. "I still think it would hurt my career, because I'm not you. Your family is so . . . so . . . cherished. There's no other word for it. Practically every family in this community has been helped by your family at one time or another. People don't forget that."

"They forgot it this morning." Erica glanced away. "I've never been so humiliated in my life. It was as if I could feel everyone in town staring at me and judging me when I left Larry's office this morning. Allen, Grady and Henrietta just sat there. They never said a word."

"Maybe they were expecting you to put up a bigger fight."

"What?"

Alice pushed her coffee away. "When have you ever just rolled over on something you believe in? When you suggested the grade school needed computers and Grady disagreed because it would cost too much, you didn't just say, 'Okay, we won't bother to get any,' and let it go. You went out, contacted every organization in town and started a fund drive. Without you there would be no computers for the kids in grade school to use."

"So what are you saying?"

"I'm saying that if your position on the school board meant so little to you that you never even bothered to challenge their decision, then maybe they think they've made the right choice." Alice stood as she replaced the lid on her coffee. "We should be getting back."

They left the cafeteria and returned to their seats in the waiting room. Most of the crowd had left after they received verification that Gerti was going to be all right. Within an hour only Judith, Erica, Alice, Sara Bell and Tina remained.

Arthur arrived a while later to pick Sara Bell up. "You call me if you need anything," Sara Bell said as she hugged Judith. She then turned to Erica and gave her a hug. "You take care of your mother."

"I will," Erica promised.

After a while, a nurse came out to tell them that two of them could go in at a time to visit Gerti. Erica told Alice to go in her place this time. As soon as they were gone, Tina moved over next to Erica. "Do you know what's going on?"

Erica shook her head. "No. Not really. I'm beginning to think that we've all slipped over the edge." She waved her hand. "Maybe the entire town has finally lost that last thin thread of sanity that we've been clinging to all these years."

Tina was silent for a moment. Something in her hesitation made Erica take notice.

"Some of your ancestors were on the *Titanic*, weren't they?" she asked as she recalled the conversation she'd had with Rae.

Tina didn't seem surprised at the question. She merely nodded slightly. "Yes."

Erica suddenly didn't want to know what was in the diary.

"It's sort of odd, don't you think?" Tina glanced at her.

"What's odd?"

"The way the folks here all come together when there's a problem, but they didn't hesitate to ask you to leave the school board once they found out you were a lesbian."

"I suppose they were just doing what they thought was best for the town."

"That's bull and you know it."

Erica didn't know what to say. She was afraid that if she started thinking about it then she might walk out the door and never return. She loved Whitehall and all its quirky residents.

Tina squeezed Erica's arm. "I'm sorry. I didn't mean to upset you."

Erica shook her head. "I'm just tired of everything being in such an uproar." She looked at Tina. "Do you know what's in that diary?"

Tina stood. "I'm going to the cafeteria for a cup of coffee. Can I bring you back something?"

"A cup of sanity would be nice."

Tina smiled and winked. "I'd probably have to drive all the way into Corpus to find any of that."

CHAPTER FORTY-THREE

Judith insisted on remaining at the hospital. Erica stayed with her even though she knew Gerti had faked the entire incident.

"I'll get Joanie to help me bring your car over in the morning," Alice said as she took Erica's car keys. "Call me if you need anything before then."

Erica nodded. As she looked at her she realized that any chance for them to be together had been lost that day. The tears that had been threatening all day suddenly spilled over.

Alice misunderstood their cause. "Oh, honey, she'll be all right. You know Gerti is a tough old bird." She hugged Erica.

The contact was too much. Erica pulled back. "You shouldn't do that," she whispered. "People will talk."

Alice seemed surprised and then saddened as she nodded slightly and left.

Once they were alone, Judith and Erica stood in the middle of the waiting room for a long moment. "Let's go get something to eat," Judith said at last. "Otherwise, we'll be collapsing."

They walked to the cafeteria together, where they each chose a salad before finding a table toward the back of the room.

As they picked at their food, Judith began to talk. "What happened with the school board this morning?"

Erica told her what she knew and even told her about her conversation with Walt earlier at the restaurant.

Judith slid the food aside. "I wonder who started that rumor."

"I don't know, and truthfully, except for any trouble it may cause you and Grams, I really don't care. The closet was beginning to close in on me."

Judith stacked her packets of crackers. "Don't worry about us. We'll be fine. I'm sorry you felt as though you couldn't come to me sooner."

"No. I'm sorry. You've always been there for me. I guess I was a little ashamed that I hadn't turned out more like you. Camille was always so pretty and liked all that girly stuff."

Judith nodded. "Camille is pretty, but God bless her, the girl can't count to twenty without taking off her shoes."

"Mom!"

"Well, it's the truth and you know it. The poor thing struggled so hard in school. She studied twice as hard as you ever did and still barely passed." She continued to play with the crackers. "That's why I never pushed her as hard as I did you." She shrugged. "I guess it's my fault you turned out the way you did."

Erica set her nearly untouched salad to the side. "No. It's not your fault. It's not a matter of blame."

"I've always wondered if you and Camille would have been better off if I'd remarried." She glanced at Erica. "I had other offers, you know."

She couldn't help but smile. "Mom, I'm sure you had plenty of offers." She realized she'd never asked her mom why she hadn't remarried and did so.

"I supposed I was afraid that I'd make another mistake."

"Why did you leave Dad?" Erica had only the slightest memory of her father. In fact, they were so dim she couldn't be positive if she really remembered them or if she had simply made them up. Judith had never liked talking about him. After the divorce, he never came around.

For a moment, it seemed as though she didn't intend to answer. "As you know Thomas wasn't from around here. It was the year after Daddy and the boys died that Thomas came to Whitehall. His car had broken down. He didn't have the money to pay for the repairs so he went to work out at Mr. Ayer's ranch. One day he came in to the store to pick up some supplies for the Ayers and that's when I met him." She smiled. "He had black, curly hair and the bluest eyes I've ever seen. I fell for him the first time I saw him." She glanced at Erica. "You look a lot like him." She continued to stack the cracker packets. "Mother didn't like him, of course. She kept telling me to stay away from him, but I was a silly girl and thought I knew everything." She shrugged. "One thing led to another and the next thing I know we're running off to Mexico to get married. I was only sixteen. I know now that it almost killed Mother, but after we came back and told her we were married, she took it pretty well. She gave Thomas a job at the store and started giving me my share of the profits. Up until then a certain percentage of the profits had always gone into a separate account for each of us kids. Thomas didn't like living here, so we moved to Houston. After that, nothing seemed to go well for us. He drank a lot and couldn't keep a job. Every month Mother would send us a check and he'd go on a bender. Finally, I decided I'd had enough. I wrote Mother and told her to stop sending me my share of the profits. I had her open an account for you and Camille and put my share into it. I thought that if the money wasn't handed to him every month, he would grow up and start taking some responsibility for his family." She shook her head. "When he found out what I'd done he was so angry. Then one night he just left and never came back. I called Mother and she sent me the money to come home on. I filed for a divorce and took back my own name." She stopped for a moment. "Maybe I shouldn't have done that."

Erica rubbed her forehead. "Mom, us not having the same last name didn't turn me into a lesbian."

"Then what did?" Judith hissed as she suddenly crushed the crackers beneath her fist.

"What made you straight?"

Judith looked at her as if she might have lost her mind. "Well, that's the way I'm supposed to be."

"And I'm exactly as I'm supposed to be," Erica replied.

Judith studied her for a long moment. "It's that simple, huh?"

"I'm afraid so. There's no one to blame, nothing that caused it, and I sure as heck didn't choose it."

"Then I guess I can't blame it on your crazy grandmother," Judith replied wryly.

"No, you shouldn't, but after today if it would make you feel better to blame her, I'd probably back you up on that one."

"It nearly scared me to death when she collapsed." She brushed a hand over her eyes. "I don't know what I'd do without that crazy old coot."

Erica knew she shouldn't betray Gerti's trust, but she wasn't going to sit here and let her mom worry. "I need to tell you something about Grams."

"Don't bother. I know she faked the entire thing."

"What!"

"I had my suspicions when I noticed that damn diary had disappeared off the floor where you dropped it beside her. She must have scooped it up when we were distracted by the arrival of the ambulance. Then the doctor couldn't find anything wrong with her. The clincher was when she called you back into the room and you came out of there walking like you had a board up your butt. I figured she had pulled you into her little charade."

"I wanted to tell you, but—"

Judith waved away her protests.

"Mom, what's in the diary? I promised Grams I wouldn't read it."

"I wish I knew."

"You mean you don't?"

"No. I didn't have time to read it. I saw what it was and wanted to rub Sara Bell's nose in it, so I told her to read it." She made a small face. "I suppose I should have read it first."

Erica struggled not to roll her eyes.

They sat in silence for a moment before Judith spoke again. "I can put some pressure on the school board if you want to stay on it."

"No. Don't do that. I don't want to be there if they don't want me."

"You know they'll come around as soon as they need something," Judith said. "Well, they can look elsewhere for their funds. I'm not going to give that group another red cent."

"Mom, don't be that way. You know most of them were only doing what they felt was right. I know Larry felt bad about the whole mess. In fact, I think everyone except Ramona Cox was upset."

"I've heard that she intends to run for mayor again next year."

"I doubt she'll be able to defeat Alice."

Judith looked around discreetly. "Maybe not if those same rumors were to get started about her."

Erica froze. "Why would they?"

"Erica, please. Give me some credit."

"Have you heard other people talking?"

"No, but I'm sure it's only a matter of time now."

"But we tried so hard to not be seen together. How did you know?"

"I suppose it's the way you look at her sometimes." She patted Erica's hand. "And the way she was looking at you tonight."

"Well, you're wrong on your last observation. She ended the relationship a few days ago."

"Pooh! She may have said go away, but I saw the way she looked at you out there. That woman loves you as surely as I'm sitting here."

"She loves her job more. I don't know what she would do if people found out and asked her to resign."

Judith tapped her fingers on the table. "I think it's time Mother and I settled our differences and joined forces." She stood up. "Come on. Let's go drag the old warmonger out of bed."

When they entered Gerti's room a few minutes later, she was

sitting up in bed watching television. As soon as she heard them she started to scoot back down into the bed.

"Give up the charades, old woman," Judith said as she reached over to turn off the television. "I know you're a big faker."

Gerti glared at Erica.

"I figured it out all on my own, so don't start pelting us with those eye daggers," Judith said.

"What is it now?" Gerti demanded as she stopped her pretense and sat up.

"It's time for you to tell us what's in that diary," Judith said as she found a comfortable spot on the end of Gerti's bed. "Erica, pull that chair over here beside the bed." She turned to Gerti. "All right, start talking."

CHAPTER FORTY-FOUR

The three women talked for hours. There were a couple of minor battles of will, but by the time they were finished, they were in agreement about what needed to be done.

They started with Gerti checking herself out of the hospital late that afternoon. Doctor Lewis, the physician on call, finally agreed to let her go, but only after she promised she would make an appointment with her own doctor.

As soon as Gerti was released, Erica called a cab. Back home they worked together to prepare dinner and for once even Judith forgot about her figure and ate a hearty meal.

After dinner, Judith started making calls to check on the last-minute preparations for the women's luncheon. Since Gerti's fake collapse ended the meeting before a decision had been reached as to whether or not she should be removed from the board, Judith continued with the planning as though nothing had happened.

Gerti disappeared into her room, saying she needed to make

some phone calls.

Erica went to her room and called Larry Collins. "I've changed my mind," she said as soon as he answered. "I'm not going to resign. If you want me off the board, you're going to have to vote me off, and if you do I'm going to fight you on it."

There was an audible sigh from Larry. "Thank God you finally came to your senses. I told you this morning that I didn't want you to go. It's basically Ramona who's doing all the bellowing. As soon as she started talking about all the calls she received from parents—well, you know Grady—he folded like a cheap chair. Then Allen started waffling. Henrietta practically decked her." He hesitated a moment. "I was shocked when you gave in like that."

"You can tell the rest of the board that after thinking it over, I'm ready to hire a lawyer if necessary."

There was a lighter tone in Larry's voice. "I think we should meet again in the morning. Tomorrow will be a busy day for everyone, so I'll tell them to be here at eight. We should get this ironed out as quickly as possible. The longer it drags on, the more rumors there are going to be."

"Larry, I don't want any misunderstanding. I want you and everyone else to know that I'm a lesbian. I have been for as long as I can remember. It has never affected my job on the school board and I see no reason why it ever should." She stopped for a moment. "Do you?"

He didn't hesitate. "No, I don't, but there may be parents who see things differently."

"If that becomes a problem, then I'll ask for a town hall meeting. I want those parents to look me in the eye and tell me to leave."

After hanging up with Larry, she called Alice and told her what she had done.

Alice was silent for a long moment before she finally said, "I'm proud of you. I wish I had your courage."

"It wasn't courage," Erica said. "I'm pissed at myself for giving in to my own homophobia. How can I expect others to respect me if I don't respect myself?"

"Do you want me to bring your keys over?"

"No, we'll bump into each other sometime tomorrow and I have a spare set around here somewhere if I need to use the car before then."

After hanging up she began to empty her pockets, intending to take a shower. As she removed her cell phone, she remembered she had turned it off at the hospital. When she turned it on, she noticed a call from Rae. She called the number on the screen. Rae answered on the second ring.

"How is Gerti?" she asked before Erica even had a chance to speak.

"She's fine." Erica told her all about the meeting and how Gerti had brought it to an early ending.

"She's a clever old bird," Rae said through her laughter. "If I ever get into a jam, I'll have to remember that trick. Of course, with my luck, they'll just let me lie there and go on with the meeting."

"Ouch, that would be cold."

"I heard you had a problem with the school board."

Erica blinked in surprise. "Gosh, it didn't take you long to build your own gossip network."

"Tina called me."

"Tina?" Erica smiled as a thought hit her. "Isn't that interesting? How is it that Tina happened to have your phone number?"

"I never kiss and tell, but don't be too surprised if you walk into Jimmy's some morning and find me there."

"With one of those atrocious vegetable dishes in front of you, no doubt."

"I promised Jimmy that I would bring her a stack of vegetarian cookbooks on my next trip down."

"I can already hear Miss Wilkerson grumbling about a second Yankee invasion."

"No. I think she likes me. I'm doing some research on her family for her."

"You'd better not find anything but good old Confederate gray in her bloodline."

"Hey, I'm no fool." Rae hesitated. "Listen, are you okay with

275

that school board business?"

"Do you have time for a long story?"

"I've got until eight o'clock tomorrow morning," Rae said. "Tell me everything that's happened since I left."

The next morning Gerti, Judith and Erica went to Jimmy Kwan's for an early breakfast. There were a few curious stares and low mutters when they came in. The three ignored them as they sat at the table Jimmy pointed out.

Walt arrived with three cups of coffee. "Miss Gerti, I'm surprised to see you out and about so soon." He set the cups on the table.

"I'm a miracle of modern-day medicine, young man."

He smiled. "Yes, ma'am. What can I get for you all today?"

"I'm going to need something a little more substantial than my usual bowl of fruit," Gerti said. "I think I'll have one of those artery-clogging specials that Erica normally has."

Walt looked concerned. "Are you sure?" he asked.

Gerti squinted at him. "Do you know what the secret to a long life is?"

"No, ma'am. I guess not."

"The secret is not to piss off persnickety old women like me. Now hurry up and get my food. I have some serious butt-kicking to attend to."

He quickly took the other two orders and scurried off.

"Mother, you scared that poor kid half to death," Judith said as she stirred cream into her coffee.

"Oh, he'll get over it. That's what's wrong with this world—too many fainthearted people." She turned to Erica. "What time did you say you had to be at Larry's office?"

"At eight."

"Do you want me to go with you?"

"No, thanks. I need to do this on my own."

"You call me," Judith said, "if that Ramona Cox continues to give you trouble." She looked at Gerti. "When it comes to that woman, I wouldn't mind dispensing a little of that butt-kicking myself."

Walt soon appeared with their food. As they ate, several people stopped by to say good morning and to share their relief at Gerti's quick recovery.

They were almost finished with their meal when Judith suddenly gave a low curse.

"What's wrong?" Erica asked.

Judith was dabbing at the front of her dress. "I dropped jelly on my dress. Now I'll have to go home and change." She threw the napkin down. "I'd better hurry or I'll be late getting to the hall."

"Is there anything I can do to help?" Gerti asked.

"No. I can still make it if I hurry."

Judith stopped and took Erica's hand. "You call me if you need me."

"Thanks. I will."

Gerti and Erica finished their breakfast and afterward remained at the table drinking their coffee.

"Are you nervous?" Gerti asked.

"I guess I am a little, but not about confronting the board. I hope we can settle this and there aren't hard feelings afterward. Except for a few minor run-ins with Ramona, the members of this board have had a good working relationship and I'd like to maintain that."

"If everyone acts like adults, you can disagree and still preserve the respect you have for one another." Gerti tapped her fingers on the table. "You realize that you may not be allowed to stay on the board."

"I know, but at least I'll know I didn't just roll over and slink away." Her cell phone rang. She glanced at the screen. "Christ, it's Ed Raines." She answered the call. "Ed, I'm at Jimmy's. Where's the fire?" When she heard his reply she nearly dropped the phone as she jumped up. "Call Arthur for me." She turned to Gerti. "I want you to stay here."

"What's going on?" Gerti demanded.

"Our house is on fire."

Gerti paled. "Judith is there."

Erica started running and didn't slow down until she slid to a stop by the fire engine in front of her home. The fire seemed to be confined to the garage and the back wall. She looked around for her mom. When she didn't see her, she grabbed one of the spare hats and jackets from the truck and threw it on before she started running toward the house. Ed Raines grabbed her as she ran up on the porch. "My mom is in there."

"No, she isn't. I saw her back by the truck earlier."

Erica looked around frantically. "I don't see her."

About that time, Judith came from Miss Wilkerson's house carrying General Lee and helping the older woman along.

Erica ran to her. "Are you all right?" There were streaks of soot on Judith's ivory-colored jacket.

"Yes. I'm fine. They were worried about Miss Wilkerson's house, so I went to help her with General Lee." She set the dog down. "Where's Mother?"

"I told her stay at the restaurant." Erica turned to the house. "I need to go help them. Will you two be all right?"

"Yes. You go on, but please be careful."

As Erica ran to the engine and grabbed an ax, she struggled to ignore the sick feeling in her stomach. She couldn't allow herself to think about this being her home burning. Emotions led to mistakes. She had to stay calm and focus on the fire.

A crew was hosing down the front of the garage and house. The worst of the smoke seemed to be coming from the rear of the building. She ran around to the back and saw that the entire garage wall was ablaze. Arthur Hogg was struggling to snake a hose around from the opposite side. She rushed to help him.

"We need to get to the inside wall," he shouted.

She nodded. There was no time to go inside and unlock the back door. She used the ax to splinter it and allow them access. The kitchen wall against the garage was smoking. She motioned him forward and grabbed the hose as he fed it in. Carefully, she made her way farther into the room, spraying the wall as she went. Her lower legs grew warm from the heat radiating from the wall. She cursed herself for not taking time to pull on a pair of protective pants.

She was about halfway across the kitchen floor when suddenly a loud explosion filled the air and the wall slowly exploded toward her. She somehow managed to hang onto the hose as she dropped into a squat and prayed the oversized coat would cover her legs. A searing ember landed on her hand. She shook it off and tried to duck-walk her way out the door, all the while struggling to keep the water trained on the burning wall. Smoke filled the room. Her vision blurred as her eyes and nose began to run freely. Her throat ached so she could barely breathe. She continued to waddle toward the door, ever vigilant to keep her legs beneath the coat. An unusually loud crack sounded from over her head. She looked up in time to see a large chunk of ceiling start to collapse. By now, the smoke was so dense she could barely see, but she knew she had to be near the door. With what little breath she could muster, she turned and threw herself in the direction where she thought the door was. Almost immediately, the heat began to sear her legs. Her jeans were burning. For one long agonizing second she seemed to hang in the air, and then hands clamped down on back of her jacket. Someone threw her to the ground and something dark fell over her. She screamed as they began to roll her across the backyard. The last thing she remembered was hearing someone crying her name. It was Alice. As she drifted into a black haze of pain, she hung on to the sound of Alice's voice. Without it, she knew she might never make her way back.

CHAPTER FORTY-FIVE

Erica slowly floated toward the sound of Alice's voice calling her name. She tried to respond, but her throat was raw and no sound would come. The back of her hand felt as though a cigarette was being held against it. She tried to shake it off, but none of her muscles seemed to be working properly. The dim scream of sirens gradually grew louder. She pushed the noise away and concentrated on Alice's voice. With agonizing slowness the voice pulled her back to consciousness. When she opened her eyes, Alice was leaning over her. Tears fell on Erica's face. They felt cool. Her eyelids seemed to be made of lead. She struggled to keep them open.

"You're going to be okay," Alice said. "Hang on. The ambulance will be here in a minute."

Erica tried to turn to see the house, but there were too many people standing around. She realized that Gerti and Judith were also kneeling beside her; both had tears in their eyes. "House," she finally managed to croak.

Gerti patted her shoulder. "Don't worry about the house. The fire is under control. The damage was confined mainly to the garage and kitchen."

Judith held Erica's injured hand across her palm. "It was that damn dryer. I should have listened to you about it. I rinsed the jelly stain from my dress and threw it into the dryer. When I went back in a few minutes later, the wall behind the dryer was on fire."

The siren ground to a halt. Erica could hear the clank of a gurney hitting the ground.

Alice leaned closer. "I love you." She looked into Erica's eyes and smiled slightly. "I'm going to say this now, so you can't argue. When you're feeling better, I want you to come to live with me." A small ripple of surprise ran through the crowd as she kissed Erica's lips. "I want a life with you and if it means giving up my position as mayor, then so be it."

The paramedics swooped in and pushed everyone out of their way. Erica closed her eyes as they slipped an oxygen mask over her face. Was she hallucinating? She opened her eyes and twisted her head until she found Alice standing between Gerti and Judith. As she stared at the three of them standing arm-in-arm, she tried to smile. God help anyone who had to battle those three. The sharp prick of a needle stung her arm. She lay back and closed her eyes.

Two hours later, she was preparing to leave the hospital after being checked over thoroughly. She had a second-degree burn on the back of her hand. Her legs had minor burns. The blanket that Arthur had thrown over her had extinguished the flames before they did any serious damage. Smoke inhalation had left her throat raw. It would take a few days before it healed; until then she was under doctor's order not to talk.

"You can borrow these to wear home." Lily Buchanan, a nurse, handed her a pair of scrub pants. They had to cut her jeans off her in the emergency room. Lily was Sara Bell's cousin. She and Camille had gone to school together.

"Thanks. I'll get them back—"

Lily shook her finger sideways. "You shouldn't be talking. Don't worry about returning them. I'll pick them up the next time I'm by the store."

Erica nodded and stood to pull on the pants. Lily stayed nearby in case she fell.

"Any dizziness when you stand?"

Erica started to speak but remembered in time and shook her head. She pulled the tie on the pants.

"Good. Hop in the wheelchair and I'll take you out to the waiting room." After Erica was seated, Lily released the brake on the chair. "There are quite a few people out there."

"Anyone with rocks?" Erica whispered.

Lily laughed. "No. We don't allow rock throwing in the waiting room." She hesitated. "I believe most of the rock throwing is happening over at city hall."

Erica looked over her shoulder. "Lots?"

"No. Just a handful of jackasses who don't have anything better to do. Now sit back and stop talking." Lily pushed the chair toward the door. "I don't really know how many, but I wouldn't worry too much if I were you. I think you might be surprised at how much support you and Alice will find here."

Something in her voice made Erica turn back to look at her again.

"What?" Lily asked with raised eyebrows. "You know we're everywhere." She winked. "Now, I'm not going to tell you again to turn around. How's it going to look on my evaluation if you fall out of this chair and crack your head?"

Erica quickly complied. When she was rolled into the waiting room, the number of people there overwhelmed her. Besides Gerti, Judith and Alice, she spotted several of the firefighters, Sara Bell, Tina, Miss Wilkerson, Jimmy and a couple of dozen other people from around town. There was a general sigh of relief when they saw her wave to them.

Lily parked the chair beside Alice. "Now, folks," Lily called out. "Erica is under strict orders not to be talking for a couple of days, so I'm putting everyone here in charge of making sure she minds the doctor's orders." She patted Erica's shoulder. "Good luck." She winked again when Erica looked up and nodded.

Erica smiled as people crowded around her. She nodded as waves of well wishes and offers of help poured over her. As she looked at the faces of people she had grown to love over the years, she realized that this was what home and family was all about. She peered around heads until she found Alice. As their gazes met, Erica said a silent prayer of thanks to Bridget and Ann, who had given up so much in search of the very thing she was now experiencing. The love, respect and strength they had shown had helped build this community, and while an outsider might find the residents of Whitehall a bit eccentric, to Erica they were family.

As the crowd milled around, Erica saw Judith shaking her head adamantly as she talked with Sara Bell. She wondered if it had anything to do with Judith's big luncheon today. The groundbreaking ceremony for the new town square was supposed to start at two, just after the noon luncheon. She glanced at the clock on the wall and saw it was already a quarter past ten. She got Gerti's attention and pointed to the clock.

Gerti said something to Alice, who came to stand behind the wheelchair. "Okay, folks," Gerti said. "It's time to start heading on over to the town square. Since everyone has been busy fighting fires this morning, everything is probably a little behind schedule already."

Erica stared at her family with a sense of pride. She knew how much her mother and grandmother were hurting over the damage to the house, but they weren't going to let it stop them from fulfilling their obligations to the rest of the community. She also knew that the community would be there to help them.

There were a few chuckles as the crowd began to disperse. Sara Bell waved good-bye and left with them. Judith came to stand by the wheelchair. "I need to get home and change again." She stared down at her ruined jacket.

"Everything at the house will reek of smoke," Gerti said.

"Can it be washed out?" Alice asked. "If so, we could go back to your place and get whatever clothes you'll need, then wash them

283

at my place." She stopped for a second. "You won't be able to stay in the house until the smoke and soot is cleaned away. I have two spare bedrooms. You're welcome to stay with me as long as you need to."

Gerti nodded. "Sounds good to me, and since you two will probably want to double up, Judith and I will each have our own room. I can't sleep with her snoring all night."

"Mother, I do not snore."

"Oh, please, Judith. The windows rattle every time you inhale."

They continued to bicker as Alice started moving the wheelchair toward the door.

When they arrived back at the house, the car grew silent. Arthur Hogg and Ed Raines were still there. Erica knew they had stayed behind to extinguish any hidden embers that might flare back to life.

Both men approached as the women got out of the car. Erica felt a little nauseous and reminded herself to move slower.

Arthur removed his helmet and wiped his face with a large handkerchief. "You okay?" he asked Erica.

"I'm fine," she whispered and was instantly scolded by the other three. She ignored them long enough to ask one more question. "Dryer?"

He nodded. "It looked as though a mouse or something had been chewing on the wire and some lint had probably built up over it."

Erica nodded and gave herself a mental kick for not checking it rather than simply complaining about it.

"Larry Collins came by already," Ed said. The house was insured through Larry's agency. "So, if you want I can get a couple of guys and put up some plywood to block this mess off from the rest of the house."

"We'd appreciate that, Ed," Gerti said. "Tell Fred to give you whatever you'll need from the store."

He hooked a thumb back toward the house. "We've double-checked everything and nothing looks hot, so I guess we'll get out of your way."

"We're going to be staying with Alice," Judith replied. "If you need anything, let us know."

He ducked his head slightly as he glanced from Alice to Erica and nodded. He tapped Erica's shoulder as he walked past. "Hope you're feeling better soon."

Arthur did the same as he left.

They went inside and were immediately assaulted by the strong odor of smoke. "Maybe you should wait in the car," Alice said as she turned to Erica. "Tell me what you want and I'll find it for you."

"It's not like there's a big selection to choose from," Gerti said. "With her, all you have to choose between is jeans and a shirt or a shirt and jeans."

Alice waved Erica toward the car. "You wait out there. I'll pick some things out."

Erica nodded, but as they all rushed off to gather things, she went to the den and removed the three albums she had shown Rae. Except for the smoke, this area had received no damage. She took the three albums and went to the car to wait.

There was another hectic flurry of activity as they washed clothes and showered at Alice's house. Erica washed her hair twice and could still smell the smoke in it. She had to be careful to keep her burned hand away from the water and quickly discovered it wasn't easy to wash her hair with only one hand.

Alice was getting dressed when Erica came out of the bathroom. "Are you sure you're up to this? I really think you need to stay home and rest."

Erica shook her head. "I have to go to the groundbreaking ceremony," she whispered. She didn't add that she wanted to be there in case all hell broke loose. She got another whiff of her hair. "Stinks." She pointed to her hair.

Alice sniffed Erica's hair. "It's hardly noticeable."

Erica sat on the bed and patted the area beside her. "Did you mean what you said earlier?" she whispered.

"Yes, I did, but you shouldn't be talking."

"I'm whispering, not talking."

"I think that's still cheating."

"What about your job?"

Alice shrugged. "I love being mayor and I won't lie to you. It will hurt if they ask me to step down, but when I saw you lying on the ground—" She stopped and looked away for a moment. When she turned back, tears glistened on her eyelashes. "When I saw you, I realized that without you nothing else mattered. I've been lying to myself. I thought being able to see you every day would be enough, but"—she shook her head—"I was such a fool." She leaned forward and kissed Erica. "Can you ever forgive me?"

"Nothing to forgive."

A door closed somewhere nearby.

"You'd better hurry and get dressed," Alice said. "Gerti will be pounding on the door if we're much later."

A large crowd had already gathered in the town square for the anticipated groundbreaking ceremony. When Alice stepped onto the podium, she received a mixed response from the crowd. There were a few boos, but they were quickly overshadowed by the applause.

Erica couldn't help but admire Alice's grace and courage as she stood before the group. She held up her hand to silence the crowd.

"I'd like to welcome everyone and say how happy I am that—"

"We don't want our mayor to be a dyke." A voice rang out from the back of the crowd.

"Then move somewhere else," someone else shouted to the heckler.

Alice held up her hands. "You're welcome to bring any and all complaints to city hall on Monday night. We'll have a town meeting then and if the majority of the community wants me to step down, I'll certainly do so. Until then, if you would be so kind as to let me continue, there have been a lot of folks toiling hard to bring you today's events. Let's not ruin all their hard work."

Her announcement was met with applause and shouts of approval. She continued her introduction and went on to give a brief history of Whitehall.

"When we decided to rebuild the town square we knew we wanted it to reflect the spirit of love and family this community holds so dear. There were many ideas presented. In the end the proposal we agreed on was to erect a statue in honor of Howard and Bridget Franklin." There was another round of applause. "As most of you already know, the community of Whitehall was severely hit by the Depression. Without the generosity and kindness of Franklin's Mercantile many members of this community would have suffered much more." Murmurs of agreement floated throughout crowd. She looked around at those gathered before her. "It's my pleasure to introduce a member of the Franklin family now, one who would like to say a few words to you." She turned and nodded to Judith. "Actually, very little introduction is needed, so, ladies and gentlemen, I present Ms. Judith Boyd."

Surprised, Erica looked at Gerti, who just shrugged. Apparently, she hadn't known either that Judith would be speaking today.

Judith approached the stage and waited for the applause to die down. "The city council had a model of the proposed statue that they were going to show you today, but as many of you already know, it was recently discovered that Bridget and Howard Franklin were just as colorful as those of us living today."

The audience began to laugh and cheer.

"Did you know she was going to speak?" Erica asked Gerti in a hoarse whisper.

"No. She never said anything to me."

The crowd grew silent and Judith continued, "I believe our uniqueness is what binds this community together as a family. We may argue and fuss at one another, but when things get rough we all come together. I look around at all your faces and know that before the day is over I'll probably be fussing at some of you." An exaggerated glance in Sara Bell's direction caused another wave of giggles. "But I also know that when times are bad I can depend on you."

Erica smiled and thought about the luncheon they had just left. Despite the fire and all that had happened over the past few days, the luncheon had been a success, and Sara Bell had been the first in line to congratulate Judith. Erica turned attention back to her mother.

Judith seemed to stand a little taller as she stared into the crowd. "Howard and Bridget Franklin will forever be my great-grandparents. Nothing, absolutely nothing, will ever change that fact for me. Without their sacrifice and bravery, I wouldn't have had the honor of calling Whitehall home. I realize that not everyone would feel about Howard and Bridget as I do, so I've asked the city council to let all of you decide what statue, if any, should be placed in the town square. The ballot will be available Monday night at the town meeting." She placed her hands flat on the podium and beamed a smile at the crowd. "Now, it's my pleasure to announce that two of our community's leading ladies have been selected to be the honorary groundbreakers for the new Whitehall town square. Miss Janie Wilkerson and Miss Ida Sue Hudson will remove the first two shovels of dirt."

Gerti leaned closer to Erica. "Let's just hope they don't turn those shovels on each other."

CHAPTER FORTY-SIX
One Year Later

Erica stood before the mirror and made a final adjustment to her jacket. In a few minutes she would walk over to the town square and say a few words before the statue was revealed. Satisfied that she looked all right, she picked up the stack of note cards and slipped them into her pocket. As she made her way through the house she had shared with Alice for the past year, she smiled.

The first few weeks after the fire had been hectic and stressful. A handful of people insisted that special elections be held for both her position on the school board as well as for the mayoral office. She and Alice had decided that it was best to get the matter settled quickly and agreed to the election. Both had been overwhelmingly reelected. A few diehards like Ramona Cox still hounded them, but for the most part Whitehall residents had continued with their live-and-let-live attitude.

The fire damage to the house had been repaired. Gerti and Judith moved back and seemed to adjust to not having a referee for their occasional bouts.

Rae Richardson had been spending more and more time in Whitehall. Now when she came in to visit, she stayed at the Delaney home with Tina.

Erica went into the library and removed Howard's diary from a shelf it shared with the new archival binders that now housed the photos from the old albums. She flipped through the pages of the diary, stopping to read short passages until the grandfather clock in the hall chimed. It was time to go. She slipped the diary into her jacket pocket and left the house.

As she walked along the sidewalk, she remembered that last horrendous night that she had snuck through her neighbors' backyards to see Alice, only to be chased home by Jason Moore's Doberman. The dog had never returned and no one seemed to mind.

People waved and called to her as she went. The sound of music from the brass band playing in the square filled the air. She found herself wondering what Bridget and Ann would think about the events of the day. How would they feel about the path their decision to leave London had taken? In the last few months of her life, Ann had written out the story of her and Bridget's life. Her account of that horrifying night when the *Titanic* sank was still difficult for Erica to read. She had read the diary many times during the last year. It had kept her going during the darkest days immediately following the fire. With Gerti and Judith's permission, she had loaned the diary to Tina to read and was surprised and pleased when, in turn, Tina had shared Betty Delaney's diary with her. The two chronicles had painted an all-too-clear picture of what had happened on that fateful night.

The crowd grew thicker as Erica approached the town square. She found a cool spot beneath an oak tree where she could see the podium and still people-watch. When Alice started speaking, Erica slowly began to work her way toward the podium. She would be the next speaker. She had heard Alice rehearsing her speech so many times she already knew it and used the opportunity to observe her lover. A year ago she couldn't have imagined how happy she could be. Life with Alice was more wonderful than she could have ever dreamed. Alice was slowly losing the inhibitions that had once threatened to drive Erica crazy. Whenever they could arrange time off together, they headed to Alice's beach house where they continued to make memories. A warm glow of desire sparked as she thought about some of them. She was so engrossed in her memories that she almost missed her introduction.

When Erica stepped up to the podium, she removed the diary and placed it to one side as she looked down at her note cards and waited for the applause to fade. Her stomach fluttered with an unexpected nervousness. She focused on Alice, who stood beside Gerti and Judith. As soon as Alice smiled, Erica began to relax. She took a deep breath and began the speech she had spent the past two weeks working on.

"I'd like to thank everyone for being here today." She glanced at two empty seats in the front. "Unfortunately, the governor couldn't be with us today. He sent his regrets, along with his congratulations for Whitehall's sesquicentennial celebration." She moved her stack of note cards to the side of the podium and looked out over the crowd. "I was asked to say a few words before the statue is unveiled. I had one all worked out until just before I left the house this morning. That's when I remembered something that I thought would be more appropriate for today. I'd like to read the final passage from my great-great-grandfather Howard Franklin's diary." She picked up the book and opened it to the spot she had marked. "It was written the night before he died." She cleared her throat and began to read.

I find myself thinking a lot about the past recently. I ran from a family who neither knew nor understood the love I carried in my heart, a love that burned so bright and warm it carried me through a long frigid night when so many brave souls perished around me. That terror is etched so deeply into my being that nothing short of death can remove it, and there are times when I fear that even death itself will not be enough. It was a night when mankind's arrogance and greed sent hundreds to a terrifying, watery grave—a night when a class system condemned the poor to an early death. In the midst of all that horror, there were glowing moments as well. There was the look of love and trust in Bridget's eyes as they lowered her lifeboat into the sea, and the courage of a man who gave his life jacket to a woman who had lost her own in the chaos. There was the music of a band that began playing at midnight when the captain ordered the lifeboats lowered. These courageous men continued to play beautiful melodies to try to calm us all even after it was obvious that most of us had only minutes to live.

As I clung to my perilous raft that night, I vowed that should God see fit to spare my life I would strive to live it with the same bravery and honor that I saw displayed that night.

It has been more than fifty-two years since that tragic event and I have begun to feel that I have little time left on this earth. I find myself thinking about my family. I'm sure my parents have long since died, and although I shall always love my brother, Hayden, I have no true desire to see him again. I hope he has had a good life, but I fear he was already too far along on the road to alcoholism.

I feel myself to be most fortunate, because I have had the most extraordinary fortune to have so many people to call family. We found a home here, a place to raise our beautiful baby girl. It was here among these wonderful people that we found our true family. I shall never forget our dear friends Miles and Louise. They were as much a father and mother to us as our own parents. I miss them deeply, as I do our dear Rachel. Betty is the only one of our old friends to survive. She will be the only one here to help Bridget keep my secret. At times, I worry what shall happen to my family should my secret be discovered, but in my heart I have to believe that the community shall continue to embrace them with love, if not complete understanding. When my time comes, I pray I face the end with the same courage as those brave men who continued to play their beautiful midnight melodies even after all hope was gone on that cold night so long ago.

Erica looked up. "I hope Howard is looking down upon us today." She turned and watched as Gerti and Judith removed the large cloth covering that had been used to hide the statue. As it slid down, there was a collective intake of breath before the crowd began to cheer and applaud.

Erica stared at the sculpture of a couple holding a small child. At a quick glance, it would be taken as a man and a woman. Only after a closer examination did you notice the man's delicate facial features and small hands.

About the Author

Megan is an award-winning artist and freelance nature photographer. In her spare time she likes to rummage through flea markets and junk shops in search of broken treasures in need of repair. Her hobbies include woodworking, metal detecting and genealogy.

Authors love to hear from the readers. You may contact Megan by e-mail at MCarterBooks@aol.com.

Author's Note

Within this book I reference two stories by William T. Stead. By ill luck or, dare I say it, destiny, William Stead was a passenger on the Titanic. Tragically, unlike the heroes of his tales, he did not survive the sinking. For anyone interested in reading his work, the first story, "How the Mail Steamer Went Down in the Mid-Atlantic, by a Survivor" can be found online at http://www.attackingthedevil.co.uk/pmg/ steamer.php. Be sure to read Stead's note regarding lifeboats at the end of the story. An excerpt from his second story, "From the Old World to the New," is also available at http://www.attackingthedevil.co.uk/ reviews/oldworld.php.

The following Web sites provided valuable statistical information about the Titanic:

http://www.titanicstory.com/titanic.htm#titanic
http://www.titanic-online.com/
http://www.titanic-nautical.com/RMS-Titanic.php

Publications from
BELLA BOOKS, INC.
The best in contemporary lesbian fiction
P.O. Box 10543, Tallahassee, FL 32302
Phone: 800-729-4992
www.bellabooks.com

PAST REMEMBERING by Lyn Denison. What would it take to melt Peri's cool exterior? Any involvement on Asha's part would be simply asking for trouble and heartache . . . wouldn't it?   978-1-59493-103-1 $13.95

ASPEN'S EMBERS by Diane Tremain Braund. Will Aspen choose the woman she loves. . . or the forest she hopes to preserve.   978-1-59493-102-4 $14.95

THE COTTAGE by Gerri Hill. *The Cottage* is the heartbreaking story of two women who meet by chance . . . or did they? A love so destined it couldn't be denied . . . stolen moments to be cherished forever.   978-1-59493-096-6 $13.95

FANTASY: Untrue Stories of Lesbian Passion edited by Barbara Johnson and Therese Szymanski. Lie back and let Bella's bad girls take you on an erotic journey through the greatest bedtime stories never told.   978-1-59493-101-7 $15.95

SISTERS' FLIGHT by Jeanne G'Fellers. *Sisters' Flight* is the highly anticipated sequel to *No Sister of Mine* and *Sister Lost, Sister Found*.   978-1-59493-116-1 $13.95

BRAGGIN' RIGHTS by Kenna White. Taylor Fleming is a thirty-six-year-old Texas rancher who covets her independence. She finds her cowgirl independence tested by neighboring rancher Jen Holland.   978-1-59493-095-9 $13.95

BRILLIANT by Ann Roberts. Respected sociology professor, Diane Cole finds her views on love challenged by her own heart, as she fights the attraction she feels for a woman half her age.   978-1-59493-115-4 $13.95

THE EDUCATION OF ELLIE by Jackie Calhoun. When Ellie sees her childhood friend for the first time in thirty years she is tempted to resume their long lost friendship. But with the years come a lot of baggage and the two women struggle with who they are now while fighting the painful memories of their first parting. Will they be able to move past their history to start again?   978-1-59493-092-8 $13.95

DATE NIGHT CLUB by Saxon Bennett. *Date Night Club* is a dark romantic comedy about the pitfalls of dating in your thirties . . .   978-1-59493-094-2 $13.95

PLEASE FORGIVE ME by Megan Carter. Laurel Becker is on the verge of losing the two most important things in her life—her current lover, Elaine Alexander, and the Lavender Page bookstore. Will Elaine and Laurel manage to work through their misunderstandings and rebuild their life together?   978-1-59493-091-1 $13.95

WHISKEY AND OAK LEAVES by Jaime Clevenger. Meg meets June, a single woman running a horse ranch in the California Sierra foothills. The two become quick friends and it isn't long before Meg is looking for more than just a friendship. But June has no interest in developing a deeper relationship with Meg. She is, after all, not the least bit interested in women . . . or is she? Neither of these two women is prepared for what lies ahead . . .   978-1-59493-093-5 $13.95

SUMTER POINT by KG MacGregor. As Audie surrenders her heart to Beth, she begins to distance herself from the reckless habits of her youth. Just as they're ready to meet in the middle, their future is thrown into doubt by a duty Beth can't ignore. It all comes to a head on the river at Sumter Point.   978-1-59493-089-8 $13.95

THE TARGET by Gerri Hill. Sara Michaels is the daughter of a prominent senator who has been receiving death threats against his family. In an effort to protect Sara, the FBI recruits homicide detective Jaime Hutchinson to secretly provide the protection they are so certain Sara will need. Will Sara finally figure out who is behind the death threats? And will Jaime realize the truth—and be able to save Sara before it's too late?
                                            978-1-59493-082-9 $13.95

REALITY BYTES by Jane Frances. In this sequel to *Reunion*, follow the lives of four friends in a romantic tale that spans the globe and proves that you can cross the whole of cyberspace only to find love a few suburbs away . . .   978-1-59493-079-9 $13.95

MURDER CAME SECOND by Jessica Thomas. Broadway's bad-boy genius, Paul Carlucci, has chosen *Hamlet* for his latest production and, to the delight of some and despair of others, he has selected Provincetown's amphitheatre for his opening gala. But Alex Peres realizes the wrong people are falling down, and the moaning is all too realistic. Someone must not be shooting blanks . . .   978-1-59493-081-2 $13.95

SKIN DEEP by Kenna White. Jordan Griffin has been given a new assignment: Track down and interview one-time nationally renowned broadcast journalist Reece McAllister. Much to her surprise, Jordan comes away with far more than just a story . . .
978-1-59493-78-2 $13.95

FINDERS KEEPERS by Karin Kallmaker. *Finders Keepers*, the quest for the perfect mate in the 21st century, joins Karin Kallmaker's *Just Like That* and her other incomparable novels about lesbian love, lust and laughter.   1-59493-072-4 $13.95

OUT OF THE FIRE by Beth Moore. Author Ann Covington feels at the top of the world when told her book is being made into a movie. Then in walks Casey Duncan the actress who is playing the lead in her movie. Will Casey turn Ann's world upside down?
1-59493-088-0 $13.95

STAKE THROUGH THE HEART: NEW EXPLOITS OF TWILIGHT LESBIANS by Karin Kallmaker, Julia Watts, Barbara Johnson and Therese Szymanski. The playful quartet that penned the acclaimed *Once Upon A Dyke* are dimming the lights for journeys into worlds of breathless seduction.   1-59493-071-6 $15.95

THE HOUSE ON SANDSTONE by KG MacGregor. Carly Griffin returns home to Leland and finds that her old high school friend Justine is awakening more than just old memories.   1-59493-076-7 $13.95

WILD NIGHTS: MOSTLY TRUE STORIES OF WOMEN LOVING WOMEN edited by Therese Szymanski. 264 pp. 23 new stories from today's hottest erotic writers are sure to give you your wildest night ever!   1-59493-069-4 $15.95

COYOTE SKY by Gerri Hill. 248 pp. Sheriff Lee Foxx is trying to cope with the realization that she has fallen in love for the first time. And fallen for author Kate Winters, who is technically unavailable. Will Lee fight to keep Kate in Coyote?
1-59493-065-1 $13.95

VOICES OF THE HEART by Frankie J. Jones. 264 pp. A series of events force Erin to swear off love as she tries to break away from the woman of her dreams. Will Erin ever find the key to her future happiness?   1-59493-068-6 $13.95

SHELTER FROM THE STORM by Peggy J. Herring. 296 pp. A story about family and getting reacquainted with one's past that shows that sometimes you don't appreciate what you have until you almost lose it.   1-59493-064-3 $13.95

WRITING MY LOVE by Claire McNab. 192 pp. Romance writer Vonny Smith believes she will be able to woo her editor Diana through her writing.
1-59493-063-5 $13.95

PAID IN FULL by Ann Roberts. 200 pp. Ari Adams will need to choose between the debts of the past and the promise of a happy future.   1-59493-059-7 $13.95

ROMANCING THE ZONE by Kenna White. 272 pp. Liz's world begins to crumble when a secret from her past returns to Ashton.   1-59493-060-0 $13.95

SIGN ON THE LINE by Jaime Clevenger. 204 pp. Alexis Getty, a flirtatious delivery driver is committed to finding the rightful owner of a mysterious package.
1-59493-052-X $13.95

END OF WATCH by Clare Baxter. 256 pp. LAPD Lieutenant L.A. Franco Frank follows the lone clue down the unlit steps of memory to a final, unthinkable resolution.
1-59493-064-4 $13.95

BEHIND THE PINE CURTAIN by Gerri Hill. 280 pp. Jacqueline returns home after her father's death and comes face to face with her first crush.   1-59493-057-0 $13.95

18TH & CASTRO by Karin Kallmaker. 200 pp. First-time couplings and couples who know how to mix lust and love make 18th & Castro the hottest address in the city by the bay.   1-59493-066-X $13.95

JUST THIS ONCE by KG MacGregor. 200 pp. Mindful of the obligations back home that she must honor, Wynne Connelly struggles to resist the fascination and allure that a particular woman she meets on her business trip represents. 1-59493-087-2 $13.95

ANTICIPATION by Terri Breneman. 240 pp. Two women struggle to remain professional as they work together to find a serial killer.   1-59493-055-4 $13.95

OBSESSION by Jackie Calhoun. 240 pp. Lindsey's life is turned upside down when Sarah comes into the family nursery in search of perennials.   1-59493-058-9 $13.95

BENEATH THE WILLOW by Kenna White. 240 pp. A torch that still burns brightly even after twenty-five years threatens to consume two childhood friends.
1-59493-053-8 $13.95

SISTER LOST, SISTER FOUND by Jeanne G'Fellers. 224 pp. The highly anticipated sequel to *No Sister of Mine*.   1-59493-056-2 $13.95

THE WEEKEND VISITOR by Jessica Thomas. 240 pp. In this latest Alex Peres mystery, Alex is asked to investigate an assault on a local woman but finds that her client may have more secrets than she lets on.   1-59493-054-6 $13.95

THE KILLING ROOM by Gerri Hill. 392 pp. How can two women forget and go their separate ways?   1-59493-050-3 $12.95

PASSIONATE KISSES by Megan Carter. 240 pp. Will two old friends run from love?
1-59493-051-1 $12.95

ALWAYS AND FOREVER by Lyn Denison. 224 pp. The girl next door turns Shannon's world upside down.   1-59493-049-X $12.95

BACK TALK by Saxon Bennett. 200 pp. Can a talk-show host find love after heartbreak?   1-59493-028-7 $12.95

THE PERFECT VALENTINE: EROTIC LESBIAN VALENTINE STORIES edited by Barbara Johnson and Therese Szymanski—from Bella After Dark. 328 pp. Stories from the hottest writers around.   1-59493-061-9 $14.95

MURDER AT RANDOM by Claire McNab. 200 pp. The Sixth Denise Cleever Thriller. Denise realizes the fate of thousands is in her hands. 1-59493-047-3 $12.95

THE TIDES OF PASSION by Diana Tremain Braund. 240 pp. Will Susan be able to hold it all together and find the one woman who touches her soul?
1-59493-048-1 $12.95

JUST LIKE THAT by Karin Kallmaker. 240 pp. Disliking each other—and everything they stand for—even before they meet, Toni and Syrah find feelings can change, just like that. 1-59493-025-2 $12.95

WHEN FIRST WE PRACTICE by Therese Szymanski. 200 pp. Brett and Allie are once again caught in the middle of murder and intrigue. 1-59493-045-7 $12.95

REUNION by Jane Frances. 240 pp. Cathy Braithwaite seems to have it all: good looks, money and a thriving accounting practice . . . 1-59493-046-5 $12.95

BELL, BOOK & DYKE: NEW EXPLOITS OF MAGICAL LESBIANS by Kall-maker, Watts, Johnson and Szymanski. 360 pp. Reluctant witches, tempting spells and skyclad beauties—delve into the mysteries of love, lust and power in this quartet of novellas. 1-59493-023-6 $14.95

ARTIST'S DREAM by Gerri Hill. 320 pp. When Cassie meets Luke Winston, she can no longer deny her attraction to women . . . 1-59493-042-2 $12.95

NO EVIDENCE by Nancy Sanra. 240 pp. Private investigator Tally McGinnis once again returns to the horror-filled world of a serial killer. 1-59493-043-04 $12.95

WHEN LOVE FINDS A HOME by Megan Carter. 280 pp. What will it take for Anna and Rona to find their way back to each other again? 1-59493-041-4 $12.95

MEMORIES TO DIE FOR by Adrian Gold. 240 pp. Rachel attempts to avoid her attraction to the charms of Anna Sigurdson . . . 1-59493-038-4 $12.95

SILENT HEART by Claire McNab. 280 pp. Exotic lesbian romance. 1-59493-044-9 $12.95

MIDNIGHT RAIN by Peggy J. Herring. 240 pp. Bridget McBee is determined to find the woman who saved her life. 1-59493-021-X $12.95

THE MISSING PAGE A Brenda Strange Mystery by Patty G. Henderson. 240 pp. Brenda investigates her client's murder . . . 1-59493-004-X $12.95

WHISPERS ON THE WIND by Frankie J. Jones. 240 pp. Dixon thinks she and her best friend, Elizabeth Colter, would make the perfect couple . . . 1-59493-037-6 $12.95

CALL OF THE DARK: EROTIC LESBIAN TALES OF THE SUPERNATURAL edited by Therese Szymanski—from Bella After Dark. 320 pp. 1-59493-040-6 $14.95

A TIME TO CAST AWAY A Helen Black Mystery by Pat Welch. 240 pp. Helen stops by Alice's apartment—only to find the woman dead . . . 1-59493-036-8 $12.95

DESERT OF THE HEART by Jane Rule. 224 pp. The book that launched the most popular lesbian movie of all time is back. 1-59493-035-X $12.95

THE NEXT WORLD by Ursula Steck. 240 pp. Anna's friend Mido is threatened and eventually disappears . . . 1-59493-024-4 $12.95

CALL SHOTGUN by Jaime Clevenger. 240 pp. Kelly gets pulled back into the world of private investigation . . . 1-59493-016-3 $12.95

52 PICKUP by Bonnie J. Morris and E.B. Casey. 240 pp. 52 hot, romantic tales—one for every Saturday night of the year. 1-59493-026-0 $12.95

GOLD FEVER by Lyn Denison. 240 pp. Kate's first love, Ashley, returns to their home town, where Kate now lives . . . 1-59493-039-2 $12.95

RISKY INVESTMENT by Beth Moore. 240 pp. Lynn's best friend and roommate needs her to pretend Chris is his fiancé. But nothing is ever easy. 1-59493-019-8 $12.95